THE TIME RIDER

REBEL WITH WINGS

BOOK 2

GAGE COPELAND

Publishing Coordinator – Sharon Kizziah-Holmes

Paperback-Press
an imprint of A & S Publishing
Paperback Press, LLC
Springfield, Missouri

ISBN -13: 978-1-964559-74-2

DEDICATION

Now, to begin. I dedicate this work to the most complicated, yet endearing friend one could ask for, Justin A. Bartnicki. We have often fought, bitterly even. If one were to see us on the outside, I would not blame them for thinking we were bitter enemies. I am an opinionated, often ignorantly judgmental human being. But you show me the beauty of a parallel, the value of an opposing side. I do not agree with everything you believe in this world. And I pray through all hardships that we both endure, whether they have already happened or will happen. That you will see the beauty of this world and the goodness of this life outside of statistics and unpleasant experiences and choose to be happy. Choose to live. Long live the true Rebel with Wings.

Forever May He Reign

*Disclaimer: The goal of every party involved in the creation of **Time Rider: Rebel with Wings** is to provide a flawless and mistake-less text for the story. But at the request of the author, who felt the need to clarify. If any mistakes are found, whether grammatical or otherwise, they are not the fault of Lael Kennedy or any proofreaders. They are the fault of an author who at best should have his computer bashed over his head for his incompetence. Or worse, should be thrown off the Gateway Arch for comedic effect. Thank you for your understanding.*

My final dedication is the most important to me, this is to the one I too often forsake. I have much to say, never enough time. I know I've never made enough time for You. I can only hope, only pray that Your anger towards me is not too great. I am plagued with fatigue and bitterness. But in a moment that is easier to write it then it could ever be to speak it, I wanted to say thank You. Whether I've made You proud and happy, or if I've disgusted You. Your hope, and Your way is what is right. And even in my turmoil, I hope You find happiness in the things that are good in this broken place. I hope to honor You in my existence, Lord. Let me leave the anger behind and find the light at the end of the tunnel. Let dreams of You be made manifest and let all who hear be saved and redeemed in Your blessed presence. You made a promise, and it will be made true. That is enough, that is everything.

Amen.

ACKNOWLEDGMENTS

A shoutout to my editor for this venture, Lael Kenndy. Writing is an activity that fluctuates in difficulty for me. And like many in the world of arts, it is easy to get disillusioned. I just wanted to thank you again for your hard work and your kind words.

The world of *Time Rider* is an ambitious one. It is filled to the brim with characters and concepts from various creeds, races, and ages. Admittedly, I feel like I'm a madman for tackling it as my first real project. To go headfirst into it without context and previous knowledge and still come through with flying colors.

Your work was worth every second and every cent. Thank you so much, Lael.

CHAPTER 1

The Ne'er-Do-Well

Markus

The world was always a place that was constantly moving and never ceasing. People saw many faces and passed by with casual disregard. As a result, some faces got lost in the blur, fading into obscurity until they are invisible. And there was a young man amongst the blur that feels more invisible than anyone. That boy's name was Markus Daniels. A sixteen-year-old who was currently struggling with his current predicament of being moved in with yet another set of foster parents.

His young life could only be described as being plagued by an abundance of bad luck. For starters, he never knew his parents. They dropped him off at an orphanage when he was just a baby, leaving him only an old adult-sized sweatshirt to his name. Even as a young boy, trouble was always something Markus seemed to actively pursue. Even when he didn't, it seemed to find him. He'd often joke to others about it, saying something to the effect in an ironic way that in the grand card game of life, he'd drawn the dead man's hand.

He had gone in and out of many foster homes throughout his life, they all ended up having the same sad story, one thing would lead to another, and he always ended up where he started back at his foster center. At the beginning, Markus was hopeful he would find a family and a place to call home, but no matter how promising the start, something would inevitably go wrong. Sometimes it was Markus doing wrong, sometimes he just wasn't what they were looking for, sometimes even money wasn't a good incentive to deal with him.

One night, Markus sat in his small room at the Baymore home, a hot wave of anger fresh in his mind. Earlier in the day had proved to be quite the ordeal. In typical fashion, he had partaken in endeavors that proved to be troublesome and was caught while he was supposed to be in school. A rookie mistake he called it. He had to be picked up from the police station by his current foster parents, Don and Beatrice Baymore. They were less than pleased with him. They gave him perhaps the most earsplitting scolding Markus had ever experienced in his life, and that was saying something given his past. He was used to it, and most of it was in one ear out the other.

The ordeal made Markus feel especially spiteful; there was a part of him that wished to retaliate for the annoyance. He thought about his last conversation with his case worker before he set off to this home. She had pleaded with him to behave and try to make this new family work permanently. He didn't want to disappoint the one person in his life that didn't treat him like a scourge, but at this point he was convinced it wasn't possible. It was just his nature to cause trouble. He hated it, he didn't understand it, but it was just the way he was.

Markus took his smartphone off its charger and dialed her number into it. It was late, and she likely had already gone to sleep, but he had to try. He was way too pent up to just sit by and deal with it on his own. He pushed the green call button and put the phone to his ear. After a few tones, Markus heard his case worker pick up the phone on the other end.

"Hello?"

"Heya Cass, it's Markus."

"Markus?" she asked surprised. "What are you doing? It's almost midnight."

"Yeah, sorry about that. I just wanted to talk for a bit, and you said I could call whenever so… yeah."

"What's going on?"

"I just… I screwed up again, okay?"

"What was it this time?"

"I mean, it wasn't really all *that* bad, I just skipped school."

"And?"

"I nicked a few bags of chips from the store and tried to book it with a cop on my tail."

"Markus!" Cassandra said in frustrated disbelief.

"I didn't have any money, and I was hungry," Markus said. "The Baymores barely feed me as is."

"Shoplifting is not the right thing to do in that situation! You know that," Cassandra scolded. "If you have issues, you call me. I've told you multiple times."

"I know…" Markus said solemnly.

"Why do you do this?" she asked. "You'll be eighteen in less than two years. An adult. If you keep this up prison will be your home, don't you get that?"

"I know," Markus repeated.

"Then what are you doing?" Cassandra asked. "You had me on my knees begging you to get your act together. What do you need me to do?"

"I just want you to listen, that's all," Markus said.

"I have been listening, but you haven't been doing your part. I can't bail you out forever," Cassandra said. "You could do such great things if you would stop acting like a little thug. I know you're better than this."

"Why couldn't you take me in?" Markus asked. "Why do you keep pairing me with people who only want the paycheck?"

"Because you scared everyone else away!" Cassandra answered. "You know I would take you in if I could, but I can't. I'm already strapped for cash just trying to raise Jamie and Emma. I couldn't afford to take anyone else in."

It stung hearing Cassandra say those words, but Markus knew they were all true. That was the worst part for him, knowing he made this bed and now had to sleep in it.

"I'm just so damn sick of it all, I don't know what to do," Markus said.

"Language," Cassandra scolded. "And I'm sick of it to. I'm sick of you throwing all my hard work away because you can't stop acting like a criminal. I want you to succeed so badly, but you couldn't seem to care less,"

"That's not true!"

"Then prove it! Stop the nonsense. Enough is enough," Cassandra said.

This was not what Markus wanted from this conversation. "Thanks for nothing Cass…" Markus said.

"Get huffy and puffy all you want," Cassandra scoffed. "But you know I'm right."

Markus let out a quiet growl. "Did you at least find anything about my real parents yet?"

There was a pause. "I'm risking my job to do it, but I've done some work. I haven't found anything concrete about their identity. There are a few leads, but nothing more than that."

"Well, throw it on me!" Markus exclaimed.

"Not now, especially not now." Cassandra said.

"Why not?!"

"Because tomorrow I'm going to have to put out the fire you started, like I always do. Maybe once things simmer down, I'll tell you what I know. Just refrain from any more wrongdoing for the time being, or is that too much to ask?"

"It's not…" Markus mumbled. "Cass, please tell me what you found."

"Not tonight," Cassandra said. "We'll talk tomorrow, It's late."

Markus clenched his teeth together. "Fine."

"And Markus?"

"What?" he growled.

"There's always a new morning, don't forget that."

"Whatever," Markus said flatly, hanging up the phone.

He had hoped talking to her would calm his nerves, but now he felt even more aggravated. Cassandra was right. Markus normally regretted his foolery, but by the time that was the case there was rarely a chance of taking it back. From his perspective, being with the Baymores beat the hell out of being back at juvie, but at the moment he wasn't feeling especially grateful.

He sat in a wooden chair in the middle of his room letting the anger within him boil. No one else seemed to get it. If no one was going to provide him with what he needed, then he was going to take it for himself. If no one bothered to even acknowledge he existed, he would make them see. It wasn't rocket science. He wanted to please Cassandra, but he just couldn't bring himself to sit around and act like a saint, especially since no one else did.

He wanted to lash out, really causing some damage. The desire caused his mind to drift to an old intrusive thought that came around from time to time.

He didn't look it, but Markus fancied himself as a form of artist—a street artist, to be precise. Although his canvases of choice often led to a plethora of angry property owners, he was very proud of his work. He had a unique tag of his own creation. It was a cardinal bird, like the one used by the local baseball team, but it had Markus's own spin on it. It depicted the bird with feathered hands as opposed to wings. In each hand the bird had a segment of chain, the tag showed the cardinal in the action of breaking it.

He calls it, "The Rebel with Wings." It was mostly inspired by the sweatshirt he wore almost daily. The sweatshirt itself was an old, faded St. Louis Cardinals sweatshirt speckled with patches of dried paint. It was the sole thing he was wrapped up with when he was left by his biological parents. He hadn't the slightest clue why they did that, but the sweatshirt had ended up being his most prized possession. He wore it everywhere, even on the hottest of summer days.

The Rebel with Wings was Markus's calling card. He always left the tag behind when he wanted to leave a message. Seeing the shop owners and cops all riled up made it worth it. Who were they to criticize the work of an aspiring artist? He always saw his work as an improvement to the usual boring colors that littered the city anyway.

He usually picked local shops and plazas as his canvases, but Markus had much bigger ambitions. He had a driven desire to tag some of the higher end buildings around town. Specifically, Oracle Tower and the plaza erected in front of it.

The tower belonged to a corporation carrying the same name. Oracle Incorporated was St Louis's darling. They had shown up in the city in the early 1990s and grew like a weed into the international enterprise they are now. They were mostly a technology and computer company, building software and artificial intelligence for everything from smoke detectors to navigation systems in 747 airplanes. They had even released their own version of the smartphone not even two months earlier.

Markus had fantasized for years about tagging their buildings, but it was always too open, too many eyes watching. He never had the nerve to go for it. But tonight, perhaps he was feeling dangerous enough to go for it.

He grabbed his sweatshirt that hung on his bed, picked up his bag and skateboard, then began to slowly open the creaky window in his room, doing it in a manner that could only be described as surgical. Once it opened enough, he jumped out of it and hung on the window frame. After letting himself hang for a few seconds, he let go and fell to the ground, landing flat on his feet.

A single quiet voice in Markus's head urged him to return to his room and start the fresh day tomorrow. The voice warned about Cassandra, and how she told him to get his act together. He quickly disregarded it. What was the incentive to being law abiding citizen anyway? No good deed goes unpunished after all. Others might be able to live their whole lives living by the book, but not him. He needed more, needed some fire—and that's exactly what he planned on doing—bringing that fire. Even if it meant spending the rest of his youth in prison.

Markus kneeled with his backpack and brought out a small pair of earphones, then plugged them into his phone. Bringing it up, he turned it on and clicked on his usual music app, looking to turn on some music for his journey. He scrolled through his favored playlist of early 2000's pop rock and alternative metal until settling on a song he felt fit the mood. He put his headphones on his ears and dropped his skateboard to the ground. Starting with one foot on he pushed forward and began gliding down the street. His heart rate began to rise, and a chitter like laugh began to emanate from his throat; he had a feeling this was going to be a night to remember.

CHAPTER 2

Taken

Markus:

Markus cruised along the streets and sidewalks of the dark city on his skateboard getting lost in his music and the night air, occasionally passing by other night dwellers and some homeless people. Most tried to get his attention in one way or another, but he just cruised along ignorant of them. He headed to an alley adjacent to an old liquor shop on the far side of town, he had hidden his bag of paint cans by a dumpster. He hoped they were still there; it had been a good amount of time since he had used it.

He arrived and skidded into the alley quickly and looked to the side of the foul-smelling container, and sure enough, to the side of it, his red paint smeared backpack was still right where he left it. A mischievous smile curled on his face. He knelt and began to examine the bag's contents. Some of the cans in it were empty, and he threw them aside disgruntled, but others still had liquid within them. The slow-moving piece within them still moved through the paint as he shook them. There wasn't much, but there was enough, enough for one last rebel with wings.

He put the paint cans in a shopping bag and jammed them into his backpack, slung it over his shoulder, and left the alley and returned to gliding down the street on his skateboard heading toward Oracle Tower. He had not been there too often, but occasionally he would find himself in the large shopping plaza that was in front of the large tower. Some old foster parents had brought him here a few times, and other times he was just passing by. He never had the funds or desire for the lavish lifestyle offered by the shops there. He always bet that those who did were almost certainly the most snobbish kind of people imaginable. For him they were fun to mess around with, but not much else.

No, what had his interest was the tower itself, specifically the large blank walls that served as the foundation of the building. To Markus they were like a fruitful crop waiting to be harvested, a perfect canvas, an artist's dream come true. That dream was what his heart was set on this fateful night.

He arrived deeper into the city and could finally see the tower and continued to proceed with haste. It got easier as the sidewalks turned to downward walkways leading to the plaza. He kicked up his board once he reached the bottom and made his way up the steps towards the tower, passing by the ugly eye statue that was positioned in front of it and ended up at one of the large walls. He quickly looked around to see if there was any security. When he saw none, an excited laugh exited his mouth as he began to pull out his paint.

He began to work his magic on the wall of the building, a canvas nicely lit by the surrounding lights. There was plenty of red there, some black there, a little orange for the legs. After about an hour of working it was coming along beautifully. Eventually, he added the finishing touches and stood back with his hands at his hips admiring his handiwork.

The cardinal on the wall stared defiantly back at him. A chain was being snapped in its hand wings like a common twig. Breaking chains was something Markus admired, something he wanted. He wanted to be that bird. He wanted to be that rebel, the rebel who could soar, soar above everything else. Every time he saw his work, he swelled with pride. For a moment he could pretend to be something more, something worth something.

"Hey you! Stay where you are!"

Markus whipped his head around in a startled panic to the source of the voice and was met by a figure shining a Maglite flashlight back at him. It was hard to tell but it was likely a security guard. He didn't hesitate to grab his bag and sling it over his

8

shoulder as he bolted in the opposite direction and jumped down the staircase leading into the shopping plaza. Not even looking behind him.

"Stop!" the guard shouted as he began running towards him.

Markus was ahead, but more guards showed up and joined the pursuit. There was no gap in any of the shops, and he had to run down the main street with the guards right behind him. He just kept running as fast as he could with the guards not slowing down in the slightest. He was so focused he almost didn't notice the guards that had arrived in front of him trying to cut him off.

One of the guards managed to grab his arm and pull him into a headlock. Frantically he used all his strength to get loose. It started to work, and the guards' grasp became progressively weaker as the others closed in. When he found an opening, he lifted his right foot and slammed it down on the guard's shoe. The guard hollered in pain and grabbed his foot, letting him go. He began running again when another guard in front of him went for a clumsy grab, but he sidestepped sharply causing that guard to fall to the ground with a hard thud. One last member of security made himself known in front. Markus whipped his bag over his shoulder and threw it as hard as he could at him. The guard caught it with both hands instinctively, and Markus rammed him hard with a shoulder charge knocking the older man off his feet and onto the ground. He recovered his bag as the guard lay winded on the ground.

He eventually made it to the parking lot with the guards getting even closer. Quickly he rushed onto one of the cars and began hopping along the row, causing a few alarms to trip in the process. The guards managed to catch up but struggled to reach him because of his higher elevation. Eventually there were no more vehicles to jump to, and he leaped down onto the street. There was a tall fence surrounding the area that was nowhere near the exit. Markus sprinted with all his might until he came to one of the corners of the lot. He saw a light pole near him and began to shimmy up it as the guards just about reached him.

"It's over kid, there's no way out now!" a guard called out.

"Give it up!" another guard said.

Markus ignored them and kept climbing the pole until he reached the top. At the top he began to stand up and to balance, slowly moving along the structure until he reached the light itself.

Something was shot at him with an electric hum accompanying it and it startled him, causing him to lose his balance and fall over the side. He held on with only one hand.

"Don't use a taser! That's at least twelve feet high!"

"You got any other ideas? He's getting away!"

Markus grabbed hold with his other hand and managed to pull back up onto the pole. He walked gently towards the end with the guards yelling at him. Once there he began a few pre-movements and jumped with all his strength. He flew through the air and landed his feet on the top of the fence and tittered back over the side. He suddenly went into a freefall but had no idea there would be more distance to fall on the other side. He screamed as he fell an uncomfortably long time until he slammed painfully into some trash bags.

When he realized he had not fallen to his death he got out of the pile and fell clumsily onto the ground. He groaned with annoyance and got back to his feet, as he had managed to fall into a dumpster. A sheer concrete wall scaled the entire distance he fell; the fence was at the top.

"Man, *screw* whoever designed that," Markus said to himself in a short breath.

He could hear the guards above and see a few of their flashlight beams scattered about. They were yelling and cursing loudly at one another. A smile formed on Markus's face.

"Heh, suckers."

He brushed himself off and began walking the other direction down an alley, feeling like a king. He walked down the alley with almost a swagger and an obnoxious amount of confidence to boot. Thoughts of guilt tried to slip into his mind, but he closed them all out. Why should he be feeling guilty? The raw excitement of pulling off a caper was the best part, and he wasn't about to deprive himself of it. Tomorrow he could deal with the fallout. But for now, there was only the burn of adrenaline and the sweet taste of victory.

He continued down the unusually long alley holding back a laugh and skipping along when he felt an odd sensation. He had felt it before and he hated it, it was like someone was looking at him, but he couldn't see anyone around. He turned around quickly and still saw nothing.

"Who's there?" he called out as intimidating as he could.

No response. But something knocked off one of the dumpsters along the wall and crashed onto the ground. He sprinted forward looking to get the jump on whoever did that, but once he got past the container nothing was there but rubbish. A cold chill ran down his spine.

"The hell?"

Markus looked down to see a thick fog surrounding his feet, it bellowed in quickly and surrounded the whole alley, and the fog arched up making walls at the entrances, blocking visibility. He looked around and saw he was boxed in, then he heard another noise down the way he came. When he focused his attention on the source, he saw some sort of light down the way obscured by the fog. It was a rich blue color, like bright headlights on a misty road. The light got brighter and brighter until something else emerged. It looked like a human head, with bright blue eyes staring back at him. The head came forward, revealing a strange person emerging from the foggy wall. He knew right away it was no ordinary human being. It lacked any clothing or any skin at all. In its place seemed to be a body comprised of shiny black flesh and a pair of blue bright lights could be seen in place of traditional eyes.

Suddenly, instinct took over and Markus bolted away from the figure and down the other end of the alley. He took a second to look behind him and ended up slamming into a metal fence. He saw the figure had begun to run down the alley towards him in a mad sprint, moving with strife. He scurried up the fence trying to get a good grip on it and began to scale it. He latched his hands on it and began to climb. He almost made it over the top when something grabbed his backpack and pulled hard causing him to lose his grip and be thrown back into the alley. Another one of those things loomed over him and began snarling at him like a rabid animal. He backed up quickly and scrambled to his feet. There were at least four of them now, all of them covering his way out. He moved against the wall and grabbed the first thing he could find. He gripped a plastic crate and began to wildly swing it at the creatures, screaming as he did so. His attackers backed away from the flurry.

"Back up! Back up!"

One of the creatures swiped at him with its hand causing the crate to go flying away. He then attempted to flee but one of the creatures hit him in the leg causing him to fall to a knee. Another grabbed him from behind and covered his eyes with its boney hand. He struggled in place unable to see.

"Get your mitts off! Let me go! Let me go!"

Markus thrashed around with all the strength he could manage; desperation quickly arrived and exceeded a boiling point. He felt his arms getting grabbed and restrained by the others. One last frightened scream left Markus's throat as his vision filled with an unnaturally bright light and suddenly faded to black

CHAPTER 3

Erased

Markus:

Blackness. Endless. Empty. Nothingness. Then without warning the light appeared. Markus woke up with a start accompanied by an intense sense of vertigo. He was lying flat on his back looking up through the crevice of the buildings leading to the early morning sky. He lay there propped up on his bag and struggled to move, feeling like he had died and come back to life. He made the mistake of looking into the bright sky and was met with a sharp stinging pain behind his eyes. He covered them quickly and fell to his side groaning weakly. He tried to get to his feet and ended up slipping and sliding down the brick wall to his right. His vision alternated between bright white flashes and wave-like blue light. This was like the abusive father of all hangovers.

After a bit, Markus managed to gain enough strength to stand. He sat leaning against the wall trying to piece together what happened. He remembered tagging the building, getting chased and ending up in the alley. Then there were those weird people, or things... he tried to remember if he had messed with anything before hand—drugs, booze, anything like that. But he didn't remember abusing anything, and it had been a good long while since he had done so. So, was that some kind of dream? It couldn't be, he was still in the alley. He pulled out his phone to call for somebody but noticed the screen had a large crack and it wasn't responding. He figured it had gotten damaged during the fall. He threw the damaged device to the ground in frustration. He held his head and struggled to think clearly. All he knew was that he had to try and get home to the Baymores. He wasn't afraid of the consequences, but he just couldn't shake the feeling he really needed some help.

Markus stumbled out into the city and back onto the sidewalks. People were going about their business as usual, but the morning light made Markus's brain feel like it was melting. He pulled over his sweatshirt hood and began walking, the only thing visible was the sidewalk from beneath the hood. He walked slowly down the sidewalk, occasionally bumping into people and getting chastised for it, but he didn't pay them any attention. This continued for an excruciating amount of time until he ended up back at the Baymore home.

The rundown house was as it always was. Chipped white paint, rusty fence, and an overgrown yard. Definitely the right place. Markus made his way up the staircase and opened the screen door and started to pat down his pockets for his house key. He couldn't find it. He swore under his breath, had he lost another one? He knocked on the door a few times and got no response. He did so again with the same result. The Baymores were heavy sleepers, so this didn't come as much of a surprise.

"Figures…" he mumbled.

Markus went around the side of the home and looked up at his window, which to his surprise was still open. They may not have noticed his absence. He was thankful he had at least that going for him. There was a fence surrounding the home that he had once used to jump up to the window before, but it was a move that proved to be tricky if his balance wasn't right. He wasn't sure he could pull it off in this state, but he had to try. He went over to the fence and slowly scaled it. At the top of the fence, Markus was extremely wobbly, but he managed to even his stance. Once he managed to turn around, he aimed his vision at the window. He pushed all the strength he could into his legs and jumped forward. His fingers found their mark and grabbed the window frame, then he scrambled up the wall a bit trying to plant his feet. Once he had a good foothold, he pulled upwards with all his might and pulled himself through the window and landed on the floor of his room awkwardly. He sat up and rubbed his head, and when he looked up, he saw something that he would never have expected. There was a girl lying in his bed staring at him like he was a ghost, she had a blanket pulled up around her.

"Oh hey, how's it hanging? I uh, wait a sec. Do I have a girlfriend right now?"

The girl let out a blood-curdling scream and a sharp ringing flooded Markus's ears. He covered them trying to shield them. Don Baymore, Markus's balding adoptive father, burst through the door. Wife beater, beer gut, and all.

"Hey!" he bellowed.

"Mornin' Don, do I have a sister now?" Markus asked weakly.

The large man didn't answer, he rushed over and grabbed Markus by the hair and began dragging him out of the room.

"Ow, whaddya doing?! It's me! It's Markus!" he screamed frantically.

"Beatrice! Call the cops! We got a house invader!"

"House invader? What?!" Markus yelled in confusion.

In a panic, he broke loose of Don's grip and ended up slipping down the stairs. He plummeted all the way down and lay on the floor. The pain became even more unbearable. Beatrice Baymore, a pudgy aged woman was in the kitchen punching a number on her phone. She jumped and screamed at the sight of the boy crumpled on the floor.

"Heya Bea, what's up?" Markus said on the floor, waving a hand at her. He looked up to see Don rushing down the stairs with a golf club.

"Woah! Not good! Not good!" Markus exclaimed as he rushed to his feet.

He backed up until he opened the front door and got it open just as Don made his first swing; Markus ducked right as it sailed over his head. Don accidentally lost his grip and sent the driver flying into the living room television. Beatrice cried out like she had just watched her own child die.

Markus rushed onto the porch in the commotion and jumped the porch staircase and bolted down the sidewalk. Don's yells could be heard behind him until they were barely audible. Markus sprinted and sprinted for as long as he could until he stopped by an old gas station out of breath, then he sat down on the sidewalk in disbelief.

What was that all about? Don never liked him to begin with but he had never gone that far. And why was there a chick in his bedroom? Did he bring one home and forget all about her? No, no he hadn't. Also, home invader? They acted like he had never met him before, like he was a stranger. The situation was way too confusing.

Markus needed to talk to Cass, or at least somebody. His adoptive father had just tried to turn his head into a hole-in-one, and he didn't trust the police. He looked around and saw an old, dirty, payphone over by the street, and he had a passive thought about how he was surprised to see that payphones even still existed, but past that he didn't question his fortune. Markus dug around in his bag and brought out four quarters that rested on the bottom. He went into the kiosk and inserted the coins, then began to dial Cassandra's number onto the metallic buttons and brought the phone to his ear. After a few tones she picked up the line.

"This is Cassandra Underwood; how may I help you?" she asked.

"Cass! Cass, it's Markus. Something weird is going on. I need you to pick me up!" he exclaimed.

"I'm sorry, who is this?"

"Markus! It's Markus, you've known me since I was just a little kid. Come on!"

"I'm sorry young man, but I don't know anybody by that name," Cassandra said plainly.

"Come on Cass please…" Markus pleaded. "It's me."

"You seem hysterical, would you like me to call somebody?" she asked.

Markus tried to think of something, anything to prove they knew each other. "Jaime and Emma!" he said quickly. "Your kids, we used to play together, remember when we set fire to the dumpster outside? You were furious, come on! You have to remember!"

"No, I do not remember such a thing," Cassandra said sternly. "I do not know how you know my children, but I will contact the authorities if you press further," she said.

This wasn't happening. This wasn't happening. Why didn't she know who he was? Why didn't she remember?

"I'm sorry Cass," Markus said as he hung up. He ended up

slamming the phone repeatedly into the console until it broke. He just stood there resting his head on a propped hand. He felt defeated and empty. But more than anything, he felt alone.

"The hell is going on?"

A police cruiser pulled up next to the payphone and two male officers exited the vehicle, knocked on the glass of the phone booth and began to speak.

"Excuse me, young man, we are looking for someone who fits your description. We would like to speak to you for a moment," one of the officers said.

Markus knew what they wanted to talk to him about. This was the nice phase of this usual song and dance. He exited the booth quietly and walked over to the squad car.

"It was me, take me in."

The two officers looked at each other in confusion, but one of them opened the back door for Markus and he climbed in without struggle. The officers filed into the vehicle and began to drive. He didn't care where he was going. He had no idea what to do, he just rode this wave not sure where the current would take him.

CHAPTER 4

Oracle

Markus:

The police officers brought Markus to the local police station and led him into the building. They took his bag and placed handcuffs on him, though the officers seemed to do that as more of a protocol than out of belief that Markus would try anything. He told them his name, and they did some of their sobriety tests on him. After that he was brought to a small cell where he sat quietly with his head down. His mind was blank, yet restless. It was like he was in a waking nightmare. He felt like a phantom, like he wasn't even there. Almost like he was dead.

A female officer eventually came to his cell door around an hour later. Markus looked up at her and she jumped back startled. Her eyes went wide with a shocked look.

"What?" Markus asked.

"Why are your eyes like that?" she asked.

Markus wasn't sure what she meant, but considering how much they hurt he figured they looked pretty rough. "I don't know, they don't feel right," he said.

"They don't look right either," the officer said. She unlocked the cell and opened the door. "Come on, it's time for your interview."

Markus got up and followed her until they arrived at an interrogation room, once inside he sat down, and the officer attached his cuffs to the table.

"Officer Holt will be in shortly to ask questions, okay?"

Markus nodded his head, and she exited the room. He began to scan the room. It was about what one would think an interrogation room would look like. He sat in a steel chair facing a table. It had white floors and walls, and a mirrored window was installed to his right. He looked over at his reflection on the wall and saw two bright eyes staring back at him.

He jumped up and ended up moving the whole table. His eyes weren't the light gray they usually were—now they were an unnatural blue. They almost seemed to be glowing, which became even brighter as he became progressively more unnerved. They were the same color of eyes that those things had. He reached out with his free hand and placed his fingers under his eyes, diligently examining himself.

"Okay... that's new."

The door to the room opened and Markus quickly sat back down. An older male officer with graying hair came and sat opposite to him.

"Good evening, I'm Captain Holt," the officer said. "You said your name is Markus Daniels?"

Markus was familiar with this guy, as he had met him on multiple trips downtown. He didn't seem to remember who he was though.

"Yes, first name is spelled with a K instead of a C," Markus answered. He didn't want to drag this out.

"Right," Holt said. "We received a report of breaking and entering with the perpetrator having shaggy blond hair, a red sweatshirt and jeans, as well as a bag with a skateboard. Snuck in through the daughter's window, broke the living room TV, and escaped out the front door. Gave the Baymore family quite the scare from what I hear."

"I didn't break the stupid TV, but I did come in through the window," Markus said.

Holt raised an eyebrow. "And why did you do this?" he asked.

"I thought it was my home," Markus answered.

"A common mistake?" Holt asked.

"No."

Holt looked a bit perplexed. "Well, you didn't have any

narcotics or alcohol in your system, and you're admitting to what you did. So, you did so with a clear mind. Are you being truthful when you say your name is Markus Daniels?" he asked.

"Yes."

Holt looked around. "Well Mr. Daniels, I admit to being confused."

"How so?" Markus asked quietly.

"We searched thoroughly, but we could find no documentation pertaining to a Markus Andrew Daniels fitting your description. No criminal record, no school record, not even a birth certificate. It's like you don't exist."

Markus knew he had extensive documentation. He had it rubbed in his face almost constantly. This wasn't normal.

"Care to explain why this is the case?" Holt asked.

"I have no clue."

Holt didn't look satisfied with the answer. "Listen son, you did the right thing by turning yourself in, but it is a major offense to lie to an officer," he started just as the door to the interrogation room swung open. Holt and Markus turned their attention to the doorway. Three suited men were standing there. Two of them were tall with the one in the middle being shorter, and they all entered the room at the same time.

"Thank you for your assistance, Captain, but we will take it from here." the shorter man said.

"Well hold on, who are you with?" Holt asked loudly.

"None of your concern, just know that the proper paperwork has been filed, and funds distributed," the shorter man said. "Your services are no longer required."

Holt got up from his chair and rushed out of the room like he needed to get somewhere quickly. The suited men came in and the shorter one took a seat at the table and crossed his hands together. Markus immediately disliked him. He could tell this was one of those born with a silver spoon types he loathed. His hair was perfect to the point where it looked fake, and his suit fit him all too perfectly. He seemed as charming as a lawyer and as trustworthy as a politician.

"You say your name is Markus Daniels, correct?" he asked.

"Um, yeah," Markus answered. "And who might you be Suit?"

"My name is Alvin Bernard. I am a representative on behalf of the St. Louis branch of the Oracle Corporation."

Oracle. They were the last people Markus wanted to deal with, especially now. "Look, if it's about that graffiti, I'm sorry," Markus said casually, not really sure how to respond. "What better way to screw up and make mistakes than when you're young and ripe right?"

"What graffiti?" Alvin asked. "No Mr. Daniels, our interest in you has nothing to do with street painting. We believe something quite extraordinary has happened to you. That you're special."

"No need to tell me," Markus said smugly. "But why do you say that?"

"Have you seen abnormal things lately? Outlandish things? Perhaps you believe you've seen strange people or what can only be described as monsters?" Alvin asked. "Has your life been changed in a drastic way? Do people not recognize you anymore? Do things you've done seem like they didn't occur? Does it feel like you don't exist?"

Markus's jaw dropped to the floor. Somehow, they knew. But how? "Do you know what's happened to me?" he asked.

"Assuming that you can relate to what I just described, yes." Alvin answered

"Well, what happened? None of this is making any sense," Markus asked quickly.

"It's very complicated. We will explain it all back at HQ. You will need to come with us. We can help you."

Markus trusted Oracle about as far as he could throw them, but they were his only lead. Besides the two agents behind him were making him nervous, they seemed about as nice as fighting dogs. He knew going against the grain wasn't going to grant him any favors.

"Alright. Fine. Do I have any other option?"

"No, you don't." Alvin looked over at the two men behind him. "Amos, Marsh, please escort Mr. Daniels to the van."

One of the two agents brought out a key for his cuffs and unlocked them. The other took hold of Markus's arm, forcing him to his feet.

"Easy, Cupcake," Markus said annoyed.

The agent sneered at him and pushed him forward. Markus was already regretting this. Both agents got ahold of him and led him out the door with Alvin taking the lead, Markus's bag gripped in his hands. Captain Holt tried to get to them to ask more questions but was rudely shoved aside as they made their way through the hallway. The four of them made their way outside to a parked black van. The agents opened the van and threw him in the back and locked a black steel gate that was installed in the vehicle. They slammed the doors behind it. He got up and shook the gate, but it was solidly built.

"I would sit down Mr. Daniels," Alvin said climbing into the vehicle. "Agent Marsh can be quite the aggressive driver."

CHAPTER 5

Apex

Markus:

The four of them drove in the van quickly through many streets, turning frequently. After about ten minutes Markus had no clue where they were. More black vehicles had joined them on their journey. He could see one vehicle in the back and one in the front. They didn't look like normal vehicles you would see every day. They looked like something the military would drive around, and they seemed to be turning this into a convoy of sorts. The Amos agent sputtered off their status repeatedly into a handheld radio. Markus stood up in the van.

"What is all this? Am I some terrorist or something?" Markus asked loudly.

"Something like that," Agent Marsh said. The agent hit the brakes hard, and Markus slammed into the metal barricade between them and fell back onto the base of the van. Amos and Marsh began to laugh.

"Knock it off you two! Marigold wants the Time Rider in good condition when we deliver," Alvin barked.

"What did you call me?" Markus asked from the floor.

The agents ignored him. Amos lifted his radio to his ear. "Trojan to Praetorian, we're coming up on Ead's bridge," he said into the radio.

Markus could hear a response from the device, but it was too garbled to make out from where he was sitting. They were going to Ead's bridge. This was no surprise. Oracle tower and the plaza were on the other side.

He felt the vehicle continue onto the bridge with the military vehicle following close behind. It continued until it stopped abruptly in the middle.

"What now?" Alvin asked loudly.

"Traffic Jam," Amos answered. "Looks pretty backed up."

"Any way to make this go faster? We have a deadline," Alvin asked tensely tapping his expensive looking watch.

"Even yuppies like you have to deal with traffic Bernard. We'll have to wait it out." Agent Marsh said with contempt.

Alvin shrunk back into his seat with a huff. Markus looked at the situation himself. "Traffic jam" was putting it mildly. In the front and back were cars as far as Markus could see. Fifteen minutes passed, then thirty, forty-five, sixty. The car line barely budged. The two agents sat idling in the front seats, passing a whiskey flask between them. Alvin sat in his seat looking mad enough to urinate dried superglue.

"Marigold's gonna have my neck," Alvin said through his teeth.

Markus thought this would be a good opportunity to try to coax some info out of these men. "So, Al," Markus started, putting his arm up on the seat. "What was that you called me earlier? A Time Rider? Care to explain what that means?"

Alvin looked over at him. "I needn't tell you anything." he said.

"Needn't?"

"Pretty much a damn superhero." Amos said from the front.

"Quiet Amos! Or I'll have *your* head on the chopping block!" Alvin snapped.

"Whatever," Amos said.

"A superhero?" Markus said perplexed. "Like what? I have powers or something?"

"Shut up," Alvin growled.

"Do I have super strength?" How about X-Ray vision? Can I fly? C'mon Al, tell me I can fly!"

"SHUT UP!" Alvin bellowed. "All you need to know is that your existence will lead to life-changing research, so stay quiet and maybe I won't…."

Alvin was cut off by a deafeningly loud crash that shook the entire vehicle. Everyone in the van went deathly quiet. Markus felt a bizarre chill down his spine. He hadn't felt anything like this before. It was like a caffeine rush going up and down his back. Another crash occurred just behind the van, and everyone fixed their eyes and saw the vehicle behind them had been damaged, like something large had landed on it. Then Markus began to hear screaming of people outside as they fled away towards the end of the bridge. Then a handful of armed men that looked like soldiers of some kind filed out of the vehicle yelling in a panic. Once they adjusted themselves something in the front caught their attention. They began yelling again and firing their weapons at something past the van, the gunshots loud and earsplitting. Instinctively, Markus and the others looked forward and saw something large hit the vehicle in the front causing it to back up into the van. The sudden collision knocked everyone backwards and shattered the windshield.

Amos and Marsh lay in the front winded and confused. Alvin had fallen between the seats and Markus was back on the floor. He tried to collect himself, but he could hear Amos's radio going insane with chatter, among that the gunfire and screaming could also be heard in unison. Amos and Marsh got out of the vehicle with their own weapons drawn, and Marsh swore loudly at something Markus could not see.

"The hell is that!" Amos yelled

"Shoot it! Shoot it!" Marsh bellowed.

They began firing their weapons until Amos got hit by something and could be heard yelling as he went flying off the bridge. Marsh continued firing until he got slammed into the van causing it to rock again. Afterward, the screaming could still be heard, but it was distant. All the gunfire had stopped, leaving the area silent. There was no sign of the attacker that Markus could make out from his position. He lay on the floor of the van afraid to make a noise. The chill in his spine was so strong it felt like it was burning. Alvin lay quietly as well, silent as a corpse.

All of a sudden something hit the van hard causing it to titter on its suspension, it came back down hard on all four wheels, then it got hit again causing the van to fall to its side violently. Markus got thrown and slammed back down to the Earth with a pained groan, and Alvin was starting to whimper in the unorthodox position he landed. Then a large muscular arm punched through the van and began reaching around until it got ahold of Alvin's leg. Whatever the limb belonged to began to pull as Alvin desperately held on to a seat.

"No! Please God no! Help me! Help me!" he yelled to Markus, but there was nothing he could do while he remained in the cage.

Alvin got pulled out of the van screaming, and Markus quickly looked out the hole the arm made, and just managed to see a red mist plume up in a thick cloud. He moved away breathing heavily and began dry heaving. Whatever was out there was big, he could feel and hear its footsteps outside get closer to the van. He looked forward past the windshield. The large being knelt down so it was looking through the shattered vehicle. A long, tooth filled snout peaked into the windshield. It had a set of those eerie glowing eyes, and it was missing its nose, leaving only the bony holes of its skull. In its mouth was a set of razor-sharp looking teeth, all of them jagged and as sharp as needles. Markus backed up quickly until his back was against the cage. It sat there still, staring at him with that hideous smile, and he felt frozen in place. After an uncomfortable amount of time, it lifted its head away.

There was nothing but silence for a moment. Then the van got lifted in the air and slammed back on the ground, which happened over and over again, with the creature lifting and throwing the van down trying to get the cage open. Markus cried out each time. The door to the cage eventually came loose and swung open and his bag plopped down into the cage with him. Once the vehicle came down to the ground again, he grabbed his bag and threw himself out onto the street. The creature effortlessly lifted the vehicle off the ground again as he rushed to his feet, and his heart felt like it was about to explode.

He got his first clear look at his attacker. It was an extremely tall humanoid figure, around eight and a half to nine feet tall. It had a chiseled armored and muscular build with no hair in sight. At the end of each of its fingers seemed to be a sort of dull claw, like those on a wolf. And like a crocodilian it had a snout and a long muscular tail on its posterior. Alongside that, the creature had boney growths akin to horns on its head. This thing was shaped like an armored werewolf, but the white plates all over its body gave it an appearance that seemed reptilian, like a large lizard.

Altogether, it was a twisted amalgamation of both.

The creature looked up and saw Markus below it and dropped what remained of the van onto the ground, its eyes and teeth making it look especially unnerving. Markus bolted as fast as he could under one of the abandoned cars trying to get out of harm's way. The creature lifted the car and tossed it aside like it was nothing. It lifted one of its legs and Markus rolled away just in time as it came down and stomped the ground hard enough to leave a crater. Left with no other option he began to run the other way down the bridge. He heard the creature let out an otherworldly howl into the air and begin to sprint after behind him. Markus moved quickly jumping from car to car to keep the momentum, his adrenaline ran on full blast.

That creature was coming at him in a full athletic sprint, knocking away cars like they were made of Styrofoam. He ran and jumped with all his effort but the heavy footsteps behind him kept getting faster and closer.

After pushing through an intense amount of effort, Markus's vision began to change. Everything started to glow blue and abundant with some kind of energy, and time itself began to feel slower. Or was he moving faster? He relaxed and his vision returned to normal. He stopped dead in his tracks in confusion.

"The hell...?"

He focused again in the same manner and his vision became engulfed by rapidly flowing blue waves. It was breathtaking, but uncomfortably alien. He quickly looked at his hand and saw all the energy flow over it like water. He became transfixed, but the sound of destruction, car alarms, and harsh roaring brought Markus's focus back to the moment.

The creature sprinted towards him, bright blue light accompanied by it. Markus focused and returned to the waves. He saw that the creature seemed to slow down when he was there but not by much, but it was much faster without him focusing. He kept going through with the energy vision, resuming his car hopping and sprinting. Despite its large size the creature kept pace with Markus. He had to push hard in order to stay ahead.

But the creature evidently had the same ability he did. Even while moving through the bright blue waves, the creature proved to be faster than Markus, who only delayed the inevitable at this point. Despite his best efforts the monster eventually closed the distance and snatched him up like a child with a small doll. Markus winced and groaned as the massive hand lifted him up and constricted his whole body. He began to struggle with no success, desperation and panic clouding his mind. He was forced to look the beast right in the eye as it brought him close to its face. Eyes of hellfire stared into him like dull daggers, its ugly set of teeth bared at him. It might have been the heat of the moment, but Markus swore he could hear a subtle, monotone laugh of triumph coming from its throat.

Everything stung with pain. He struggled with every attempt feeling like he was trying to escape a solid vice. The creature just held him there, seeming to savor catching its prey. It opened its jaw wide and moved its head towards his, ready to bite down.

In a panic, Markus threw his one free hand forward through the blue waves and landed a punch against its teeth. The creature's head lurched back in unexpected pain. A plan formed quickly in Markus's mind upon seeing this, and he began to swing his fist against its teeth over and over again as hard as he could. Again, he jabbed against its jaw, even when the creature moved its head trying to dodge. After one especially solid punch, Markus felt its teeth come loose and shatter against his fist.

The creature howled in pain and flung Markus away from him out over the bridge. Deathly cold air enveloped him as he began to plummet. He barely had enough time to scream as he hit the surface of the water and sank down into the Mississippi river.

CHAPTER 6

Sweet Sixteen

Charlotte:

Charlotte Rowes sat at her kitchen counter in her **apartment** working on a school assignment. She sat there with one hand, writing, the other propping her head up on the countertop. The assignment was fairly simple, almost boring, but she didn't mind. She tried to keep her mind off things anyway. She was once again being haunted by the bittersweet memories of the events that happened three months ago. Haunted by memories of him, the Time Rider.

The television in the living area currently played in the background as she worked. A game show was broadcast until it switched over to a commercial that made Charlotte peer over to the screen absentmindedly at the sound of a familiar music sting she recognized. The commercial depicted men and women of various races and sizes dressed in business clothes and happily typing away at computers or working on team projects next to sterile white looking backgrounds. A chipper woman's voice could be heard over the footage talking about the value of ethics and the groundbreaking research of the local corporation.

It ended with an aerial shot of similar people smiling as a purple eye insignia rose above their heads while they recited their motto. "Oracle: We foresee the technology of the future."

There was one man near the front that Charlotte recognized. A middle-aged man in a lab coat suffering from aggressive balding and an overblown smile. Almost as if on cue, her right hand began to shake rapidly, causing her to mark on her school assignment accidentally. She secured it until the shaking stopped. The commercial went away just as she scowled at the television.

"Good for nothing jerks…" she muttered to herself.

Her train of thought came to a halt as her mother had entered the kitchen deep in conversation on her phone. She was dressed in her usual button-up shirt and had her red hair pulled tight into a bun.

"Yes, that will be fine. No, we'll figure out appointments next week," Mrs. Rowes rambled off into her smartphone. "Yeah, talk to you then. Bye," she said hanging up.

"What's that all about?" Charlotte asked casually.

"Oh, that was Thomas, just setting some things up."

Thomas was a counselor that had been paired with Charlotte to help her through some emotional problems she'd been contending with. She thought he was nice enough but obviously couldn't divulge the whole truth about her "friend" to him. If she did, they would likely put her on something a bit more powerful than Prozac, if they didn't institutionalize her first.

"I'm not sure how much I need a therapist, Mom."

"It's just to help you feel better," Mrs. Rowes said positively. "Life's too short to be blue all the time."

"All they've done is do basic stuff and shove pills down my throat. I feel more like a customer than a patient."

"It's the serotonin sweetie, just chemicals. A lot of people take medication for that."

"I'm not like everyone else," Charlotte said grumpily.

"I know you don't like it, but it'll help, you'll see," Mrs. Rowes said cheerfully leaning her arms on the counter. "So, how are we feeling today?" she asked brightly.

"Fine, I guess," Charlotte said. "Why? You taking notes on my mental state now?"

"Well, I just happened to notice the date and saw it was a very special day today."

"What's so special about it?"

"You tell me," Mrs. Rowes said.

Charlotte looked up, confused. "Tell you what? Did Dad call or something?"

A disgruntled look formed on Mrs. Rowes's face. "Charlie, you're kidding, don't tell me you forgot."

"Forgot what?"

"Your birthday!" Mrs. Rowes exclaimed. "Oh honey, how can you forget your own birthday?"

It might have seemed odd, but Charlotte had in fact forgotten her thoughts had been elsewhere for so long she didn't even think about it. "Yeah, I guess it is my birthday, sorry."

"Well, I'll never forget!" Mrs. Rowes declared. "That was the happiest day of my life, I remember the day you were born like it was yesterday."

"Happier than the day you met Dad? Or the day you married him?" Charlotte asked.

"It's not a competition Charlie," Mrs. Rowes said brightly. "I love both of you," she said. "Ever since I was your age, I always wanted to be a mother. After I met your father and a nine-month pregnancy I got exactly what I wanted."

"Weirdo…"

"Am not!" Mrs. Rowes exclaimed. "I was a normal girl with a normal dream. Your birth was a great blessing to me when that dream of mine came true."

"Not to your schedule, your sanity, or your finances. *Especially* your finances." Charlotte said flatly.

"Stop that!" Mrs. Rowes retorted. "You're worth more than all the money in the world."

"All the money in the world? I don't know, that's a lot…"

"Quit it, it drives me up a wall when you talk like that," Mrs. Rowes scoffed. She seemed annoyed but still brought out a warm smile. "Anyway, you're now sixteen! How exciting!"

The cynic in Charlotte seemed to be working overtime today, and she had to really try to keep the atmosphere friendly. "Yeah!" Charlotte said as bright as she could. "Do I have a party or anything?"

"Well, you know how it is, all the family we have are out of town. They did send you cards though! And of course, your father will call you as soon as he's done with his duties for the day," Mrs. Rowes explained. "And you don't have too many friends. It's a shame that Ryder friend of yours isn't here. I would have liked to meet him."

"Yeah…"

"But I did get you a cake! And a gift," Mrs. Rowes said.

Charlotte looked up with curiosity. "A gift?" she asked. "What did you get?"

A youthful look out of character for someone as old as Mrs. Rowes formed on her face and she ran up the stairs. Charlotte got up and looked up the staircase with anticipation. Her mother came back down with a large, gift-wrapped box and laid it on the floor.

"This was your father's idea, I didn't know when to give it to you, but I figure now is a good as time as any."

Charlotte knelt and examined the container and looked up at her mother.

"Go on," Mrs. Rowes urged waving her hand.

Charlotte began to tear the wrapping paper revealing a cardboard box with a lid on top, she took off the lid and looked inside. Inside the container was a small puppy matted with black and white fur. It was sitting in the corner and looked up at Charlotte when she opened the box. Her whole body jolted.

"Aw, no way!" Charlotte said happily as she picked up the small animal and clutched it tightly to her body. The puppy began to lick her face playfully causing her to giggle.

"There's that smile," Mrs. Rowes said. "You like it?"

"I love it!" Charlotte said happily as she dodged another barrage of puppy licks. "What's his name?"

"Actually, she's a girl. Her name is Millie. She's a Siberian husky."

"A husky? I thought you said you didn't want a dog."

"I changed my mind, and pulled some strings with the landlord," Mrs. Rowes said. "I thought you could use a new friend."

"Thank you so much!" Charlotte exclaimed; she began to rub her head against Millie as the dog started yapping happily.

Mrs. Rowes knelt and began petting Millie herself. Charlotte let the puppy go and it began wandering around the apartment, exploring her new home. Charlotte went over and hugged her mother tightly.

"Happy birthday Charlie," Mrs. Rowes said as she hugged her daughter back. "Oh, and just so you know Maxine from that coffee shop you liked called, they wanted to wish you a happy birthday and said you have a free drink from them if you want it."

Charlotte backed away. "Really? That's nice of them."

"It is. If you want to go grab it, just let me know." Mrs. Rowes said.

"A macchiato sounds good, but what about Millie?"

"She'll be here when you get back. You want to go over there?"

"Yeah, if that's alright."

"Of course, just don't be gone all day, you still have cake and a puppy to spend time with."

"You got it," Charlotte said as she got to her feet and grabbed her jacket. She put it on and tried to get to the front door, but Millie came over and started nipping at her feet and jumping on her leg.

"Hey! I'll be back," Charlotte told the puppy as she knelt and rubbed behind her ears. She yapped louder as she got out the front door.

Once outside she began walking to Sebastian's coffee shop, her favorite dive for caffeinated beverages. The outside air had become brisker over the last few days with fall was on the horizon. Her favorite time of the year. Walking through the city felt euphoric as the cooler air cycled through her lungs and the happiness from meeting Millie lingered. Perhaps not the most exciting birthday ever, but Charlotte didn't mind. Only one thing could make it better in her eyes, but she chose not to think about that.

After her walk she arrived at Sebastian's. She went into the small coffee shop to see the two employees of the shop working at the counter. There was Maxine, the worker Charlotte was most acquainted with, the other was her husband, Sebastian himself. The shop was quiet, and only one other customer was in there. The darker colors and landscape paintings around the shop always helped Charlotte feel comfortable. She got along with the owners well enough they could be considered friends.

"Hey Seb," she greeted walking up to the counter.

"Hey Charlotte. Happy birthday!" Sebastian said. He was a gentleman in his late thirties with a dark tan and shiny black hair. His demeanor was as warm as the coffee he masterfully brewed.

Next to him was his wife, Maxine. She was always just as bubbly as her husband.

"One caramel macchiato with white chocolate shavings, coming right up!" Maxine called out.

"I can still pay for that," Charlotte offered.

"No, you can't, it's on the house. Special treatment for our most loyal customer!" Sebastian said.

Charlotte smiled. "I'll take a seat."

"Yeah, go ahead! Max will get that drink over to you as soon as it's ready. And just be warned," he pointed at the only other customer there and lowered his voice. "That young man over there is smelling something foul. Might be best to sit away from him."

"Will do, thanks." Charlotte went over and sat to the right side of the shop waiting for her drink to be ready. She looked around at the walls and the paintings, then to the boy Maxine mentioned that she saw sitting in the corner. He stood out sitting alone wearing an old Cardinals sweatshirt and a cheap looking set of aviator glasses. Maxine wasn't being hyperbolic, even from where she was sitting a raw scent of what could only be the smell of sewage wafted over to her. She was surprised Sebastian and Maxine even let him into their business.

He nursed a coffee that was placed in front of him, looking down at it aimlessly. Charlotte figured she probably shouldn't stare, but there was something about him she couldn't put her finger on. He briefly took off the glasses and rubbed his eyes. The moment he opened his eyes for a split-second Charlotte froze in place. She knew his eye color by heart. That vibrant blue was something she would never forget anytime soon, she saw that shade every time she dreamed. They were the same eyes of the Time Rider.

The boy quickly put the sunglasses back on and stared at Charlotte. She didn't even budge, she just sat still as a statue staring at him.

He gathered his bag and bolted out of the shop, leaving his drink behind. Charlotte began to get up and go after him when Maxine called out to her.

"Don't forget your drink!" she said.

"Oh, right." Charlotte said quickly grabbing the coffee. "Thanks again!"

"Happy sixteenth!" Sebastian called out.

"Thanks!" she called out as she left the shop in almost a sprint.

This was the worst time possible to have a hot coffee in her hand.

CHAPTER 7

Old Friends

Markus:

diot. **That's what Markus kept muttering to himself. After** the bridge incident and somehow surviving that plunge into the river he was stricken with paranoia. He kept moving around the city as much as he could. He was deathly afraid that large, monstrous thing would show up and finish the job it started. There was too much to process. Markus had never seen anyone die before today, he disliked Alvin and his bodyguards the moment he met them, but now they were dead and gone. And the way they went out hadn't been pretty, even for Markus that was too much. Those macabre scenes felt like they were carved into his brain.

He managed to nab a pair of sunglasses and some food from a local shop and did his best to lay low while he figured everything out. He had gone into that coffee shop and bought himself a simple black coffee with the little money he had left. The joint felt out of the way, out of trouble. But of course, he ended up flashing his new night brights at the only other person in there. That girl had stared him down like he had tentacles coming out of his ears. He had to get out of there. He wasn't willing to risk getting anyone else involved. He was quickly walking the sidewalks trying to get lost in the crowd.

"Hey! Hey wait!"

Markus looked behind him to see that girl running towards him, coffee in hand. "Oh for the love of—" Markus grumbled throwing his hood up.

"Wait up!" she called out.

He just kept walking doing his best to ignore her. "I'm not here. I'm not here. I'm not here," he muttered over and over.

"Ma-Markus! MARKUS!" the girl cried out hysterically.

He stopped in his tracks. The girl caught up to him out of breath, still holding that coffee. "How do you know my name?" he asked.

She lifted a finger to give herself a moment. "You are Markus, right?" she asked once she gained some stamina back.

"Yeah…"

She grabbed the front of his sweatshirt and pulled him into an alley to their right. "Easy Doll Face, I've been thrown around enough today as is," Markus said with annoyance.

"Do you know Ryder?" she asked.

"Wha—who?"

"Ryder," She repeated. "You know anyone with that name?"

"No," Markus answered. "Should I?"

She slowed down for a moment with a disappointed look in her eye, silently staring off into space.

Markus took a good long look at her. She had long, relaxed messy hair that seemed to be leaning more towards a hearty red color. She was small and petite, with a set of bright green eyes and some patches of light freckles beneath them. She was clothed in a light hooded jacket, a T-shirt, tight denims, and a well-worn pair of converse sneakers. She looked like the quintessential tomboy. She wasn't really Markus's type, but she was appealing in her own way. For him she was better company than what he had to deal with over the last twenty-four hours.

There was something about her he couldn't put his finger on, something familiar. He turned it over in his head again and again until it finally clicked. Once it did Markus felt his eyes light up. As luck would have it, they had actually attended school together. He attended their high school like anyone else his age and met a plethora of students in the process just passing through the hallways going in between classes. Her hair ended up being the dead giveaway.

In the sea of heads topped with brown, black, and blonde hair.

Her head always stood out with its red color. Slowly he began remembering who she was. If he recalled correctly, she was the same grade he was. She was a smaller, more reclusive girl that kept to the outskirts of any social circle. Not necessarily because she was anti-social, she just never went out of her way to participate with others.

He'd heard some girls whisper snide gossip behind her back, stuff that would cause a fight if said by a boy. Things like how she always dressed like one, or how she was clearly single. Or just a freak in general. Markus never paid it even half a thought. She was cute, but quiet. That was abnormal. And the girls at school didn't like abnormal things, so they talked. But whatever was said never seemed to affect her. She coasted along every day, minding her own business, and going off into the city after the final bell had rung.

"Wait a sec... it's Charlotte Rhodes right?" Markus asked.

Her eyebrows shot up. "It's Charlotte *Rowes*. Like row your boat."

"Right yeah, sorry."

"How do you know who I am?" she asked.

"We go to school together," he said brightly.

Her eyebrows started shifting again. "No, we don't."

"I remember. You played Annie in that school play back when we were in the sixth grade."

Her eyes went wide in anger. "Don't you *ever* bring that play up again. I've spent years trying to forget about that."

"Regardless, proof enough, right? We are in the same grade. I was there when you were prancing around in that red dress. I also remember you going for a nosedive off the stage when you missed your footing."

"All right! I got it."

"We pass by going to class all the time. Come on, surely, we know one another just a bit. Just a teeny bit?"

Charlotte blinked. "No, we don't."

Markus was alarmed, then he quickly realized this was exactly what she was always going to say. "Yeah, gotcha, of course we don't..."

"Wait a minute," she said biting her lip. "That's right, you've been erased."

"Erased? What are you going on about? How do you know me? Hmm? Because ever since I've woken up this morning, instead of people wishing I weren't born, it's people *acting* like I was never born, not to mention all the other weird things going on. You are the only person who knows my name."

"Well, that's just the thing, you... kinda don't exist."

"*Kinda don't exist*? Care to elaborate?" Markus asked.

"Look, I'm not really the expert, but I know someone who is. You need to follow me," Charlotte said as she began walking out of the alley.

"Woah! Hold up a sec, Sweet Cheeks, they aren't with that company, are they? Cause if they are I'm turnin' heel."

"What, Oracle? No! He's no friend of Oracle believe me, and neither am I," Charlotte said.

"Not a fan of them, eh? A dissatisfied customer?

"More like arch-nemesis."

Markus liked the sound of that. "Sounds like we'll get along just fine," he said pompously. "Lead the way."

Charlotte nodded and continued onto the sidewalk with Markus tagging along close behind. He followed her down the sidewalk for a bit. She looked ahead occasionally taking a drink from that coffee she drug around. The last person Markus expected to get answers from was someone like her, but at this point he just hoped he wasn't digging an even deeper hole than he was already in.

They arrived at an old convenience store, called Rudy's. Markus actually knew the place. He used to lift stuff from here all the time until the owner started recognizing him. He was this older, hefty African American with a thick southern accent. If Markus even dared to stick his nose in there again, he would threaten him with a healthy dose of yee-haw justice. It was admittedly funny, but terrifying. Markus followed Charlotte into the store as she went over to the counter where the owner worked the register. He was currently tapping away at his registers' monitor.

"P.O.S system," he muttered. "Ain't that the truth..."

Charlotte walked up to the counter, stood up slightly on her toes, and placed her arms on the counter. Markus kept a healthy distance behind her.

"I'll be with you in a moment," Rudy said acknowledging their presence. "I'm currently booting this thing back up. It went and overheated again. Piece of crud."

"Hi Rudy," Charlotte greeted.

The owner looked up from what he was doing and his eyes shot open. "Ms. Charlotte!" Rudy exclaimed.

He let out a hoarse laugh and walked quickly around the counter to the front and hugged her. She returned the affection by hugging him back and grinning warmly. Markus just rubbed his head awkwardly, feeling like a third wheel. After a moment they moved away and faced each other.

"Been awhile, how you been honey? I missed you," Rudy said.

"Doing just fine," Charlotte said warmly. "Is Spencer around?" she asked.

Rudy looked up. His eyes incredulous. "He's down where he usually is. Why?" he asked.

Charlotte went over to Markus and yanked his glasses off.

"Hey! Rude," Markus retorted.

Rudy looked at his face and his eyes went even wider. "Wha— another one?"

"I think so," Charlotte said.

"Another what?" Markus asked impatiently.

Charlotte shoved his glasses back in his hand and grabbed his arm ignoring his question.

"I need to bring this guy to Spencer. I'll be back."

She started moving with him before Rudy called out. "Hey, wait a minute. Be careful stomping on down there," he said.

"Why?" Charlotte asked.

"It's just… he's been in a real mood lately. Might not be a good idea to show up all willy-nilly."

"When is Spencer not in a mood?"

Rudy's eyebrows went low, but he didn't answer.

"I'll be careful, pinky promise."

Charlotte began to drag Markus back out onto the street and into the cluttered alley behind the store. Markus took his arm back and began to rub it.

"Man, we haven't known each other long enough for you to be getting rough like that," he scoffed.

Charlotte wasn't paying attention to him. She looked at the wall facing the right of the back door. Markus saw there was some kind of large metal door installed on the side of it. Charlotte went over to the right of it to some kind of control pad, then she pressed a button on it and a feminine voice sounded back.

"Please vocally state authorization ID."

"Charlotte," She recited. The door began to open upwards like a bunker, revealing a staircase going down into the building. "Good, he didn't change it. Come on," she told Markus.

She began walking down the staircase with Markus doing the same apprehensively. When they both made it to the bottom, Markus saw it was some kind of basement set up as a living area. It had a kitchen, living area, and a bunch of other necessities. And for whatever reason, the place reeked of musk and stale booze.

"Spencer!" Charlotte called out.

Suddenly, a loud bang could be heard and the wall above Charlotte shot out a cloud of dust. She screamed and ducked down onto the floor while Markus stood frozen in place.

"Dammit Charlotte!" an older male voice yelled.

Markus looked over and saw a man wearing slacks and a white dress shirt. He was an older guy with slick black hair and gray sideburns. He had a handgun raised, and the barrel still smoked from the gunshot.

"What are you doing?!" Charlotte yelled angrily. "You could have killed me!"

The man dropped the gun with an annoyed look on his face, then he walked over to her and offered her a hand. "Sorry kid, you alright?" he asked.

"No!" Charlotte snapped. She took his hand and pulled her to her feet.

"What in the blue blazes was that?" a voice from outside boomed. It was the Rudy character from earlier. "Was that a gunshot I just heard?"

Before Rudy got too close, the man pushed a button on a keyboard next to him and the bunker door at the top of the stairs closed. The sound of his beefy fists and multiple protests began to emanate around the base.

The man rolled his eyes and drew in a deep breath. "That's another fire to put out later," he muttered. "Happy birthday by the way."

"Thanks Spencer," she replied bitterly. "Perfect day to get shot!"

"Look, Oracle's been snooping around. It's a piss poor time to come barging down here. I really need to install an intercom system..." Spencer turned his attention over to Markus. "And you—I was wondering when you would show up, Markus."

"Okay, seriously how do you two know my name?" Markus asked.

"Very long story," Spencer said. "I got an inkling you have some questions?"

"Ya think?" Markus said. "I got a helluva lot more than an inkling. You mind giving me a rundown of why I'm so popular all of a sudden?"

Spencer put his gun on one of the desks and began to lean against it. "For starters, you're what we and Oracle Inc. call a Time Rider, meaning you have the ability to pass between our dimension and another that passes parallel to our own. Oracle calls it dimension Alpha-2; we call it the Time Stream." he explained.

"Okay... parallel dimension..." Markus said deep in thought. "It wouldn't happen to be like really blue, would it? And space-like?"

Spencer crossed his arms and raised his eyes; then he took a glance over at Charlotte who sat propped against the back of the sofa. She remained silent but did seem to indicate she knew what Markus was talking about.

"Yes, exactly," Spencer confirmed. "So, you have passed into it before?"

"I guess, If I hadn't, I'd probably be dead on that bridge," Markus explained. He stood up straighter. "Oh yeah, about that! What was that big freakin' thing that tried to kill me?"

"Wait the bridge?" Charlotte asked. "You were there?"

"Yeah! Those Oracle guys tried to haul me off and that boney werewolf-looking thing attacked and tore through em' like tissue paper."

Spencer turned around and started typing away at his computer on the desk. One by one the monitors above him turned on and began to show documents and footage. They all showed the monsters that Markus had encountered the night before. All were arranged neatly as description files. Markus quickly scanned the screens, reading off their names and diagrams.

"They're called revenants," Spencer said. "They live in the

Time Stream. Only thing that does. They also like to visit our dimension and kidnap people."

"For what?"

"It's how they multiply. They drag people deep into the Time Stream and their victims become one of them. I think it's safe to assume they tried to do the same to you."

"I guess. They grabbed me, and after I woke up, everyone I know forgot who I was."

Spencer stayed quiet for a second. "They didn't forget, you were erased."

"Erased? That's what she said too." Markus gestured towards Charlotte. "What's that supposed to mean?"

"It means that your existence was wiped from reality. Everyone who knows you never knew you. Everywhere you've been, you've never been. You were never born."

"What are you talking about? I'm still here!"

"It's the same thing that happened to anyone who became a revenant. They got taken and erased. In your case you're still you, but you became like those things.

"What are you saying? That I'm one of them?"

"Yes and no. You got captured and taken into the Time Stream, but it wasn't a smooth transformation since something went wrong. That's why you're still human, at least mostly…"

"Then what's the beef? If I'm like them what's the issue?"

"They don't see you as one of them. If anything, you're a threat."

"A threat? What did I do?"

"It's not anything *you* did but believe me they have a good reason to believe that."

Markus tried to get his finger around all this. At this rate he was so open-minded he could believe in the Easter Bunny or Santa Claus.

Spencer raised a hand and gestured towards the files on his monitors. "As you can see, revenants come in many different variants, each having their own strengths and weaknesses," Spencer explained. "Knight revenants are armored and clawed, spikers will shoot crystals at you, raptors can fly, and that's barely scratching the surface," Spencer explained.

"What kind of revenant attacked me on that bridge?"

Spencer grimaced his teeth and stayed quiet for a moment. "I don't know," he finally answered. "That one is new, never seen anything like it. Shrugged off armor-piercing rounds like nothing, knocked around automobiles like they were made of plastic, not to mention its massive size..." he explained. "Admittedly, that one's got me a little scared."

This didn't instill Markus with much confidence. "Oracle agents are the ones that nabbed me, what does a tech company know about this stuff?"

"A lot actually," Spencer said. "They research both the revenants and the Time Stream. I'm at odds with them, been that way for over a decade now."

"Why?"

"Another long story," Spencer said as he stood up from the desk. "Does the name Ryder mean anything to you Markus?" he asked.

"No," Markus said. "She asked me about that too, who is that supposed to be?"

Charlotte had her arms crossed and looked down at the floor. Even Spencer seemed a bit uneasy, which Markus thought was strange, but the feeling of the whole room seemed to change.

"Ryder was... is... a Time Rider also. I worked with him for a good long while, combating Oracle and the revenants. He's been missing for three months now; and we have reason to believe you might have some clues as to his whereabouts," Spencer explained.

"Hate to disappoint, but I have no idea who that guy is."

"I see..." Spencer said quietly.

Charlotte remained where she was, still as a statue.

"Markus, you've had a long day. You can use the empty room down here if you need a place to rest your head, and we'll talk more tomorrow. It'll give you a chance to get that musk off you too," Spencer said.

"Yeah, no," Markus said quickly.

A look of confusion shot onto Spencer's face. "What do you mean, 'no'?"

"I mean no, 'I'm going back out there on my own.' Thanks for catching me up to speed, but no."

"What do you mean?" Charlotte stood upward on her feet; a heated look simmered in her eye. "Don't be stupid."

"What would be stupid is trusting random strangers again. Made that mistake once today. No thanks," Markus said, irritation rising in his voice.

"We're not your enemy son. Stay here, let me teach you what you need to know. You will be capable of doing some real good once you know what you're doing."

"Is that what this is about? Using my new bells and whistles to become some hero?" Markus asked spitefully. "Well, news flash, I'm not exactly a good Samaritan. I don't wanna be."

"You are in danger Markus," Spencer pleaded. "Oracle is still out there looking for you and they're not alone. This new variant is out there too. It tore apart an armed convoy trying to get to you. You're the one it wants. It would only be a matter of time before it finds you again. I have deterrents here, ways of masking your presence. You can't be anywhere safer."

"I'll take my chances," Markus said adjusting his bag, about to leave the basement. "I'm better on my own anyway."

"How can you be so selfish?" Charlotte cried out.

Markus turned back to look at her. "Don't take it personally Princess, but I learned the hard way that being the nice guy is the best way to get screwed. I don't plan on that happening again." Markus began ascending the staircase. "Toodles," he said just as he went through the door and left, leaving Charlotte and Spencer alone.

CHAPTER 8

Neglected Longing

Charlotte:

"**J**ERK!"

Charlotte fumed. What was that guy's problem? Princess? Who did he think he was? She wanted to run up those stairs and slug him in the mouth, but she settled for kicking one of Spencer's desks, hurting her foot in the process and falling to the floor.

"Yeah, desks hurt," Spencer said.

"Shut up!" Charlotte yelled as she sat on the ground nursing her foot and whimpering.

Spencer didn't pay her anger any mind, he just took a seat in an office chair next to her as she sat there rocking back and forth on the ground.

"I'm sorry kid," He shook his head. "He wasn't what I was expecting either."

"Ryder signed his name in that letter Spencer. Why? What does that jerk have to do with anything?"

"I don't know. We're just going to have to see."

"Why did you let him go?"

"Well, what was I supposed to do? Point a gun at him?"

"Sure, didn't stop you with me!"

"Stop, I feel bad enough about that as is!" Spencer bit back. "Besides if I did that he would never trust me or you again."

"He already doesn't."

"Yeah, it's clear he has some bad blood in that department. He's clearly not as much of a people person as Ry was."

"Is," Charlotte said quickly.

"Is," Spencer repeated.

Charlotte started to calm down, trading anger for sorrow.

"Are you okay? I worried about you kid. You stopped coming around," Spencer asked.

"I'm sorry. I just had to get away. This place brings back a lot of memories, and not all of them good."

'I know," Spencer replied.

Charlotte dipped her head down again and Spencer placed his hand on her shoulder.

"Keep going. Keep believing right?"

"Right," Charlotte said. "I just want to know what happened. I don't know what else to do."

"I get it. I really do. The undercroft, and this job, it all feels empty now."

"Yeah," Charlotte replied.

"So, what have you been up to, anyway?" Spencer asked.

"Pfft, same old, same old," she answered. "Yourself?"

"Not much I can do on my own, but I've made a hobby out of picking on Oracle in my time. Some embezzlement, leaked files, just general buffoonery."

"Sounds like fun."

"It has its moments." Spencer smiled, like he was recalling a good memory. He patted Charlotte's back "It is good to see you again, though."

"Likewise." Charlotte looked up at him with a warm grin. "Assuming the undercroft doesn't turn into a firing range."

Spencer rolled his eyes. "Yeah, I'll get to work on the intercom system tonight, it'll keep me busy."

"Can you do me a favor while you do that?" Charlotte asked.

"What?"

"Lay off the liquid courage a bit," she said. "You smell like a bar."

"Spencer groaned. "That obvious?"

"Duh, it stands out like a wardrobe malfunction."

Spencer groaned. "Fine, probably best to stay alert anyway.

Plus, it'll get Rudy to back off a bit in that department."

"Even with the gun going off?"

His face went still. "You let me worry about that okay?"

"Yep, no problemo." She stood up from the floor and brushed herself off. "I'm gonna head back home, are you alright down here?"

"I'll live; I got to keep an eye on our new Time Rider as well. Make sure he doesn't get himself killed."

"He didn't even know who Ryder is, why did he want us to know about him?" Charlotte asked.

"No clue, but the fact that he's here now is a good sign. We're just gonna have to reign him in. I can't believe you found him yourself."

Charlotte shrugged. "I guess I got a knack for finding Time Riders. What are you going to do?"

"I'm already playing with a few ideas. It's gonna be a delicate operation though. Say the wrong thing and Markus is gone."

"Yeah, wouldn't want that..." Charlotte said sarcastically.

"I know kids like him. The wannabe anarchists. I used to be one myself believe it or not. They get a kick outta trying to get under people's skin. Try not to let it get to you."

"Too late," Charlotte said.

She walked over to the staircase and stopped at the first step, then looked back at Spencer to ask something.

"You don't mind me hanging around for this, do you? You trying to rein him in?" she asked.

"Just don't do anything to drive Markus away, and you should be fine," Spencer said. "Be safe getting home and enjoy the rest of your birthday."

"Thanks."

"Oh, and one last thing," Spencer called out as she began to climb the stairs. "Yeah?"

"Drop by and let Rudy know you're all right, would you?"

Charlotte sighed. "I'll drop in and say hi."

Spencer resumed his work, and Charlotte went up the staircase, and visited with Rudy briefly, then began the journey home. This was not how she had expected her birthday to go. But she still looked forward to some cake and seeing Millie again. All things considered she chose to think of the day as a win.

She developed a sort of distaste for Markus, but she hoped with a little luck meeting him was the first step to getting Ryder back. Maybe. Just maybe. She was trying not to get her hopes up, since she and Spencer still had no idea how he fit into all this. Charlotte let herself have faith and let herself dream. It was all she had, but it was serving her well. She would see Ryder again. She chose to believe that, and that was enough.

CHAPTER 9

The New Face

Artemis:

Farai Omari is an active lieutenant within the Oracle Corporation's private military contractor sector. A woman hailing from Africa, inside the company she has gained a reputation for being someone of unshakeable focus and unnerving intelligence. Farai was the PMCs resident tracking and trap expert, skills she had acquired over many years of hunting big game and other quarry all over the world. Her work earned her the codename Artemis: named after the mythological Greek goddess of the hunt.

On this day Farai had been summoned by the chief executive officer of Oracle, a woman by the name Esther Marigold. She had called for an emergency meeting at Oracle tower. She and all the lieutenants that lived on sight were expected. Farai woke up that morning and quickly went through her usual rituals and exercises, putting on her usual attire of a fresh black tank top and cargos. After she pulled her braided hair back into a knot she began making her way to the meeting room.

As she walked, she tried to deduce what the meeting could be about. It was an uncertain time for the company as a whole. Three months ago, Project Witching Hour, an attempt to open a gateway to the alternative dimension, code named Alpha-2, was executed using the massive Gateway Arch. It had been successful, but Marigold was the only person with the information pertaining to the true goals of the operation. To bring forth the revenant matriarch, an entity known as The Progenitress. Once she arrived, she attacked Marigold and sent her hell spawn to attack everything else in sight. She and the other lieutenants were forced to enlist the help of the Time Rider, someone that actively opposed them to close the gateway. They had joined forces and were successful, but the Time Rider had not been seen since.

Marigold had somehow survived the incident, albeit not without injury. She has been on the mend since the incident and has not been able to assume her position in full capacity since then. Company operations have been agonizingly slow, as they have only been able to do basic routines and haven't been able to make any real progress.

Farai made it to the meeting room on one of the higher floors of the tower and opened the door. She entered a bright room lit by the early morning sun that came in through the large windows that surrounded the room. The middle of the room was occupied by a large desk made of a beautiful polished dark chestnut, and the other two lieutenants, agents Spartan and Legion, were present at the end of the table.

Farai took a seat next to Legion, with Spartan across from her. Spartan, whose true name was Edgar Talon, was a muscular military man sporting a buzzcut, wearing his usual tight black undershirt and camouflaged cargos. He had a lengthy career as a member of the United States military. He commanded all the operators that were in the employment of Oracle. He was the one person that Farai could rely on when it was needed.

"Farai," Spartan greeted.

"Talon," Farai said back.

To Farai's left was the lieutenant, code named Legion, clothed in a hooded cowl and mechanical mask. "All four of us are present," they said in their usual Germanic accent, the mask's eyes glowed yellow. They switched over to a green color. "Speak for yourself, I can't process anything with this exhaustion,"

The mask's eyes then changed over to purple, a child's voice followed. "I'm so sleepy…"

The eyes now changed to red, a malicious voice boomed forth. "It was your incessant singing that kept us up all night!"

"I'm sorry… I was bored." The purple eyed Legion member

said.

Farai shook her head. "I don't know how you four do this."

Legions eyes went yellow. "Don't have a choice, we're stuck with one another."

The eyes returned to red. "Unfortunately."

Legion was the oddest member of their team, or more specifically members. The entirety of Legion was one body, but four different people. The original identity of Legion is classified, but the four personalities inside took turns occupying it. They were given a mask that would have the eyes change color depending on who was in control at one given time. Annike: a female that often served as the voice of reason and unofficial leader, was indicated by yellow. Eckard: a violent spirited male who served as the enforcer and damage dealer, was indicated by red. The purple eyes belonged to Klara, a childlike female who serves as a moral antithesis of Eckard and likely stemmed from a desire for the days of childhood innocence. And finally, Fritz. The green-eyed member of Legion. He is an intelligent male that serves as the narcissistic strategist and problem solver. All together they acted as one lieutenant, and multiple all at the same time.

Esther Marigold herself finally came into the room, her right arm bound tightly in a brace. Farai noticed she looked worse than usual. Marigold was an aged woman with a wrinkled face and a dead looking blonde color for her hair. She also had a notable boil or infection on her face that always stood out like a sore thumb. It had gotten so bad now that noticeable decay had begun to form and go through her right eye, causing the eye to go blank and dull. Her face was also sprinkled with various bruises and cuts, making her appearance seem even more ghastly. Marigold was not a kind woman, but Farai couldn't help but pity her in this state.

"Good morning," Marigold stated in an English accent as she walked to the back end of the table. "You must be wondering why I called you all here today." Everyone in the room looked at her but didn't say anything. "As you are all very aware, our operations have been sluggish during my recovery, but I am delighted to report a groundbreaking development."

"And what would that be Ms. Marigold?" Fritz asked.

Marigold grabbed a small handheld radio from her waist and brought it to her mouth. "Doctor Yorkshire, bring in the equipment."

The door opened again and a small brown-haired balding man in a white lab coat started to wheel in a projector. Farai knew Yorkshire as the head of research for the company, in both research and development and Alpha-2. He wheeled the device over and began to set it up so that it was displaying its contents on the gray screen set up in the back. Once it was all set up it showed a picture of a blond teenager sitting in an interrogation room of some kind. He seemed completely average with one glaring abnormality. His eyes shined brightly with an all too familiar color. Farai's heart felt like it dropped to her feet.

"Wait a minute," Spartan started. "Is that..?"

"Yes, Talon," Marigold interrupted. "What you're seeing is a Time Rider, a new one. At the moment all we have is information on his appearance and his name: Markus Andrew Daniels."

"A new one?" Klara repeated.

"You've got to be kidding," Eckard followed up.

"When did you find this out?" Spartan asked.

"Eleven hours ago," Marigold said. "He was picked up by local authorities."

"And where is he now?" Farai asked.

"His whereabouts are currently unknown," Marigold answered. "A collection team was dispatched but they were unsuccessful."

"Unsuccessful?" Annike exclaimed.

"What happened?" Fritz asked.

Marigold started looking sour. "Yorkshire," she said.

The doctor lifted a small remote and clicked it once, and the screen changed over to another screenshot. What Farai saw sent a chill down her back. The screenshot showed a very tall and strongly built humanoid being with a large tail. It had the usual flame-like eyes and a thick snout of sharp teeth. The first thing that came to Farai's mind was the word "predator." There was something about it that seemed to exude natural power, like the large lions back in her home country. It looked strong, fearsome, designed to kill.

"What the hell is that?" she asked.

"Look at those teeth," Klara said with shock.

"We are unsure at this time," Yorkshire said. "Once again, a new variant has made itself known. But it does not take a scholar to see this one is quite different from its siblings. It's far larger in terms of height and mass. It's stronger, and it seems to hold much higher cognitive ability. And its resilience to traditional attacks is exponentially higher. This isn't a throw-away unit, it stands above all others we have seen. The best way we can describe it is that it is—"

"An Apex," Farai said. "The highest in the food chain. The ultimate predator."

Yorkshire's eyebrows arched upwards "At this current junction, I'd say that's a valid description." He stepped forward, clipboard in hand. "This new variant, this 'Apex' as Artemis has coined it, made itself known yesterday when a collection team captured the new Time Rider. When crossing Eads bridge the variant appeared and attacked the convoy. Despite the team's best efforts all twelve operators as well as one of our representatives and his security detail were eliminated. The Time Rider himself only escaped because of his ability to enter Alpha-2. He was last seen plummeting into the river below in his attempt to escape."

Yorkshire switched over the projector again and showed a new picture of the Time Rider. It looked to be a still of him walking down a sidewalk in the city. "As you can see, the boy survived and was last seen here in this still near North Leonor K Sullivan Boulevard. His current whereabouts are unknown."

He flipped over to another still of the massive revenant variant. "This new subject has quickly become a budding interest for my department, but it needs to be known that it produces a great threat to us. This Alpha-2 revenant has shown great resilience and strength. The standard issue armor piercing rounds fired by the operator issued battle rifles did little to harm or negate the subject in any meaningful way. It has shown itself strong enough to lift the conventional automobile with ease; even vehicles are not suitable protection. With what we have learned, as well as respecting the fact there is much we currently don't know, it is highly recommended that if any Oracle personnel encounter this new variant, don't engage, merely observe from a safe distance and report what you learn back to the appropriate avenues. Thank you."

Yorkshire stepped back, letting Marigold step forward. "When it comes to this new Time Rider, now is the time to act. The largest reason the previous one proved to be such a threat was he survived long enough to become one. This new one is less than a novice, a nonexistent threat. He shouldn't provide too much trouble, but that may not be the case if we give him too much time. He needs to be located and dealt with, whether it be through capture or elimination. This is our top priority."

"Sounds easy enough," Spartan said. "What about Spencer Carter?"

Marigold gave him a cold look. "What about him?"

"He provided the original Time Rider with gear and information; do we know if this new one has made contact with him?"

"Negative," Marigold responded. "But knowing Carter, it's likely he has reached out to the Time Rider to some capacity," she explained. "All the more reason we need to act now."

"And what about this Apex variant? What if it shows up again? If what the doctor says is true, nothing we have can make a dent in it, not even our own unique equipment." Fritz asked.

"Through our analysis we believe this variant shares the same goal we do: to do away with the Time Rider," Marigold said. "If it appears again, you don't get in its way. But don't make the mistake of relying on it. The Time Rider escaped it once before and he can do so again. I'm expecting all that come into contact with the Time Rider and this new variant to act and adapt accordingly. Capture or kill, that is the mission," Marigold said.

"What are our standing orders?" Spartan asked.

Marigold stepped forward and placed her good hand on the table. "Spartan, rally your men and women and make sure they are up to speed. Make sure they are ready to take on orders at the drop of a hat. We are going to need them."

"Affirmative," Spartan said.

"Artemis," Marigold said.

"Yes," Farai responded.

"Go out there in the field and track the Time Rider down, however you can. You know the drill. Once you find him, if you encounter the new variant do not engage. Report it back to HQ as soon as possible."

"Understood," Farai answered

"Legion," Marigold called out. They had their head on the table half asleep. "Legion!" Marigold yelled, slamming her hand on the table.

Legion shot up in alarm, their mask changing eye colors rapidly. "Wha-yes?" one of them asked.

"Get all of yourself in order! There are four of you in that one body and none of you can seem to take care of it!"

"It's that brat! She's the one keeping us up," Eckard snapped.

"Yeah, it was Klara!" Fritz followed up.

"Leave me alone!" Klara screamed.

"I don't care whose fault it is! Stop acting like helpless children! Get this under control or I will do away with you!" Marigold said vitriolically. "Klara!"

Legion's eyes shot over to purple. "Yes!" Klara answered.

"I know it is you causing all these issues to crop up," Marigold told her.

"What, me?" Klara asked skittishly.

"Yes, you!" Marigold snapped. "The singing, the complaining, the complete humiliation of your kindred! Legion is the lieutenant that our personnel feared the most, the ones the Time Rider feared the most. And now you're all a laughingstock because of you, the cutesy little girl...."

"'Please stop... all I want to do is help."

"You've done everything but help!" Marigold scolded. "Annike is the leader, Eckard is the muscle, Fritz is the brains. What are you?"

"I... I... I don't." Klara started.

"Don't know?" Marigold finished. She walked over to Legion and looked directly into the eyes of the mask. "Your excess Klara, and I would dispose of you if I could. You will not get in the way of the others again. Are we clear?" Marigold asked coldly.

"Yes," Klara said. She sounded like she was in tears under the mask. Legion dipped down and quiet sobbing could be heard as they sat in their chair.

Legion was always an awkward pill to swallow, but after spending enough time around them all the lieutenants got used to their unique predicament. All four personalities were treated like their own independent people. Marigold was not lying when she said that Legion had initially been feared. They showed very early on they were capable of extreme violence and there was real concern amongst the staff about letting someone with an obvious case of extreme mental illness be not only an active operator, but a lieutenant that could command others when necessary.

The hard light holographic generator technology they used proved to be extremely effective in keeping all four of them satiated. They used the holograms to separate from the original body and move around independently. They had proved themselves to be efficient and useful in many situations, making themselves a crucial pillar in the PMC structure.

The body of Legion was that of an adult, yet there was Klara, this child persona wrapped in with everything else. She was obnoxious at times, but no one truly hated her. She was the closest thing the team had to something innocent. That was something of a scarcity within Oracle, even if she came from perhaps the most violent lieutenant.

Seeing Marigold drill into her like that made Farai feel defensive. Maybe it was some previously dormant maternal instinct within her, but she could hardly watch that. Farai got the impression that Marigold herself had something far more mentally broken within her, something that even put Legion to shame.

"Before we disband, there is one last thing you all need to know," Marigold said. "Due to these current events, I will be adding a lieutenant to our line up."

Everyone in the room stared at her in surprise.

"And who is that gonna be?" Spartan asked.

Marigold looked over at the door. "Come on in Smirnov."

The door opened and a massive man walked through it, clothed in a tucked in olive button up shirt, slacks, and a belt. He was over seven feet tall and built like a professional bodybuilder. He had a thick beard and head colored in a healthy looking brown.

He came in and took a seat next to Spartan. Spartan was not a small man, but now he may as well have been a stick bug.

"This is Gleb Smirnov. He is a former member of Spetsnaz, and he will be our crowd control expert here at the company," Marigold explained.

"What's his code name?" Spartan asked.

"Quake," Marigold said. "His alias here will be Quake."

"Pleasure to make your acquaintance," Quake said with a thick Eastern European accent. "Mr. Talon, Ms. Omari. Legion."

Spartan and Artemis nodded in acknowledgement.

"You do not scare me big man," Eckard hissed.

"Not now, Eckard," Annike scolded.

"He's as big as a house!" Klara said astonished.

"I assure you Mr. Eckard, I am no threat to you. We are allies. There is no need for hostility," Quake said.

"We will see about that…" Eckard said.

"Eckard," Annike hissed.

"Enough, all of you," Marigold butted in. "Like I said, Quake will be our breaching and crowd control expert," she explained. "Yorkshire and his men are still working out his equipment situation, but we have the utmost confidence Quake here will be a vital component in our operations.

"Mr. Smirnov, are you aware of our work—what we do as lieutenants here at Oracle?" Farai asked.

"And its unusual nature? Yes. I am all too aware of Alpha-2 and the revenant creatures. As well as these "Time Riders," as Ms. Marigold called them. Admittedly this is not uh, familiar territory for me. But I learn quickly, you will see," Quake said with a smile.

"Spartan, Legion. You're dismissed, get back to your duties," Marigold ordered.

Legion got up and left the room immediately. Spartan seemed hesitant. but got up and left the room as well, leaving Farai, Marigold, and the new lieutenant alone in the room. Quake sat across from Farai, Marigold stood at the end of the table closest to them, tracing her finger along the smooth wood of the table.

"Artemis," she began. "This is a very important time for all of us, we can't afford mistakes, not now."

"I am in agreement, but why do you say this?" Farai asked.

"For the longest time, Edgar Talon, or Spartan, was my right hand. He served me well in that time, but he did not pull through when I needed him most. He failed countless times to stop the previous Time Rider. And now with this new one present, we desperately need reliability. If you are able to complete this mission, you will take his place at my side."

Farai thought on it for a moment, but it didn't sit well with her. She and Talon had a complicated relationship, but she had no desire to take his position, she knew it gave him purpose. Plus, his position was not exactly one to be envied. The Time Rider was not easy prey, which was always something Marigold failed to understand. She had locked fists with him a fair number of times as well. Only bad memories stemmed from those encounters.

"I am grateful for the opportunity, but I can't imagine I would be a better fit for the position than Spartan," Farai said.

"Farai, I'm not suggesting," Marigold said. "You will get this done. There is no other option."

Farai didn't say anything.

"I know you are capable of dealing with Markus Daniels, but this new variant will be a different case. Quake here, will be tasked with combating it."

"Is that even possible? We don't even know how to hurt it. Can we really task a new lieutenant with this?" Farai asked.

"I appreciate your concern Ms. Omari," Quake interjected. "While I will not divulge my personal history at this time, I do have experience in fighting and crowd control. I was put in a dangerous position and Ms. Marigold offered me a way out. I am grateful and have no intention of failing here. I have trained all my life to make the most of my physique, and my strength is unmatched. I am certain I can not only stand toe-to-toe with this variant but beat it as well. You are a hunter, yes? I am a fighter. We will combine our strengths and emerge victorious," Quake explained.

Quake was practically leaking with confidence, which was admirable, but Farai herself wasn't feeling so optimistic. All she could think about was how much she hoped Spartan wouldn't find out about this.

"Do we need some time?" she asked. "Quake here doesn't have his equipment yet, whatever that might be."

"Don't worry about that, your orders still stand," Marigold said. "Do your part, and I'll keep you informed."

Farai looked over at Quake. He had an obnoxiously charming smile on his face.

She stood up from the table. "May I be dismissed?" she asked.

"Yes Artemis, you're dismissed."

Farai stood up and exited the room. She walked down the empty hallway outside, her mind feeling scattershot. She would do what she did best, and maybe they could finally get a win. But she couldn't shake her feeling of guilt, like she was betraying Spartan by doing this. She reminded herself that she didn't have a choice, but it didn't matter. Farai didn't have much resentment for him. He had moments where he would be worthy of admiration, but he was just a colleague, even if he had playfully pushed the envelope to something more flirtatious at times.

He had asked her out for drinks from time to time but she always politely refused. He always respected that and there was no bad blood between them. But they had known each other for years, and it made this feel like a betrayal. Even so, she chose to put these worries in the back of her mind for now, she resumed her duties for the day, doing her best to focus on those alone.

CHAPTER 10

Purpose and Pizza

Charlotte:

Charlotte awoke the following morning to a warm, sticky tongue licking her face. She struggled a bit awkwardly as her new dog stood on her chest and she found it difficult to get away. She managed to push her off and the puppy plopped off to her side and rested her head on her stomach. She tried to wipe the dog slobber from her face with disgust.

"Ugh, Millie," Charlotte whined.

The dog barked once in response.

Charlotte had let her sleep in her bed overnight with her. The puppy had taken a shine to her quickly and didn't want to leave her side. Charlotte was more than happy to accommodate, though a small detriment had just made itself known. She managed to sit up in her bed and get her hair out of her face. Millie started jumping on her back.

"Millie! Seriously..." she said with a laugh.

Charlotte took Millie under her arm and began to pet her. Afterwords she got to her feet and started to get ready for the day, trying to avoid tripping over Millie the whole time. When she finished, she went downstairs with her furry friend tagging along behind her. Mrs. Rowes was in her usual spot in the kitchen, fixing some breakfast. Charlotte sat down and Millie went over to the food and water bowl that had been set up and started lapping up water with her tongue.

"You two sleep okay?" Mrs. Rowes asked.

"Yeah," Charlotte answered.

"How are you feeling?" Mrs. Rowes said as she started putting food on a plate.

"Like crap," her daughter grumbled.

"I told you about eating too much of that cake."

"I love cake, though."

"I know! When you were little, I could never give you any because when we ran out you would always start crying. I swear you could eat a whole bakery."

Charlotte groaned and let her head fall down to the table, causing the silverware to clang. Mrs. Rowes brought over a plate of food and placed it in front of Charlotte. She picked up a fork and began eating.

Mrs. Rowes turned her back to the counter and put her hands on it, leaning. "Got any plans today?" she asked.

"I'm gonna head out and meet with a friend," Charlotte said with a full mouth.

"Chew your food," Mrs. Rowes scolded. "Is it Ryder?" she asked brightly.

"No, someone he knew though."

"Who would that be?"

Charlotte chose her words carefully. "He's kind of an... adoptive father for Ryder I guess."

"You guess?"

"Yeah, Ryder lived with him while he was here. He's been on his own since then, thought I would visit. He's good people."

"Well, that's sweet of you. What's he like?"

Charlotte scrunched her face a bit. "He's kind of a grump, but he's super smart and can be a nice guy, if you catch him being so."

"Hmm, fascinating."

Charlotte finished her plate, and Mrs. Rowes collected it.

"Maybe you should consider staying home for a weekend, spending time with Millie."

"Oh yeah, definitely," Charlotte said, wiping her mouth. "Just not today."

"Are you sure?" Mrs. Rowes asked. "Millie already likes you so much."

"Believe me, I know," Charlotte said. "It's just that somethings come up and I want to be there for it. But I promise I'll spend time with Millie, I really do want to."

Mrs. Rowes shook her head. "Alright, have fun out there."

"Yup, yup," Charlotte said hopping down from her chair.

She turned to leave the apartment when Millie charged her down and began pawing at her leg and whining. Charlotte kneeled and Millie started licking her aggressively again. She held the puppy in place and planted a kiss on her head. This sent the dog into a bit of a frenzy, causing her to keep jumping and yapping at Charlotte.

"Geez, love you too. I'll be back don't worry." She went to open the door but stopped where she was when she felt a scratchy sensation rise in her throat. She coughed harshly into a fist she had formed over her mouth.

Millie continued making noises at her until she started doing something that confused Charlotte, she immediately stopped yapping and then suddenly went deathly quiet. She began to stare at Charlotte stiffly, eyes wide open, ears perked up sharply, not a muscle on her small body moving.

She began to growl and back up. Charlotte examined her and reached out a hand to the small dog. "Millie? What's wrong?"

When she got too close the puppy immediately turned around and began running on the tile as fast as it could until she bolted up the stairs and out of sight.

Charlotte had to blink a few times to process what had just happened. "Well, okay. That was weird." She looked over at her mother in the kitchen. She had a wide-eyed stare on her face that Charlotte would bet ten to one was identical to the look on her own face.

"That's odd, she bolted like a spooked colt," Mrs. Rowes said. "I guess that cough of yours scared her."

"My cough? I guess so," Charlotte said.

"Only thing that would make sense," Mrs. Rowes said. "Are you sure you are feeling good enough to go out today? It sounded like you were about to hack up a lung just now."

"Yeah, I'm feeling fine. It's weird, I had a coughing fit but now I'm fine. It's like it never happened."

Mrs. Rowes stared off for a minute, then shrugged. "Let me

know if it happens again, I don't like the sound of that."

"I will."

In spite of being plagued by sudden confusion, Charlotte opened her apartment door and hastily began her journey, walking to the undercroft as the morning was ending. She arrived at Rudy's convenience store and made her way behind it, where she came to the bunker door. She examined the pad on the side and saw some sort of extension had been installed.

She saw the button on the side and reached her hand out to touch it. For reasons that were unknown to her she hesitated, acting like the console would explode like a dead man switch if she hit it too fast. She eventually just quickly tapped the button.

"Doofus," she said quietly to herself.

"Who is it?" Spencer asked through the intercom. Charlotte jumped, putting her hand over her heart, then rolled her eyes at herself and spoke into it. "It's Charlotte Spencer."

After some silence Spencer spoke again. "Come on down."

The bunker door opened, and she went down the steps. Spencer was seated at his usual station by the monitors spinning a pen in the fingers on his right hand.

"How's the intercom?" he asked.

"Very um, intercommy," Charlotte said, not sure how to answer.

"How observant."

Charlotte took a seat next to him and looked up at the monitors. It took her a moment to see, but it was footage of Markus sitting in a pizza parlor. Charlotte recognized it as an Imo's pizza, a parlor that specialized in the style of pizza that originated in the city. He was just sitting there, eating.

"This kid man..." Spencer said twirling the pen even faster.

"What? What'd he do?" Charlotte asked.

"He's a complete menace!" Spencer exclaimed. "I've never seen so much thievery and stupidity in my life!" he explained. "He took a bunch of stuff from the shop upstairs, setting Rudy off in the process. Broke into a vending machine, got caught by police, then went on a merry chase for like an hour before he got away. Robbed paint from a supermarket for some reason. Spent most of the day cruising around on that skateboard of his, then he nicked the bag off some poor overweight bastard in a motorized scooter. And that isn't even the worst part! He taunted the guy for like five minutes, running ahead of the cart just out of reach, before jetting. He teased a guy in a motorized scooter after he robbed him, playfully hopping along just to show how much faster he was. Who does that?"

He was pretty fired up, and Charlotte just kept looking back at him and the screen "So, have you figured out how to reign him in?" she asked.

Spencer chucked his pen down on the desk and threw up his hands in defeat. "I don't know. This kid is *not* Ryder. Ry believed in being someone better, this guy... he needs a drill sergeant, or a damn exorcist..."

"I mean, what was Ryder like when he first started anyway?"

"Well, in typical Ry fashion he was just really mopey all the time, it was a bad time for him, but I didn't blame him. He was like that until well... he met you."

"Me?"

"Yeah, one night he went out into the city and when he came back, he had that beat-up bat and yeah, I'll never forget what he said. He was like "Spencer, I want to fight those things, I want to help people, stop them from taking others." He shook his head. "That was where it all started. That's when he became the Time Rider, and you were his first rescue. He didn't tell me about what happened till later, but yeah it all started with you. That was when he became brave enough to stop groveling about the undercroft all the time."

Hearing this gave Charlotte an idea. "Say Spencer, has he been messing with any girls? Like in a flirty way?"

Spencer gave her a skeptical look. "Now that you mention it, yeah. It's like he can't help himself," Spencer said. "Wait a minute, what are you thinking?"

"I think I might go join him for some pizza. I do love me some Imo's."

Spencer turned his chair to face her "Are you going to woo him?"

"I wouldn't say that. More like smooth talk," Charlotte said. "If he's got a soft spot for the ladies..." she shrugged. "Maybe I can use that."

Spencer's eyebrows dropped. "I don't like the sound of it, but it might work. Just don't do anything stupid. Don't let him feel you up or anything."

Charlotte stood up. "Don't worry, femininity can be powerful tool if used properly," she said tilting her head and twisting her foot.

Spencer snorted through his nose. "Yes, that's something I learned the hard way, Knock em' dead."

Charlotte twisted her head and gave Spencer a cheesy, girly smile, then turned on her heel out of the undercroft. She set out for the pizzeria playing out a few scenarios in her head. She'd had to play off overeager crushes before, she just never imagined she would reverse the roles. She knew plenty of girls her age that would go for a troublesome boggart like him, though her preferences lay elsewhere.

She passed by the pizzeria and looked in the window. Sure enough Markus still sat in that booth eating his food. Charlotte went inside and quickly plopped into the booth sitting opposite Markus. He was in the middle of a bite of pizza.

"Heya, Charlotte!" Markus said with a mouth full of pizza. "Small world, eh?"

The pizza he was gorging on was St Louis style pepperoni thin crust. Charlotte quickly grabbed a slice without asking and started eating. Markus lifted a hand to protest but settled with a look of mild annoyance on his face.

"Always have the good stuff here," Charlotte said mid bite. "Wouldn't you say? Believe it or not it's my favorite."

"Sure, always been a safe dive," Markus said. "How did you know where I was?"

"Girl has her ways," Charlotte said. "I hear you've been having some fun."

"Oh yeah? What kind of fun?"

"Oh," Charlotte said propping her head on her hand and staring up at the ceiling. "Some thievery, running from cops, teasing fat guys in scooters."

Markus had to stop himself from bursting out laughing. "You don't understand…" He let out a laugh into his right hand. "That was hysterical."

"A real stallion, aren't ya?"

"Oh, absolutely."

"That's a little amateur, don't you think? Just picking on civvies?"

"Well since I got friggin' erased from existence, I have to start from scratch."

"So, Rudy, vending machines, and McDonald's enthusiasts?"

"Wherever, whoever," Markus said casually. "And McDonald's enthusiast are easy targets. Plus picking on them is well... hilarious.

"How noble," Charlotte said sarcastically.

Markus shrugged. "I guess that old guy is tracking me. Hmm? How else would you know I'm here?"

"Good question, I…"

"Cut the crap, Freckles, I know why you're here. The answer is still no."

"Have you thought about it?"

"Nope."

"Well, what are you going to do?" Charlotte asked. "Just going to be on the run for the rest of time? You know you don't age?"

He looked up with a statue-like gaze. "That so? Haven't thought that far ahead."

"I mean you got Oracle, the revenants…" Charlotte said shifting her head from side to side with each point.

"I can handle it. Oracle might as well just be cops cosplaying soldiers, and those revenants… I dunno, like I said I'll work it out."

"You'll 'work it out?" Charlotte said in disbelief. "They're hunting you Markus, and they could be anywhere. You don't know how they work; you don't know anything. Why are you so casual about it?"

"It's par for the course at this point. Could you give me a sec? I'm trying to finish my pie here," Markus asked resuming his eating.

"How can you sit there and eat pizza?"

"I dunno, I like pizza. Nothin' like good ol' pep y'know?" Markus said casually grabbing another slice and dropping it on his plate. He took a deep breath. "Look, I'm the invisible guy alright? Mr. friggin' Cellophane. Even before this whole thing happened I might as well have not existed to begin with. Now it's official. All I ask is to disappear like I always do."

"You don't have to settle for that. Don't you want to be more?"

Markus let out a small laugh. "Me? More? That's funny." He took another bite of pizza. "Look I've got nothing against you. You do seem nice and all—certainly easy enough on the eyes, even if you're almost as flat as Kansas..." Charlotte quickly crossed her arms over her chest and felt her face turn hot. It took every bit of will power she could muster not to slap him.

"But you're tugging on the wrong sweatshirt," Markus continued. "I'm just a punk. I'm not gonna pretend to be anything else. Just let me go, it's not worth it." He rose to his feet ignoring his new slice and started to exit the shop. Charlotte scrambled to her own feet.

"Wait a sec," she called out.

Markus stopped reluctantly.

"I don't see a punk; I see someone lost."

"Aw, cut the crap..."

"No, just hear me out!" Charlotte pleaded. "You'll die out there, Markus. Come with us and we can help you! You don't have to just fade to black."

"That's how this was always going to end for me," Markus said quietly.

"Are you sure about that?" Charlotte asked. "Just think about it. Please? Maybe you're not at the end yet. Maybe it's another beginning."

Markus was quiet for around ten seconds, then spoke. "Sure. Whatever you say Red," he said as he exited the shop.

A waitress came behind Charlotte trying to get her attention.

"Here's your ticket. Have a nice rest of your day," she said, handing her a black case with a receipt. Charlotte was confused until she realized, long after the waitress had gone, that Markus hadn't paid for the pizza.

"He was gonna dine and dash," Charlotte said in disbelief. She face-palmed and groaned.

CHAPTER 11

Zenaphosphorus

Charlotte:

"Let me in Spencer!"

The undercroft door opened, and Charlotte stomped down the stairs and angrily sat down in one of the office chairs and crossed her arms. Spencer was sitting in his usual spot, fiddling with a beige device in his hand, casually not even looking up at her as he did so. "So, did femininity work?"

"No!" Charlotte exclaimed. "He owes me eighteen dollars and forty-nine cents!" Spencer laughed out loud. "It's not funny! I'm still in high school; I'm not made of money! That was almost twenty dollars for one stupid pie!" Spencer was trying to stave it off, but the laugh still lingered.

Charlotte blew through her teeth. "Glad you're happy," she said. "Do you have any other ideas?"

"Well, we tried femininity, now we try masculinity." Spencer said.

She scrunched her eyebrows. "What do you mean?"

Spencer looked over at her with a mischievous smile on his face, then put the device he had on the desk next to him. "Come here, I wanna show you something." He got up from his chair and walked over to his workshop.

Charlotte got up, too, and walked over to him. He was opening a large worn military-looking case. He opened it and icy air escaped the container and spilled out onto the floor. He reached inside and brought out a large, shiny blue crystal.

"You know what this is?" Spencer asked.

"Is that… a spiker crystal?"

"Precisely," Spencer said.

"I thought those disappeared after a few minutes."

"They do, unless they're preserved in the right conditions."

Spencer went back and put the crystal back in the box. "Back in my days at Oracle, we made a pretty nifty discovery early on. We discovered an entirely new element that was exclusively found in the Time Stream. We named it zenaphosphorus. It's normally found in gaseous form, but we discovered that some variants of revenants produce this stuff naturally in abundance, specifically molders and spikers. That's why they can do what they do. They have the ability to make the zenaphosphorus into other forms of matter instantaneously, hence molder weapons and spiker crystals. Then I thought of something." Spencer turned around to face Charlotte. "Can you tell me the three states of matter?"

"Solid, liquid, and gas?"

"A plus," Spencer said positively. "So, I figured, if the revenants can change its form, maybe I could too."

Spencer went over to the refrigerator over in the kitchen area and started rummaging through it. "I managed to get it into a solid easily enough. Liquid however was a little trickier."

Spencer brought out a dark foam square filled with vials of a bright blue liquid and brought it back over to the workbench. He took one out gently and placed it into some kind of Bunsen burner. He brought out a spark lighter and scraped the two prongs together causing a bright blue flame to ignite and burn steadily.

"Zenaphosphorus is a very potent fuel, something that I found even puts standard petroleum to shame," Spencer said. "I had one vial take twenty days to burn out in this burner. *Twenty*. It's like candle wax on steroids."

"That's neat, but how is this gonna convince Markus to join us?" Charlotte asked.

"Well," Spencer started going over to one of his contraptions. "I noticed that Markus is quite fond of that skateboard of his, so I've been making this in my spare time."

Spencer lifted a skateboard shaped device from the table. It was covered in black material and didn't have any wheels. Instead, it had a nozzle and canister compartment installed on all four sides of the board, every component connected by a series of tight, colorful wiring. There was also a piece on the front that started at the sides and met in the middle to form a point, and two more near the back jutting upwards. The pieces all together gave it an appearance similar to a rocket.

Spencer took four vials of zenaphosphorus out of the foam and began to install them in the compartments on the board. "This started out as an old hobby project I started three years ago. At first, I thought about dragging out an old A.M.R prototype as a peace offering, but I figured this would be more Markus's style. Plus, it gave me a chance to play with this new fuel," Spencer explained.

Once Spencer finished installing the fuel canisters, he put on a strange fingerless glove on his left hand. It had some sort of gauge resting on the top of it. He pressed down on it with a distinct click. The four nozzles began to shoot out calm blue flames, and the board straightened out and began to hover above the workbench.

"Presto," Spencer said in victory.

"Is that a hoverboard?" Charlotte asked with bewilderment.

"Fuel-Based Propulsion Board, or the F.B.P Board Mark One. But yes, it's essentially a hoverboard. Or the skysurfer, as I like to call it."

"That's awesome! It's like that one from *Back to the Future*! It's floating off the ground and everything!"

"Back to the Future had a hoverboard?"

"The second one did," Charlotte said. "In that one they went *into* the future, to 2015. They had them for kids."

"They had hoverboards in 2015? For children?"

"Yeah, they were like floating scooters for little kids and adults. They also had flying cars and stuff."

Spencer's eyebrows shot up. "Flying cars? In 2015?"

Charlotte's face went still and she looked around. "It was retrofuturism. That's what they thought 2015 would look like. Their view on the future was... optimistic, to say the least."

"Clearly," Spencer said. "Nice to see you like the board. Let's hope Markus sees it that way."

"You're going to give it to him?"

"If he agrees to work with us, yes."

"Will that work?"

Spencer pulled the gauge on the glove and the board dropped down onto the table. He leaned against it and brought up three of his fingers. "Three words, boys with toys. We men like our little knick-knacks. You find something that'll pique our interest, and you can keep us busy for hours, maybe a lifetime. Boys are experts in finding fun in the most random things. And a little device like this? There's a lot of fun to be had. Just looking at him, I could see the kid has a thirst for chaos, I'd bet every dollar I got that Markus isn't the type to be convinced by preaching honor and valor. No what he's looking for is adrenaline, something that'll get his blood pumping. Mixed with revenants and Oracle, yeah, then you got chaos."

"So, you want to entice him with a fancy floating skateboard? That will convince him to risk his skin? What are you going to do if he just takes off with the board?"

"Well, the board will be useless without the zenaphosphorus fuel. Only I can make that for him. He can take off with it if he wants an oversized paperweight," Spencer explained. "Plus, there's a reason I'm calling it the skysurfer. Once I work out a small fuel injection flaw, the F.B.P will be able to fly, albeit at the expense of burning excessive fuel. A flying hoverboard, Charlotte. Do you know how many boys would kill for something like that? This used to be a thing you could only pretend. And now it's real. I would try it myself if there wasn't a guarantee I would break my neck."

"*I'd* kill for a flying hoverboard," Charlotte said. "So that's the idea? A flying Time Rider?"

"That's right," Spencer said excitedly. "I'll admit I'm actually kind of excited about this. Makes me feel somewhat young again."

"Groovy, but are you sure this will work?" Charlotte asked apprehensively.

"Remember, boys with toys."

Charlotte looked over at the F.B.P and back at Spencer again. "Are boys that simple?"

"Charlotte, you would be astonished how simple boys can be."

He pressed the gauge on his glove one last time and the F.B.P board came to life. Spencer responded by letting out a giddy laugh.

CHAPTER 12

Predator and Prey

Markus:

After his unplanned lunch date with Charlotte Markus spent most of the day cruising around town on his skateboard. All he had was his thoughts and boredom to keep him company. He really wished he had his music to drown it all out and allow himself to think about something else entirely.

But instead, he played his conversation with the girl in his head over and over like a broken record. He wasn't sure why. He knew she was just trying to butter him up, or at least that's what he told himself. But near the end of their conversation, he could detect what he thought was genuine generosity. "Don't you want to be more?" and "You don't have to fade to black" were phrases that stood out. It bothered him like an itch. Whenever someone talked to him like that there was always a catch, always another angle.

He wasn't sure what he wanted, or if there was anything left to want. There was just nothing in front of him now, nothing to pursue. That old guy Charlotte brought him to, he talked about using this Time Stream to help people, to be some sort of hero. The idea seemed laughable at the time. Markus Daniels? A hero? He was the one the so-called heroes chased. He was a thief, a vandal, a scourge on society. He was the villain, what could he do to help? Yet those annoyingly calming words slipped back into his mind intrusively, challenging him.

The day was coming to an end, and Markus didn't know where to settle for the night. He had slept out in the city on days he either didn't or couldn't afford to go home. It wasn't ever a desired outcome, but he didn't have any other options. He briefly considered going to find Spencer, but he quickly pushed the thought aside. Not now. Maybe he would think on it.

Markus was in East Downtown St. Louis, a place not exactly safe at night. His search for shelter became a panic as he struggled to find something that would work. To put it lightly, there were always people that roamed out in this part of the city that made Markus's disruptive activities look like child's play. They were not people you wanted to stumble across. No matter how much Markus searched for a place half-way decent, eventually the sun came down completely and the area became covered in the dull orange lights coming from the streetlights. Markus was out of time.

"Great," he mumbled angrily.

He settled next to a dumpster in an alley and sat out of sight. Between the smell, the cold, and the hard concrete he sat on, Markus wasn't confident he was going to get much sleep. He closed his eyes and tried to relax as much as he could. As he sat there, he lost track of time, not sure of when he slept or not. Minutes and hours passed without him paying any mind.

Occasionally Markus found himself drifting in an out of feverish dreams. He dreamed about revenants. He dreamed about losing control, not being able to fight back. As he slept, he saw himself lying flat on his back looking up at a dark sky, a horde of those revenant monsters surrounding him, looking down at him as he lay. Those cold glowing eyes beaded down at him hungrily. The dream had him closing his eyes in fear, hoping to spare himself the bloody image of his body being torn apart, but nothing happened. When he opened his eyes, he saw a different revenant. The same one from the bridge looked down on him. It towered over him like a building, and its snout still locked in a macabre smile. Then it lifted one of its massive feet above his head and brought it down hard.

Markus awoke with a panicked breath. He was still curled up next to the dumpster, cold and filthy, one foot still within the dream. He tried to steady his breath to calm himself down. He had awoken from one nightmare and reentered the real one he now faced. As his mind remained in limbo, everything came flooding back to him. Cassandra, all his misdeeds, all the times he ruined his chance to live normally. All the events that led to him going to Oracle tower and facing the revenants. Everything that led to him being erased and alone here in the cold Illinois night, sleeping next to a dumpster with nowhere to go. For the first time in a very long time, he was scared.

As he lay there, a noise in the alley made Markus's head shoot towards the source. Then he began to see something moving towards him, blocking out the light coming into the alley. The closer it got, he began to think it was a person, but it didn't move like one. It hobbled like a hunchback, shuffling awkwardly on its feet. The feet seemed disjointed and misaligned as they moved, like they weren't put together right. Eventually, it moved its glowing eyes, and the dark coloration of its head could be seen. Markus's heart began to beat faster upon the realization that this was yet another revenant.

But this was not like the ones Markus had met before. It was humanoid and covered in masses of what looked like gray wax or some kind of clay. All of it had the appearance and texture of a hornet's nest. The large mass accumulated on the back and head of the creature, causing it to bend over. It was surrounded by a cloud of unusual-looking blue gas. An imposing, crude crystalline spear was grasped firmly in its hand.

"You! Filthy! Filthy!" the creature yelled in a raspy voice, pointing at Markus with its free bony hand.

Markus was dumbfounded it talked. He shot to his feet, grabbed his bag, and tried to flee out the other side of the alley when another wax revenant dropped down in front of him, causing him to fall off his feet trying to recoil. The gas around this creature seemed to congregate around its hand, and a crude-looking object resembling a blade materialized out of thin air into its hand. The revenant swung downwards toward Markus and cut into his left arm.

A searing pain shot through him, and he screamed. He reached for it instinctively and brought forth a batch of hot blood on his hand. He backed away quickly and almost backed right into the original revenant. They surrounded Markus on both sides. He knelt nursing his arm, wincing through the pain.

He felt like screaming again, but no sound left his throat. The intense fear and pain from his arm injury immediately gave him a stinging headache. It was difficult to breathe or collect his bearings. The revenant with the spear brought its weapon back and thrust it forward towards Markus. Quickly coming to his senses, he managed to dodge out of the way and jumped towards the wall to his left, making him slam into some piping that had been installed on the building. The impact caused parts to break off and land on the ground with metallic clangs.

The other revenant with the sword rushed forward with a mighty shriek, knocking its compatriot over in a clumsy mad dash. Markus grabbed one of the loose pipes and brought it up horizontally over his head just as the revenant's sword came down and connected with it. Markus was forced to block three more times as the revenant kept swinging in a rage, nearly cleaving his fingers off in the process.

Markus threw his feet forward and kicked the sword revenant away. He scrambled to his feet with the pipe clutched firmly in his dominant right hand. His assailant kept swinging madly at him without a hint of grace. He stepped back as the flurry of swings drew closer and closer to him, but he managed to find an opening before the rugged weapon found his flesh once again. He focused as much as he could and swung the pipe like a one-handed baton, connecting it with the revenant, knocking it back onto one leg and forcing it to lose balance, leaving it open to attack.

As the revenant tried to recover, Markus rushed forward and began hitting it with the pipe in an adrenaline-fueled tantrum, each hit sending high pitched metallic clanging throughout the alley. After a series of successful hits, he channeled one last powerful swing through the Time Stream and connected with his targets head. Upon impact, the revenant's head shattered like old pottery and what remained of its body fell onto the pavement and dissipated into thin air like a lit fuse.

The other revenant was on its feet now, inconceivably angry at the fate of its kin. It raised its spear in a defiant taunt. "You'll pay, vermin! You will pay!"

Markus raised his pipe, expecting another attack, but before anything else could happen, something extremely large dropped down at the entrance and landed on the spear revenant. The collision slammed it into the ground causing it to vanish into a fine blue miss. After the mist dispersed, Markus got a clear view of the assailant. It was the revenant that attacked him earlier on the bridge. It was standing in the alley-way entrance with utmost malice. Its massive size blocked out all light.

Markus's heart was now in overdrive, and he didn't hesitate to drop the pipe and break into a lengthy stride going the opposite direction. He didn't look behind him, but he could hear the massive revenant slowly gaining momentum, each footfall sounding like thunder striking the earth. Markus tripped over some trash bags and lost his footing, then briefly saw it barreling after him like a track runner. One glance and he was back on his feet with no intention of slowing. He scanned the area desperately trying to give himself options, but he was never going to evade that thing in a straight shot like this. Somehow that thing was still faster than him.

He scanned obsessively until something caught his eye. A fire escape. It was too tall for Markus to reach by jumping normally. He thought quickly. He'd gotten that high before, by jumping wall to wall, but he wasn't confident he could gain enough momentum to push himself up there. He began to close in quickly, running out of time. Then he remembered something. The Time Stream! It had helped Markus move quickly earlier, so there was no reason to think it wouldn't this time. He channeled all his focus and took a bold leap toward the left wall, flying into the Time Stream simultaneously. He landed and pushed off high to the right, then landed and pushed left again. He flew forward and caught the fire escape ladder with both hands, then searing pain shot down his left arm again. He lost his grip.

Markus hung suspended in the air connected by his right hand. The Apex caught up and put a giant foot forward, braking its entire body. It looked up at its prey dangling just above. He struggled to get up the ladder when it suddenly gave away and began sliding down toward his pursuer. Frightened, Markus swore loudly and frantically tried to pull himself up as the revenant started jumping and trying to bite him. Its mouth snapped like an alligator each time. Markus managed to get up onto the fire escape, but it grabbed the ladder and began forcefully pulling and shaking the entire structure. He rushed up the ladder, barely keeping his footing. Once at the top he jumped with all his might and landed clumsily on the roof as the whole structure came down with a crash that could be heard for miles.

He reeled from pain and shock, just sitting there on the roof as he heard the Apex roar defiantly from below. For a moment, the night went quiet. Markus's lungs worked like an aged engine, going in and out painfully. He took a moment to let the cool night air temper his body

At the exact moment Markus let himself calm down completely, he felt a powerful rush of air behind him, and the Apex landed a mere few feet away from him on the rooftop after a mighty jump. It spun around and glared at the boy on the ground.

It opened its mouth wide and Markus could see the inside of its throat become brighter. He shot to his feet and sprinted as much distance as he could just as the Apex shot out a steady stream of bright blue flames in its path, setting the whole roof ablaze. Markus came to the end of the rooftop and jumped across to another below passing over another alley and breaking into a tactical roll at the bottom. The Apex followed behind and jumped to the rooftop as well. It took a swipe at Markus, just barely missing him.

He backed up quickly and bumped into something. The revenant rushed toward him causing him to fall over the side onto a pane of glass. Then, he rolled over quickly as a massive foot came down on the glass and tried to stomp on him. It missed and glass shattered beneath him. He ended up in freefall again screaming as he fell through a set of spiral staircases. He managed to grab a few of the railings but failed to keep hold, slowing his descent but not stopping it. Before he could even process it, Markus hit the floor hard.

His vision became blurry from the pain, and he could barely think. He looked up from where he fell and saw the Apex still on the roof, looking down at him on the bottom floor. All Markus could manage was to lay on the cold tile floor and look up at the creature. The revenant stood there still as a statue, staring down and breathing heavily. He felt like it looked right through him, gazing into his soul as he lay there, almost as though he was still deep in a nightmare.

The creature eventually moved its head out of sight and Markus summoned all the energy he had left to get to his feet and stumble out of the building and onto the street. He fell to a knee as he heard fire truck sirens blaring in the distance. That big revenant had made itself scarce last time people were around, so Markus bet that he was safe, for now. He examined his arm and found it difficult to look at. It was still bleeding badly.

He needed to get medical attention. Maybe there were paramedics with the firefighters? That was possible.

No, they would want to take him to a hospital. Oracle would no doubt pay him another visit, just like at the police station. And he didn't want to test how bold his new biggest fan was. Markus thought hard about his predicament but couldn't think of anything. It became progressively harder to think about anything as the moments passed. Between the pain and blood loss his vision had gotten so bad it was like he was underwater. He began stumbling away from the apartment building with as much vigor as he could muster, eventually getting far enough away to evade any attention. Back out in the dark street he began to limp, his good arm grasping his injured one as he moved. He was still going, but he felt shattered. All he wanted to do was sleep.

He did everything in his power to keep moving, but eventually the burden of his injuries became too much and Markus collapsed in the street. He sat there grinding his teeth and breathing roughly, incapacitated and close to shutting down completely.

As he lay there, a vehicle pulled up right next to him, white in color, bulky in scale. Markus didn't have any energy left to pay it any mind. The only thing that he could process was the headlights lighting up the area. The driver's side door opened and a pair of feet wearing dress shoes hopped down onto the street. Within a moment he was turned over onto his back and looked up at a dark-haired figure just above him. The figure scanned him over with its eyes and hands. Its head began shaking back and forth.

"Why didn't you just stay with me back at the undercroft, kid? Would've saved you one helluva near death experience," the figure mumbled. "Come on, let's get you somewhere safe and away from that thing out here."

It registered in Markus's mind that this was Spencer, the older man from before. He helped him to his feet and guided him to the passenger seat of that van; the interior lights stung his eyes the moment they contacted his retinas. Spencer followed into the driver's seat, started the vehicle, and drove away, most likely back to that basement. If he were in a better state, Markus would have refused assistance right then and there. But right now, he remained curled up in his seat like a ball, looking at the door absentmindedly. Every time he closed his eyes all he could see was his pursuer, eyes shimmering and mouth spewing flame. Anything or anywhere away from the beast that wanted his life was where Markus wanted to be.

CHAPTER 13

Sanctuary

Spencer:

Earlier that night Spencer had stayed up watching his monitors while sitting reclined in one of his office chairs, propping his head on his hand. It was a pretty standard night. There were a couple of packs of revenants roaming about and just doing what they did. If they took anybody, Spencer would be none the wiser; that was something he only realized when he started working with Ryder. If they caught anybody, they didn't exist anymore.

Oracle operator teams did their usual patrols, moving around the sectors and checking their capture cages, nothing too abnormal. A fire had broken out in East Downtown, which was a point of interest, especially since there were high levels of electromagnetic fields in the area, which would indicate the presence of revenants in the area. But frustratingly, Spencer couldn't make out anything. He couldn't pin it on revenants without the proper evidence. The inferno had grown to be quite the sight. As far as he could tell, no one was injured or killed from it, but he couldn't be certain. All he could see was a plethora of people either half-dressed or in sleepwear standing around outside alone or with their pets. It was something, but a very boring something.

Just as Spencer started to doze off in his chair, he heard an alarm on one of his monitors. His eyes shot open, and he leaned in to focus on it. After a moment, he pressed the button on his end. What he saw was Markus stumbling out of the very same apartment that had gone ablaze. The camera that recorded him was on a light pole a good distance away, so once the footage zoomed in the quality went down drastically. Even so he could see he was in a bad way.

Spencer's mind began to spin with a plethora of unsavory possibilities. Like if he was picked up by paramedics or the police and made easy pickings again. Or that he may die from any injuries he may have suffered. Either way, he wasted no time rushing out of the undercroft and driving over in his van.

Luckily, that side of town wasn't more than a few blocks off, and he found Markus away from all the commotion. He was injured, exhausted, and smelling like the business end of a digestive tract. Once he got him to the van, Spencer drove recklessly fast back to the safety of the undercroft, cursing himself for allowing him to be put into this kind of danger in the first place. Spencer had opted to play a game of psychology with Markus, a mind game, having him come around to the idea of assisting him on his own as opposed to brute forcing it. But the new Apex variant was not allowing for such a delicate matter.

Spencer kept thinking about what Charlotte had said earlier, something implying having Markus at gunpoint. It was a stupid idea. There would be more problems than it was worth, but it was starting to sound more like a viable option.

Once at the undercroft, Spencer helped Markus down the stairs until they both reached the bottom. The kid was covered in dirt and muck, his bag and skateboard were missing, and his left arm sleeve was damaged and covered with blood. Markus leaned up against the wall and slid down to the floor, exhausted and weary. Spencer kneeled to his level. "What happened? Were you the one who ended up setting fire to that building?" he asked.

"No! It was the friggin' big thing!" Markus yelled irritably.

Spencer raised his hands. "Okay, calm down. Did it injure your arm?"

"No, a smaller one cut me up good," Markus said trying to nurse his arm. "It cut pretty deep…"

Spencer thought for a second. "Look, go ahead and sit up on that workbench over there; I'll see what I can do about that arm."

Markus got to his feet and Spencer went to gather his first aid kit and sutures and brought them over to where Markus had managed to climb up onto the workbench. Spencer laid out a towel and pushed back his damaged sleeve and examined the wound. It was a deep cut going down his arm and was still bleeding badly. It was a horrifying thing to look at. Spencer quickly went over to the refrigerator and brought out a ham sandwich he had prepared earlier that day and laid it at his side.

"What's that for?" Markus asked weakly.

"Eat," Spencer ordered. "God knows how much blood you've lost."

Markus grabbed the sandwich with his good hand and started to eat it slowly. Spencer began to clean around the wound and applied some anesthetic. After that he prepped a suture and started working to close the wound. Markus had his eyes closed and grimaced nervously. He looked like he was running on fumes. Spencer knew this would be easier if he could keep his mind off what he was doing.

"So, this revenant that cut you up, what did it look like?"

Markus looked over. "It was, like, weird. It was a hunchback looking thing covered in like clay or wax. It made a sword outta thin air."

"Ah," Spencer said. "We call those molders."

"Molders?"

"Yeah, they form makeshift weapons out of that gas that surrounds them."

"And that big one," Markus said, lost in thought. "You don't know what that is?"

'It's new, no ordinary revvie I've ever seen before. New variants crop up from time to time, but I've never seen one like that before. Oracle named that thing the Apex."

"The Apex? What do you mean that company named it?"

"To make a really long story short, I have eyes and ears in their database. Got a peak at the file their head of omni-dimensional research was working on. It's mostly empty with two exceptions. First, they gave its official name, "The Apex." Second, its danger level is threat level four. Considering the fact there were only three levels beforehand tells you all you need to know.

Markus scoffed. "That's stupid," he muttered. "I think Dickface would be a more fitting name." Spencer was caught off guard by the comment and ended up laughing.

"Yeah, you also failed to mention those things talk," Markus said.

"What now?"

"The molders, they talked."

Spencer leaned forward and started to stitch more diligently. "They can talk, but only you can understand them."

"What? Why?"

"Their language is called SpecterSpeak, and when I say 'language' that's a very loose definition. To normal humans it just sounds like incoherent disembodied voices and whispers, but to Time Riders and other revenants it can be understood normally. Like it's plain old English."

"Cool-gahhhh!" Markus yelped in pain as Spencer made a sloppy needle insertion. "Come on, man, that's not Play-Dough that's my friggin' arm!" Markus complained through his teeth.

"I'm an engineer, not a doctor," Spencer said defensively. "That's machines, not people."

"Then how do you know how to do this at all?"

"Ryder," Spencer answered flatly, taking a pair of medical scissors out of the first aid box. "He used to get torn up all the time, had to patch him up when it happened since hospitals aren't a luxury we have," he said. He changed the subject. "So, you were attacked by molders and the Apex?" Spencer asked changing the subject.

"Um, yeah. The Apex didn't seem to like the molders very much."

"How so?"

"It killed one of them," Markus said quickly. "Smashed it like an egg. Guess it got in the way."

"Interesting," Spencer made a distinct snip with the scissors and began cleaning them with a rag. "How does it feel?" he asked.

"Still stings like hell."

"Yeah, well at least you're not leaking all over the place," Spencer said, putting his tools back in the box.

"Thanks," Markus said lethargically.

"I know you like to play lone wolf, but my offer still stands. There's a shower and a bed down here if you want to use them.

You'll find fresh clothes in the chest-of-drawers in that bedroom over there," Spencer said pointing.

Markus hopped down from the bench and hobbled over to the bedroom and closed the door behind him, not saying a word.

"Okay then," Spencer said. He went back over to his computers and began typing and clicking when necessary to bring up the footage from the Eads bridge incident that he had saved. Considering its horrifying nature, Spencer was reluctant to pull it up again. This Apex revenant made him feel uneasy. All known revenants with the exception of one could be eliminated with traditional weapons, it could not.

On the bridge it tore through men and machines alike to get to its mark. And if Markus was telling the truth, it even turned on its brethren that stood in its way.

Spencer pulled up a few stills of the massive revenant and took a good look. Staring at them too long would steadily chip away at his composure. It terrified him, but at the same time there was something almost awe-inspiring about its feats. He had never seen anything like it. He wondered what Oracle was making of this thing. Were they looking to study it? Or kill it? This was the most frustrating part of this three-way war: the uncertainty.

Oracle were looking for their ageless factor, the cellular stasis that allowed them to not deteriorate. Spencer and Ryder wanted to prevent more people from being victimized by both Oracle and the revenants alike. The revenants were driven by what could be described in two words: procreation and colonization. They desire to make more of their kind and inhabit Alpha-1, the normal dimension inhabited by humanity, like ravenous parasites breeding and killing the host they latch onto. They want to assimilate Alpha-1, make it a second home. Almost certainly at the expense of all living organisms that reside there, especially humans.

Spencer could play espionage and dig into some Oracle info through a few sneaky back doors he installed in the database during his time in the company, but there was no way of knowing what the revenants were doing or what they knew.

The last big play made by them was Project Witching Hour. The Progenitress, the ominous revenant matriarch, orchestrated it. With her failure, there was no way to predict what would happen next. However the existence of the Apex made one thing clear, The

Progenitress, was not pulling her punches anymore—she was starting to play hardball.

Spencer had installed a few countermeasures around the undercroft so revenants wouldn't show up unannounced. There were some electromagnetic scrambler systems, electromagnetic readers, and the bunker door. He had to make a few adjustments so they wouldn't affect Ryder, but they were successful in hiding them from the revenants, or at least in keeping them away.

Spencer questioned their integrity now. He knew if the Apex wanted into the undercroft, it could get in. Its massive size might be a deterrent, but that would certainly not diminish its drive. To his dismay there was simply not much he could do. He needed to convince Markus to assume the same position Ryder did. He needed a Time Rider, especially now. But he knew better than to rush this. Markus needed to be eased into it. Spencer would be asking the kid to assume immense responsibility and danger, so he couldn't let himself forget that Markus was still a human being. This needed to be done gently, and one step at a time.

Spencer switched off the monitors and sunk back into his chair, trying to unwind. Tomorrow was going to be an important day. He didn't have the energy to think about it any longer. He got up and made his way back to his room to settle in for the night.

CHAPTER 14

The Turbulent Road

Artemis

Farai awoke early in the morning and did her usual routines. Around one hundred sit-ups and pull-ups inside her room to start, then she had a small breakfast and proceeded to go to one of the service elevators located on the eleventh floor of Oracle tower. Once she got there, she inserted her unique service card into a small slot at the bottom of the elevator panel, and a familiar awkward mechanical noise could be heard as the elevator began to descend. Farai was always annoyed by the unusually long elevator journey downwards.

Sitting still for too long made her mind wander, often to nothing comforting. It was a bad habit of Farai's. She tended to overthink even the simplest of situations and determine the most disastrous outcomes. Maybe it was her instinctual nature as a huntress, or maybe it was the chronic fear of failure instilled in her ever since she was a little girl, but Farai always found herself stricken with stress in one form or the other. It was exhausting, but when she considered that she worked under a secret private military contractor for someone like Esther Marigold, she didn't blame herself for any of it.

Farai headed down into the PMC's headquarters and research hub. It was a sprawling underground base designed like a small city with a variety of functions. It acted as weapon storage and research development, specimen containment, and varied research into dimension Alpha-2, and much more. There was seldom a department within the base not in frequent use.

She had plans of going to the base's armory and checking on her unique equipment. The elevator arrived at its destination and Farai stepped out into a carved-out tunnel with a few motorized carts moving by on the built in roads inside them. She walked along the outer walkways until she arrived at one of the base's tram stations. From there, the entire sprawling facility could be seen. There were rows and rows of equipment stacked high and low on an incomprehensible number of shelves and rooms, all lit up with bright white ceiling lights. The sheer scale of the place always took Farai's breath away in uncomfortable awe.

She stood on the platform amongst a group a male operators. They all backed away and showed signs of nervousness. It was an odd thing seeing a group of armed militants getting uneasy, but for Farai it was always like this. While Oracle hired men and women alike for the PMC, it came as no surprise to anyone that most active operators were men. Initially when she had been recruited as a lieutenant, Farai couldn't go two feet without some pompous overpaid soldier boy trying to flirt her up. The harassment had gotten so bad that Farai had to put her foot down one day and ended up breaking all the bones in an operator's arm when he couldn't keep his hands to himself.

She caused quite the commotion when it happened, but funnily enough Marigold was quite pleased that she did. In retrospect, Farai wasn't surprised, knowing her nature in a contemporary context. While she was no fan of violence to prove a point, she knew that it was important for the alpha to show their subordinates a display of strength, just like predators in the wild. When the tram arrived, she stepped on with a handful of operators. The familiar feminine AI voice announced its next location.

Next Stop: Armory

Farai grabbed hold of one of the top rails as it began moving, and everyone in the car did the same. The usual prerecorded messages played on a screen in the front and back of the car. It displayed what meals were offered in the mess hall, news and events, and Marigold's best attempt at sounding grateful for all the hard work they did each and every day with an altered photo of her in the background.

When the tram stopped at the armory Farai hopped off and the tram sped off quickly behind. She walked up to the large door and opened it, stepping inside the dimly lit room. The armory mostly consisted of rows of black metal shelves housing the standard-issued battle rifles and high-caliber handguns. Farai went over to two metal tables which lined the back of the room. Doctor Yorkshire and Quake were near them discussing something. Farai went up to them.

"Ah! Artemis, pleasant morning," Yorkshire said turning around to face her.

"Ms. Omari," Quake greeted afterwards.

"Morning," Farai said. She noticed a weapon she was not familiar with laying on the table and a few cartridges sat near it. "What weapon is that?"

"That is what I was discussing with Quake here," Yorkshire explained. "This is the ZL23 spark rifle."

"Spark rifle?"

"Yes," the doctor said as he lifted the weapon up for Farai to see. At first glance it looked like one of the many battle rifles that could be found in there, but it was heavily modified. The barrel and the body were covered in what looked like aftermarket aluminum pieces, all connected with a series of colorful wiring. Based on the barrel alone, Farai could tell this weapon didn't fire traditional projectiles anymore.

He offered the weapon to her, and she held it in both hands. The usual battle rifles were already annoyingly heavy, but now it was just cumbersome. "This is one of those old science projects you were forced to shelve, right?" she asked.

"Correct. I've been given permission to create and use the ZL23 spark rifle conversion kits, given the unique circumstances," Yorkshire explained.

"The Apex?" Farai asked.

"Yes."

Farai picked up one of the cartridges from the box the spark rifle came in and examined it. It looked and felt like a large battery, complete with two prongs on one end and a caution label on the opposite side, as well as another tag indicating the correct way it is to be loaded. Looking even closer she noticed the hazard logo indicating a potentially explosive compound was inside the cartridge.

"Zenaphosphorus?" she asked.

"Yes, liquid form. Very tricky and volatile. Any target hit by the weapon will burn like they were hit by napalm's abusive grandfather."

"That's quite the sell. Sounds quite destructive," Farai said, holding the little box closer to the light in the room.

"Indeed, um, please don't hold it so high. I don't doubt the integrity of the magazines, but I would rather not take chances," Yorkshire said taking the cartridge from her and putting it back in the black case.

"Is my bow operational?" Farai asked.

"The bow? Yes, it is in working order," Yorkshire said brightly opening one of the display cases on the wall and bringing out her bow. He handed it over and Farai took it quickly for examination.

Farai's compound bow was originally invented by Spencer Carter, who affectionately named it the Boomslang morphing bow. It was designed and operated like a hunting-grade compound bow, complete with tension wheels, metallic string and polymer grips. A zenaphosphorus container and magnetic field generator had been installed on the weapon. This made it so whenever the drawstring was pulled back a magnetic field in the shape of an arrow would materialize where one would normally be placed, then zenaphosphorus would be released quickly into the field. The sudden change in conditions would cause the gas to solidify, forming a functional arrow that could be shot from the drawstring normally.

Farai always welcomed the fact that the arrows from the boomslang had direct advantages over traditional arrows. They eliminated the need for quivers or reloading all together, and they disappeared after a few minutes. Firing in quick succession was also much easier, a fact which proved to be immensely beneficial. Farai quickly examined the bow and saw nothing that would be a cause for worry.

"Thank you, Doctor."

"Of course, Artemis. Now for Mr. Quake here. As I was discussing with him, I'm still working out a few kinks, but we are nearly finished with his equipment."

"Take the time you need, Doctor Yorkshire," Quake said politely.

"Thank you. Um...now that I mention it, I need to get back to work. If you'll excuse me..." Yorkshire left the room with the spark rifle box, awkwardly waddling along until he left the armory, leaving Farai alone in the room with the massive man.

"I was taking it upon myself to examine the weaponry of this combative body," Quake explained walking over to one of the rifle racks. He yanked one off and began to examine it.

"7.62 by 51 armor-piercing firing battle rifles," Quake said pushing out his bottom lip. "Good weapons, but expensive. Recoil also leaves much to be desired."

He put the weapon back and walked down the aisle, picking up a large, silver colored handgun.

"Ah! Krasivyy!" he said brightly holding a box of ammunition that was placed next to the handguns. "Chambered in .44 magnum not .50 AE? Smart choice, but again expensive, very cumbersome."

"Oracle can do expensive," Farai said at the end of the aisle, crossing her arms.

"Price does not always coincide with practicality," Quake said. "Believe me, Russians like me know this better than anyone."

"You should tell Marigold that," Farai scoffed. "I see you fancy yourself a firearms expert?"

"Da, yes. I dabble," Quake said brightly. "What about you, Ms. Omari?"

"I don't care for guns. Too crude. This is more Spartan's niche," Farai answered.

"I see, you're more fond of the bow and arrow. The difficult option, but the more impressive one." He laid the weapon back on the rack and leaned against it, deep in thought. "Ms. Omari, I must admit, I find you intriguing."

Farai hoped this wasn't going where she thought this was going. "And how's that?" she asked.

"You are a foreigner to the United States, yes? You are not from here?" Quake asked.

"No, I am not from the United States," Farai answered.

"Where do you hail from?" Quake asked.

"Zaire," Farai said. "Africa."

Quake took a moment to think about that. "Africa," he said quietly. "Do you ever miss home?"

"Every day," Farai said, homesickness slipping into her heart. "I will always prefer the savannah to this concrete jungle."

Quake smiled slightly. "I miss home as well, though I am more acquainted with Siberian tundra as opposed to arid savannahs," he said. "I can see you are an intelligent woman. Out of all the paths you could have chosen, why this one?"

Farai chose her words carefully. "My father and I knew and craved the thrill of the hunt," she began. "He hunted till the day he died. I continued after he had gone. I traveled to any continent I could, hunted whatever I could. Eventually, I had taken down just about everything, legal or otherwise. Then I settled for a career in Johannesburg. I never lost that love, though. Challenging nature and besting it, there was nothing like that."

"And joining Oracle gave you new prey," Quake stated.

Farai remembered the day she met Esther Marigold. Her future employer had flown via helicopter to the hospital she worked for and offered to take her to Oracle tower in the United States, speaking of an opportunity she promised she would be perfect for. The woman had done her homework. At the time Farai worked as a physician, but Marigold knew about Farai's past as a hunter, and that it was a burning passion for her. Marigold gave her an opportunity to hunt once again. Farai didn't have any idea what she was talking about, but the idea of hunting again gave her an interest she couldn't ignore. She eventually took up Marigold's offer and came to America for a time to see what the woman had to offer.

That's when she saw the revenants for the first time. Their raw ferocity, their uniqueness, their unpredictable nature. They were a quarry Farai, and any other hunter of dangerous games could only dream of. The deal was a mutual partnership. In exchange for her services, she would be on Oracle payroll and be able to hunt the revenants at her own discretion. She accepted the offer the same day.

"Yes, the revenants became my new quarry. In exchange I became a lieutenant."

"I see," Quake acknowledged.

"Why are you here, Smirnov?" Farai asked.

Quake firmly put the handgun back in its place and moved over to face Farai, his sheer scale intimidated her. "Do you believe in redemption, Farai?"

Farai looked up and tried her best to look at his face. "I'm not sure. I feel it's more a question of if someone is worthy of redemption."

"Worthy? In that case, who is to judge who is worthy of it?"

"I suppose ourselves, case by case."

"Ourselves..." Quake said quietly. "Do you remember the first animal you ever hunted? What was it like to kill it? To take a life?"

Farai took a moment to reminisce. "It was a sable antelope. I killed it with a bow, and I cried for a week afterwards," she said.

"Not a pleasant memory?"

"No. Even now, I have no interest in killing anything defenseless, not for sport. I didn't want anything to do with hunting after that. It wasn't until a puff adder decided to slither into my bed one night that I came back to it."

"A snake? Why did that change your mind?"

"I managed to kill it with my machete before it struck. I had to kill it before it killed me. That's when I realized what it really meant to hunt. That fear, I came to crave it. Hunting hunter's, killing killers."

"I understand that sentiment," Quake said.

"You didn't answer my question," Farai reminded him.

Quake looked down at her. "I did wrong. I brought dishonor to my home, to God, and to myself. And I fear my sins may never be washed clean. But I will still try. I must. That is why I am here, to make things right as best I can."

"Well, you picked a funny company to do so."

"I didn't choose," Quake said coldly.

There was an atmosphere of tension between the two. "These Time Riders, they are children?" Quake asked.

"Physically," Farai answered. "Why do you ask?"

Quake was still and didn't say anything. He had a silence about him that seemed to speak volumes. He spoke after a moment. "Tell me Farai, these children... are they serpents? Or antelopes?"

Farai didn't know how to respond to that. Just before she opened her mouth to say something Spartan came from behind Quake with a displeased look on his face.

"Am I interrupting something?" he grumbled.

"Ah, no. Actually, that reminds me I need to meet with Doctor Yorkshire again about my equipment. He said it was nearing completion," Quake said as he began walking. "Good day to you Ms. Omari, Mr. Talon."

Quake walked away and out of the armory. Spartan grabbed one of the handguns and a battle rifle and placed them on the metal table behind them. He took a box of ammunition and began to prepare and load magazines. He was angered by something. Farai walked over beside him at the table.

"What's your problem?" she asked.

"Getting friendly with the Russki huh?" he asked, jamming another round into a handgun magazine.

"My associations are none of your business," Farai said sternly. "Besides, when did you start caring?"

"I started caring…" Spartan started slamming a magazine into his handgun. "When you started going behind my back."

"I beg your pardon?"

"Don't play stupid, Farai, I know you're out to take my spot, you and the Red," Spartan said starting on the battle rifle magazines.

Farai had no clue how he figured that out. "For your information, I don't want your position. It's being forced on me."

"That so?" Spartan responded doubtfully.

"Yes! I have no choice."

"We all have a choice Farai."

"You know I don't!"

Spartan just groaned and kept loading his magazines furiously. "I know this position is valuable to you, but I'm backed into a corner," Farai said.

"It's not just that," Spartan said, then he stopped and took a deep breath. "Farai, Oracle has a different take on terminations, you know that."

"I do. That's why I can't say no," Farai responded.

"So, it's a competition then? Survival of the fittest?"

"No, we support one another. There's no other way. Someone will be killed if we don't."

Spartan slapped a magazine hard into his battle rifle. "Easier said than done," he said. "Look Marigold wanted me to relay a mission to you."

"A mission?" Farai asked.

"Yeah, you are on babysitting duty. Got a squad of misfires she needs you to accompany."

"Why me? You have live feed from their helmet footage, don't you? It's being relayed back to the servers down here."

"Yeah, the footage is fine. Marigold still wants a lieutenant out there, so it doesn't go snafu. This batch has been known to muck things up. Especially the technician."

"Isn't that something you would do normally? That's your jurisdiction. You know those men and women more than anyone else."

Spartan glared at her. "Yeah. It is my jurisdiction, for now." He grumbled placing the handgun in his holster and lifting his battle rifle onto his shoulder.

"You got half an hour before you sail off, Artemis. Do your worst, don't strain your arm on that bow of yours," Spartan said leaving the armory.

After he left Farai stood still at the table watching the door close slowly and leave an uncomfortable silence within the room. She put her hands on the table and breathed downwards. The fact this situation was so out of her control was difficult. She didn't want to pick sides, but she had to go by the book. She gathered her bow and put on her tranquilizer gauntlets, leaving the armory behind and reluctantly making her way to the capture squad.

CHAPTER 15

Hearts and Tools of War

Spartan:

Edgar Talon stormed out of the armory, spite eating away at his sanity. His current predicament left him growling under his breath, moving through the facility. It all felt out of his control. In truth it was. Talon knew more than anyone in Oracle, failure had weight. He had underestimated the Time Rider. Initially, that kid was about as threatening as a dachshund. Every time he showed his face he would disappear just as quickly. He always ran, doing everything he could to hide or get away. Compared to the revenants, he was small fry. Talon's mistake was thinking that was always going to be the case. After enough time had passed The Time Rider became bold enough to attack Talon's men and was even successful in doing so. Talon didn't even bother with the incident reports that became more numerous by the day. Why would he believe a teenager was not only surviving against, but defeating his operators?

But regardless of who was in their ranks, The Time Rider had managed to best whoever was thrown at him. It was only when Talon faced him himself that he understood why. Alpha-2 gave him an advantage that any combatant worth their salt would kill for. The speed and power it gave his attacks was borderline incomprehensible. The kid learned how to make it his tool, learning how to dance to its tune. Revenants had the same abilities, but they were only a little more than animals. The Time Rider had the brains to unlock its full potential, making him unpredictable and strong, the most difficult enemy Talon had ever faced in a lifetime of combat.

It didn't help that he had the backing of Spencer Carter. Oracle's current head engineer, Doctor Bartholemew Yorkshire, did a good enough job as head of research and development, and the toothpick was more useful than he looked by far, but everyone, including him, knew if Carter was still with them, he would be running circles around him. Back then that man seemed more like some kind of wizard than an engineer. Every day it was like watching a kid run around a candy store. He was in his element, always engineering or tinkering with something. The tech he cooked up would have fit right at home in a sci-fi film. Talons very own VD-11 Goliath gauntlets were one of his creations.

But after he left nothing was ever the same at the company. His absence was as heavy as raw iron. His position was passed down to Yorkshire, his personal assistant and right-hand man. He was an efficient engineer himself but had admitted multiple times that Carter's designs dumbfounded him. He has examined and taken them apart multiple times but could never replicate them. All he could manage was repairs and basic instruction that was passed down to him.

The Time Rider had a device of his own that Carter made. A grappling hook system of some sort. It latched onto his body at all four limbs and had a large storage box on his back. He was able to fire and slack hooks on both arms which he often used as whips or ball in chain like weapons, paired with Alpha-2 they were a dangerous tool, something Talon had been on the receiving end multiple times. They were not experiences he wished to repeat.

He tried again and again to put a stop to The Time Rider, but he couldn't. It was frustrating, but Talon couldn't help but feel respect for the kid. It was the kind of respect only an enemy could have. He'd had more than his fair share of jarheads that thought they were God's gift to the world. The Time Rider could certainly be rude and annoying, but it became expected, a familiar song and dance. Even still, his skill spoke more than his words ever could.

But to Talon's detriment, all Marigold could see was the bottom line, and that line showed he had failed to do his job multiple times. And now there was Quake, this new lieutenant Marigold handpicked. Talon could see the writing on the walls. Marigold was looking for a replacement, and even worse they were dragging Artemis into it. Talon trusted Farai in a platonic way, even if there were times he wanted more from their relationship. But now Marigold steered her in a way he was in the way of, and Quake was starting to get friendly with her, too. It made Talon want to knock the Russian down onto his oversized hind end.

He traveled around the base, heading over to the research and development hub. Yorkshire had mentioned new provisions that he was working on, and Talon wanted to follow up on them.

He traveled on the tram system until he arrived at the vast metal staircase that led down to the R&D workstations. He stepped off the tram and began to descend, his heavy battle rifle being held in his right hand aimed upwards. At the bottom he saw the usual work ants in lab coats working on their science projects. Yorkshire spoke to one about something Talon couldn't piece together past his high school diploma education. The doctor noticed him in his peripheral vision and quickly made his way to him.

"Spartan! What brings you here today?" Yorkshire asked with obnoxious enthusiasm.

"Following up with those new wares you were working on. Anything up and going yet?"

"Oh yes, indeed! Right this way please," Yorkshire said walking over to one of the nearby tables. Talon followed him. Yorkshire took one look at him and started to get squeamish.

"What's your deal?" Talon asked.

"Is that weapon loaded?" Yorkshire asked timidly.

Talon looked at his rifle. "Yeah," he said in response to the obvious question.

"Can you put that thing down for the time being? The last thing that needs to happen is for that thing to go off in here."

"It's on safety."

"Please, I must insist."

Talon grumbled and dropped the rifle down onto the table loudly, causing Yorkshire to jump. "Anyway," Yorkshire said clearing his throat. "What you see here on this table are our new ZL23 spark rifles."

"Spark rifles?" Talon looked down at the weapons on the table.

They resembled traditional rifles, but Talon had never seen a weapon like this before. It looked like a weapon of the future. The rifle was most definitely experimental, but that didn't mean it wasn't professionally made. From what Talon could see the standard SCAR 17 battle rifle was used as a base, with a multitude of custom technology installed on it. A camera-like optical scope and digital side monitor was present. Red and blue wires snaked around the body to a battery pack on the side, and an assortment of additional metal and polymer pieces were professionally installed on the body and the barrel. Altogether it looked like a very expensive, futuristic shirt cannon.

"What do these fire?" Talon asked.

"Something special. Would you like to try it over here at our range?"

"You already know the answer to that Doc."

Yorkshire rolled his eyes. "Of course. Right this way."

The two men walked over to a practice firing range to the left of the area, only a short distance from the tables. Operators and scientists were testing out various weapons and equipment at the same time.

When they came to their station a black case filled with large custom magazines was placed open on the counter. Yorkshire took one out and handed it to Talon.

"Place this inside the weapon near the top in that open compartment," Yorkshire instructed.

Talon lifted the rectangular magazine and placed it into the compartment. It fit neatly on top with a distinct click. The monitor on the side beeped happily with two beeps followed by two higher pitched ones, indicating the successful reload.

"Okay, go ahead and point it downrange. Once you're ready to fire, disengage the safety mechanism on the backside of the trigger."

Downrange there was a plain limbless dummy set up. Talon pointed the weapon at it and flicked the switch behind the trigger. He pressed the rifles stock into his shoulder and aimed to the best of his ability using the built-in optic showing a circular blue reticle within. He pulled the trigger and the rifle recoiled into him aggressively. The weapon fired a steady, bright energy stream into the target dummy, electricity occasionally arching from the beam.

The dummy immediately burst into flames and evaporated in seconds. The two of them sat there in awe at what had just occurred.

"Okay, now take that charging handle there to the left and tug it back firmly," Yorkshire directed.

Talon did as he asked and the magazine flew upwards into the air, then fell to the floor with a distinct ping, the smoking cartridge falling to the ground sounding like an empty can. Yorkshire put on some gloves, picked it up, and put it on the counter.

"Your thoughts?"

Talon didn't even know he was smiling until he spoke. "I like what I'm seeing Doc, you've outdone yourself."

Yorkshire looked proud of himself. "Thank you, Spartan. How did it handle?"

"The recoil was inconsistent, but manageable, likely because of its weight. But to be honest, I don't think there's a weapon that's actually like this. It's like the world's most dangerous fire hose but instead of water it's... whatever that was."

"Weight-wise, it's around the same as a standard M249 light machine gun. And it fires a steady stream of highly charged electrons, all with the aid of zenaphosporus," Yorkshire said.

"That again?" Talon asked, examining the weapon once again, flipping it side to side.

"Yes," Yorkshire said brightly. "The discovery of zenaphosphorus has led to abundant opportunities for technological improvement. It's a miraculous element, able to be used as perhaps the most potent fuel this world has ever seen. It rivals even radiation in its current form in terms of electrical output and is by far safer to use. Even now I'm looking for ways to use it to power systems, weapon technology, and even vehicles."

"Ambitious. You trying to give Elon Musk a run for his money?"

"One would hope," Yorkshire said casually. "If given enough time I would imagine the company that holds the keys to the use of zenaphosporus, well... let's just say their net worth would easily surpass his."

"Bet Marigold would be happy with that."

"Indeed, but there's something else."

"What?" Talon asked.

"As you are aware, certain variants of the Alpha-2 revenants produce zenaphosporus naturally in abundance. That's how we've been able to craft this weapon. We've harvested the gas from our captive specimens."

"Yeah, spikers and molders."

"Precisely. The beam of the ZL23 obviously produces an immense amount of heat, and we've had to take great care when storing the element to make sure temperatures don't exceed a certain threshold, which if not stored correctly combustion may occur. As a result, we have concluded that if these specific revenants are hit with this weapon they would react similarly."

"They'll explode?"

"Yes or violently catch fire. You need to be vigilant if these variants are present and you're using the ZL23. If used against them, they might cause far more destruction than initially intended. But then again, you could also use this to your advantage if the opportunity presents itself."

"Noted. Thanks for the tip. Are we planning on using this?" Talon asked.

"Of course, I'd never hear the end of it if I didn't allow you to use them. But we are going to patent it and sell it as well."

"Really? You're going to sell this thing?"

"Need I remind you that Oracle at its core is a company that sells technology? Where do you think Marigold gets the funds for things like this?"

"I know what the company sells Yorkshire," Talon said with a groan. "I just can't see this being legal."

"When has the law ever stopped our operations or commerce?"

Talon knew exactly what he was talking about. Anyone with any sort of prestige in the company did. Marigold normally did a combination of legal and illicit deals to maintain the corporation's absurd net worth. Without black market and under-the-table sales, they wouldn't be half of what they were. Talon imagined weapons like the spark rifles used in conflicts in the Middle East, Eastern Europe, and even the United States. It reminded him of his days in Saudia Arabia and Kuwait during Operation Desert Sabre back in 1991. It was the follow-up ground invasion after Operation Desert Storm. It was the first major military campaign in which he had participated. Talon and the multitude of NATO forces had managed to push back and overtake Saddam Hussein's forces out of Kuwait in only three days.

Talon imagined how much faster it would have been with spark rifles, or what would have happened if Hussein's resistance forces had them instead, cutting through man and machine alike. Weapons like these could change the course of war entirely, especially if some overeager scientist decided to make a weapon of mass destruction out of it. Yorkshire here was playing Oppenheimer for profit, not caring about anything resembling consequence. Thoughts like this came and went. They always prevented him from being able to be comfortable on his own two feet, not while he was on the payroll.

"Are you satisfied Spartan? I need to check in with Quake..."

"What's he doing here?" Talon asked suddenly.

"Testing his new equipment. Let's see how he's faring."

The last thing Talon wanted to do was be anywhere near the Russian, but he did need to know how he was going to operate in the field. Talon and Yorkshire moved away from the firing range and down through the middle of the row of worktables. At the end Quake could be seen, dressed in a white tank top, his exposed muscle structure in his arms and back could be seen clearly, making him look like a statue of Atlas. As they got closer, they saw more scientists taking notes. A large slab of concrete was placed next to him. Talon could see that Quake held some kind of hammer down on the floor. It was massive, something only someone of Quake's size could use, despite the fact that it looked mundane from where Talon was sitting.

"That's all he uses? A hammer?"

"Not just any hammer. That is the kinetic friction hammer."

"Friction?"

"Yes, there is a built-in friction system there in the base. It moves rapidly inside causing a field of electricity to arc out of it. For obvious reasons we can't see it in action now, but we can see what he can do otherwise.

Quake lifted the large hammer and swung with great exertion towards the slab of concrete. The collision sounded louder than a gunshot and bits of rubble flew in every direction. After the dust cleared the slab was nonexistent; only loose pieces remained in its place. Quake dropped the hammer and lifted the safety glasses he wore onto his head. The scientists around began to murmur and whisper with awe.

"It's like we were made for each other Doctor. I salute your work," Quake said brightly.

"Thank you Quake," Yorkshire sounded out loudly. He turned around to speak to Talon. "Wouldn't want to be hit like that would you?"

Talon looked over at the strongly built man and what remained. "No, I wouldn't."

Something loud behind could be heard hitting the tables and everyone and Talon looked back to see what it was. Legion was standing at one of the workstations, fiddling with their hard light generator. It felt like they appeared out of nowhere. A new chill ran down Talon's spine. Legion was just fiddling and taking apart the device with speed and precision, the mask showed Klara was the one at the wheel at the moment, which confused Talon. Fritz was normally the tinkerer of the four. Yorkshire got one look at them, then quickly turned to hysterics.

"Ms. Klara, please don't tamper with your generator in such a manner!" Yorkshire said, walking towards them. "I've told you before that the calibration shouldn't be adjusted without my supervision!"

Yorkshire went up right behind them, but Legion paid him no mind and continued working.

"Ms. Klara, please I must insist, that is not a toy."

Yorkshire put his hand on their shoulder trying to get their attention. Within what felt like a mere second, Legion whipped around and grabbed Yorkshire's arm, pinning it to the table, before the doctor could protest, a blade was slammed down onto his hand, going through the metal table, pinning his limb to it. Yorkshire cried out in pain and every scientist in the room let out either a gasp or horrified scream.

"Do not place your filthy hands on us worm!" Legion yelled venomously.

"Legion, stand down!" Talon bellowed.

They drew another blade and pointed it at him. "Do not test me Kommandant!"

Legion's eyes still glowed purple, and that high-pitched voice told the same story. This was Klara. Talon expected this kind of aggression from Eckard, but not Klara. She was the soft one. This out-of-character episode made Talon sick with nervousness.

"Easy, Klara, what are you doing here today?" he asked calmly, trying to change the subject for the safety of everyone in the room.

Klara lowered the blade. "We have grown restless. We want to move around freely."

"Alright, I'll work with the doc to get your generator up and going. Can you refrain from stabbing anyone else in the meantime?"

Legion looked at Yorkshire, who was still groaning in pain, almost in tears. "As long as they don't give me reason," Klara said.

They grabbed the grip of the blade and yanked it out of the table. Yorkshire let out one last yelp of pain and crumbled to the floor, holding his hand.

"You will get us the generator hastily, ja?" Legion asked, cleaning the blade on a sleeve.

The doctor nodded his head quickly in fear.

"Good," Klara said leaving the area.

Quake rushed over to the doctor's side. Where he stood, Talon was still perplexed.

"Talon? Do you have a first aid kit nearby?" Quake asked.

"Uh, yes, hold on," Talon said going to grab it from a pillar nearby. He came back and quickly knelt beside Yorkshire, opposite where Quake knelt as well. Yorkshire shook and wept where he sat. Pity found its way into Talon's mind. Even as a military man he felt shaken up after that. He couldn't bring himself to judge Yorkshire too harshly for reacting this way. He was a man of science, not war.

"What did I just witness? That was completely out of line!" Quake exclaimed. "Is this how Legion normally acts?"

"They've always had aggression problems, specifically with Eckard. But even he doesn't turn to violence this quickly. It's normally just morbid threats," Talon explained as he began bandaging Yorkshire's hand.

"But Eckard is red color, not violet."

"Exactly. That wasn't Eckard, that was Klara."

"The child? I thought she was the peaceful one?" Quake asked.

"She is, or at least I thought so. Something's changed," Talon said.

Quake looked up with a glassy look in his eye. "Well, it was certainly nothing good."

"No, it most certainly wasn't," Spartan said. "Have you read their file yet?"

"Their file? What do you speak off?" Quake asked with a puzzled tone.

"Assuming Marigold has granted you lieutenant status you should have level five security clearance. That means you can access the files lesser ranks can't. Me, Farai, and Legion all have a biography and overview file that's only viewable by personnel with that level of clearance. You should take a peek at mine some time, it's quite the read."

"What makes Legion's file significant?"

"I'll give you a little spoiler. Legion wasn't always the clown car they are now. They were once just a she. One singular girl from a smaller town in Germany. She grew up in a rough home, so rough in fact she ended up solving the problem in its entirety using a sharp hunting knife."

"*Proklyatiye...*" Quake muttered in Russian. "Is that why they are the way they are? Why they are many?"

"Pretty much," Spartan said. "There's nothing like the first-time jitters when it comes to killing. I'd imagine that knocking off their own mom and pop at a young age like that had to wreck their head. Our on-site physician, Doc Watson, says they whipped up those personalities as a coping mechanism in an attempt to repress excessive trauma. Psychosomatic amnesia she called it. Their brain is doing everything it can to not face what happened."

"She is sick. Why is she here being... enabled?" Quake asked, a simmering heat behind his words. "That sickness needs to be cured, not utilized!"

"You want to tell them the truth Smirnov?"

Quake went still.

"It ain't right, but it's all we got right now. When life gives you a good killer, you make a good soldier. Here in the states we've had that philosophy since our time in 'Nam. Get them to crave blood and they'll never think twice about spilling it."

"A good soldier is a mere tool," Quake said quietly. "And when tools break or are no longer of use, they are discarded."

Spartan looked away. "I'm well aware." He pulled on

Yorkshire's bandage, causing the small man to let out a short scream of pain. "There we go, army-grade tourniquet on the house," Spartan said. "How does she feel, Yorky?"

Yorkshire lifted his hand and looked at it with disbelief. "Army-grade? I need a physician-grade tourniquet! There was no antiseptic, no soap, not anything!"

"Doc, for crying out loud. It was a fresh cut that didn't touch anything, it will be fine."

Yorkshire shot to his feet. "I must see Dr. Watson at once!" he declared, running up the stairs and towards the nearest tram stationed.

Spartan threw his hands up into the air. "Well, don't let him tell anyone I didn't try," he said. "Go on and take off, Quake. I gotta talk to Big Tyke about his little science project and make sure Legion doesn't poke holes in anyone else."

"Big Tyke? I beg your pardon?" Quake asked.

"Donovan Tyke, he's our mechanic. Deals with all the armored personnel carriers and the cover vehicles. He's been working on something called Project Charon for the last six months. He wants me to look at it. You really need someone to show you around the place, get acquainted with your colleagues."

"That was the plan. Until my would-be tour-guide got stabbed..."

Spartan stifled a laugh. "Welcome to the company, Gleb."

CHAPTER 16

Gear Up

Markus:

Markus awoke earlier in the morning stinging and **stiff.** The previous night he changed out of his old clothing and into pajama pants and decided to go shirtless. He fell into bed and passed out instantaneously. When he woke up his old clothing was gone. When he tried to sit up in bed he immediately regretted doing so. He examined his body and saw he was almost completely covered in bruises and cuts, and his arm was still in a lot of pain, but he was grateful it was stitched up. He managed to sit up and make his way to the door and go out into the undercroft.

It was empty at the moment. He wasn't sure what time it was, but he figured Spencer was still sleeping. He felt better in new clothing, but he was still filthy. He went over to the bathroom and closed the door behind him. After briefly examining the shower inside he turned it on and let the water warm up. When it was ready, he changed out of his clothes and climbed in, letting the warm water wash over him and remove the masses of grime and dirt from both the city of St. Louis and the Mississippi river from his body. After around twenty minutes of showering and using an absurd amount of soap he turned off the shower and stepped out. He changed back into his pajama pants and stepped out of the bathroom.

Spencer was still nowhere to be seen. He started to rub the back of his head, unsure of what to do with himself. Part of him wanted to leave, but he couldn't be bothered to be stupid enough to think that was a good idea.

"Spencer?" a feminine voice said by the computers to Markus's right. This caught his attention, and he walked over to investigate. "Spencer, it's me. Open up!"

It was Charlotte. Markus looked at the controls on the little motherboard on the desk and casually pressed the button that said *open* underneath it. The bunker door could be heard being lifted upstairs. After it lifted completely Charlotte descended the steps excitedly until she reached the bottom of the staircase.

"Heya, Freckles," Markus greeted.

Charlotte took one good look at him; her eyes went wide and she quickly turned around. Markus was confused at first, but then he remembered he was only wearing pajama pants, and his entire upper body was bare. He rolled his eyes upon realizing this. "Oh, for crying... I don't care if you look."

"I do!" Charlotte exclaimed.

"It's not like I'm down to my birthday suit, you ever been to a public pool before?"

"Markus, please," Charlotte pleaded.

"What are you two doing?" Markus looked up to see Spencer coming down the staircase with a bunch of shopping bags in his hands. He took a look at Charlotte and Markus as he stood there conspicuously.

"Why aren't you wearing a shirt?" Spencer asked.

"Cause I didn't want to?"

"Well throw something on! Charlotte is here now."

"Where are my threads?"

"In the dryer, but if you want something new, just—"

"No, those will work."

Markus went over to the dryer and collected his clothes and skate shoes and went back into the bedroom and changed into them. He came out fully clothed in his jeans and sweatshirt. Charlotte cowered at the end of the staircase.

"It's all right, Charlotte, your virgin eyes are safe." Markus said sarcastically.

She turned around slowly, a look of anger stretching on her

face.

"Are you sure you want to keep wearing that?" Spencer asked.

"Wouldn't have it any other way. Had this since I was a baby," Markus responded.

"Even with that sleeve?"

Markus lifted his left arm and the split sleeve slipped right off and started to dangle. Without thinking about it, he tore the remains off the sleeve and did the same to his right sleeve without the aid of any tools. This left only the torso of the sweatshirt with his beefy arms exposed. Charlotte and Spencer looked at him, dumbfounded.

"You know I could have mended that right?" Spencer asked.

Markus shrugged. "Too late now. Whatcha got in those bags?"

Spencer looked down at them. "Just basic essentials, you hungry?" he asked.

"Famished," Markus responded.

Spencer brought the shopping bags over to the kitchen and started to bring out the contents. Milk, some sodas, various food items. He then brought out two cups filled with popcorn chicken bites.

"*Bon Appetit*," Spencer said going back to unloading the bag.

"Yes!" Markus said gratefully grabbing one of the cups and gorging on its contents.

"Figured you'd be by Charlotte, so I grabbed one for you too."

"Thanks," she said quietly, taking the cup. She didn't start eating.

"How was school?" Spencer asked her.

"Fine," Charlotte answered quietly. "Got a C on a math test, that kind of sucked."

"Work on that," Spencer said. "Mathematics is the ultimate enemies-to-lovers tale. Learn it well and don't forget it."

"If you say so…"

Markus jumped up and landed on the sofa, popping off the lid to his cup and dumping the remaining pieces of chicken into his mouth rather loudly. Spencer went still for a moment, shook his head back into focus, and began walking over to the workshop.

"So, Markus," he began as he started walking with a bag in his hand. "I've been needing to see you."

"Still wanting to recruit me? It's like I told hair bomb over there; you're wasting your time."

"Not recruiting," Spencer said, dropping the bag and fiddling with something on the bench. "I want you to test some new equipment out that I've been working on."

Markus spun his head around to face him and sat up on the sofa. "What kind of equipment?" he asked.

"It's right up your alley," Spencer said. "Put these on." He threw the bag to Markus; it was a set of knee and shoulder pads. He got up and obliged, tore open the packaging, and put the black pads over his pants and arms. He then walked over to the workbench. Charlotte followed behind quietly. Spencer lifted what looked like a backpack of some kind.

"What's that supposed to be?"

"This," Spencer said smacking the pack. "Is the pack kit for the F.B.P board."

"F.B what what?" Markus asked.

"Here, let me strap you into this thing. Put your back against it here on the bench."

Markus showed some hesitation, but he listened. Spencer started to strap him into it. The pack fit neatly onto his back and Spencer attached straps over his shoulders and under his legs, connecting all in the middle with a metal buckle. For Markus it felt like he was prepping for skydiving or ziplining.

"All right, take a few steps forward," Spencer ordered.

Markus slowly moved forward. The pack was strapped tightly to his back and didn't droop at all. It had a healthy weight to it, but it wasn't oppressive.

"Fits like a glove, perfect. Okay, next." Spencer walked over to the other side of the workbench and unhooked something from a charge station and brought it over. Charlotte leaned in close to get a good look.

"That's new, what is that?" she asked.

"Is that a paintball mask?" Markus asked.

"No, it's a custom ballistics mask. My own design. A more lightweight and compact version of a helmet Ryder used to wear."

Markus looked at the mask. It was a black face mask with no top, featuring a single, blue-tinted frame that covered the eye portion of the mask. The bottom was covered in drilled holes, making the mask look lighter and more breathable. It seemed to be reinforced with some kind of hard polymer at specific points inside. A camera had also been installed on the left of it, pointing in whatever direction the mask was looking.

"Put this on," Spencer told Markus.

Markus slid the mask over his head until he was looking through the blue lens. Out of nowhere, the lens lit up with a bunch of code and commands like a computer screen. It depicted some kind of synchronization.

"Ay, yo, what's this all about?" Markus asked, spinning his head around.

"What's going on?" Charlotte asked, leaning over to Spencer.

"User interface. Ryder had the same thing in his helmet, same program just with a few updates."

"Why didn't you just make another helmet like Ryder's?"

"Because I didn't have another helmet," Spencer answered. "Ryder's was part of an old shipment that Oracle had during their more experimental phase when they tried to figure out how to equip the PMC. I nicked one and built all the technology into it as aftermarket modifications. The helmet did good for him, looked neat too. But it had some flaws. If I'm starting over, I may as well make something better, you feel me?"

"Ryder's helmet had issues? Like what?"

"Weight for one thing. Whiplash became a real problem at high speeds when getting momentum through the Time Stream. And don't even get me started with the on-board computer system I had to rig up just to compensate for the lack of peripheral vision. It didn't help that it wasn't exactly designed to be used by teenagers who could move as fast as two hundred miles an hour."

"Two hundred miles an hour?!" Charlotte exclaimed.

"Two hundred and twenty-four to be exact. Ran some tests with Ryder back when we first started. Didn't dare try again after that."

"Why?"

"Inertia, that's why. Whatever is in motion stays in motion until impeded upon by an outside force. And once Ryder found that outside force, it ended up being a brick wall. He ended up breaking his left arm and nose, he was out of commission for weeks."

Charlotte gritted her teeth and hissed through them. "Owie."

"Couldn't afford injuries like that. Time Riders have an ageless factor, not a regenerative one. Worst case scenario he'd hurt himself so badly it wouldn't heal right. It would only take one bad tendon or misaligned bone, and he wouldn't be top of the line anymore."

Markus smiled and swung his head around enjoying the mask. "It's like a video game! Ha, ha! Awesome!" Markus yelled with glee.

Charlotte and Spencer looked over at him.

"I think he likes it," Charlotte said.

"And that's just the appetizer," Spencer said, rubbing his hands together.

Spencer walked over to Markus and began adjusting the mask on his face.

"Yeah, this baby is equipped with a built-in communicator, audio speakers, global positioning system, and a helluva lot more. Might need to adjust the volume on the speakers, it's a tad bit loud..." he said through his teeth. "And this is not even the main piece."

"What's the main piece? Gimme!" Markus asked excitedly.

Spencer picked up a fingerless glove from the workbench and began to fiddle with a dial on it. Once he was finished, he handed it to Markus.

Markus slid the glove on his hand and began to examine the gauge on the top of his hand. "What's this do?" he asked.

"Go ahead and press that gauge down," Spencer said putting some kind of board on the floor.

Markus pressed down on the circular piece and the board began to hover above the ground, held up with blue flames. Markus went starstruck.

"Bruh! A freakin' hoverboard!" he said loudly.

"That's right," Spencer answered. "Go on, give it a try."

Markus placed one careful foot on the board, then hopped on with the other. He hovered off the ground and leaned from side to side, and the board responded fluidly.

"Alright, now hop off," Spencer ordered brightly. Markus got off and back on the ground. "Okay, now you should be able to switch the gauge to the left there," Spencer said motioning with his hand. Markus did what Spencer said. "Now press it again, this is the setting I'm most interested in seeing. Make sure you stand still."

Markus pressed down on the gauge and the board flew up in the air and slid into his pack, sitting vertically on his back. He began to giggle like a madman in response. Spencer and Charlotte gave each other affirmative glances.

"Boys with toys?" Charlotte mouthed.

"Boys with toys," Spencer mouthed back.

Markus pulled upwards on the gauge again and the board flew up into the air and back onto the ground. He hopped on it and began to playfully fly about, then he started messing with the gauge, pushing and spinning it randomly.

"Wait, Markus, don't..."

Suddenly the board shot Markus upwards, smashing a hole in the roof with his head. The board came down just as quickly, throwing him to the floor, and bits of the roof fell after him. He began to groan on the floor, holding his head. Charlotte had to put a hand on her mouth to keep from laughing, but even as she did air escaped through her fingers, making an obnoxious raspberry-like noise. Spencer rubbed his eyes with his index finger and thumb. He looked up and saw a hole the size of a bowling ball in the roof.

"Rudy's gonna be pissed."

CHAPTER 17

The Test Run

Markus

After a brief recovery period Markus and Charlotte left the undercroft and went outside. Past the back fence of the convenience store was around an acre of flat land. The whole area was private property and mostly consisted of gravel. Spencer asked Markus to go out there and get familiar with his new skysurfer. Charlotte tagged along because she just wanted to watch.

Markus made his way out there with the board stowed on his back. Charlotte strutted behind him. He summoned the board to his feet and placed his right foot on it. He pushed it forwards and backwards trying to get a feel for it.

"Try not to launch yourself into the stratosphere Markus," Charlotte teased following up with a suppressed laugh.

Markus rubbed the back of his head. It still hurt after he accidently sent himself into the roof of the undercroft.

"Yeah, yeah. Laugh it up Ginger Snap. But by the time I've mastered this thing you'll be singing a different tune," Markus said defensively.

"Bet."

"Yeah, bet!"

Markus jumped up and planted both his feet on the board, balancing out evenly.

"You read me Markus?" Spencer's voice asked inside the mask.

Markus could see his picture in the top left corner of his mask's vision. "Yeah, I got you."

"Okay, good. Comms are working. Okay now you should see the GPS going online in three, two, one," Spencer said, following up with a loud clicking noise.

Markus saw a map of the city appear in his vision in the upper left corner of his peripheral and zoom downwards towards his position.

"That working fine?" Spencer asked.

"As far as I can tell."

"All right... live camera feed is also going steady, yeah, we are good to go."

"Hey just so you know, I didn't agree for no partnership or nothing," Markus reminded him.

"Of course, it's just testing some equipment. Nothing more," Spencer said.

"Right..."

"Go ahead and play around with the board, get cozy with it. Just don't kill yourself," Spencer said.

"Sure," Markus said beginning to push forward on the ground like it was a normal skateboard. The board slid along just above the gravel as smooth as butter. After what felt like a lifetime of wiping out from mere pebbles causing the wheels of his skateboards to lock up, having a board that could go over any surface without getting caught on anything felt amazing. He glided around the area easily enough, occasionally doing arm gestures like air guitars and eagles in a joking fashion just to give Charlotte something to see. She just kept shaking her head and facepalmed every time he did. He came back over to her and opened his arms in a showman like gesture.

"Voila," he said brightly.

"Let me try," Charlotte said.

"Wait, what now?"

"I want to try the board, get off."

"Have you even ridden a skateboard before?"

"I rode one when I was thirteen at a park once."

Markus raised an eyebrow at her. "Were you any good?"

"C'mon, please let me try it. Pretty please?" Charlotte pleaded with a softer tone.

Girls wanting to ride his skateboard. Markus had played out this scenario more times than he ever thought he would. Most of the time it ended in feminine calamity. As amusing as it was, it also proved to make him equally sad. Regardless, he could never bring himself to say no. He stepped off the hover board and gestured to it. "By all means Miss Rowes, have at it."

Charlotte scrunched her face and tilted her head in a sarcastic gesture of flattery, then stepped forward to the suspended hoverboard. She put one sneakered foot up on the board and moved it back and forth slightly. She paused for a moment, moved it again, then she hopped up once, twice, then she jumped onto it with both feet. The board began to sway back and forth as Charlotte struggled to keep balance. With a sharp yell, the board flew out from under her feet, and she began to fall backwards in the air. Markus managed to catch her and hold her up by her arms midair and held her up as she sloped downwards. "Easy does it," he said. "Coming in a bit too hot there, eh, Frecks?"

"Let go of me," she murmured stepping away and wiping her arms with her hands.

"Okay, it looks like standard hover mode is just fine, so we're going to try something fancier," Spencer said into the mask.

"Fancier? What's that supposed to mean?" Markus asked.

"If you switch the gauge in the right direction, you'll increase the fuel output, and as we saw earlier that will increase your elevation. I want you to try that again, just don't assault the gauge this time. You don't need to go from zero to a hundred again," Spencer explained.

Markus climbed back on the board and began to move forward. He looked on his right hand at the fuel gauge and gently twisted it clockwise as he was moving. He could hear the board hiss louder and he began to elevate into the air on the board.

"Wha—whoa. Whoa!" he yelled as he went into the air.

"Don't panic, this is normal. It should operate normally up there. Lean and follow your feet wherever you move them," Spencer said. Markus leaned and sure enough, it moved just as fluidly as he did on the ground. He turned the fuel gauge clockwise again and went even higher in the air. Markus began to laugh with excitement. He looked down and saw Charlotte looking up at him, shielding her eyes from the sun with her hand.

Markus looked at the glove on his left hand and noticed a button of some sort resting in the palm of his hand.

"Yo, Spencer, what does this button on my palm do?" Markus asked.

"Don't touch that, I'm still working that out."

"You said touch it?"

"NO! Don't touch that!"

Markus touched it. The nozzles on the board could be felt moving, and he suddenly began flying forwards. He almost lost his footing but managed to keep his balance as he sailed away from the lot and into the city.

"Markus, get back here!" Spencer bellowed.

He was so absorbed by the wind and excitement he didn't even hear Spencer talking. He flew through the city quickly like an airplane, gliding without resistance and having the time of his life. He dropped down low and high, side to side. Anywhere he wanted to go. It was like the hoverboard and Markus were one in the same. He continued passing over small buildings and shops until he was high enough and out of the way of any potential obstruction.

Once he made it to a clearing he was struck with an excited epiphany. He straightened out and focused with all his energy. He sent himself and the board into the Time Stream. He flew even faster, and the area became coated in the familiar wavey energy. Markus's exhilaration reached its peak as he flew through the St. Louis skyline at top speed, bobbing and weaving and even going upside down a few times. Then he dipped down near the Mississippi River and began skimming along the surface, reaching down with his right hand and letting the water drift through his fingers. Afterwards, he eventually returned to normal and clicked the palm button again, coming to a stop in the air.

"Ha, sweet beans."

"Markus!"

He adjusted the mask a bit since his ears had started to hurt. "What's up, Spencer?"

"What's up? What's up!" Spencer yelled. "Get back here now!"

"Alright, don't grow a hernia!" Markus responded.

Markus went into flight mode again and steadily made his way back to the gravel lot, staying high in the air to not draw any more attention. Once he got back he turned the gauge counterclockwise and dropped to the ground, hopped off and summoned the board into his pack. He went over to the undercroft intercom and asked to be let in. The bunker door opened and he entered.

Spencer was leaning over the assorted monitors by his desks. Charlotte stood near the television watching a news report. Every screen in the undercroft depicted Markus's flight through the city.

He took off his mask and threw back his hair, a smile still lingering on his face. "I got to say old-timer, that was the coolest board I've ever ridden," he said laughing.

Spencer walked over to Markus; his two hands clasped together in front of his face. He looked like he was trying to keep his composure in check. "Markus," he began. "We can't be doing what you just did. We need to keep a low profile," he said calmly.

"Dude, Markus that was crazy!" Charlotte called out excitedly. Spencer and Markus looked over at her. She had her mouth opened in a half smile and an accompanied sparkle in her eye.

"Don't encourage him!" Spencer said, raising his voice. "The whole city probably saw that, and Oracle…"

"Let Oracle know!" Markus interjected. "Why not let them know a new Time Rider is in town? Let's show them we mean business and aren't scared of them!" Spencer just stared, a soft look in his eyes. "So, you're on board? Are you willing to assist us?"

"Yeah, I'm not sure about the hero stuff, but I'll run a few errands if you'll let me use the hoverboard. I mean, as far as I'm concerned, Oracle can stick it where the sun don't shine, and those revenant freaks can do the same! You can be like that techie guy from those spy movies and Charlotte could be, like, uh… the snarky, teenage sidekick or something."

"Sidekick? I'm no one's sidekick!" Charlotte exclaimed.

"Eh, we'll work on it," Markus said teetering his hand back and forth. "Sound cool?"

Spencer crossed his arms and clicked his tongue. "Yeah, sounds cool," he said. Charlotte smiled from where she stood. "We'll have to lay down a few boundaries if you're on board. One thing at a time, if we rush this it could get dangerous real fast. Even more than it already is."

"Come on, I live for it." Markus clapped Spencer's arm, and he walked over to the refrigerator and grabbed a few cans of soda. He tossed one to Charlotte and the other to Spencer. He opened the last one and began to drink it. Spencer put his soda down on the coffee table and walked over to his computers. Charlotte was tenderly drinking hers with both hands on the can. Markus walked over curiously, looking at what Spencer was working on.

"What are you tapping away at now?"

"Right now," Spencer started, still diligently tapping away at his keyboard, "I am checking on my resident zenaphosphorus factory. It's been a hot minute since I checked on my revvie pet upstairs."

"Say what?" Charlotte asked. "Did you say revvie *pet*?"

"That I did," Spencer said.

"You're kidding, right?" Charlotte asked, slight demand in her tone. "Say you're kidding right now!"

"No, I'm not. I got it upstairs," Spencer said.

"*Upstairs?!*" Charlotte asked with a voice crack.

"Calm yourself, I've got it under wraps. And keep it down, would you? Rudy doesn't need to know I have one behind his shop."

"Rudy doesn't know?" Charlotte shrieked.

Spencer brought his finger to his mouth and shushed her aggressively. After letting the tension between the two of them dissipate for a moment Markus asked. "So, you have one of those things?"

"That's what I said," Spencer answered.

"Like in a box or...?"

"A cage, I have a spiker specifically. A real moody critter. Managed to swipe an Oracle capture squad cage with it inside."

"How did you manage that?" Markus asked with a hint of amused disbelief.

Spencer bit the inside of his cheek. "It's a real stupid tale, let's just say a little cash and hardwiring led to a real solid score. And a lot of property damage..."

"Sounds like my kind of tale," Markus said.

"No doubt..." Spencer murmured.

"I can hotwire pretty good too if you ever need it."

Charlotte swung her head over with a confused look. "Are you serious?" she asked him.

"Yeah, dead serious."

"How in the world did you learn that?"

"An old girlfriend," Markus said. "Tina Shrew, a real firecracker. Just as hot as she was psycho. Man, she was something else," he said dreamily.

"Tina Shrew? Tina freaking Shrew?" Charlotte exclaimed. "Crack baby Tina Shrew?"

"Don't talk trash about Tina!" Markus exclaimed. "She might have been a crack baby, but she was also *my* baby! I loved that chick, some of my favorite memories were with her. When she taught me to hotwire, we took a car out to a part of town where we ended up, well, let's just say she left me sore for about a week and a half."

An audible dry hurl escaped Charlotte's throat as she clasped her hands over her mouth. "Gross, what is wrong with you?" she asked through her hands.

Spencer wasn't paying attention to them as he worked. He typed a command into his computer and began to look at his monitors diligently. "Okay, looks like the tanks are ready to be changed out anyway. Do you two want to see the revenant?" he asked.

"Sure!" Markus said enthusiastically.

"No!" Charlotte said unenthusiastically.

Both Markus and Spencer turned to face Charlotte. The girl looked mildly shaken up, with her limbs shaking a bit where she stood.

"What's your deal?" Markus asked.

"My deal?" Charlotte said in disbelief. "There's one of those monsters up there, that's my deal!"

"What's the prob? Spencer said the things locked up tight."

"He's right Charlotte," Spencer started. "It can't hurt you the way I've got it set up."

"Don't you remember what happened in the underground base, Spencer? It's all fun and games until the caged animals get loose, and they *do* get loose. I mean, come on! Have either of you ever seen Jurassic Park?"

Spencer rolled his eyes sharply. "You need to stop that. We're not in some movie. Believe me, I don't want the thing breaking out either. If it did, I would be the first one in its crosshairs. I've used extra precautions. It's not getting loose."

"That's what all the park workers thought too, until the power got turned off…"Charlotte murmured.

"Friggin' dork," Markus said quietly. Charlotte heard him and shot him an icy scowl. "Look, I really need to change those tanks. Whoever wants to see is more than welcome to, just keep it down," Spencer said with a huff as he began his ascent out of the undercroft, muttering incomprehensibly as he did so.

Charlotte and Markus remained behind, Markus seeming to be slightly amused. Charlotte didn't look like she felt the same way.

"I'm going up to see it," Markus said gesturing toward the stairwell with his finger. "You wanna come with?"

"No," Charlotte said hotly. Markus gave her an annoying smirk and leaned forward towards her, saying only one word. "Chicken."

He pranced towards the stairs, hands in his pockets. He began to run up the metal steps until he was out of sight. Markus didn't make it more than five steps up before Charlotte could be heard quickly moving behind him.

"Hey! Wait up!" she called out.

"Keep it down!" Spencer snapped from behind.

CHAPTER 18

Autumn

Spencer:

Markus and Spencer both came out of the undercroft and into the back alley behind Rudy's store. Charlotte eventually joined him and Spencer up top. She was huffy and puffy, but quietly so. "Nice of you to join us. Follow me you two," Spencer said.

Markus and Charlotte had trailed behind as Spencer opened the gate to the backlot where Markus practiced on the skysurfer earlier. The three of them began to walk on the white gravel heading towards a work shed on the other side of the area. It sat remarkably uninterestingly in the corner of the lot.

"Just for the sake of precaution," Spencer started as they walked. "Like I mentioned, it's a moody critter so don't expect a warm welcome. The cage is a slightly newer one so it has a nice firm chicken-wire like mesh on it to ensure nothing will fly out but keep your distance just to be safe."

They eventually arrived at the shed; the front door was secured heavily with a plethora of padlocks. All of them hung neatly in the middle going down vertically from the top all the way bottom. Aesthetically it looked absurd, almost comical. But Spencer knew better than to underestimate a revenants drive to escape any captivity that found them. They were natural cage-breakers, and hours of secretive Oracle obituaries Spencer had read were testaments of that fact.

At the door Spencer brought out a keychain that hung on one of the loops of his suit pants. After sifting through the large mass of keys he began to work on the locks one by one, carefully opening each one as quietly as he could and dropping them gently onto the gravel below. After trying to unlatch one near the bottom, the heavy lock slipped from his grasp and loudly hit the side of the door. Spencer locked up and didn't move a muscle. Markus and Charlotte exchanged puzzled looks behind him.

Charlotte began to speak "You good Spence...?"

Before she finished speaking the shed lurched forward with a sudden boom and Spencer jumped back quickly as the door flew outwards toward him, locking up on the last few padlocks. The entire shed began thrashing around on its base and ethereal screeching and painful sounding scratches could be heard coming from the inside. The commotion was so violent that Spencer worried that the entire city block would hear it.

Markus whistled loudly. "Someone needs a nap."

"Like I said, she's a moody critter," Spencer said.

"She?" Charlotte asked with bewilderment.

Spencer didn't answer her. He inched forward slowly and began to undo the last of the padlocks, opening them all slowly. Eventually, the last lock came free, and he gripped the final latch for the door. He took a deep breath and began to count down. Three, two, one. He opened the latch and flung the door open.

Suddenly a barrage of banging and high-pitched screeching came from inside, kicking up a cloud of dirt and dust in the process. Both Markus and Charlotte yelled and jumped even further back from the shed. After a moment of allowing the dust to clear, the spiker within was finally able to be seen. Its morphed humanoid body was twisted into a creature that stood on all fours. A bony crown of armor adorned its head and snout. Its mouth opened over and over revealing the bright blue magma like coloration within it. Large crystals flew from its throat outwards towards the mesh on the cage, all of which shattered against it harmlessly.

"Hello Autumn."

"Autumn? You named it Spencer?" Markus asked.

"That's right, named after the season I snagged her."

"Again with that?" Charlotte said. "Is it actually a girl? I didn't even know they had sexes."

"They don't."

Markus began to snort. "You guys can't hear it talking right now, right?" he asked. Autumn slammed into her cage again, sending a fresh wave of dust out of the shed.

"No, we can't," Spencer answered. "Since you're a Time Rider you can interpret SpecterSpeak. What is she saying?"

"Nothing nice," Markus said leaning forward slightly as Autumn began a series of hissing and screeching at him. "Yeah, I hate to break it to you, buddy old pal, but that thing sounds like a dude."

"They all sound male, at least that's what Ryder said. But as far as we know, no revenants have any kind of genitalia or sexual dimorphism. They are genderless creatures."

"Then why do you call Autumn she?" Charlotte asked crossing her arms.

Spencer found himself unexpectedly embarrassed. "I don't know. Why not?"

"Why not? Maybe because it's weird?"

"What's weird about it?"

"Eh, don't judge him too bad for it Charlotte," Markus said walking over to her and gesturing like a car salesman. "Some guys call all sorts of stuff she. Like their trucks, boats, guns, and stuff like that. Some dudes just gotta supplement with other stuff cause they can't land a babe to save their life, or they just don't like the one they have..."

If Spencer still had patience for Markus before this, it was long gone now. "Markus, I don't want another word out of you."

"Hey, I don't care one way or the other. Not everyone is as smooth with the femes as yours truly. There's no shame in that. Gimme a break."

"How about breaking my foot off in your ass?" Spencer growled.

"Okay, wow. Calm down," Charlotte said getting between Markus and Spencer. "Don't you need to collect zenaphosphorus from the rev—I mean Autumn?"

Spencer shook his head back into focus, immediately forgetting Markus's snide remarks. "Right," he said heading back into the shed. Autumn snarled at him as he got closer to her but didn't attack any further. Spencer looked over at the side of the cage and examined the large assortment of faded green gas canisters that sat upright to the side of the cage. Each of these gas canisters had a device on top of them that came adorned with small desk fans covered in aluminum foil at the top. All of them together looked like a jerry-rigged windfarm.

Spencer started examining each container for ones that were full, carefully navigating between them so he wouldn't tear his shirt. Charlotte held a hand to her nose and let out a noise of disgust. "Man, that stinks," she whined waving her free hand about.

"Really? I don't smell anything," Markus said.

"Probably another Time Rider thing smart one," Charlotte said through a pinched nose.

"Okay don't be mean about it," Markus grumbled. "What does it smell like anyway?"

Charlotte dared to take another whiff and immediately recoiled into her hand again. "It's like... cold, rotten garlic."

"*Cold* garlic? How does something smell cold?"

"I don't know, it's just cold!" Charlotte said irritably.

"It feels cold," Spencer said within the shed. He was currently adjusting the fan on one of the gas tanks. "It's like vapor rub going up your nose. I smell it too; I'm just nose blind to it."

Autumn hissed at him and butted the container again with her head, then began snarling. "Geez, you think my roasts are annoying Spencer? You would kill this thing if you heard what it was saying," Markus said.

Autumn turned her attention to Markus and began directing her snarls and hissing towards him instead. Markus's face contorted in disbelief listening to her, becoming progressively more insulted.

"Oh, really now? That's cute coming from the literal evolutionary misfire," Markus retorted at Autumn. The revenant herself retorted with another wave of ethereal shrieks and hissing. "I smell? I smell fine compared to you!" he said angrily.

"No, you don't," Charlotte said.

"I didn't ask your opinion," Markus hissed at her.

"Paging Mr. Musty," she said in a sing-song voice.

"Zip it!" Another wave of hissed and shrieked insults flew

Markus's way. "Spencer, your pet is a friggin' dick!"

"Ignore her!" Spencer barked. "I'm nearly done here; I got four full tanks that need to come out. You want to give me a hand?"

Markus groaned and started to help move the containers out of the shed. Charlotte moved forward examining the setup of the cage. "How does Oracle go about capturing revenants anyway? Are these cages like mousetraps?" she asked.

"Essentially," Spencer answered. "They have custom aerosol canisters installed in these puppies. Revvies love what they spew out."

"What do they spew out?" Charlotte asked.

"Lab-synthesized glucose vapors; Oracle scientists whipped up a scent so potent a revenant can smell it up to five miles away."

"Glucose? Like sugar?" Charlotte asked.

"That's right. If there is one human aspect those things have kept, it's a love for sweets. They're drawn to it like addicts. Ever eaten a sugar cube? Try to imagine it as a very powerful perfume. That gunk is rich. It's pleasant at first, but after a minute or so you'll likely end up passing out. It's ridiculous."

"Sounds like a good way to end up a diabetic," Charlotte said.

A laugh escaped Spencer's throat. "You're not even wrong. One of our technicians ended up going to the hospital because he couldn't take it. Poor guy didn't produce enough insulin to keep up."

Charlotte began to grimace. "Yikes, tough break." she said

"You got that right, tough break indeed," Spencer said.

"What is all this?!" A burly, southern accented voice bellowed behind Charlotte. Spencer's heart bolted in his chest. He immediately recognized the voice. He looked behind him and saw Rudy at the entrance of the shed, he had a bottle of animal repellant in his hand.

"Sweet moth—what in the—what are you doing? Why are one of them things out here in the back of my shop, Spencer Carter?!"

"What are you even doing out here Rudy?" Spencer asked.

"What am I doing?" Rudy retorted. "I heard noises. I thought it was them raccoons you kept blaming it on. But it weren't raccoons! There were no raccoons! You had one of them monsters back here the whole time? Are you outta your mind? Are you touched in the head?"

Spencer left the shed and held out a hand toward Rudy like he was an angered animal, trying to settle him down. "Just simmer down for a minute, let me explain myself."

"Explain nothin'!" Rudy yelled. "I oughta tan your scrawny white hide for this! Racoons? Are you kiddin' me?!"

Charlotte stood off to the side of Rudy, tensed up and looking like she was suffering second-hand embarrassment. She had her teeth open in a grimace and looked so uncomfortable it was like she was bound with rope. Markus on the other hand seemed delighted. He was currently failing miserably trying to hold in his chuckling. His amusement wasn't helping Spencer feel any better about the situation.

"Rudy, can we not do this in front of the kids? Can we go back to the shop and talk about this?"

"There ain't nothin' to talk about! You need to either get this thing out of here or put it down!"

Autumn rushed forward again and slammed her head into her cage toward Rudy, letting out an especially ear-splitting screech. Despite his large size Rudy jumped back like a startled cat, letting out a scratchy scream as he did so. He lost his footing and fell unceremoniously onto the gravel, adding additional frustration to the older man's temper. Markus had to duck away to hold his laughter in.

Spencer went over to the fuming shop-keep and offered a hand. Rudy responded by placing his own hand in Spencer's. He began to pull up trying to get him to his feet. It took great effort because of his size, but eventually Spencer got him to his feet. Once Rudy was all the way up, he brushed himself off bitterly, starting to gaze with a molten look at Spencer as he did so.

Even with the fresh frustration Spencer couldn't help but feel a little guilty about deceiving him, but he knew this was exactly how he was going to react. He just didn't have the luxury of storing Autumn anywhere else.

"Rudy, please. Let's go back to the shop for a bit. I did bad by you here and I want to make this right," Spencer requested solemnly.

Rudy was clearly still livid, it could be seen on his face and felt in his vicinity. He sat there quietly thinking, his hands sternly on his hips like an angered grandmother. He lifted a finger to Spencer and jabbed it toward his face.

"Alright, but you owe me. I want a raise in what you've been payin' me. At least another twenty-five percent."

"Twenty-five percent!" Spencer exclaimed.

"I know you got the paper Carter, don't be all stingy," Rudy retorted matter-of-factly, treating Spencer like he was an unreasonable child. "Plus, you keeping one of them things behind *my* shop? Not part of our deal! What if that thing gets loose? If that happens you better hope it kills me because if it don't and it wrecks *my* shop? I'll hunt you down and start layin' a biblical tier whoopin' on you!"

Spencer never liked giving up capital without reason, but Rudy wasn't wrong. They never agreed to keep anything stored behind the shop like this, especially a revenant. "Alright you have a deal, but let's not discuss it back here," he said.

"Fine," Rudy said. "Let's go back and talk about it."

Spencer looked over at Markus and Charlotte, who were both standing quietly next to one another. "I need to discuss things with Rudy, you two get the shed closed. Just don't mess with Autumn, you got that Markus?"

"Aw, but I wanted to take her for a walk," Markus whined sarcastically.

"I'm being serious."

"But look how grumpy she is. She could do well to stretch her legs for a bit."

Spencer couldn't believe this kid. "Keep an eye on him, Charlotte. don't let him do anything stupid."

"It will be done, my master," Charlotte said sarcastically.

"Ha! You're gonna have her keep me in line? You know I was just playing right?"

"I wouldn't trust you if *you* were the one behind bars," Spencer said as he began to walk away. Markus said something whiny behind him, but he chose to ignore it. Rudy didn't seem to be any happier. He began venting to Spencer as they both walked. "Oh yeah, and that's another thing. You're keeping that blond boy here, right?"

"Well, yeah," Spencer scoffed. "He's the same kind of person Ry was, a Time Rider."

"I don't trust that boy, Spencer; he's got the devil in his eye.

And it didn't take a detective to see he was the one flyin' around earlier."

"I know Rudy, he's a pain in the ass. But I'm working on it. I have to. Ryder mentioned him in that note of his."

"Are you sure it's him?"

"Certain. His name is spelled with a K and everything."

Rudy scoffed in disbelief. "I was hoping you wouldn't say that. Have you found out anything about what happened to Ryder? What does that hooligan got to do with any of this?"

"I don't know," Spencer said quickly. "That note gave us next to nothing to work with, but Ry wrote his name specifically. It was even darker than all the other words he scribbled. He needed us to know about him."

"But why?"

"God knows. I don't like it either, but I trust Ryder. If he wrote that name in that note, it was for a good reason. Markus is needed for something."

He and Rudy made it to the fence and went into the alley, both stopping at the shop's back door. "Well, I hope the reason makes itself known soon. Hopefully, it's the first step to getting Ryder back," he said.

"I hope so too," Spencer said. "Whatever it is, I just hope Markus will even be willing to do it if he even can. If this is going to be any kind of risk like Project Witching Hour, a lot of lives are in his hands."

CHAPTER 19

Charlotte's Woes

Charlotte:

Charlotte and Markus remained back at the undercroft while Spencer went to meet and discuss things with Rudy. She was coasting back and forth between Spencer's monitors and the flat screen in the undercroft. Markus had decided to lay down for a while in the guest room, saying something about how nice it was to have a bed again, then left her alone in the undercroft. She didn't mind. For her being around Markus was like being stuck with an oversized toddler. A little bit of peace and quiet sounded amazing.

She took a seat in one of Spencer's office chairs near the monitors, letting her mind wander as she spun slowly while looking up at the ceiling. Her daydreaming eventually got interrupted when a news station on the flat screen in the middle of the room started airing. For the longest time Charlotte hadn't cared much about the news as it was rarely anything uplifting for her. After she met Ryder, she found herself paying attention to it more often. In truth her newfound interest came as a surprise to her. Her best guess as to why she was interested in it now as opposed to then was because she had a different perspective on things because of what she knew about Oracle and the Time Stream. Or maybe she was hoping for a sign of Ryder's return.

She began to absentmindedly watch the news people yammer

about political strife, gun violence, and other things she didn't even bother processing. A report on a local group new to town, known as the New Martyrs, caught her interest. According to the newscaster on the television they were an unknown group of urban terrorists stationed somewhere in St. Louis. They were blamed for various attacks against Oracle, including the infiltration of Oracle Tower and the immense vandalism done to the Gateway Arch three months ago.

Charlotte knew it was all phony. There were no urban terrorists, no New Martyrs. It was Oracle running damage control. The nature of the revenants, Oracle, and the Time Riders alike demanded the utmost secrecy. It was a goal shared by all parties involved. Whenever there was clashing out in the city, a made-up story to explain it was always cooked up and spat out to the media.

Charlotte began moving left and right in the office chair she sat in. Since she regained her focus, she found herself getting a bit bored, even with the news. She got up and blew through her lips, then began to walk around and started to get nosy. She raided the kitchen and started messing around with some of the appliances. When she got tired of that she went over to the sofa in the middle of the room and fell backwards over it, watching the TV upside down. After she got too dizzy, she got to her feet and went over to the workbench and started to fiddle with the tools there.

She began to open the cabinets above and rifle around through them, curious about the contents within. She pushed aside some containers and work trays looking for anything to mess with. After opening the cabinet farthest to the left she froze upon seeing what was inside. Her heart sank to the floor.

Inside was a DevTac Ronin, a black ballistics helmet. Charlotte knew it well. It belonged to Ryder. He used to wear it every time he left the undercroft. She was reminded of that heartbreaking morning, the one when Spartan had come to them with this helmet and announced that Ryder went missing. Charlotte always tried her best not to think about it, but seeing the helmet again was like living it out all over again.

She reached up and took the helmet out of the cabinet and brought it close to her face. It reminded her of a time when Ryder visited her home one night. She hadn't expected him so when he appeared outside her window wearing that helmet, she punched him right in the face, hurting her hand in the process.

Looking at the helmet made Charlotte's face hurt. The whole situation made her feel cheated. It was like a never-ending nightmare caught where the worst-case scenario occurred, she would forget, then be forced to relive it all over again when reminded of it in some way. She felt robbed. She just wanted to see him again, to say the things she wanted to say, and do the things she should have done. Spend time with him and actually get to know him, have the chance to be close. Anger cut deeply into her soul, and longing weighed heavy on her heart. She placed her hand on the face of the helmet and moved her fingers gently over it.

"Whatcha got there?"

Charlotte spun around startled. Markus was now right beside her. She had been so transfixed she hadn't even heard him walk up.

"Nothing," she said quickly moving the helmet between her hands. "I thought you were napping."

"Tried," Markus said. "I'm tired, but I'm too worked up. Seriously what is that? That looks neat. Is that like a military helmet? It looks like it even has a bullet hole in it," he said inching closer to it, Charlotte recoiled and pulled it away from him.

He frowned and looked over at her with confusion. "Why are you always so prickly?" he asked.

"Why are you always such a jerk?"

Markus just kept looking with a puzzled look on his face. "Man, you really don't like me, do you?"

"Oh? What tipped you off Einstein?" Charlotte said, shooting him a glare.

"C'mon, what did I do?" he asked brightly.

Charlotte raised her head in contemplation and put the helmet on the workbench in front of her. "Let's see. You're a thieving bully, an obnoxious narcissist, and unapologetically rude." Charlotte listed off, counting off on her fingers.

Markus whistled loudly. "Quite a rap. You even pulled out the big words for that one."

"Plus, if memory serves, you dumped the bill for that pizza on me and dipped, not to mention sexually harassing me," Charlotte said.

"What?" Markus exclaimed. "I didn't... oh, is that about that stupid Kansas comment?" Charlotte didn't even bother answering.

"Okay, back at Imo's I was just calling it like I saw it. Sorry, I do that sometimes. If it makes you feel better most guys really aren't that picky anyway."

"All right! Enough."

"Lighten up," Markus said warmly. "I know I've been something of an... acquired taste, but how about a fresh start? Huh? Clean slate?"

He wanted a clean slate? Charlotte didn't want to give him a pass, but she knew not playing along was likely going to bring more problems than it was worth. She just looked over at him silently, then stared back to the floor and exhaled. "Clean slate."

"Sweet beans!" Markus said clapping his hands together and jumping to his feet. "I want another soda. You want one too?"

"Sure," Charlotte said.

"Gotcha," Markus acknowledged, walking back over to the refrigerator. Charlotte watched as Markus reached into the fridge and got two more cans of pop and went over and leaned on the workbench. She got up from her chair and collected hers from him and cracked it open, leaning against the workbench herself. She took a small swig of the beverage as Markus did the same. After drinking for a few minutes Markus began to stare right at her face with glossy eyes. When she noticed she made a conscious effort not to meet his gaze, lest she get lost in it.

"What?" Charlotte asked.

"Aw, screw it. Probably shouldn't push my luck, but I gotta ask you something."

"Ask me what?"

He ran his hand through his golden hair and let out an exhale. "I've just been thinking. I know I had a bit of a bad start per se. I'm not much of a people person, and I'm not good at warming up to them. And I'll admit, I did treat you and Spencer badly because of that, but being here kinda gave me a small change in perspective."

"That so?"

"Yeah, and that change was you." Charlotte began to look at him attentively. "I'll be the first to admit I didn't think too highly of you at first, but you're starting to grow on me. I wasn't kidding back at the pizza joint. You aren't the worst looking gal in the world. To be honest you're really friggin' cute."

Charlotte's heart did a somersault, but not necessarily out of flattery. "So, I was thinking. I know I'm probably gonna be real busy, but if I got some free time I had hoped we could do some stuff together. Y'know, dates and stuff," Markus explained happily. "Been awhile since I've shared company with a girl but believe me, I've had my fair share of experience. I could make it worth your while. If you're interested."

Charlotte began to think about something that her mother warned her about a while back. Something about liking boys like him. When she heard it the first time, she had told herself it could never happen to her, but now she wasn't sure. Markus was no doubt frustrating, but he seemed so authentic as a result—carefree, unshackled. It also didn't help that the memory of his shirtless body kept creeping into her head intrusively. The more she entertained the idea of accepting his offer, the better it seemed.

She eventually placed her soda can on the workbench, then she stared blankly at him for a moment and gestured with a finger for him to move closer. Markus did until their faces were extremely close. She closed her eyes and leaned forward. Markus did the same. Before anything happened Charlotte quickly opened her eyes and kicked Markus hard in the shin.

"*Ow, ow, ow!*" Markus yelled as he began hopping on one leg and holding the other. Charlotte casually walked away towards the bathroom. "Take a mental picture Markus, 'cause that is as close as you're gonna get." Markus went back to his two feet, threw his head back and let out a hearty laugh "Now I really like you!"

CHAPTER 20

Thin Wall

Spencer:

O nce Spencer finished getting haggled down by Rudy he went out to make sure Markus and Charlotte had secured the shed correctly. Lo and behold, some of the padlocks weren't locked all the way, and Autumn's tantrums of cage-mashing had caused them to come loose. Spencer wasn't even angry about it. The padlocks were finicky even on a day when Autumn was relatively calm. Rudy had made a fresh point about keeping her back in this lot. Something in the vein that if she hypothetically escaped it would have put him in mortal danger. He knew he was right.

Keeping Autumn behind there was not the brightest idea he had ever had. In truth it very well might have been his worst. Spencer had played around with the idea of getting a revenant for years, and even tried to get Ryder to secure one multiple times. But luck was simply not on his side on those occasions. Spencer and Oracle had known about zenaphosporus for over a decade, and it practically drove him mad that he had no way to harness it. The potential the element had was outrageously numerous. For Spencer it was like an itch he couldn't scratch, a craving he couldn't satiate.

The capture squad cages Ryder ended up securing always allowed the specimens to escape, meaning Ryder was always forced to eliminate them or more often they weren't in the cage to begin with. Since Ryder was gone, Spencer had needed to collect Autumn by hand. Around one month ago a rather disgruntled Oracle desk worker had tipped off Spencer on a capture squad that had gone into the city. Spencer himself traveled to it and managed to sneak into the truck they stuffed their captured spiker in. The rest felt sped up to him in retrospect. He snuck into the vehicle, hotwired it, alerted the operators upon starting the vehicle, backed into a light pole in a panic, and sped off into the street with his new prize.

Spencer ultimately considered it a win, even if it was rather clumsily pulled off. But keeping his new spiker under wraps wasn't easy. Spencer was forced to deactivate the electricity within her cage to not risk igniting the gas within the shed. Then he had tried to make some reinforcements to the foundation and sides to the cage as best as he could, but Autumn was never in the mood to settle down once he began working. When he managed to nail and slap down what he held, it was like plugging up a water pipe with tape. It was almost guaranteed to fall apart eventually.

After he opened the back of the shed Autumn went ballistic with the anger of a thousand hornets. The four-legged creature kept hitting the side of its cage and shooting crystals through its mouth harmlessly at Spencer. He finished collecting the gas canisters from earlier and put them outside, then proceeded inside to assess the damage that had been done. The cage was assembled and put into the back of the shed with the utmost assiduity, but that was not much when dealing with abuse from Autumn. Spencer knew that if for even a second the integrity deteriorated enough, the resident revenant would break out and most likely turn him into a pin cushion.

He tried to get inside multiple times to get close enough for inspection, but the spiker ensured he would never get close. Eventually, after enough time Spencer lost his cool. He had no patience for temperamental animals like this revenant. After failing to make any progress Spencer ended up just swearing and ranting loudly at the spiker. He didn't have the ability to understand SpecterSpeak, but between what Markus had said and the loud, otherworldly hisses and growls, there was enough evidence to safely assume it wasn't saying kind things to him, either.

He kept thinking about Rudy's rant about keeping aggressive

interdimensional creatures in the back of his shop. He had laid down a heavy sum of money trying to ease the situation. It had worked, but he knew he'd lost some valuable trust of an old friend. Spencer didn't have much when it came to friends, so he always tried to do right by Rudy if he could. There was a good chance Spencer would be dead if he hadn't taken him in all those years ago, but more often than not his simple life turned upside-down because of what Spencer's work entailed.

Eventually he called it even and left Autumn alone, telling himself he would deal with her later, and hoping and praying the cage would hold in the meantime. He grumpily made his way back into the undercroft and was confronted with a curious scene. Markus was leaning against the desks right next to the entrance to the undercroft. Charlotte was on the complete opposite corner by the kitchen counters, giving a stink eye in Markus's direction.

"What are you two doing?" he asked.

"She said she wanted space," Markus said casually.

Spencer looked over at Charlotte, who looked like a redheaded hermit hiding behind the counters. "What did he do this time?" Spencer asked.

"What did I do?" Markus exclaimed.

"Tell that creep to stop hitting on me!"

"All I did was ask you if you wanted to go on some dates, get over yourself!"

"No!"

"Oh, for the love of... you're teens not toddlers, show some maturity, would you?" Spencer barked.

"Tell him to leave me alone!" Charlotte yelled.

"Fine! I'm sorry I was a big enough idiot to think you were interesting enough to date! Oops! My bad!"

"*Enough!*" Spencer bellowed.

Markus and Charlotte went deathly quiet. "I am not in the mood for this. You two need to make up or so help me..." Spencer started.

Before he could complete the thought, something on the flat-screen television in the back caught his eyes. Scrunching his eyebrows, he looked at a news report that had just shown up on the screen. At first glance, the footage depicted an old building in the back with a firetruck and other first responders on sight.

"What's that all about?" he asked quietly, walking over to the sofa and looking over it at the television. Markus joined him to his left, and surprisingly Charlotte did the same to his right. A newsperson was standing in the rain giving a speech to the audience. For Spencer it all blended together, but he did hear mention of lightning strikes with a slight chance of arson as it correlated to the amount of damage to the building behind.

"I mean, lightning hit that dump," Markus said. "It's rare, but it happens sometimes."

"Shut it," Spencer said.

Charlotte leaned over the sofa to get a look at the television. "I feel like I've seen that place before. Is that the city hall?" she asked.

"No," Spencer said. "That's the municipal courts building right next to it," he said with intrigue. "That place is abandoned, been that way since 2003. Lighting hit it?"

"Like I said, it happens sometimes," Markus said.

"You don't say," Charlotte said. "Want a gold star genius?"

"Lay off, Freckles," Markus growled. "What's the big deal about it all anyway?"

"The big deal is the destruction," Spencer said. "Look at that." He started pointing. "The roof. Look at that damage. Lighting is a static discharge, just like a larger instance of zapping your hand on a doorknob. It normally targets objects that are up high, and it looks like the same thing happened here. But it's like it not only hit the roof, but it also went through it."

"Through it?" Markus asked.

"It looks like a bomb went off," Charlotte said. "Maybe that is why that newsperson mentioned arson. It's like King Kong punched a hole right through the top."

Spencer thought diligently. It could have been a coincidence, but something about this property damage felt uncanny, or rather all too familiar. He lifted a hand and moved it up and down a few times. "Thin wall…"

"What was that?" Charlotte asked.

Ignoring her, Spencer walked back over to his desk and opened one of his drawers. "Ryder's note," he said. "He mentioned something about a thin wall. Couldn't make heads or tails of it at the time. But something about this feels adjacent." He pulled out a laminated piece of paper from the desk and began to read aloud. "Far away, bad place, A-okay, miss you, Spencer, Charlotte, Progenitress gone, thin wall, come home…"

"Come home?" Charlotte asked walking over. "What are you thinking here, Spencer?"

Spencer remained quiet for the moment. "Breach theory," he finally said. "An excessive amount of energy in one given spot could cause a substantial breach into our dimension. It wouldn't be odd revvies slipping out anymore. It would be a bridge between here and there."

"Just like Project Witching Hour," Charlotte said. "Just like the Gateway Arch?"

"Just like the Gateway Arch," Spencer repeated.

Charlotte blew through her teeth. "It's not much of a theory anymore, is it now?" she asked rhetorically.

"Wait, hold up. Are we talking about when it got ransacked earlier this year?" Markus asked. "Like those New Martyrs or whatever?"

"There are no New Martyrs," Spencer scoffed. "Oracle pumped enough electricity through it to rip our dimension a new one. It was all of them. That's where Ryder went missing three months ago."

"No kidding? Well, they royally trashed that hunk of metal. To be honest, I was a little jealous learning about it. Imagine wrecking a landmark like that, man…"

Spencer remained deep in thought, casually moving his hand up and down. "Maybe, I don't know," he said quietly. Breathing out, he moved his head left to right then began moving over to a coat rack and put on a coat.

"Hey, hey, whoa, whoa. Are you leaving?" Charlotte asked, walking over with a raised hand.

"I need to be sure."

"Sure of what?" Markus asked. "Are you sure you aren't jumping Jaws here Spencer?"

"I can't sit on this," Spencer said hotly. He walked back over to his desk and opened one of the drawers, revealing his handgun. He lifted it up, pulled back the slide, and stuck it in the holster on his belt. "If I'm not back in two hours, assume the worse. Let Rudy know what happened."

"I want to come with you," Charlotte said.

"Me too," Markus followed up.

"No, you two are going to remain here, where it's safe."

"You think Ryder's going to be there!" Charlotte exclaimed. "I am not going to sit here with my thumb up my..."

"No arguments!" Spencer barked.

"At least let me come with," Markus said. "I'm a Time Rider, let me back you up."

"Yeah, let him come with," Charlotte said.

"No! You two are going to stay here and that's final."

"But..." Charlotte started.

"Not another word. I'll be back, don't get your hopes up..."

Spencer was suddenly interrupted by the sound of knocking coming from the top of the staircase at the bunker door. He stood there stupidly, like a mock statue. Knocking came from the door again. Charlotte came over and started tilting her head toward the door as well. Markus and Spencer remained still. Five more knocks sounded out, followed by two more.

Then the speaker on Spencer's desk began to emit static, and a familiar voice began speaking. "What even is this crap? What was wrong with the password system... Heyo, hello? Can anyone hear me?"

Spencer's heart jolted. The voice was that of a teenage boy, he knew this one better than anyone. So much so that he had to second guess himself. Charlotte didn't, she rushed over to the microphone and began screaming into it. "Nathan? Nathan is that you?!" she asked.

"Charlotte?"

"Yes! Yes! It's me!"

"Is Spencer in there?"

"Yes!"

"Can you tell that old fart to open the door? What did he even do to it?"

It didn't make sense; it didn't even seem possible. But that was Ryder on the other side of the door. He sounded tired, but he was here, and he was alive.

"Open the door!" Charlotte yelled to Spencer.

He ran over to his desk and slammed a button on the console next to the speaker. The bunker door at the top of the stairs opened and everyone in the undercroft looked up the staircase to see Ryder hobbling down the steps one foot at a time. Then he lost his footing and plummeted down the steps and landed at the bottom and onto the floor. Both Charlotte and Markus cried out in surprise.

The first thing that became apparent was his odor. He reeked like wet garbage and looked it, too. He wore what looked like some sort of dirty, homemade poncho over his old, armored bodysuit. His head was a tangled mess of black, greasy hair. His glowing blue eyes could be seen through the long strands.

All three of them collectively backed up to give him space. He stood up on the floor and leaned against the wall next to the staircase, then he let himself slide down to the bottom. There he lethargically closed his eyes and began to breathe harshly through his teeth. Then he opened his eyes and leaned his head back, finally gazing back at the other three in the room. "You guys are the most beautiful thing I have seen in a good long while," he said.

A chirp-like noise escaped from Charlotte, and she covered her mouth. Then, she quickly ran over and plopped herself onto the floor and threw her arms around his neck tightly, then sobbed joyfully into his shoulder. Ryder began to hug her back just as tightly, rubbing his head next to hers as he did so.

"You jerk, don't do that to me," she said into his shoulder. "I told you to come back safe."

"I did. It just took me a minute, sorry," Ryder said.

She moved away from his shoulder and looked at him right in the face. "A minute? It's been months!"

Ryder smiled nervously. "Got a little sidetracked. Won't do that again."

Charlotte let go of him. They separated but remained close.

"Let me look at you," he said as he brushed some of her hair from her face and tucked it behind her ear. "It's so nice to see you again."

"Ditto," Charlotte said. "What even happened? There was all that stuff at the Arch, that big army guy showed up. We didn't know what happened, we didn't know where you were, and it drove me crazy not knowing..."

"I know, I know. I'm sorry for making you worry. But I'm okay. Mostly." He narrowed his eyebrows at her. "Are you okay?"

"Yeah, why wouldn't I be okay?"

"Spencer Carter!" A voice bellowed from the top of the

staircase. Spencer's mind skipped a frame trying to compute Ryder on the floor and Rudy up at the top of the stairs. "That critter of yours is makin' an absolute racket!" He began to descend the staircase. "You better have a way of shutting that hellspawn up or the deal is off." Spencer remained silent. "You hearin' what I'm saying Spencer? Respond to me before I..." Rudy reached the end of the staircase and looked downward to his right to see Ryder sitting there. He went just as still as Spencer.

"Hey, Rudy," Ryder said moving away from Charlotte and getting to his feet. "I just walked in and I..."

Rudy laughed hoarsely with delight, then proceeded to scoop up Ryder in his arms and hug him even tighter than Charlotte. Ryder made notable struggling noises as he was lifted into the air, and his feet began to dangle.

"You're okay!" Rudy cheered. "You're okay! You're okay! You're okay!"

"Yeah, I'm... okay," Ryder choked. "Missed you too, big guy, but can you let up a tad? I like my spine, y'know?"

"Yes, yes. Sorry about that," Rudy apologized. He let him loose and he dropped onto his feet. Rudy placed his hands on his shoulders and the side of his head, examining him. "Good golly, boy, your dirtier than the Mississippi! Where you been? A mud derby?"

"It may as well have been," Ryder said.

Rudy started shooting off an assortment of more questions, so many it wasn't even possible to answer all at once. Spencer finally walked over and put an end to it, forcing himself to face him.

"How are you even here, Ry? It's been three months since you went missing. How are you doing physically? What's your mental state?"

"I'm doing as well as I can, Spence," Ryder said. He reached out and hugged him as well. "I'm just glad to be home with you guys."

He was still wet and that putrid stench he had lingered, but Spencer felt warm inside receiving this affection.

"Spencer gets a hug, Grease ball gets a hug, Freckles gets a hug. Where's *my* friggin' hug?" Markus asked.

Ryder held on to Spencer until he saw Markus in the room. With everyone in the room focused on Ryder, he relegated himself to the corner of the room and leaned against a desk looking moody. As far as Spencer could see he reeked of pretension in droves.

"Markus," Ryder started. "It's great to see you man, thank God you survived. Are you okay?"

"What's it to you?" Markus asked. "You don't even know who I am, pal."

"I do," Ryder said. "Just not in the way you think."

"Well, care to enlighten me?!"

Ryder jumped slightly at the harsher tone. "In due time," he said. "It's real heavy stuff."

"Markus is right Ry," Spencer said. "Talk to us here. Can you tell us what happened to you?"

Ryder backed up and let out a tired exhale and looked around the room. "Y'all might want to sit down for this one. It's a real long story."

CHAPTER 21

The Alpha and The Apex

Before Ryder's return, all Farai could think about was the cold. She sat in the back of an Oracle cover vehicle, specially designed by Donovan Tyke and his team of engineers at Oracle Towers laboratories. Superficially mundane, the modified moving van was housing both Farai and a squad of Oracle operators on the inside.

It had begun to rain earlier, causing the air to cool. Farai sat with four others, seated inside on the custom seats like a patron in a subway car. The air inside had turned frigid, making her regret wearing her usual tank top and cargos with only a black raincoat to cover her whole body. Such cold was once foreign to her, but not anymore.

She was here on the mission that Spartan had relayed to her back in the armory, to oversee a squad of operators as they did their routine asset collection route. She was to go around under the cover of one of the modified vehicles, check the cages, and report any successful snags back to a separate squad with the proper equipment for collection. Though conceptually elementary, she found the task unbearably uncomfortable on a wet fall evening. All Farai could do was remain as still as possible to keep the moisture off her face and use her coat to catch the colder air.

The squad with her was something of a pack of misfits, subpar in performance most of the time, but essential. There was a reason they had earned the name of "Renegade Squadron."

There were four members. First, one of two point men, a former military man named Kane Merkel. He had history with Spartan himself—he had fought alongside him in Afghanistan on multiple occasions, earning the nickname "The American Rasputin" for his ability to avoid death.

The same couldn't be said for the man that sat beside Merkel, an Irishman with a buzz cut who wore a set of goggles on his head. Seamus Killian, squad engineer. Ironically, he was an immense piece of work himself. An illegal street racer-turned-mercenary who eventually ended up on Oracle's payroll. He was the one Farai was eyeing like a hawk more than the others.

The team lead was Finley Tabard, an old guard soldier. He had fought in every conflict from Korea to the Gulf War. He always reeked of cigarettes and something like a used bedpan. There was always a reason to keep a wide berth from him.

Finally, there was the second point man, who just so happened to be the only woman on the team. Mallory Tumen, a former policewoman from St. Louis Metropolitan Police Department. She wore an old police cap on her medium-length blond hair to honor her past.

Farai and the squad had been working out in the city for close to two hours at this point. It wasn't pleasant, but it kept Farai's worries on the back burner. So far, it had been what Oracle mercs called a dud run. None of the cages had captured any revenants. She didn't care; this was more so a babysitting run to make sure Killian didn't muck things up. But he was mellowed out, almost bored. It could have been the cold slowing him down. Farai couldn't be bothered to figure out which it was.

They traveled to the third to last container, and Farai leaned over, resting her arms on her legs as the truck tittered back and forth as they traveled. Her mind idled. It wasn't until Mallory kicked her boot from in front of her that her focus came back to the present.

"You hanging in there, lieutenant?" she asked.

Farai blinked; her eyes began to sting from the cold air she let into them. "I'm fine, I'm just not fond of the cold."

Seamus Killian let out a hearty laugh. "You should try Dublin on for size, love. Cold and rainy is the Irish way of life."

"I think I'll pass…"

"Land of the plaid-skirted men," Finley said with a laugh. "Sounds like paradise."

"Oi! Don't be talkin' like that. You've always got to oust yourself as the bitter old bastard, don't you, Finn?"

Finley just responded with a groan.

"At least Afghanistan didn't have the damn rain," Kane said, chipping in. "I'd take getting holed up in a foxhole over staying out in the water for another minute."

"I grew up in the Congo," Farai said. "Rain is a commonality to me. Though, admittedly it was far warmer there."

"You don't say," Kane said plainly.

Mallory slammed her hand on the side of the truck two times. "Driver! How far are we to the next package?"

"Less than five minutes!" the driver's voice sounded from the metal sheet separating the front from the back.

"Thank God," Mallory murmured. "If I get hypothermia from a capture run, I'm going to be pissed."

"You're always pissed, Mal." Finley said. "Ever since your dearest Todd got shish-kebabbed by a spiker."

"Talk about Todd again and I'll shoot your damn kneecaps," Mallory growled.

Farai put a reassuring hand on her leg. "Easy, ignore him. There is no need for hostility."

"You gonna write me up, Teach?" Mallory spat.

"I'll do worse," Farai hissed. "You are a good friend, but I am not going to let you off the hook because of that. Stay cool."

Mallory grunted. Before she could respond further, the truck's brakes screeched. Everyone inside shifted forward, rocked back, and then sat upright.

"Looks like we're up," she said.

"Back out into the stupid rain…" Kane grumbled.

The operators yanked their firearms out of the carriers installed to the right of their seats. Farai unlatched her boomslang bow from hers. Everyone took a moment to examine their equipment. Kane flicked the safety of his weapon off, Seamus adjusted his goggles, Finley stuck a crumpled pack of cigarettes in his vest pocket, and Mallory racked her shotgun.

Farai reached down and pulled the latch at the bottom of the door, and it came loose and rose all the way to the roof of the truck, exposing them to the grayish rain-soaked world outside. She lifted the hood of her raincoat over her head and gripped her bow with her left hand, jumping off the truck and landing on the pavement outside. Everyone followed her from behind, each one leaving the vehicle with their weapons raised, assuming a formation with each of Farai's sides covered by two operators.

The downpour outside made her feel like she stood in her shower. Her ears were enveloped by unending pitter-patter of the rain hitting her hood, and her vision was more impeded than usual. Regardless, she was able to make out where she was.

It was a smaller area than the other capture zones, a back area of a supermarket. There were rows of white garage doors to the left, and a chain link fence to the right. Up ahead was supposed to be what they were there for, but all five of them immediately realized it wasn't.

"Where's the cage?" Mallory asked, dumbfounded.

Up ahead, past the barrage of rain, was a concrete road leading as far as they could see. The metal cage that had been deployed was missing without a trace.

"What?" Seamus exclaimed. "Did those...?" He didn't finish what he was saying. Instead, he ran forwards in a sprint towards the open area.

"Killian, stop!" Farai yelled.

He didn't listen. He stopped running past the back end of the semi-truck and looked to his left to something no one else could see from where they stood. Then he waved them over, letting one of his hands loose from his rifle.

Farai took point, bow at the ready. Her right hand on the bow itself, the left on the draw string. The other three operators moved through the rain beside her, rifles aimed high. Once she was closer to where Seamus was, she saw what he had responded to.

The cage they sought was up on the concrete platform past the truck, smashed to pieces. Bits of metal piping, wiring, and what was left of the power generators were strung about like uncanny confetti. Farai had seen revenants break out of these containers before, but she had never seen a container be what she would describe as obliterated. The other operators met her where she stood, gazing at the debris themselves.

"What in the fresh hell?" Kane murmured.

"That's a new one," Mallory followed up.

"Keep looking at it, I want your helmet cams to record it," Farai ordered. "Kane, Seamus, on me."

"Affirmative," the two of them said.

Farai went over to the platform and climbed up onto it. Kane did the same while Seamus used a staircase to the right. She bent down over the remains of the cage, lifting one of the loose bars in her hand and letting it drop back onto the concrete. Kane knelt beside her as Seamus examined everything from his side.

Kane shook his head. "These things aren't on the light side. What the hell kinda revvie moved it all the way up here?"

Farai tried to drown everything else out and slow her thinking. She looked back at the container's original spot, then where it landed. It was forcibly moved at a horizontal angle with such force that it flew into the air and landed at a platform of a higher elevation. Unless it was deliberate, it would take a large number of revenants to move it in such a manner. But Farai doubted it was the work of multiple subjects.

"I think I know the kind of revenant that could do this."

"Lieutenant!" Mallory called out.

Farai looked over at her. "What is it?" she asked.

"We got a cadaver!" Mallory screamed over the rain. "Civilian!"

Farai jumped from the platform back into the rain and came over to where Mallory was. Just past a crate, Farai saw what she was talking about. A pair of legs was seen sprawled on the ground; murky crimson was carried by the rain from it down the road. Looking past the crate, Farai saw that the legs were pretty much what was left.

She stood back up. Mallory had her head turned away, holding the top of a hand against her nose.

"What are we dealing with, Farai?" she asked.

"The Apex."

Mallory moved her hand away from her face. "The new variant? It did this?"

"Yes," Farai answered.

"How do you know?"

"It's the only revenant big enough to move the container like that."

"What even happened? Do you have a clue?"

"Food aggression," Farai said.

"Food aggression? Like that thing dogs get?" Mallory asked.

"Something in that vein," Farai answered. "My bet is it was triggered by the pheromone dispenser."

"Why?"

"The Apex smelled the sugary scent, got frustrated when there was nothing to consume, and it hit the container. Then it took out its hunger on the first thing it could eat. That's my working theory."

"Seems pretty accurate to me," Mallory said.

The Apex was here, and Farai knew it. She found herself feeling something she had not felt in a long time, excitement. This was something she was familiar with, the site of a mauling. And now there was a man-eater loose in the city. A man-eater to hunt.

"Seamus! Get down here and flip your goggles. I want to know when our culprit was here."

"Aye!" Seamus said jumping down from the platform and running back into the rain. He touched a device on his glove and goggles on his head came down on his eyes with a mechanical sound. The eyes of the goggles began to glow yellow. Seamus kneeled and looked around the area with them. The rain pattered against the glowing lenses as he moved. He touched his wrist again and the goggles returned to the top of his head.

"Got a good EMF plume," he said. "Real big, dissipating pretty fast, but it's fresh. It had to have been less than an hour since whatever was here was here. What was it, lieutenant?"

"Give me the hand-held," Farai ordered.

Seamus opened the pocket on the front of his vest and pulled out a black device. He extended it and Farai plucked it from his hand. She went down on her knee and opened it up. A small, beige counter with numbers came up as she turned it on. A green light began to pulsate on the side in response to the electromagnetic field in the area. She stood back up, still looking at the device.

"Finn."

"Yes lieutenant," Finley said, walking over.

"Take charge, get the rest back in the van and complete your run. I'm going to track the Apex variant."

"Alone?" Mallory walked up. "You can't kill that thing with a bow. Let four guns back you up."

"It's bulletproof. If I can't take it down, four guns aren't going to make a difference."

"And you don't think it's arrow proof?" Kane asked.

"I'm not going to explain myself!" Farai snapped. "Follow the order."

"That little tracker won't do any good," Seamus said. "The range is dog water, and it'll only pick up a signal from a big field. Only revvie packs have that much.

"That's what I'm looking for," Farai said.

Seamus moved his mouth rapidly but didn't say anything.

"Finn, follow the order," Farai repeated.

All four operators looked at one another. After some hesitation, Finn circled his finger in the air with a "rally up" gesture. "Form up, let's get back to the cover vehicle."

"Affirmative," the other three said.

They all began walking together towards the truck at the end of the road, leaving Farai alone, standing in the rain. She looked at the small reader in her hand being splotched by the rain. The green light on it began to oscillate, feeling almost like a taunt.

Farai began to follow the invisible field in whatever direction caused the numbers and light to change. Slinging her bow over her shoulder, she climbed through moats, ran across streets, and crouched by drainpipes. She was unaware of all sense of time, lost in the act of hunting her target. Occasionally, she would find large three-toed footprints embedded in the mud, like the toes of the avian cassowary but far larger. And the distance between the tracks was profound. The Apex was moving fast, faster than any normal terrestrial creature could.

Farai drew her bow, keeping the EMF tracker pinned to her hand and the base of her weapon. She moved in stride along a field, splotching water and mud on her boots. Then the tracker began to whir, the green light remaining solid and the electromagnetic wavelength excessively high.

Farai looked around. She had managed to find her way to an open field. It was vast, with some large ponds being visible, and another rounder one with an old gazebo structure erected in the middle of it.

Farai had arrived at Forest Park, now vacant because of the

weather. She looked at the tracker again. It hummed steadily, like a drowning scream. There was nothing but grass and a few man-made structures. Farai muttered a French obscenity under her breath. Where was this thing? And what was it doing?

Something caught her eye, a mere glimmer of light over the hill. Looking over to it, Farai saw nothing. But she kept her eyes trained, her hands gripping the base and drawstring of her bow firmly. Then the glimmer came back, starting at the top of the field then disappearing below it, like a bright blue cloud. She gripped her bow tighter. She counted her breaths. One, two, three. Her eyes remained unflinching, like a panther among jungle ferns.

Five, six, seven… she dove out of the way in a tactical roll. A large, clawed hand suddenly flew past her. On a dime, Farai turned around, crouching low. The Apex skidded on the grass and looked back at her. Its eyes glowed demonically against the gray sky. It let out a shrill roar as lighting cracked loudly behind it.

Farai lifted her bow, ready to fire, but the Apex swung at her again and forced her to evade. She slipped on the wet grass and fell, rolling down the hill. She tumbled over and over, powerless against the momentum until she stopped suddenly, in pain and covered in muck. She heard the Apex roar once more.

Clenching her teeth, Farai forced herself onto her knees with her bow. The Apex slowly began to descend the hill; its mouth opened it hissed like a snake. Farai put her left foot in front of her and leaned back on her right. She lifted the bow horizontally and pulled back the drawstring. A crystalline arrow formed between the string and the bow. She took aim with timely precision and let the string fly.

The arrow slammed loudly into its leg. The Apex howled and slipped on the grass as well, tumbling down toward Farai as an organic avalanche. She jumped out of the way as the beast landed right where she did.

Off her feet again, Farai sat right next to the Apex's head. It snapped at her once, then again as she got out of the way. She shot to her feet, readying another arrow vertically. The Apex began to climb to its feet, leaning on its knee that had the arrow embedded in it.

Farai let another arrow fly, and it landed in the revenant's shoulder. Another cry escaped its maw as it held its newly injured limb. It sniffed and looked at the arrow, then took it in its opposite hand and pulled it out. Looking at it one more time, it trained its gaze on Farai, tossing aside the arrow without breaking its sight. Then it ripped out the arrow in its leg and righted itself.

Farai readied another arrow as it inched close, slowly. She stepped back in tandem. She could hear a rumble over the rain, a sound emanating anger and aggression. It was subtle, but its maw was gradually opening, like a crocodile. Then came the inferno growing ever-so-slightly inside its throat. Thinking quickly, Farai realized she was at almost the right distance to be in the trajectory of the flames.

Whether it was impatience, or it realized she was onto it, the subtle inferno in the Apex suddenly grew large, and Farai fired off one more arrow right at it as she ducked out of the way of the firestorm aimed right at her.

The Apex growled and hissed simultaneously, ripping the arrow from its nose. Tossing it aside, it ran forward, enraged. Farai began moving just as fast. She sprinted toward the round pond and the gazebo, seeking any bit of shelter she could. She landed in the pond and waded towards the structure, hearing another shrill roar from the Apex that made adrenaline pump in her veins. She climbed up into the gazebo and stood in the middle of it. The Apex walked through the pond after her.

She lifted her bow and readied another arrow. The Apex suddenly stopped moving. It stood still, its mouth open and sniffing. Then it slowly began to pace around the round pond. Farai kept her bow trained on it the whole time. This creature could easily topple her poor excuse for a shelter over like a Jenga tower. But now it was merely encircling the round pond that surrounded the gazebo, almost as if in contemplation.

Again, it walked through the pond for another circle around. It had a posture that was too human for Farai's liking. It was agonizing. This was a predator that knew it would get hurt if it was too rash. The Apex was a lion gambling on when to expend its energy. And this time, Farai was the antelope.

It circled repeatedly, too many times to count. Then, another crash of lightning came down, loud and true. It stung Farai's ears as she fought the urge to bring her hands to them. Instead, she kept her bow raised. Her voice contorted in pain as her hearing began to ring. The Apex looked up at the sky and sniffed again. Then it looked toward Farai again, roaring once more before it sprinted through the pond and back onto the grass. Then it went into a blue blur once more and disappeared out of sight. Farai ran through the pond herself and looked out over the hill. Outside of a few fresh footprints, it was nowhere to be found. It was on the move again.

She pressed a button on her earpiece and spoke into it.

"Finn, you copy?" she screamed over the rain.

"Go ahead, Artemis," Finley said.

"I've found the Apex variant. I am in pursuit. Make sure your driver is ready to receive a new location. Do not return to base. I repeat, do not return to base."

"Affirmative," Finley said.

Nodding to herself. Farai took out her EMF tracker again and turned it on, running and following the tracks the Apex left behind.

CHAPTER 22

Return to Sender

Ryder:

Twelve hours ago, Nathan Ryder returned home. In what felt like mere moments ago, he felt himself spinning and turning, unable to determine what was up or down. He sat strapped inside a metal container that tumbled about like it was caught in a tornado, traveling through the very Time Stream itself. The whooshing noise inside of it proved to be earsplittingly loud. His mind shook violently in his head, his thoughts mere frames. All he could do was close his eyes as tightly as he could and pray to God it would all be over swiftly.

And as quickly as it started, his request was fulfilled. The tumbling suddenly stopped, and Ryder felt himself go lopsided. His back ended up pinned to the bottom of the container and his feet were perched high in the air above him. Trying to bring his mind into focus, he squirmed a bit. The container began to rock back and forth like it was stuck on something. On what he did not know. He squirmed even more, with more effort. The container rocked back and forth like a rocking chair caught in the wind. He continued until all of a sudden, the container came loose.

Ryder's stomach immediately lurched into his skull and his heart stung as both he and the container plummeted down. His screams echoed throughout the inside until a loud crash emanated as it slammed into the ground, sounding like a frying pan. He gritted his teeth and groaned, taking time to slam a balled fist into the side of the metal box to vent the anger that came from being hurt by the fall.

"Would it have killed you to put some cushions or something inside this thing Markus?" he asked rhetorically.

Ryder reached down and pulled a stiff metal lever on one side of the container and pushed forward, the door opened slightly but stopped abruptly, caught on some solid debris. He began pushing against it with annoyance. It budged forward ever-so-slightly with each push. Once it was open enough, he brought his face forward and peered out of the open crevice and looked into the world outside.

It was difficult because of the storm of kicked-up dust, but he deduced he was inside a reasonably large building. There was an abundance of clutter and a dark, foreboding hallway he couldn't see beyond. Coughing once, Ryder readied himself for another round of hitting the door. Using the Time Stream, he bashed the door with his foot until it flew forward with a metallic screech, causing him to fall out and land on a mass of burnt wood in front of him.

He lay flat on his back and blocked out the white light and obnoxious levels of water coming from the hole in the roof. He felt the dirt and muck stuck to him and his long, greasy hair began to cling to it. He sat up and took in his surroundings in a feeble attempt to find his bearings.

He deduced that he was in some sort of office or state government building, but it looked abandoned. Beyond the container and the hole it made was an old, massive staircase that led to the second floor of the building. Various bits of roofing, papers, and other clutter were scattered where Ryder sat and spread out all over the floor. A distinct, unpleasant odor of rotting wood and mold lingered on his nose. Nothing about this place brought any comfort.

He began to second-guess himself. He didn't know what to expect if Markus's plan worked. But it wasn't this, the building didn't look any different. It still looked run-down and broken, just like the St. Louis he left behind. He looked around hoping to find Markus or the device that had sent him here, but there was nothing or nobody around. Ryder was alone.

His body began to ache again. Was he still in the tribulation? Had he not gone far enough? His thoughts were muddled by worry. But before anything conclusive presented himself, he felt something. A spine tingle had returned. It felt hot, like a branding iron against the nerves in his back. Then he heard and felt massive footsteps in the hallway to his right. They were so heavy the building began to shake. Some loose debris from the roof fell and landed around Ryder. He looked up at the ceiling, which was rumbling and shaking above his head. Thinking quickly, he grabbed his bag right next to him, managing to find its straps, and swung the bag over his shoulder before grabbing the chain of his grappling hook. Ryder jumped out of the hole the container made just as debris fell from the roof down into the hole and covered the doors in front of him.

Before anything else could be done, something growled down the same hall the footsteps were coming from. Two bright blue eyes emerged from the shadows and drew closer to him. Until a snout full of teeth and a massive body made itself known. Whatever this thing was, it was ducking down in the hallway because of its height. Ryder felt paralyzed with fear. This was a revenant, but not one he had ever seen before. It was too big. Too ferocious looking. It resembled something like a dragon cobbled together in the frightened logic of a night terror. Looking at it made him feel like a small child waiting to be consumed by the monster under the bed. Even in the dark, Ryder could make out a crooked smile on the ends of its mouth.

"Hello, Nathan," it sneered in SpecterSpeak. The revenant opened its mouth and blue fire shot out at him. Ryder managed to duck out of the way, but not far enough to prevent his arm from getting partially in the blast, resulting in his poncho catching fire. He immediately began to pat it out with his hands, then he began to feel the revenant moving again, the building shook with each step. He ran into the building ahead.

Despite low visibility, he rushed forward through the dark hallways with his hands out as the beast behind him found its stride and began chasing him throughout the building, occasionally shooting off flames from its gullet and engulfing entire hallways in fire. Ryder moved along as best he could, trying not to lose himself in the darkness. He moved just to move. He had no idea where he was going. All he knew was that he had to put distance between the heat-spewing pursuer.

There was no chance to stop and catch a breath, but Ryder didn't stop. Eventually, his endurance paid off when he saw there was light ahead. It all came from a large hole formed in what looked like the back of the building.

A loud noise behind him caught his attention and he looked behind to see the revenant catching up. It had just noticed there was an exit available and now fired on all cylinders trying to catch him, its large and hefty movements causing the building to feel like it was wobbling on stilts. Both Ryder and the revenant used the Time Stream to move towards the opening in the building. Ryder made it outside, but the revenant shook the foundation of the building so much it caused a collapse of the roof. Debris came tumbling down on the monstrous being and covered it before it could leave the building.

Ryder sat up on a grassy ground, backing away from the building as the creature howled in anger and struggled to get loose from the rubble. It bulged as it tried to move, but it didn't budge. As of now, it was trapped. Taking a moment to breathe deeply, he climbed up off the grounds and brushed himself off, his mouth still open from being out of air.

"A revenant like that?" Ryder said. "That's not good, not good at all."

Not expecting it, Ryder felt a sting into his neck. He closed his eyes and winced, reaching for his neck with his right hand. He pulled some kind of dart out of his neck adorned with red piece of feather. His face went wide in realization as he wobbled on his feet.

"Arta, Artem..." Ryder said as his legs turned to jelly, and he fell to his knees.

Looking up quickly at the parking lot caused his gut to wrench further. Across the parking lot was what looked like a moving truck. Four operators were stationed around, weapons pointing directly at him. There were three men and one woman in a police cap. In front of them was Artemis, the Oracle Lieutenant. She wore a raincoat with her bow strung over her shoulders.

Ryder began to feel too weak and fell to the ground and onto his stomach. His vision slipped in and out as Artemis began talking on a radio.

"Ms. Marigold? Prepare for our return to base. I believe you will be pleased with what we have acquired tonight, quite pleased indeed." she said.

He breathed rapidly, fighting in vain against the concoction shot into his neck. All the armed men and women in front began moving toward him until a loud noise behind him near the building caused everyone to give their undivided attention. Their heads all shot up toward the source. The noises continued behind, sounding like massive rubble and wood were breaking apart. Ryder couldn't even move to see what was happening, but the loud high-pitched roar behind him made it apparent that his pursuer wasn't taking having a building fall on it too kindly.

"The Apex variant!" one of the operators yelled in an Irish accent.

"Prepare to fire!" a gruffer voice screamed.

"No!" the woman in the front said, swinging her bow around off her shoulders. "Do not engage! It's the Time Rider it wants; that's its prey. Kane, Mallory. Get him back to the truck, and the rest of you follow suit back to your vehicle. We are leaving. Make haste before it breaks through the rubble. Don't delay!"

"Affirmative!" every operator sounded off. The woman in the cap and one of the male operators immediately grabbed Ryder by the arms and pulled him away from the building. He got a good look at what he previously couldn't see behind him. The large revenant fought viciously, its head poking out and occasionally shooting flame and lighting up to the sky as it struggled. The woman with the bow fired at it with her weapon, striking it with glassy looking arrows. Each one that struck caused the Apex to howl in pain like a dog, then hiss like a reptile in response.

Ryder tried to stay awake, but the tranquilizer mixture in the dart finally had its way with him. His eyes became heavy, and the last thing he heard before he lost consciousness was the two operators yelling to each other and slamming the vehicle door on him as he slipped to black.

Chapter 23

Homecoming

Ryder:

Next thing Ryder knew, he was lying on a cold flat floor with bright lights bearing down at him. He put his hand out to block the light and slowly sat up on the floor. Thick, see through glass surrounded him. He was in a small room that felt more akin to a cooler or small bunker.

The door into the room opened with a sharp noise. Ryder focused on the source. Artemis stood in the doorway and proceeded to enter the room, her bow slung over her shoulder.

Spartan walked in behind her with a strange-looking rifle stowed on his back. They stood outside the container while Ryder himself remained on the floor.

"You know I never thought I would say this..." Ryder started pointing his index finger in the air. "But it's actually kinda nice to see you guys."

"How in God's name did you survive that incident at the Arch?" Spartan asked.

"Because the God in question wanted me to? What do you want me to say?"

"You threw yourself into the Arch like a damned martyr. You should be dead but you're not. Explain yourself."

"Nice to see your eyes still work," Ryder joked. "But I'll spare you the details. Might not make it into that thick skull of yours."

Spartan grumbled and rolled his eyes. "Just when I got used to you not being a thorn in my side…"

"Can you two help me get up to speed? I can't help but feel like I've been gone for a hot minute."

"What do we look like, your drinking buddies? We don't have to tell you squat," Spartan said. Ryder exhaled loudly. "Okay, so still not on the best of terms, gotcha."

"What happened to you? Where have you been?" Artemis asked.

"How long was I gone?" Ryder asked.

"What?"

"How long was I gone?" he repeated.

"We are the one's asking questions!" Spartan barked.

"Throw me a bone here, Meat-Head." Ryder said. "Humor me a little bit, and I'll return the favor."

Spartan and Artemis shot each other a disconcerting look. Artemis was the one to speak up. "It has been three months and four days since the failure of Project Witching Hour."

"Three months?" Ryder asked.

"Yes," she replied.

"That was it…?"

"Your turn kid. Start talking before I make you," Spartan threatened.

"Can your stupid threats," Ryder groaned throwing him dismissive gesture. He got to his feet and leaned against the container. "I didn't go anywhere. I was here in the city the whole time."

The two lieutenants looked confused by the answer. "What's that supposed to mean? Were you hidden?" Artemis asked.

"Out of reach, somewhere only I could go."

"Within Alpha-2?"

"Something like that."

"Care to elaborate?" Spartan asked.

Ryder paused for a moment. "Wouldn't be safe to do that."

"Safe?"

"And where is that woman? That Progenitress. What is her status?" Artemis asked.

"No clue. She disappeared after I threw her through the gateway."

"K.I.A?" Spartan asked.

"M.I.A," Ryder replied. "That means, 'missing in action' so you know."

"You think I don't know that? Don't get smart with me, I have half a mind to shut you up for good right now," Spartan growled.

"Half a mind is right," Ryder groaned. "Why are we still doing this? I've been through too much to have to put up with this hero and villain crap all over again. Can we find some common ground here?"

"Will you participate in aiding us in our research?" Artemis taunted.

"You still hunting for that stupid ageless factor for Marigold?" Ryder pointed at her from inside the container. "Get this through your head, and your boss can do the same. This ageless thing is not a gift, it's a curse. I am doomed to an eternity where all I know will fade and die, and the only way out is death. Does that sound ideal? Does that sound preferable? Because believe me when I say this, it's not."

Artemis didn't answer.

"So, I'm guessing you didn't tell her about our little team up?" Ryder asked.

"Of course we didn't. She would have strung us up by our Achilles tendons. If we were lucky..." Spartan said.

"That partnership was a result of circumstance. We are still ordered to perceive you as a threat," Artemis said.

"Shame," Ryder muttered. "It was kinda nice having you guys try not to kill me for once."

"Like she said, it was circumstance," Spartan interjected. "This has got to be some sort of sick joke. Why does there have to be two of you?"

"Two?" Ryder asked. "Are there *two* Time Riders now?"

Neither Spartan nor Artemis moved their mouths. They didn't need to.

"Markus," Ryder said quietly. Then he let out a holler. "He made it! The note worked!"

"What are you speaking of?" Artemis exclaimed.

"Nuh-uh, nope. That's gonna stay a secret."

"I can loosen your tongue if it's needed," Spartan growled.

"Are you really going to pop the lid on this thing and risk me darting out?"

"The odds would still be in my favor, kid."

"Favor? Don't make me laugh. You never were one for good luck, Edgar." Ryder said.

Spartans' whole body locked up. "True that," he said. "Probably won't be around long anyway since Artemis here is the one who brought you in. The original Time Rider in the flesh, that's quite the haul."

Artemis looked away. Seeing her made Ryder rub the back of his head. "If I had a dollar for every time I got hit by one of those stupid tranquilizer gauntlet darts of yours, Farai, my net worth would easily surpass Oracle's," he moaned.

"The alternative would be to just simply kill you," Artemis said. "I pursued the new variant hunting you, and I got a visual on it while I tracked it. I followed its path until it arrived at your location. Perhaps your luck isn't the best either."

"Most certainly," Ryder said.

As they spoke, the room's lights dimmed and turned red, then the alarm began to blare. Artemis and Spartan were taken aback by the sudden transition.

Attention: Security breach detected. All personnel be on alert.

"Real bad luck..."

"What is going on now?" Artemis asked.

"I don't know," Spartan said quickly, taking his rifle from his shoulder. He flicked some switches on the side of it, causing the weapon to hum to life. "We need to get out there. It could be the new Apex variant."

"What about him?" Artemis asked.

"Those containers are used to hold revenants. He is not getting out, come on!" Spartan yelled.

He an Artemis ran out of the room leaving Ryder alone. The alarms continued. He slapped his palms against the glass and kicked a few times, his actions soon becoming frantic. The glass was so thick it felt like being stuck in an aquarium tank. The impact he made caused merely dull vibrations through the thick layers.

He paused when he felt a familiar feeling trail up his spine—his revenant sixth sense—but this was different. It was quicker, stronger, almost panicked. It was the same sensation he felt when he first arrived.

Out of nowhere a horrible roar echoed around the room he was in. Ryder's heart felt like it fell into his stomach. A loud crash outside sounded off outside the room. He walked back and pressed himself to the back of his container, his breaths becoming shaky. There was a moment of slow silence, broken only by the sound of exhales. Then the room became filled with the horrid sound of metal being torn and sliced. He let out a startled yell as something forced a hole to form in the middle of the room. Two clawed hands began pulling the room apart.

A large head came into the room, adorned with glowing eyes and a long jaw full of razor-sharp teeth. Ryder backed up into the little room he had left.

The large Apex variant poked its large head into the room looking around before it fixed its gaze on him. For a frightening amount of time, he and the creature met each other's gaze.

"Oh. Hello again," Ryder said. "How are you doing buddy?"

The creature smiled grotesquely. "Splendid," it sneered "We have unfinished business, Nathan." It pushed itself inside, forcing the hole it made even wider, and it reached in and grabbed his container.

"Oh No!" Ryder yelled.

It pulled Ryder's container out of the room and into the open area. Once outside it picked up the entire container and slammed it onto the ground in an attempt to break the glass of the container. Outside of a few cracks, the integrity of the cage remained. The Apex repeatedly hit the container in frustration, with its arm knocking the container over a few times and causing Ryder to tumble inside like he was stuck in a washing machine. He immediately found himself in a debilitating amount of pain, groaning loudly and grimacing on the floor of the glass box.

The Apex grasped two sides on top of the box and opened its mouth widely. Ryder gazed into its throat as he lay there, a bright light becoming bigger by the second inside its chasm of a throat. When it got large enough. A storm of angry blue flames hit and encircled the entire container. Ryder let out a scream as the heat and light enveloped him. When the flames dissipated, he noticed a large orange hole formed where the flames had touched it. The Apex slammed its beefy arms on top of it and the glass began to crack and give way. After one more blow the glass caved in completely, raining shattered pieces down onto Ryder. He forced himself to shield his eyes from the oncoming barrage.

Just as the Apex reached in to grab him something bright hit its shoulder. It let out an angry roar in surprise and looked over at the source. Ryder did as well.

An entire formation of Oracle operators was there, holding the same kind of rifle that Spartan had earlier. They were kneeling, weapons in hand. Spartan stood right behind him, his own rifle in hand. He lifted a hand and pointed at the Apex.

"Fire!" Spartan bellowed.

Another barrage of bright electric beams flew forward, slamming and burning into the Apex. The revenant was knocked back forcefully and almost lost its balance, hobbling on one leg before coming back down. After a moment, the entire front part of its body was covered in black scorch marks. The Apex examined itself and let an even louder roar from its body as it rushed toward the operators in a blind rage.

"Fall back! Fall back!" Spartan ordered.

Most of the operators followed the command, but one of them didn't. He tried to reload his rifle while moving, pulling a charging handle on the weapon and ejecting a spent cartridge onto the floor. He placed a new one into the weapon and closed the hatch readying the rifle to fire. The Apex grabbed him quickly and took him up high in the air before he could do so. The operator screamed as it bit down hard on his head and threw his dead body to the side like a rag doll.

"Suppressive fire!" Another round of beams hit the Apex only adding to the creature's fury. It chased after Spartan and his men as they made their escape back through the shelves. Ryder took advantage of the opportunity. He climbed up through the hole and jumped out of the container, plopping onto the ground awkwardly in the process. He lay down against the container among the shattered glass and held a hand to his heart, grateful he was even drawing breath. Once he collected himself, he looked around, trying to figure out where he was. The shelves, boxes, and rooms that surrounded him ended up being a dead giveaway.

"Aw, not this place again..."

He was in the underground base below Oracle Tower, where he

had been only once before when Charlotte Rowes had been kidnapped by Oracle. He barely managed to escape last time with her. It all came back to him. With the lockdown in effect he would have to find the main lift in order to escape. But first, he needed his duffel bag.

He knew about Doctor Yorkshire and where he likely brought his only possession. He would have keen interest in what was inside. A simple plan of vague absolutes presented itself in Ryder's head. Find his duffel, get to the main lift, don't get killed in the process. It was as good a plan as any.

He stood up from his spot and brushed the glass off him. Taking a deep shaky breath and swallowing his fear, Ryder proceeded into the base.

CHAPTER 24

Clash of Titans

Spartan:

Sartan and his operators quickly went from hunters to the hunted. They began to back up, firing the ZL23s and their battle rifles as they did so. The Apex stomped along and moved towards them, not showing any sign of slowing down and growing increasingly more agitated.

Eventually all the operators lost their composure completely and just began running as fast as they could, despite Spartan barking orders telling them to do otherwise. He was forced to begin sprinting along with them so he wouldn't be left alone with the large revenant.

They backed away into a large open area. All the operators ran into the next narrow path between the shelves and Spartan turned around and swung his own ZL23 around off his back and fired at the creature the moment it came into the area.

The beam hit the Apex leaving a smoldering layer of burnt tissue in its wake. The revenant roared a harsh and loud drone that seemed to shake the very earth and made Spartan's vision turn blurry. He realized that all the combatants under his command had deserted him, leaving him alone with the angry monstrosity in front of him.

He discarded his spark rifle and readied the gauntlets on his wrists, ready for a close-quarters fight. The Apex slowed down, readying its claws, growling like an oversized reptile. Before it got too close, the Apex got pelted from above with crystalline arrows. They hit the solid parts of its body and became stuck in its body, making the revenant even more unhappy.

Spartan knew those arrows by heart. He looked up to his left and saw Artemis up on the catwalk using her bow like she had done countless times before.

"You're a sight for sore eyes, Farai!" Spartan called out.

"So I've heard!" Artemis called back. "Don't focus on me, focus on that thing!"

The Apex's attention turned to the catwalk. It opened its mouth wide, and a storm of blue flames flew from its gullet. As the flames sailed through the air, Artemis became impossible to see.

"FARAI!" Spartan cried out. He ran and smashed his gauntlet-guided fist into a scorched part of the Apex's leg. The leg buckled and it let out a high-pitched wail. With the creature at a lower angle. Spartan continued his assault, treating its abdomen like a punching bag, and exploiting its newfound weakness. Each punch into the burned tissue reduced the Apex to a whimpering animal in distress.

Spartan threw a large swing that collided with the Apex's head, but he realized too late that its head had not been hit by spark rifle beams. It took the blow, barely even moving. In retaliation, it threw its left hand, hitting Spartan and making him fly into the air and slam into a catwalk, then he plummeted down to the concrete floor below.

Spartan writhed in pain on the ground. He held his arm and tried to crawl, but his movements weren't fast enough to get away.

The Apex began to walk towards him, each step like a thunderclap. It walked slowly, its twisted teeth resembling the smile of a psychotic murderer. It seemed like it savored this, basking in the joy of a turned table. It may have been the pain or the panic messing with his head, but Spartan could have sworn he heard a crooked laugh sounding out from its throat.

Once it got close enough it leaned over and stared down at him on the floor, twisting its head side to side like it found him to be something garnering curiosity. Talon used all the energy he could to move, but he might as well have been a slug on pavement with a child holding salt over his head.

The Apex stood back up and opened its mouth, a flame starting as a small cinder that grew into a contained inferno. Spartan closed his eyes and braced for the heat to cook him alive.

Preventing the inevitable, a large hammer slammed into the Apex's head knocking it back, frizzy electricity lingered in the air. Spartan looked over and saw Quake above him, fully kitted in his new gear. He wore an electricity-proof jumpsuit, gloves, and a custom respirator-protective glasses hybrid. The massive kinetic hammer was held in his hand. He dropped to the ground and offered Spartan a hand.

"I'm sorry I'm late my friend. Are you able to stand?" Quake asked.

He threw his hand into Quake's "I'm still kicking."

"Good to hear! Let's get to work comrade."

The Apex let out another harsh roar. Quake and Spartan turned to face it, weapons at the ready.

"*Bozhe, zashchiti menya...*" Quake muttered in Russian. "You're injured Talon, stay behind me!"

Quake lifted his hammer in the air and rushed forward, howling a battle cry to get the Apex's attention. The creature roared in response. Quake and the Apex squared up and circled one another, waiting for the moment one of them would take the first bold strike. Despite Quake's absurd size, the Apex was even larger. Spartan had never felt so small in his life.

Quake swung forward first, hitting the creature and knocking it off its feet. He lifted his hammer and slammed it down onto the creature's body. The Apex's body jolted unnervingly; electricity coursed through its body. It managed to power through and push the hammer away from its body. Quake kept his grip but was forced to defend himself as the Apex got to its feet and began swinging madly at him with its dull, clawed hands.

Talon recovered his spark rifle, ejected the spent magazine, loaded a new one, and took aim. Quake and The Apex pranced around in a clumsy dance. They both took wild swings at each other and were audibly trying to intimidate the other. The prototype nature of the ZL23 left the rifle with only a mid-range scope as its aiming optic. Between the erratic movements of the target, and a friendly in the vicinity, using the spark rifle now would be far too risky.

Spartan tried to think of another solution quickly. He scanned through the area for any other options, desperate to get the edge on the revenant. He managed to strike paydirt. He saw three forklifts parked neatly to the right of the area. He hobbled as fast as he could manage. The Apex and Quake were still interlocked in combat.

Once he got there he immediately climbed in and checked the keyhole, hoping that the driver's had missed the memo again in regard to the keys. Fortunately, the key sat invitingly in its spot with a shiny metal tag attached to it.

A dastardly smile formed on Spartan's face as he turned the key and the vehicle roared to life. The smell of propane fumes wafted into the air as he drove it into the middle of the area and aimed it toward the two large figures butting heads.

"Make wake Quake!" Talon yelled. "I ain't OSHA certified!"

Th Russian moved quicker out of the way faster than Spartan thought was possible for someone his size. Once he was out of the way, he slammed the gas and sped towards the Apex, which seemed confused as the two prongs of the lift wedged into its body, carried it, and slammed it into the shelving units.

The Apex began to thrash around and snarl angrily. Spartan slammed the gas even harder and started yelling, digging deeper into its tissue. The revenant opened its mouth and began to summon another batch of flames, but before it did, Spartan jammed his spark rifle into its mouth as far as he could.

"Bite down on this!"

Spartan pulled the trigger and fired a hot beam of electrons down its throat. He backed up the forklift and Apex dropped down onto its knees holding its chest. Its insides could be heard boiling and flames erupted from its mouth and started shooting all over the place, far more powerful than what the revenant had done on its own. Both Quake and Talon took cover to not get incinerated. The blast emanating from its gullet pushed the Apex into the shelving units again before the flames stopped in their entirety, turning its mouth black like a spent road flare. It stood up, with mouth aimed high in the air, before collapsing onto its knees, then falling facedown onto the ground. The shelving unit behind it came crashing down onto its body with a mighty crash, its contents flying around the area.

It took a minute to piece together what had happened, but Spartan realized he had won. The Apex had been defeated by him.

"Someone's going to need an antacid..."

"Well done, Talon!" Quake exclaimed. "You've killed the creature!"

"It's dead?" a voice from the catwalk called out.

Spartan looked up and saw Farai up there, alive but badly burned on her arm. She leaned against the railing, tenderly holding her injured limb.

"Ms. Omari!" Quake yelled.

"Farai!" Spartan called out. "Are you okay? I thought you were toast, literally!"

"Injured!" Farai yelled. "I need medical attention!"

"Rodger! Get to the infirmary! I'll meet you there!"

"Wait!" Quake exclaimed walking over to Talon. "The Time Rider! Is he secure?"

Spartan wasn't sure. He had gotten so focused on fighting the Apex he had no way of knowing. Then he heard a few gunshots being fired and voices echoing off the walls. Flashes of vibrant blue light emanated over the top of the shelves, followed by silence. The blue light flew in one direction quickly and disappeared out of sight

Quake looked over at Spartan, anticipating a command. "He's going to make a break for it. The only way is the main lift, so he's going to go for that." Spartan tried to get to his feet but couldn't, it was likely he had some broken ribs from colliding against the catwalk. He slammed his gauntlet into the ground in frustration and swore loudly. "Every damn time!"

Quake knelt next to him, dropping his hammer beside him. "You need medical assistance, as does Ms. Omari. Get yourselves to the practitioner. I will deal with the child."

"No, I can power through this," Spartan said making a second attempt to climb to his feet but immediately fell back down.

"You are in no condition to remain in combat my American friend. You've slain the Apex, that is enough."

"You haven't fought him Smirnov," Spartan said, making pained breaths. "There's nothing like it. He's going to..."

"We are not left with choice here Edgar," Quake said. "I beg you, seek help. I will deal with him, he'll relent, or I will be forced to destroy him."

This was a gamble that Spartan didn't want to roll on. He hoped against everything that Quake would be enough to stop him, because he wasn't left with a choice. This was the only play.

"Do you think you can pull this off Quake?" he asked.

Quake lifted his hammer and twirled it a few times, letting sparks dance along its surface. "Consider it done."

CHAPTER 25

Research and development

Ryder:

Ryder moved rapidly through the sprawling complex through the vast city of shelves, but with how similar it all looked he was getting confused. It was difficult to not let panic seep in. He had been here only briefly a long time ago, and any memory of this place drew the same conclusion he faced now. It was all a whole lot of the same.

He had heard gunfire and roaring coming from the other side of the base, but all Ryder knew was that he needed to be as far away from that as possible. He kept moving until he collided painfully with a chain-link fence. After groaning in frustration, he noticed a white sign with white lettering hung from two plastic zip ties on the fence. It read:

Oracle Research and Development
Department Lead: Doctor Bartholemew Yorkshire
All personnel unable to present level 5 security clearance must gain authorization prior to entry.
Any personnel failing to do so will be subject to disciplinary action
By order of Esther Marigold: Chief Executive Officer.

Ryder smiled "Here we are."

He opened the gate and walked into the expansive workshop, making a circular glance around. Ryder had never been in this area before. It was a large space, something that reminded him of a school gymnasium. Two rows of six metal tables sat parallel to one another, leading to a large metal staircase in front of a platform of some kind. A long row of booths sat to the right of them, pointing towards a shooting range.

The place was fascinating, but off-putting. It had an aura of mad science and smelled like an unholy combo of a traditional factory and a meth lab. The scents of chemicals and burnt wires lingered aggressively on his nose. At each table there seemed to be a station dedicated to a project one of Yorkshire's scientists worked on. What those projects were could not be seen. Many of them had various clutter ranging from glasses and beakers to various wires and electronic scrap. All of it made Ryder laugh under his breath.

"Are all men of science absolute slobs?" he asked rhetorically.

He scanned the room until he saw more metal tables arranged in the back near the lockers next to Doctor Yorkshire's desk. Ryder's duffle bag was placed neatly on top of them. He went over to his gear and began to put it on.

Ryder picked up his makeshift chain grappling hook and put it onto a climbing clip on his pants, then he picked up his canvas duffel bag. He opened it and peered inside, where a device lay in its rectangularly-shaped collapsed mode. It was adorned with weathered metal and withered polymer. A sigh of relief escaped his mouth.

"Okay good," he said. "I'd hate to lose you old friend."

Alarms began blaring which caused Ryder to jump. Marigold's voice began screeching over the base's intercom system. "Five million dollars to any person or active squad that detains the Time Rider! Do not let them escape! No excuses. Not one!"

"Love you too Marigold," Ryder groaned. Taking this as a cue, he sprinted to the fence and opened the gate. Maneuvering through many designated areas and shelves, he eventually ended up in a relatively open area. After a moment to process where he was, he recognized it. He ran over to the painted yellow railing where the base's main lift began and prepared to climb onto it, only to meet an empty man-made cavern that led high above him.

"Aw what? Come on!" Ryder yelled slamming his hand into a

guard railing. He looked over at a button that stood beside them, standing tall with a convenient flashing light on it.

"Oh yeah, button. Duh." He jumped down and hit the button. Some alarms blared and yellow light oscillated. He could hear the lift at the top coming down on its track, far too slow for his liking.

"Stop right there!" A thick, bombastic voice sounded out behind him. Turning around there was an absurdly large man dressed in a grey mechanical jumpsuit that covered his head and entire body. On his hands were what looked like dark electric-proof gloves. His face was covered with a large respirator or gas mask. A giant metallic hammer was being held by both of his hands.

Ryder looked on in shock, then groaned. "A new one?" he said. "Aw, come on..."

"Surrender now, while you still can." The man said with a thick eastern European accent.

"What's your deal?" Ryder asked loudly. "You're big enough to have your own TLC show."

The man in front showed no sign of amusement. "Mocking my size will get you nowhere child."

"I can only imagine what your mom looks like, unless she was normal sized... in that case she has my utmost sympathy."

"Silence!" Quake bellowed.

"What are they calling you?" Ryder asked.

"Quake," the man muttered.

"Alright Quake, I'm giving you one last chance to get out of here before I turn you into something you could stick in some pelmeni. I've had a real stinker of a day, and I've got way bigger fish to fry."

"No! Stand down or I will be forced to kill you!" Quake yelled.

"I am so not in the mood for this..." Ryder muttered. He quickly undid his grapple hook from his pants and readied it in both hands. The hook itself was a common chain with a homemade hook on the end of it, and Quake took notice of this when he looked in Ryder's direction.

He let out a low-pitched laugh. "And what would you be doing with that? Scale me?" he said.

Ryder spun the hook around his head a few times and threw it through the Time Stream. It swung around and smacked Quake right in the head. He yelled out in abrupt pain and growled, moving towards Ryder in a rage.

Angered, the large man collected his tool and rushed forward, hammer in hand. He slammed it down on the ground in front of him, a torrent of electricity was emitting from it and flying towards Ryder. Every nerve in his body felt like they were screaming. His body shook with the electricity coursing through him and after it dissipated, he was pushed back, and every hair on his body stood up.

"Electricity? What is it with Oracle and electricity?" Ryder exclaimed.

"Courtesy of Research and Development," Quake said. "It would be a true shame to have to use this device to its full potential. Wouldn't you agree?"

"The real shame is what I'm gonna do to you pal," Ryder growled under his breath.

He rushed through the Time Stream toward Quake. Right as he got close enough, Quake lifted his foot in Ryder's direction and kicked. It connected with him and the Time Rider flew back in the opposite direction landing on his back on the floor, sliding until his head hit a maintenance toolbox.

Ryder held his head and began thrashing about, angered. He yelled loudly, getting up from the floor. He rushed through the Time Stream in a red haze and jumped high into the air, connecting a punch right into the obscenely large man's head. Once he fell back down to the ground, he immediately began nursing his hand, which was now stricken with pain.

Quake swung toward Ryder letting out a mighty roar of exertion. Ryder rolled clumsily out of the way, the nearby impact caused chunks of the floor to spray toward his face and body. Quake swung again rapidly three times, kicking up fragmented concrete all over the place. Ryder managed to dodge each one.

He didn't pull his punch in the slightest. Somehow the brute took all that force from a Time Stream-guided punch and shrugged it off. That punch should have been enough to knock him out cold and even done much worse. Shocked, Ryder couldn't help but question if this man was even human.

The large lieutenant prepared one last mighty swing, ready to bring it down on Ryder.

Before the hammer dropped, he quickly crawled backwards. He

ended up scurrying over many large chunks of smashed rubble; after finding an especially round piece he suddenly had an epiphany. He took his grappling hook and slammed it onto the piece so that it was solidly attached to it. Then he got to his feet and lifted his hook up, rubble hanging from it.

He backed up and lifted his hook up and swung it above his head like a lasso, sending it through the Time Stream. The hook turned into a blue blur above him sailing around in a circle like a spinning blade. The lieutenant looked confused as Ryder threw the hook forward with great strength and launched the cement chunk right at him. It sailed through the area in a straight line and hit Quake right in the head, shattering on impact. His head went backward, his entire body went stiff, and he plummeted to the floor onto his back. The impact caused Ryder to bounce slightly off his feet.

After his thoughts recentered, Ryder stared in awe at the large man passed out on the floor. He cautiously went over and lightly kicked Quake once, and the large man didn't respond at all, out cold. He was still in disbelief at how efficiently he had dispatched his adversary.

Alarms began to blare again, and the main lift finally came into view and stopped at the bottom of the cavern. Its yellow guard rails opening outwards, beckoning him forward.

"Right on time," Ryder said as he walked over to it.

But as he moved his leg got grabbed from behind. He swung around to see Quake conscious again. Ryder got loose with a yell but fell over doing so. Quake got to his feet quickly and tried to stomp on him while he was on the ground. Ryder barely managed to get away. He tried to get back up off the ground, but Quake was now on his feet, towering over him.

"I am not your Goliath little David. You're not leaving here, not while I still stand!" he bellowed.

Without even thinking, Ryder kicked hard through the Time Stream toward Quake. His foot sailed like a missile and collided into Quake right between his legs, making the most definitive and unsatisfying noise he had ever heard. The lieutenant howled in pain and dropped to his knees holding his groin. Ryder threw his hands into his hair and gazed at Quake on the ground, mortified.

"Crap! What have I done? No!" he yelled afterward.

Quake was completely immobilized, but he kept panting hurt grunts and breathing rapidly

"Dude, I am sorry, that was literally a low blow! Crap!" Quake fell over onto his side and kept whining. "All is fair in love and war I guess, and unfortunately for you there wasn't a whole lotta love to go around today," Ryder said, making a cross gesture with his hand. "Lord forgive me."

"Little cretin. I crush you!" Quake screamed.

"I would deal with what's already crushed first, you're gonna wanna get to a hospital, like ASAP."

Desiring to get away from his crippled foe, Ryder jetted away and proceeded up to the platform, occasionally taking a guilty look at Quake. He hit the manual override switch where it rested just where he remembered from last time.

The platform began to ascend, leaving Quake behind just as he managed to get to his feet. Slowly he began to go up on the large platform. Ryder closed his eyes again as the fatigue and nausea he was feeling were allowed attention. Every time he closed his eyes, he saw flashes and figures. He was tired and drained, but even so he wanted to go home. He needed to see Markus, he needed to see Spencer, but most of all he needed to see *her*.

After a few prolonged minutes, the platform reached the top and Ryder rushed out and into a large, inclined service tunnel. Once the security gate opened, he rushed out into the rest of the cavern and ascended the ramp and back out into the city. Being close to the end, Ryder didn't stop moving until he arrived at the undercroft.

CHAPTER 26

Destiny

Markus:

In the present, Ryder explained in detail what happened to him from the moment he returned back into the city. Once everyone was satisfied with the new information, he wasted no time getting changed and taking a lengthy shower at the undercroft. Markus, Spencer, and Charlotte waited for him to do what he needed to do.

Charlotte looked like she had won the lottery with how giddy she was. Even the usually stone-faced Spencer seemed to be in good spirits. Markus was indifferent. He was all right, as far as he could tell. There was some comfort in finding another Time Rider, but just as quickly as he arrived, it felt like everything had gone full circle. Once again, he had gone invisible.

Markus knew it was petty, but being a Time Rider meant he could imagine himself as more than just a street rat. He got to stick it to that corporation and make some new friendships in the process. Shaky friendships, but friendships, nevertheless. And now that the kid of the hour himself was back in the picture, it already felt like he was being pushed aside.

He could normally handle it well enough, but it was Charlotte that set him off. It was mostly envious annoyance but seeing that big smile and excited demeanor on her face made Markus want to put a hole in the wall. He wouldn't have minded if she got that excited over him, but at the same time he knew he had done nothing to earn it.

Ryder eventually came out of the bathroom wearing clean jeans and a long-sleeved shirt. He seated himself at the kitchen table with Spencer and Charlotte grouping up on him. Markus remained behind them leaning against the refrigerator.

"Hey, Markus, you got anything to drink in there?" Ryder asked.

Markus was lost in his own world. "What?"

"You have any drinks in that fridge? Like water or soda?"

"Uh... yeah," Markus said, reaching into the fridge and grabbing a canned soda. He casually threw it over to Ryder and went back to leaning against the fridge.

He opened the soda and began ferociously drinking the beverage, Markus had never seen anyone drink anything so aggressively. He thought there was a chance he would eat the can afterwards. Ryder eventually finished the beverage and let out a refreshed sigh. "Do you have any idea how long it's been since I had anything with sugar?"

"What even happened to you Ry? There would have been no way to even know if you were alive if you didn't send that note," Spencer asked.

"Long story, that. I um... don't even really know for sure."

"Do you know anything?" Charlotte asked.

Ryder looked like he was trying to find the right words to say, casually drumming his left index finger on the table as he did so.

"Back at the arch, the Progenitress was there. I had to throw her into that gateway, and she took me with her."

"Project Witching Hour, they pulled it off?" Spencer asked.

"You bet they did," Ryder said assertively. "It was bad, man. There were revenants everywhere. She planned a full-on assault on our world. A lot of people were taken or killed..."

"But you stopped it?" Spencer asked.

"Not alone. I had help from the lieutenants."

"Wait. Oracle lieutenants?" Charlotte asked.

"The same. They closed the door after me," Ryder said. "They stopped it."

"On purpose?" Charlotte asked tensely. "Of course they did."

"It was my call. I had to close it one way or the other. I knew the risks."

Everyone took a minute to process that. "You mentioned you were in the city, but you were out of reach," Markus said. "What did you mean by that?"

Ryder's tapping became even faster. "Look, we all know the Time Stream has a kind of depth to it, and I fell… *really* deep into it," he explained. "The things I saw, it was so much faster there. Like what me and Markus can do? That's just scratching the surface. Where I was minutes, hours, days, even years passed by as quickly as you could breathe. An entire human life could end in old age in mere minutes. When I finally got out of there, I ended up back in Louie, but it wasn't the same."

"How so?" Spencer asked.

Ryder looked up, a dead look in his gaze. "The future, I ended up in the future."

The other three's eyes went wide in disbelief.

"The future?" Charlotte said loudly.

"You time traveled?" Markus asked.

"Pretty much," Ryder said.

"What did you see?" Spencer asked.

Ryder grimaced. "I was warned not to talk too much about it. It's like those movies y'know? Where there are consequences for knowing your own destiny and all that. It's dangerous."

"You can't say anything?" Spencer asked.

"Wouldn't be a good idea."

"Just like the Back to the Future movies," Charlotte said, drifting off. "Mess with one thing, you could change everything. Like Biff did with the sports almanac in part two."

"Isn't that the one flick where that guy made out with his mom?" Markus asked.

"That was the first one. Why is that what you remember from it?"

"Cause his mom was kinda hot?"

"Enough." Spencer took a step back and rubbed his mouth with his hand. "What can you say Ry?"

"It was not a fun place. I tried to tell you in the note. I'm glad you got it, and it was even legible. The pen I had was crap."

"How did you even send it?" Charlotte asked.

"Well for starters, there's a good reason we call it the time *stream*. It flows, like a river or stream, in one direction. That's why Oracle ops even started calling me the Time Rider. That flow is time itself, and me and Markus can ride that flow. Just like a canoe on a river, it's much easier to go in one direction than the other. So, when it comes to quote-unquote time travel, in layman's terms, it is much easier to go forward, much harder to go backwards. We were able to use a contraption mixed with my Time Stream abilities to launch it into the past. It's extremely hard to do, but we could literally use the Time Stream to shoot objects into the past at specific places. The way I was able to send the box and have it land in the past came down to the presence of electricity. Same concept as the arch. A device had to be rigged onto it which would channel enough electricity to cause a mini breach to occur. When that happened, the box would fall back into Alpha-1, as opposed to just flying back into the future. Think of it like Skee-ball—the ball rolls onto the ramp and then just rolls back down, unless it lands in one of the holes which means it would fall straight down. Same concept."

"Alpha-1?" Markus asked.

"Our dimension." Spencer answered. "So, time travel is actually possible."

"As crazy as it sounds, yeah. It is." Ryder said.

"Hot damn, those quantum nuts were actually onto something."

"And you turned yourself into a metaphorical ski ball?" Markus asked.

"Basically. We cobbled together a metal box that would carry me through it. But I couldn't create the hole on my own, not like the boxes. Unless I wanted to be vaporized."

"That's why you needed the lightning strikes," Spencer said quietly.

"Yes, exactly, but I was told what I needed early on. Cost me an arm and leg to get the records I needed to know when the bolt would touch down, and some good people died for me to pull it off. The one that happened was the earliest one I could find. It doesn't happen as much as you think. That window when the breach occurred and would subsequently close was a stupidly small window, but I pulled it off. Thank God."

"What about the Progenitress?" Spencer asked.

"I don't know. We got separated when we fell through. Haven't seen her since."

Spencer's eyes scrunched together. "Not once?"

"Not once," Ryder answered quietly. "I tried to write that in the note, I hoped I could at least give you some of the picture, put you at ease a bit, y'know? I don't know if it worked though."

"Why did you write my name?" Markus asked.

"Your name?" Ryder asked.

"Yeah," Markus said, getting up from the fridge and walking toward them, a stone-like look on his face. "How do you know me?"

Ryder resumed his finger tapping and rubbed the back of his head with the other. Nervousness practically leaked out of him. "I wrote it because you were there, Markus. You were different but you were there. You wanted to be found early. It was your idea."

"Found?" Markus exclaimed. "What about all that crap about not messing with the future?"

"This is the one great exception, the one risk," Ryder explained. "You needed to be here. You needed to get your footing."

Charlotte and Spencer gazed at Markus with concerned looks.

"Why?" Markus asked.

Ryder remained quiet, his silence deafening. "I can't say a word as to what will happen, I refuse. But something very bad could happen if you hadn't."

Markus felt his heart quicken in his chest. The way Ryder said this was scary. Horror could be heard in every word. He could tell this came from a place of genuine fear.

"I'm guessing there's nothing you can say?" Markus asked.

Ryder looked right at him. His gaze cold. "All you need to know is that a lot of people will die if you don't stop it."

Suddenly every eye in the undercroft trained on Markus. He just stood there boredly.

"So, if I don't stop this mystery event from happening a bunch of people are gonna die?"

Ryder grimaced and looked around. "Yeah, pretty much."

Markus let out an exhale. "Gnarly…"

CHAPTER 27

What Lies Latent

Ryder:

Ryder's little catch-up conversation didn't exactly go poorly, but he still felt awkward laying all that out the way he had, especially to Markus. He couldn't talk about much—he wouldn't let himself—but dropping a bombshell saying the lives of an unspecified number of people lay in his hands? Ryder felt stupid and unsympathetic. It was all the truth, but that didn't make it any easier.

After they talked, Ryder sat and chatted with Charlotte for a bit on the sofa in the middle of the undercroft. Markus merely stood around quietly, lost in his own thoughts. Spencer examined the contents of Ryder's duffel bag he had been dragging around since he had been back.

"Ry, what did you do to the A.M.R?" Spencer exclaimed.

Ryder turned around and looked at him. It may have been his eyes playing tricks, but he could swear he saw sadness in his eyes.

"A.M what?" Markus asked.

"It's like his hook-shooty thingy." Charlotte gestured with her hands closed vertically and made trigger-pulling movements with her index fingers.

"Hook-shooty thingy?"

"Advanced Mobility Rig," Ryder answered. "My go-to gadget, or at least it was…"

"Seriously, what happened? It's all rusted and worn. Did you give it a bath every night?" Spencer asked.

Ryder got up and walked over to the workbench. The device was in its collapsed mode, looking like a large black box. There was indeed an abundance of orange rust on it. It was so filthy it probably shouldn't have even been placed on the worktable for the sake of cleanliness.

"Well, for starters, it crapped out on me back at the arch, so the grappling hooks don't work. Second, I haven't used it in a long while for that very reason. And third, the conditions weren't exactly optimal for the storage of advanced technology."

"Even in a climate of above-average moisture it shouldn't have gotten like this. I designed it so it could operate in rain and snow without falling apart. The only thing that could have worn it down like this is well, time. An extended period where it wasn't properly maintained," Spencer explained.

"Well, I was gone for a while," Ryder reminded him.

"But in only three months? The metal I used to make it was galvanized, it should have lasted way longer than that," Spencer said confusedly. He blinked a few times and looked down at the A.M.R. "I guess it doesn't matter. I'll see what I can do. We're gonna have to give it at least a day or two before I can draw any conclusions. I really hope I don't have to start from scratch. This thing wasn't the easiest thing to cook up."

Spencer turned and looked over at Ryder's face.

"What?" Ryder asked.

"Are you gonna keep that hair? It's getting into your eyes and everything. You even have a little beard going with that stubble. Isn't that scratchy?" Spencer asked.

"Haven't really thought about it. I normally kept my hair short because of the helmet. What do you think, Charlotte?"

"I like your shorter hair, and without the facial hair. Now you just look like a bum."

Markus snorted.

"Well… okay then. Original style it is," Ryder said, slightly hurt by Charlotte's brutal honesty.

"Hey, wait a sec. My hair is around that length. You saying I look like a bum?" Markus asked.

"Yes," Charlotte said plainly.

Markus scowled at her. "You're a real piece of work, Freckles. Don't even get me started on that fire hazard on your own head."

"Fire hazard?"

"Knock it off," Spencer said, trying to defuse any potential strife. "I'll have Rudy break out the old kit here in a bit. And you—" he added, pointing at Charlotte. "You should head home for the night."

"What? Why?" Charlotte asked.

"It's half an hour till nine, that's why."

Charlotte checked her phone to see for herself. "Shoot." A look of unease formed on her face. "I... don't wanna go."

Ryder went over to her. "Hey, I'm not gonna disappear on you again I promise. I'll be here tomorrow."

"I mean... I know, I'm sorry," Charlotte said.

She slipped her phone into her pocket and threw her arms around Ryder's neck for one last hug. Ryder returned the affection and that fuzzy feeling returned. Markus turned his head away at the sight of them. She quickly dropped back down to the floor afterwards.

"I can't believe you're...." Charlotte started before starting to cough rather harshly, quickly turning louder and rougher.

Ryder immediately became concerned. "Hey, you okay?" he asked quickly.

Charlotte stopped and smiled. "Yeah, sorry. I think my mouth is dry or something, but I'm good."

"You sure?"

Charlotte snorted out a laugh. "I can handle a little cough, Nathan. You don't need to save me from everything."

"All right," he said slightly embarrassed.

"See you soon," Charlotte said, smiling. She skipped over to the staircase and left the undercroft. Ryder was hit with a fresh dose of gratefulness.

"I need to go find Rudy, I'll let you know when he's ready, okay?" Spencer asked.

"Yeah, sure."

Spencer went over to the staircase and also left the undercroft, leaving Ryder and Markus alone in the room together. He was leaning on the refrigerator, staring off, a sense of tension lingering about him. Ryder went over to him hoping to strike up conversation.

"So uh, Markus." He didn't acknowledge him. "I just wanted to say I'm happy I'm not the only Time Rider around anymore y'know? I'm, honestly kinda excited to—"

"Stop talking to me."

Ryder was surprised to hear that. "Are you okay? Is there a problem?"

"Nope, none at all."

He didn't buy it. "Please don't lie to me. What's the issue? Is this about what I said earlier?"

"Like I said, there is no problem." Markus spoke with heat in his words.

Ryder couldn't help but feel slightly unnerved. "Well, clearly there is. Come on, talk to me. You can trust me. We're a team now, right?"

"Wrong," Markus growled. "Now keep that nose of yours out of my business Prince Charming, you got that?"

"Wha—seriously, wh…"

"Just go back to being the class favorite, pal. I'll go back to being Mr. Cellophane, I'm used to it."

"Cellophane? What are you talking about?"

Markus didn't answer, he just walked by Ryder and bumped him hard in the shoulder with his own, then stormed into his old room and slammed the door behind him. Ryder rubbed his shoulder and attempted to process where that outburst came from.

"You okay Ry?" Ryder awoke from his loose trance. He hadn't even noticed Spencer back in the undercroft. "Yeah, I'm fine. A bit tired I guess."

He looked at him, at the door to his room. "Did Markus give you trouble?"

Ryder was still shaken, but he chose to keep it close to his chest. "Nah, it's fine."

Spencer had a serious look on his face. "Don't let him give you any grief. He might be a Time Rider but his attitude and recklessness has worn out their welcome. I'm at my limit."

"Take it easy on him. My patience is a bit thin too, but I don't want any grudges."

"I know you said he was important, but you haven't seen him, Ry. He's a troublemaker, a rebellious brat."

"Let's cut him a bit of slack. Take it from me, being a parallel being isn't the easiest thing in the world to get accustomed to."

Spencer let out a groan. "I forgot how sympathetic you can be," he lamented. "You know what we're dealing with here, more than I do. We can't have a loose cannon sputtering off doing whatever he wants to do and being defiant."

"He's figuring things out, I don't know what's going on but he's in a bad state right now. We need to be patient with him and figure out what's wrong. I didn't handle it all this easily when I started, either."

"I've been patient, but with you here there's no room for chaff."

"Chaff! Just because I'm here doesn't make him chaff!"

"Keep it down!" Spencer hissed. He clenched his fists and took a deep breath. "We'll figure it out tomorrow, and we'll do it your way for now. But something has to change."

"Fine," Ryder said bitterly.

Spencer took another deep breath. "I'm sorry. Do you still want that haircut?"

Ryder loosened up a bit. "Yeah, I don't know if the boy band look is really my thing. I think I'm a few decades late to that party," he said.

Spencer chucked slightly. "I would agree. Plus, Charlotte likes your hair short anyway."

"Yeah, gotta keep her happy I suppose."

Spencer blinked a few times. "That reminds me. Not tonight, but we got to talk about her."

"What's wrong now?"

"Nothing, just want to lay out some guidelines, that's all. Make sure we all see eye to eye."

"Well, whatever floats your boat."

"Did Markus run into your room?"

"Yeah, I don't really care," Ryder said casually.

I can make sure he gives it back to you," Spencer said.

"Really it's fine."

Spencer's face went still, but his demeanor conveyed that he wasn't going to press forward. "Rudy is ready for you upstairs. Go on and get cleaned up, then come back down and get some rest. You look like you need it."

"I do," Ryder said with an exhale. He didn't have to be told twice. He had become painfully self-aware of the mass of hair on his head and was ready for it to be gone. Helping himself out of the undercroft he left and walked through the back alley at the top of the stairs. The cooler night air stood out prominently in his mind as he knocked on Rudy's back door. After a moment of standing outside, Rudy opened the back door. He now wore a different, black-colored apron, casually snipping a pair of barber's scissors in his right hand. A goofy, yet hearty smile was stretched on his lips. If he chose to be honest, Ryder would say it was slightly off-putting.

"Crapsnacks…" he muttered.

"You ready for a trim son?" Rudy asked heartily.

"I guess..."

"Come on in and sit in the back, I'll get you cleaned up." Despite the hesitation on his mind, Ryder eventually climbed the stairs into the back of his shop and took a seat on the usual wooden dining room chair that he expected to find. He sat down and let Rudy get to work

CHAPTER 28

Rescue

Markus:

The following morning Markus went from the calm thoughtless state of sleep to his anger flooding back to him the moment he opened his eyes. It was like his brain was paused and suddenly started playing again right where he left off. Once he woke up, he was angry at Ryder, Charlotte, Spencer, and himself. He knew that starting beef would put him at fault, but he was too frustrated to even care. This anger was like an animal waiting for the opportunity to spring from its cage, and spring it did.

He lie in the secondhand bed and spun around so his face was buried in the pillow, then he dug his arms under it, wanting to scream into it. Under the pillow he could feel something metallic slithering against his fingertips. His head rose in surprise, and he brought out the object and sat on the bed with his legs crossed. He opened his palm and examined it. It was a twine-like necklace, likely made of a cheaper kind of metal. It was composed of very small, interlocked chains. The centerpiece was not something that Markus expected—a small, yet bold looking golden cross.

Markus knew for certain he hadn't put that there, and he couldn't imagine Spencer put it there either. He knew this room had once belonged to Ryder, so it had to be his. Markus scoffed and shook his head. Was he one of *those* kinds of people? Those holier-than-thou clowns? Markus himself didn't really believe in much of anything, never had a reason to. To him, those religious institutions were no different than corporations like Oracle. They preached virtue and love all day and "morality" till their throats ran dry, then broke that morality behind closed doors. Then proceeded to do that song and dance all over again.

Yeah, Markus wasn't worthy of sainthood. He'd done things that would give a normal coffee-sipping Sunday school student an aneurism, but he told himself it would be better to be that way and be honest about it than to pretend to be the moral superior every time he walked outside. The potential of Ryder being one of those kinds of people made him even more resentful of him.

Markus jumped up from the bed and went out of the room and into the undercroft. Ryder was already up and doing something in the kitchen and nearly jumped to the roof when Markus barged out of the room. He took one look at him and his eyes flared up like a severed powerline. His hair was shorter now on the sides and the back, with loose medium length strands resting on the front of his face. A scar he had was much more noticeable, streaming down his right eye and cutting into his eyebrow and down his face. On his otherwise blemish-less face, it stood out quite a bit.

"Hey, uh... good morning Markus," Ryder greeted brightly. Markus chose to ignore him and started to rifle through the fridge. Ryder just stood there, unsure what to do. "Yeah, uh... Spencer normally doesn't cook anything, so I don't know if there's anything good in there. Rudy has some pretty good breakfast grub upstairs, though, if you want some of that. He makes these really good breakfast croissants by hand every day and...."

"Dude... just shut up," Markus said shooting him down.

Ryder began scowling. "Would you be so kind as to remind me what your problem was again?"

Markus slammed the fridge door loudly. "Get this through your skull, we're not friends."

Ryder's eyes started to glow. "Seriously, what's the problem?"

Markus huffed in annoyance. "Leave it alone, you're not winning this."

"Come on, man."

"What's the appeal anyway? You trying to forgive me? Be a good little Christian boy?"

Ryder's eyes went wide. "What? How do you even..." Markus quickly brought out the neckless, letting it hang from his right hand.

The blue hue of Ryder's eyes lit up brighter at the sight of it. "Markus. Give that to me." He rushed forward and tried to grab it, but Markus pulled it away before. "Stop screwing around!" Ryder barked.

"Do you really believe in that stuff?"

"What difference does it make, give it back!" Ryder said desperately. As he kept reaching for it, Markus continued to play keep-away.

"You do, don't you! Come on, tell sky daddy to make me give it back!"

"Markus! My parents gave that to me. You need to give it back now!"

"Your parents? They didn't have a lot of money, did they? Considering how cheap this thing looks."

Ryder let out an enraged growl, almost a roar, then he grabbed Markus by his sweatshirt and threw him through the Time Stream, where he slammed him into the wall. Markus's lungs immediately felt like they were gripped and deflated. Ryder gazed at Markus, eyes ablaze. He looked like he wanted to kill him.

"Don't... push me."

Markus didn't show it, but this terrified him. He wasn't expecting a move like this. One minute Ryder played peacekeeper, the next he played warlord. Markus had never misread someone so badly. Despite his heart feeling like he had just ran a marathon, He just opened his mouth in a dumb smile.

"You got it, buddy."

The necklace slipped slightly out of his hand and caught Ryder's eye. His expression went from aggression to disbelief. He looked back up at Markus and let him go. He slid down to the floor and began letting out choked coughs. Ryder backed up and his demeanor changed instantaneously, he stared at his hands in shock and backed even farther away.

Markus was even more perplexed now, it was like Ryder was possessed by some sort of benevolent spirit, almost like he was another person entirely. He knew everyone had a bad side; he'd just never seen such a sharp contrast between the two like that before.

"Can I… please have my necklace back?"

Markus didn't even hesitate to give it back. Ryder took it from him and clasped both his hands around it, then pressed it against his forehead and closed his eyes tightly. Markus scrambled to his feet and stood in front of him, not sure whether to accept the apology or return the brute force. A voice in the room sounded out before he could make up his mind.

"Morning!"

Markus and Ryder turned toward the staircase on the other side of the room. Spencer walked down it, hands shoved in his pockets. He paused when he touched the floor and gave a confused look to both of them.

"Why are you two glowing?"

"Glowing?" Markus and Ryder asked at the same time.

"Both of your eyes. What are you fighting about?" he asked hotly.

"Us? Nothing!" Markus said brightly. "Just saying to Ryder how good it is to have him back!"

Ryder gave him a look of contempt. To Markus's frustration his eyes seemed to glow even brighter.

Spencer clearly didn't buy it. "Now you're lying to me?"

"Leave it be, Spence," Ryder interjected. "It wasn't anything serious."

Spencer looked like he wanted to instigate but didn't have the energy for it. He stood there and let out a quiet sigh. "You two sleep well?"

"Slept better than I have in a good long while," Ryder answered.

"On the couch?" Spencer asked.

"You bet."

Spencer blinked a few times like that was incomprehensible. "Well, I'm glad that's the case. Markus?"

"Slept fine," Markus said casually, the previous incident still lingering about in his mind.

"Super," Spencer said. He walked over to the workbench, and gestured for the two boys to come where he was. They did so and looked at what was on the table. That A.M.R device was still on top of it.

"Played around with this for far too much time. It might be salvageable but it's gonna be awhile Ry. Can you manage in the meantime? Or do you need a bit of time to get readjusted?"

"Nah, I would rather be out there. Don't really feel like sitting still right now."

"Out there?" Spencer asked. "Without the A.M.R?"

"I have my grappling hook, it'll be fine. I've had to make do without it for a while anyway."

"It's not just that, how are you expecting to keep a low profile? Looking to swing through the city like Spider-Man on that hook?"

"That sounds like fun," Ryder said brightly. "You know, now that you mention it, do you think you can make a real web-shooter Spencer? I bet you could."

"Stay focused, Ry. Besides creating a wrist-worn device that can shoot a line of fluid stronger than steel would be a nightmare. Well, maybe with a polymer base and microscopic metallic alloy but then again, reasonable fluid capacity and enough pressure to be fired would be hard to come by, maybe if compressed CO_2 was used, or maybe propane..." Spencer trailed of after before he saw Ryder and Markus staring at him blankly.

Spencer shook his head out of his engineer's dream world and realigned his focus on the present. "Anyway, my point still stands. You wouldn't have the same level of maneuverability as a basic grappling hook. Besides, I doubt you would even swing off anything consistently."

"Can you just drive me to the locales?" Ryder asked.

"Are you joking?"

"No," Ryder said. "You know I can't drive. It's been years since I've sat behind the wheel."

"It's not like I would ever let you take the van out anyway," Spencer scoffed. "And rolling up to an Oracle body—or revenant hunt— like a soccer mom wouldn't exactly be preferable, either. It's not just about getting there, it's getting out. I can't monitor you and be there to make a quick exit."

"Well, what do you suggest I do?" Ryder asked.

Spencer reached into his pocket and pulled out his wallet, then took out a few large bills and handed them to Ryder. "Spend time with Charlotte today, take her and do something fun. She's missed you something fierce, and I think it would do you some good before we start getting back to work."

"Oh, so he gets to chill and spend time with his cute little tomboy girlfriend while I get stuck back here doing nothing?" Markus complained.

"Markus, she's not my…"

"Can it Markus, you've caused enough of a scene. I don't want to hear any lip about it, you especially have to lay low. You got that?" Spencer asked.

"Yes, mein Führer," Markus mumbled under his breath.

"What was that?!"

Markus straightened himself. "Nothing."

He quickly decided he didn't want to deal with the two of them. He just shook his head and stormed back into Ryder's room, slamming the door behind him for dramatic effect. He just sat on the bed and looked at the plain-looking wall. The silence that followed was painful, outside everything was quiet, inside him was anything but. All Markus could do was simmer and marinate in his anger, growing more resentful by the moment. Part of him wanted to go out and see Charlotte as well, another part wanted to break Ryder's nose. At the moment, it couldn't be more than dark thoughts, but he had yet to see if he would make them reality.

CHAPTER 29

Past, Future, And Now

Ryder:

After Markus stormed into his room, the sinking feeling in Ryder's stomach came back full-swing. Part of him wondered if being so forgiving was more of a detriment to this problem than it was beneficial. It was the double-edged sword of his personality. He handed out second chances like free samples at an ice cream shop. Come one, come all. That was how he was raised, that was who he wanted to be.

But Ryder wasn't always so sugary.

He showed a part of himself to Markus he didn't want anybody to see. For better or for worse he kept that part of him locked up tight, out of harm's way. But sometimes it got loose regardless. Sometimes it was too difficult to hold back.

"Ry? You still here?"

Ryder shook himself awake. He had ended up daydreaming deep in thought as he stood there in the undercroft. "I, uh, yeah I'm here, sorry."

"You're fine," Spencer said sitting down in one of his chairs. "Can I keep you here for a minute before you take off?" he asked.

"Of course," Ryder said brightly moving towards the desk and leaning against it. "What's on your mind?"

Spencer took a minute to think, then spoke. "I just wanted to catch up with you. I know you gave us the sitrep on your little time travel adventure, but I'll be the first to admit not having you around was just depressing."

"Miss me, Spence?"

"Guilty as charged."

"What even happened while I was gone?" Ryder asked.

"A whole lotta nothing," Spencer answered grumpily. "I was only one man. I couldn't really do anything. Made some bribes and blackmail to beef up the pocketbooks, but there has been zip in the field work department."

"Using that leverage?"

"Yeah, footage of a little teenage girl getting shocked up for info still tugs on heartstrings, and I made sure Oracle remembered that."

"Is the revenant activity getting out of hand?" Ryder asked.

"Yeah, unfortunately it's skyrocketed. Since Oracle has been licking their own wounds for the quarter of the year, they haven't been much help either. It's gotten bad. I just didn't have a Time Rider for all that time. I have no idea how much damage that caused."

"I see," Ryder said quietly. "But let's put that on hold for now, that wasn't all I wanted to talk about," Spencer said.

"What else?"

Spencer raised an eyebrow. "You know what."

"No, I really don't."

Spencer rolled his eyes. "Charlotte, Ry."

"Her?"

"Yeah, her," Spencer said. "She missed you bad. You know that."

"Yeah, I could tell. I missed her, too."

"We didn't have time to really talk about her back then, it was all complicated and moving too damned fast. But we really need to figure out what your relationship with her even is."

"My relationship with her? Does it even matter?"

"Yes. It does matter," Spencer said coldly. "Is she a friend? A lover? A sister from another mother?"

"What?" Ryder asked confusedly.

"Are you drawn to her because of looks? Personality? Libido?"

"Woah! Libido? Slow down with that crap!" Ryder exclaimed. "It's not like that at all!"

"Calm down, I'm just trying to be thorough." Spencer said calmly.

"Be a little less thorough! Geez."

"Well, you tell me, what is she to you?"

Ryder thought about the question. He cared for her deeply, and that care was legitimate. He'd first met her when she was only five years old. When he first saved her, it made her a catalyst for an idea, a mission. A mission to continue to fight Oracle and the revenants to protect good innocent people like her. Somehow, against all odds, they had met again three months ago. Even after all that time he still felt obligated to protect her. That was one of the biggest reasons why he was so willing to give his life back at the Gateway Arch in the first place. It made Ryder nervous. There was something about her that made him lose control of himself, lose composure. That was a dangerous thing for someone like him.

"I care about her, with all my heart. That's all I can really say."

"What do you want from her, Ry?" Spencer asked.

"What do I want?" Ryder repeated. "I just want her to be safe and happy. It's not rocket science."

"Is that all? Or is there more to it? Do you have feelings for her? Do you love her?"

Ryder suddenly felt nervous, even angry. "Do I love her?" he asked heatedly. "Spencer, Charlotte isn't some high school crush to me. She's so much more than that."

"Then what is she?"

Ryder shook his head in frustration. "I don't know, she's... my light. My hope. She's my reminder that not everything in this world is violence and monsters. I need her; everyone needs someone like her."

Spencer leaned back in his chair quietly, Ryder took steady breaths, trying to calm down. "Look, back when we started working together, I knew this was always gonna be the minefield we would inevitably have to traverse. I made sure you kept to yourself, didn't get too attached to anyone. It was all a precaution. A cruel one, but it *was* a precaution," Spencer said.

"What do you mean?"

"I mean I made sure you were alone. I thought it would keep you less distracted, keep liabilities from forming," Spencer explained.

Ryder tried to remember how things were back then. Spencer had been much colder and strict. He was like a drill sergeant. It had been an agonizing experience, but it had toughened up Ryder significantly, or at least, that's what he told himself. Now that it was mentioned, it did seem like he had actively been keeping him away from people. He was always ordering Ryder to return and make himself scarce when saving people, and he never let him off on his own unless it was for the field work. Spencer did loosen up a bit as time went on, but he still had his moments of bitterness. It was part of his personality. Ryder never gave it thought enough to find an underlying motive to it.

"Did you stop doing that precaution?" Ryder asked.

"It only stopped because Charlotte skipped down our doorstep one day. I never anticipated that happening. Next thing you know, you showed up at her apartment, then everything after that took place. This may come as a surprise, but I contemplated letting you have this. Letting you two spend time together."

"Really? What about all that liability and distraction stuff?" Ryder asked.

Spencer took a deep breath. "You're a human being; I didn't respect that initially. I thought I could turn you into a soldier, a drone. That's not who you are. You've worked hard, gone the extra mile. Yes, having Charlotte in your life puts you and her in danger, but I can tell this is something you really want. I'm leaving this up to you, you make the call. But you need to understand, there's a price for everything. Don't forget, you don't age. You can get as close as you want with her, but it will hurt like hell when you have to break it off. And you will have to break it off one day. This is the one thing that won't go on forever Ry. You need to be careful. This kind of thing can change you; it can lift you up or destroy you. Do you understand?"

"Believe me, I do."

Hearing this made Ryder think of the Progenitress and the words she had said back at the Arch. She had said something like this, her words slithering around like worms in his subconscious mind. "What do you think is going to happen? You two remain until she grows old and returns to the dust? Could you do that Nathan? Could you watch her die?"

Those words played over and over in his head like a broken

vinyl. He thought of an older Charlotte, far past Ryder's physical age, her youth faded by time. Her smooth skin turned wrinkly; her red hair turned grey. Then out of nowhere his thoughts changed to her in a far more disturbing state. Her body lying lifeless, cold to the touch, the color gone from her eyes. He quickly tried to discard the thought completely. It was far too incomprehensible to think about, and his occasional existential dread threatened to burst forth. "Yeah, yeah I get it, hundred and ten percent," Ryder managed.

"Good," Spencer said. "But for now, carpe diem, as they say, seize the moment. Go have fun with her, don't worry for now. We'll get back to work soon."

"Hey, wait a minute, what about that Apex thing? It's still out there, right?"

"Apparently not. Combed through the Oracle database again last night, yada, yada, yada, you know the deal. Checked the electronic journals, but they took it down somehow."

"Took down, like killed it?"

"More of a coma from the looks of it. They've been running tests on it all night, making sure to keep its internal levels of zenaphosphorus to a minimum. Thing is built like a tank and weighs about as much too. You said it came after you too?"

"Yeah, twice," Ryder answered. "I guess the Progenitress took her time with this one. I hate to admit it, but it's solid work."

"It's a pièce de résistance if I've ever seen one," Spencer said. "I can only imagine what poor bastard had to get snatched up in order to make a revenant like that."

"You said the lieutenants brought it down? For good I hope?"

"Here's hoping. It's not dead yet, but at the moment, it's only as dangerous as it usually is."

"Yeah, okay," Ryder said quietly, followed up with an exhale.

"Take it easy. Sorry if I scared you." Spencer apologized. "When are you going to tell me about your little field trip?"

"My what?" Ryder asked.

"Your time off the grid?"

Ryder was suddenly stricken by frustration. "Never, that's when."

"What do you mean never?" Spencer asked hotly.

"Did you not hear what I said last night?" Ryder asked. "It's dangerous."

"What's dangerous is leaving the future up to someone like Markus Daniels. I don't like it Ry, the kid's a loose cannon. It's a miracle he hasn't gotten himself killed yet."

"You're just going to have to trust me on this one, Spence. This is not something you want to screw around with."

"Is there going to be substantial danger? Are lives at stake?"

"I'll handle it," Ryder said coldly.

"I thought we trusted one another."

"I do, I just... I'm not telling. Not now, not ever. Okay?"

"What was one of the things we talked about when we started all this? We don't keep secrets. Secrets put me, and everyone else in danger. You need to talk."

Ryder's face began to feel hot. "No, I won't."

Spencer had a tense look in his eye and held it for a good long while. "Ryder, if people are in danger here, are you willing to accept their deaths if things go wrong? Could you live with knowing there was a chance to anticipate and stop them?"

Ryder's brain felt like it was constricting. "I don't have a choice but to live with it. I've never had a choice. Sometimes you can't take things back."

"And what about the things you could stop prior to..."

"Spencer, please not now. It's difficult to even process what's in front of my eyes right now. Can I just go see Charlotte now? I'll think about what I can fill you in with, but I'm warning you right now. It won't be much."

Spencer eventually exhaled in defeat. "All right, go on and see her. But this isn't over."

Ryder stormed away and obeyed his request. After slipping on his old pair of dark sunglasses he left the undercroft in his street clothes, exiting through the alley and onto the sidewalk. Beginning his journey toward Charlotte's home.

After he left the undercroft the early-morning sun hitting his face and skin felt like a warm embrace, and the hustle and bustle of St. Louis citizens was a welcome change of pace. Even before Ryder very rarely walked the streets like this. Normally he had all his equipment and zipped around using his A.M.R to keep a low profile. Just walking the sidewalks made Ryder dream of just being a normal teenager again. Someone who wasn't always in danger, someone who actually had a future in front of him. They were sweet white lies, but they brought some comfort.

Thoughts of Markus, Charlotte, and the current situation in general passed through his mind as he walked. It felt like only yesterday it was only him and Spencer against Oracle and the leagues of revenants. And now, two other people had come into his life that he felt extremely strongly about for very different reasons. Charlotte went without saying, but Markus was a whole other world. Ryder always felt like an anomaly, out of place. Seeing someone else with those shiny blue eyes and incredible abilities was vindicating, especially coming from someone as confident and bold as Markus. Briefly, Ryder felt like they were going to get along, maybe in the most unorthodox way possible, but they could work together. But just as quickly Markus started to hate him. It wasn't a good way to start a relationship with someone who you were likely going to spend a better part of eternity with, assuming he didn't try to kill him first.

Ryder wanted to fix it. He always wanted to fix things, but he had been blindsided by this sudden malice. When the heat turned up, he couldn't really focus. As far as priorities were concerned, it was at the top for Ryder to mend this relationship. He knew there was pain behind that tirade, that anger came from a hurt heart. He just didn't know how to appeal to it.

Ryder found himself in a familiar area surrounded by a plethora of pristine, orange-roofed apartment buildings. An older playground sat in a grassy median in the middle of the area, and a swing moved about slowly being pushed by the wind. Seeing it brought back memories that spanned many years of Ryder's life, in a strange way it could be considered a center piece for it. A common occurrence.

He climbed up a small concrete staircase and went up to Charlotte's apartment door, nervousness creeping into his mind one last time as he raised his finger to the doorbell.

CHAPTER 30

Boyfriend

Charlotte:

C harlotte had spent most of the morning messing about in a restless state. It might have been either Ryder's return or the fact her mother had the thermostat at an arid temperature, but she didn't sleep very well and woke up fresh out of a fever dream only a few hours after laying down for the night. Even after she woke up, she felt stuck in it. All her limbs felt strange, and her mind was still in the dream. It took her at least half an hour before she returned back to normal. After that she decided to quickly shower just to bring some coolness back to her body, then she threw on some jeans, a dark undershirt, and a cozy red plaid shirt with rolled up sleeves. She couldn't bring herself to lay down again, so she just browsed her computer or played with Millie. Time passed by steadily, and the sun gradually returned to the sky with every hour, beckoning the morning.

Eventually her idle state was interrupted by the sound of a doorbell blaring about her home. Millie's ears shot up, and she bolted from Charlotte's room. Yapping as she went down the staircase.

"No Millie!" she exclaimed, wincing with each loud noise the puppy made, that racket was almost certainly going to wake her mother if the doorbell hadn't.

"Dumb dog…" she muttered under her breath bolting down the

staircase towards the front door. Once she got there, she saw Millie clawing at the door loudly, making unsatisfying noises. Charlotte pushed the dog gently aside and looked inside the peephole to see who rang the bell in the first place. She saw Ryder dawning his old haircut and wearing sunglasses.

She opened the door without even thinking, and Millie bolted out the door and started jumping on Ryder's leg, yapping excitedly.

"Oh! Hello there doggy," Ryder said seeming both enthralled and nervous being jumped on by the small animal.

"Millie!" Charlotte hissed, scooping up the dog in her arms and holding her close. "I'm sorry Nathan, she's not really trained yet," she explained before getting pelted by a few of Millie's licks. Charlotte squirmed a bit in response but couldn't do much with the dog in her arms.

"You didn't tell me you got a dog!" Ryder said happily.

Charlotte set Millie back inside and closed the door behind her, pressing her back against it and blowing through her lips in embarrassment. "Yeah, that was Millie."

"Heh, that's awesome."

Charlotte took a look at him. She was over the moon that he went back to his short hair, it was a way better look for him, even with the glasses. Soon one thing did stand out, however, a large scar that went down his face.

"Nathan, what happened?"

"What do you mean? The scar?"

"Yeah," Charlotte said sadly. She walked over and began to trace it with her index finger. Ryder gently took her hand and moved it down.

"Did you get hurt?" she asked.

"A bit ago. Don't worry it wasn't bad," Ryder said reassuringly.

"I don't like it, your poor face…"

Charlotte ended up getting hit by the door behind her and was pushed. She stumbled forward and would have fallen down the front stairs if Ryder hadn't caught her in his hands.

"Oh! Charlie, are you okay?"

Mrs. Rowes was on the other side of the door, wearing silk pajamas and holding Millie in her arms. Charlotte readjusted herself and stood next to Ryder. The door swung open completely and Mrs. Rowes saw Ryder in his entirety. Her eyebrows raised in surprise.

"And who might you be?" she asked.

Charlotte swallowed deeply. "Yeah mom, this is Ryder. That boy I told you about. He's my..."

"Boyfriend!" Ryder exclaimed. Charlotte's eyes shot opened completely. He laughed nervously and wrapped an arm around her. She just looked at him with an unflinching glare. "Yeah, she didn't tell, did she? She's cute like that, always shy and gets embarrassed easily. But yeah, I've been gone for a while, and I just wanted to check in. I missed her," Ryder explained, nudging her a little bit.

Charlotte still gawked at him, less than pleased.

Mrs. Rowes' eyebrows somehow went even further up. "Is that so?" she asked, Millie yapped exactly once afterwards. "It's good to finally meet you, Ryder, Charlotte always spoke highly of you."

"Did she? Aw, that's sweet of her. And ma'am? Please call me Nathan, Ryder is my last name."

"Will do," Mrs. Rowes said positively.

"Mom, can you give me and Nathan a minute?" Charlotte asked, holding in her frustration, and putting on a happy face, getting out from under Ryder's arm.

"Okay, I'll get dressed and start breakfast, would you like to join us, Nathan?" Mrs. Rowes asked.

"Sure! That sounds..."

"No, he doesn't." Charlotte interjected.

Ryder and Mrs. Rowes looked at her with surprise. "Charlie! How rude! Do you always treat him like that?"

"Wha-no, I was just..."

"If he would like to join us, he is more than welcome to," Mrs. Rowes declared. "I'm going to get started, and he better be here when I get back." Mrs. Rowes said closing the door. Charlotte went back to pressing against it with her back, she was still giving Ryder a death stare, he just shot her a guilty smile.

"Boyfriend?!" Charlotte hissed through her teeth.

"Oh boy, what have I done?" Ryder muttered quietly.

"What were you thinking? My mom is gonna be on my tail about this for months!" Charlotte exclaimed.

"I don't know I mean... would she have believed anything less?" Ryder asked.

"Wha-that's not the point! It's not even true!" Charlotte retorted.

"Look, I'm sorry. It just popped in there. I'm not expecting you to smooch on me or anything. I mean, it's not like you haven't done it before…"

"That's not the point you dumb…!" Charlotte said catching herself. She flattened both of her hands and brought them to her face, meeting her fingers at the top of her nose. She closed her eyes and tried to collect herself.

"Hey, I wasn't being serious, it was just a cover, I didn't really mean anything by it."

"No, I just… I've never dated before Nathan. My folks are like really weird about it, especially my dad. Because she's hearing all this now my mom is gonna assume we're sleeping with each other or something."

"What! Again, with that? I would never… is it so weird to *not* want to have sex these days?"

"I know you don't, you've been good to me. But she doesn't know that, please, you need to fix this."

"I have to fix it?"

"Yes you!" Charlotte exclaimed. "You started it!"

Ryder shook his head around and blew through his mouth. "Alright, you're right. I got it. I don't want to take advantage of you in any way and that's the honest to God truth. I would never force you into that."

"Good, now prove it to my mom."

Ryder gave a goofy affirmative nod. Sharp knocking could be heard behind Charlotte, and she backed away from the door. It opened and Mrs. Rowes could be seen wearing one of her favorite dress shirts and pants.

"Come on in! It'll get started here in a few minutes."

Charlotte and Ryder looked at each other for a second and proceeded back into her apartment, Charlotte gritted her teeth and hoped for the best, but she wasn't feeling optimistic.

CHAPTER 31

Sarah

Ryder:

Ryder regretted calling himself Charlotte's boyfriend, at the time it just popped into his head, likely because his conversation with Spencer was still on his mind and it just seemed like the most believable answer.

It was amusing seeing Charlotte all flustered, but Ryder would never say that to her face. He didn't enjoy getting her like that in the first place. It was the most absurd thing. Countless times he had his life threatened by everything from militant operators to alternative dimensional monsters, but he had never felt more intimidated and nervous sitting there about to talk to Charlotte's mother. Doing dangerous field work somehow felt preferable. Would it be easier to face a pack of revenant knights or Mrs. Rowes? Knights. Definitely the knights. At least he had experience in that department.

Ryder and Charlotte sat alone in the living area of the apartment for about fifteen minutes. He had always been casually curious about her home. It was a nice place; everything felt neat and tidy, and the decorations and walls gave off positivity and lightness. There was even a lingering scent of what smelled like laundry detergent in the air. The living area had two fabric sofas and a coffee table with a fireplace installed diagonally to both of them.

He kept peering at a photograph that sat up on a mantle above the fireplace positioned to his right. Even with the sunglasses, the details didn't allude him. It looked like it was Charlotte and both her parents at the local Six Flags park, all three of them smiling with glee. She was younger in the photo, between five and seven years old, standing between her parents' legs with a pinwheel hat on. Mrs. Rowes stood to her left, almost a carbon copy of the woman he had just met outside.

To her right was a modestly handsome man with brown hair. Ryder assumed this was her father, the military man. His eye color was gem-like green, Charlotte's eye color. He couldn't help but be transfixed. He couldn't forget that color even if he tried, seeing the color in someone else's eyes made him obsessively more interesting. He only stopped looking when Charlotte kept making strange movements.

She sat there on a sofa opposite to where he sat, popping her knee up and down nervously. Her small dog had come over and tried to hop on his leg, so he decided to lift her up onto his lap and began to pet her. She was full of energy and struggled to sit still, but Ryder loved it. He always had a soft spot for dogs, and it helped that she was a cute little husky.

"I think she likes me," Ryder acknowledged happily.

"I think she likes everyone," Charlotte said.

"Did you trade in your jacket?" Ryder asked, avoiding Millie's tongue.

"It's fall, thought I would start wearing my favorite kinds of shirts," Charlotte answered casually. "Do you like my jacket more?"

"Nah, I like plaid," Ryder answered with a smile.

"Is that so?" Mrs. Rowes came in behind Ryder, a sly smile on her face. He got one look at Charlotte, who was glaring blades at him again, he was happy there was nothing close to her that she could throw at him. "Come on in and sit at the counter you two, it's nearly ready," Mrs. Rowes said.

Show time. Ryder gently moved Millie off him and onto the floor, but she still insisted on jumping on his leg as he walked.

"Millie!" Mrs. Rowes barked at the puppy.

It jumped off not because of being scolded, but because she smelled food in the kitchen. "Sorry, our little family member's enthusiasm knows no bounds."

"It's fine, always nice to have a fan. Right, Millie?" Ryder asked. Millie yapped once in response, almost like she could understand exactly what he said.

Ryder seated himself at a high table in the kitchen and Charlotte took a seat next to him looking nervous. Mrs. Rowes dropped a plate in front of the two of them. He looked at its contents and saw it was some sort of white bread cut into squares. Honey-like maple syrup drenched on top of it. "French toast," Mrs. Rowes said. "Personal recipe of mine."

Charlotte began to gorge on her food like she was malnourished, it was nasty the way she went about it. Both Ryder and Mrs. Rowes stared at her with dumb gazes.

"Charlie! Good Lord, where are your manners!" she scolded.

Charlotte stopped, embarrassed. She leaned back slightly with her face covered in syrup. Even Ryder had no idea where that behavior came from. She let out a quiet belch and opened her mouth to speak. "Uh, yup, sorry," she said awkwardly. For her sake Ryder held in a laugh.

"Good grief, you're sixteen years old, not sixteen months! Go get cleaned up right now!" Mrs. Rowes ordered. Charlotte looked over at Ryder and winked at him. He was confused for a second, then it all began to click. She had done that on purpose so he could talk to her mother. She hastily left the counter and sprinted up the stairs, Ryder's vision following behind her.

"I apologize. I have no idea what's gotten into her, I certainly didn't raise her like that!" Mrs. Rowes said.

"It's fine, she's always been a unique flavor."

"Flavor?" Mrs. Rowes asked, puzzled.

Ryder swallowed hard. "I guess just 'unique' would be a better way to put it. She's one of a kind," he said.

Mrs. Rowes returned to normalcy. "Yes, I would say she is unique."

Ryder mentally congratulated himself for a smooth recovery. "Yeah, I've always liked that about her."

"You don't need to wear sunglasses indoors Nathan, you can go ahead and take them off," Mrs. Rowes suggested.

"Bright light hurts my eyes unfortunately," Ryder said.

"And why is that?" she asked.

He was suddenly afraid he'd just implied he'd been drinking or something in that vein. "I had an accident," he began. "It involved a lot of bright lights. My vision is mostly back but I have to wear these everywhere I go," he fibbed, pointing to his glasses. It pained him to lie in any capacity, but it was more of a half-truth, a lie of omission. Which was still objectively a lie, but Ryder chose to omit that particular fact as well. He knew his eyes were probably glowing like floodlights under the glasses, and he did everything he could to not make eye contact.

"I see, I'm sorry about that, Charlotte said you've been gone for a while. Was it because of that accident?" Mrs. Rowes asked.

"Yes!" Ryder said loudly, Mrs. Rowes seemed shaken by the response. "I mean, yes I was away because of that."

"What happened?" Mrs. Rowes asked.

"I was at the Gateway Arch three months ago," Ryder said in quick-draw fashion.

"Really? When those horrible New Martyrs attacked?" she asked.

Ryder felt himself going into the danger zone. Yes, it was the truth, but she couldn't get the full picture, and at the rate he was going, he was going to blurt out all his secrets without even thinking about it. He had never heard the name "New Martyrs" before, but it reeked of an Oracle coverup.

"Yes," Ryder answered. "I was there when it got damaged."

"There was a big blackout that night, but there was also a big flash there, right?" Mrs. Rowes asked.

"Yes, and I got caught in the middle of it," Ryder said.

"Oh no," Mrs. Rowes said, bringing her hands to her face the same way Charlotte had outside.

Ryder noticed that Mrs. Rowes was like her daughter in many ways. For one thing, she looked nearly identical to her. It was almost off-putting—she had the same rich color of reddish-brown for her hair, and freckles peppered her face. The only exception was her eye color. Hers were warm brown, like chocolate, but Charlotte's were green. Ryder had a hard time gauging what her age was. Considering her daughter was in her teenage years she assumed Mrs. Rowes had to be at least in her mid-thirties, but she did not look like that at all. It was like she had an ageless factor of her own.

In the most respectable way possible, Ryder thought she was

stunning. Her hair and face looked healthy, and her demeanor radiated warmth. Only her skin would indicate her age, but even so, it was certainly not a blemish of any kind. Ryder was grateful Markus was not in the same room as them, as he almost certainly would have made a mess of things with someone like her there.

"I'm so sorry to hear that, Nathan. Are you recovering well?" Mrs. Rowes asked.

"Yeah, I heal easily enough," Ryder said smiling. "Good," Mrs. Rowes said, leaning her arms on the counter. "How did you meet Charlotte?"

"I met her when she was five, at the playground outside."

"Really?" Mrs. Rowes asked.

"Yeah, she was almost abducted that day."

"What?"

Ryder cursed himself harshly. "There were some unsavory characters around," he started, shakily trying to find his next words. "I protected her."

"Protected her? You would have been around her age; how did you do that?"

"I had a bat on me," Ryder said. "A metal one. I, uh… hit them with it."

"You hit them with a metal bat?"

"Yes, ma'am."

"As a child, you fought off abductors with a bat?"

"Yes," Ryder said with uncertainty, gritting his teeth. "What can I say? Being clobbered with an aluminum bat still hurts." Despite being the truth, this story sounded more like a fabrication with each word uttered. Mrs. Rowes appeared to share this sentiment. It didn't look like she believed any of it.

"And why do you think she didn't tell me about this?" she asked.

"It was late in the night. She probably thought she would get in trouble if she told you. I guess she didn't bother bringing it up later."

Mrs. Rowes looked like she was trying to process that. "I'll ask her about it later," she said.

Ryder wanted to move away from that topic, it was too close. "But we somehow met again three months ago. It was one of the happiest days of my life," he said.

"And nights?"

"Sorry?"

"You were in her room that night, three months ago. I heard you." Ryder was flabbergasted hearing this, almost impressed. He thought he had pulled that off without detection. "Yeah, I was there."

"You snuck in through her window. You were in her room, late at night."

"Yeah," Ryder said slowly, knowing full well how bad that looked. "But I just wanted to catch up, nothing more."

"Uh huh," Mrs. Rowes mumbled. "How did she hurt her hand that night?"

"She punched me in the face."

Bringing it up so casually almost made Ryder burst out laughing.

"And why did she do that?" Mrs. Rowes asked.

"I scared her, that's all," Ryder answered.

Mrs. Rowes raised an eyebrow. "Are you telling me the truth?"

"Yes ma'am."

Mrs. Rowes leaned forward a bit, a tense look in her eye. "Nathan... you do seem like a nice boy, but as her parent I'm admittedly still suspicious of you, especially since Charlotte had been so secretive of you till now. I think you know where I'm going with this. What are your intentions with my daughter Mr. Ryder?"

There was the bombshell question he hoped he wouldn't hear. Ryder had beat this drum twice today already and was already tired of it, but at the same time he couldn't bring himself to blame her for asking.

He thought of something and reached into his pocket to bring out his crucifix he got back from Markus. It glimmered brightly in the kitchen lights. Mrs. Rowes formed a look of glee on her face.

"You're religious?"

"Yes, ma'am, born and raised."

"What denomination?"

"Protestant at most. Never found my footing in a specific sect, just believe the words of the Bible," Ryder explained. "Are you a believer as well?"

Mrs. Rowes frowned. "Back out Midwest I was raised Baptist,

but after I met Charlotte's father I moved here, and I never found time to settle down in a local church. Parenthood is taxing. We do swing by for Easter and Christmas, but that's about it."

"Maybe you should consider going there more often," Ryder suggested.

"Maybe we should," Mrs. Rowes agreed.

Ryder started to feel a bit more comfortable. He never really had a chance to talk about his faith in any capacity without getting scoffed at, or at least without the potential for scoffing. "But yeah, I want to take the teachings seriously. That means no fancy stuff till marriage."

Mrs. Rowes smiled pleasantly. "I hope your sincere about that."

"I am," Ryder said firmly. "Mrs. Rowes, Charlotte came into my life when I needed someone like her the most. Life hasn't been good to me. I lost my parents a long time ago and I've tried to hold on ever since, but it's been difficult. If I'm being truthful, I genuinely didn't want to deal with any of it anymore. If my future had anything good in it, I couldn't see it. Then we met again, and everything changed. I felt happy again, learned to love again. I don't know if you believe like I do, but I do believe she is a gift from God. He gave her back to me, and I would rather die than do anything to hurt her. If anyone tries to, they are going to answer to me. She means the world to me. She's my girl. The light of my life."

Ryder told himself that what he said was an attempt to not blow his cover. He was supposed to be her boyfriend, her lover. He was meant to say something sappy like that. But something about how the words came out seemed too easy.

Mrs. Rowes had a glassy look in her eye and a few tears escaped from them. She quickly brought a hand up to wipe them away. "I'm sorry, I didn't mean to get you emotional," Ryder said guiltily.

"No, honey, you're fine," she said happily, laughing off her emotions. "I'm just glad you said that. I worry so much about her. It's definitely not good for my health, but... her father isn't always home, and she used to spend so much time holed up here in our apartment, it scared me. There is a whole life she has seemed so disinterested in. She used to go off on her own a lot, but I didn't like that, either. It wasn't safe."

"She told me about her dad, Navy SEAL, right?" Ryder asked.

"Yes, Elliot. He's a wonderful man and an even better husband. But he's always on deployment and I'm normally the only one raising Charlie. I was happy when she told me about you. I thought she had finally found a friend, but then you were gone. I'm guessing because of your accident, but she just became so sad. I had no idea you two were closer than that. I thought you were only going to be trouble, but Nathan, I don't think you are. I'm glad you met her."

Hearing this filled Ryder with comforting vindication. It wasn't hearing her say she cared for Charlotte and trusted him, but he could feel it. That was something he took a minute to learn when it came to caring deeply for someone. It all had to do with the heart. Beforehand this was obvious for him, but he'd never seen it work before. It was so powerful he could feel Mrs. Rowes's passion for her daughter and his own. It was an invisible chain, linking them together.

"Thank you, Mrs. Rowes."

"Please, call me Sarah," she said warmly.

Ryder let his mouth form a grin. "Thank you, Sarah."

"You're welcome, Nathan," Mrs. Rowes said. "Are you going to eat your food?"

Ryder had forgotten all about his plate. "Uh, yeah, absolutely!"

He said a very quick prayer and began chowing down. He immediately tasted the sweet syrup, bread, and sugar. As it turned out, it seemed like the bread had been dipped in egg. It was the most delicious thing he had eaten in years.

"Any good?" Mrs. Rowes asked.

"Oh my, you're like my favorite person right now!" Ryder said, continuing to eat.

"Don't let Charlie hear you say that, speaking of which," Mrs. Rowes started. "Come back over here, sweetie."

Ryder looked over and saw Charlotte poking her head out from behind the wall behind the staircase. She blinked and moved out from behind it, Millie followed suit.

"I got to say, Charlie, you have good taste,'" Mrs. Rowes told her.

Charlotte blinked a few times again. "Are we okay?" she asked.

"Yes, you're okay," Mrs. Rowes said. "Did you and Nathan

have plans today?"

"Did *you* want to do anything Nathan?" Charlotte asked slowly with uncertainty.

"I thought I'd leave it to the ladies' choice," Ryder said.

"Oh, such a gentleman." Mrs. Rowes chided in.

Charlotte scratched her hair and thought about it for a moment. "We just ate, so we probably shouldn't go to a restaurant or anything. Do you wanna grab a coffee?" she asked.

"I don't drink it often, but I'm game," Ryder said.

"You want to go to Sebastian's?" Mrs. Rowes asked.

"Yeah, are you cool with that?" Charlotte asked, leaning her head to communicate directly with her mother.

"Of course! You two have fun. Just not too much," Mrs. Rowes said.

"Yeah, yeah. Easy-peasy," Charlotte said quickly.

Ryder saw his cue and hopped down from the chair, then went over by Charlotte.

"Thank you again, Mrs. Rowes."

"Remember, it's Sarah. And you're welcome, the pleasure's all mine."

"Right, yeah, sorry. Let's go, Charlotte," he said tugging on her sleeve. She got dragged away and started walking out the door after Ryder.

"Be safe!" Mrs. Rowes called out as the door closed behind them.

CHAPTER 32

Dark Evening

Charlotte:

Outside Charlotte leaned on her knees and breathed deeply like she'd been holding her breath the entire time.

"You good?" Ryder asked, laughing.

"I think," she mumbled. "I only got to hear the last bit of that. Did it go okay?"

"Yeah, she kept asking me when we were going to give her grandkids."

"What?"

Ryder laughed out loud. "Okay, that was a filthy joke, sorry."

Charlotte hit him in the arm. "Ow!" Ryder exclaimed, his laugh growing louder.

"God, I freaking hate you!"

"Hey, watch it! Don't use his name in vain like that," Ryder scolded.

"It did go okay?" Charlotte asked.

"Yeah, your mom's awesome," Ryder said. "She's like your cool older twin or something."

Charlotte groaned loudly. "I know she looks like me. I get reminded of it every other day!"

"What's wrong with that?"

"It's just... I'm me! You know?" Charlotte exclaimed.

"Yes, I'm fully aware you're you, Charlotte Rowes," Ryder

said. "The coolest gal in St. Louis. How could I forget?" Ryder said.

Pleasant warmth rushed to her cheeks hearing that.

"What was that coffee shop called again?" Ryder asked.

"Sebastian's," Charlotte answered.

"Oh yeah! I used to pass by it a lot. Any good?"

"The best. But first, away with those," Charlotte said, snatching Ryder's glasses from his face. His eyes lit up in slight frustration.

"Hey! Don't be yanking stuff off my face like that!" he whined.

"I want to see your face."

"I appreciate that, but I don't just wear those for looks. My eyes aren't exactly factory- made you know?"

"Just for a bit, please? At least until we get there?" Charlotte pleaded.

Ryder looked like he wanted to argue, but he mellowed out the moment he looked at her. "Fine, but if an Oracle bum rushes us don't run to me asking to pull your butt out of the fire."

"I won't need to ask." Charlotte said playfully.

Ryder gave her a side-eye. "That's not funny."

Charlotte gave him a sly look. "Come on, hero," she said smugly as she began walking. Ryder tagged along behind.

The two of them walked together, traveling through the city on the sidewalk. She took the lead with Ryder right next to her, casually taking in his surroundings. It felt good being with him again like this.

"Can I ask you something?" Ryder eventually asked.

"Huh?" Charlotte asked, not paying attention.

"Can I ask you a question?"

"Well yeah, sure."

"Why does your mom keep calling you Charlie? Isn't that a boy's name?"

Charlotte sighed and rolled her eyes. "Charlie can be used as a nickname for girls, too. It's a long story. When my mom and dad were trying to have a baby, they both wanted a boy really badly. They even had a name picked out and everything."

"Let me guess, Charles?" Ryder asked.

"Bingo," she said. "Charlie Rowes—my mom and dad were dead set on that name. So, you could imagine the disappointment when they found out I was a girl. It wasn't even a big deal for the most part, they just named me the female equivalent of Charles. But of course, since the moment my mom found out you could call girls 'Charlie,' I've never heard the end of it. Annoys the ever-living heck out of me."

"Seriously? I can't imagine you as a boy," Ryder said.

"I can," Charlotte said. "Considering how I dress and what I'm actually into. Makes me feel like there was a mix up somewhere."

"I wouldn't envy it all that much," Ryder said. "Being a boy isn't a picnic, either."

"True that. I could've ended up like Markus," Charlotte said with a small snicker. Mentioning him seemed to pique Ryder's attention "What's he been like?"

Charlotte scrunched her nose in disgust. "I don't want to talk about him."

"What did he do?"

"He's just a pervert. Tried hitting on me and everything."

"For real?" Ryder asked, surprised.

"Unfortunately. No interest in him, no thanks."

"That's it? I mean what about the general Time Rider stuff?"

"He's fine, I guess. Seriously, can we just forget about him for now? I just want to get to Sebastian's."

"I want to learn more about him, it's kinda important."

"You'll have time later!"

Ryder seemed put off by that. "Are you okay?"

"I'm sorry, I just want to focus on you right now. That's all."

"What's gotten into you? I've never heard you like this. You sound... cold," Ryder responded with concern.

"Nathan, Markus is not a good person. He's not like you."

Ryder's eyes glowed even brighter. "Me? Good? All I do is try to be a better person. Don't judge people like that."

"Just... please, Nathan, I don't want us to be angry," Charlotte said.

Ryder looked forward again. "Fine, you're right."

Charlotte looked straight ahead, feeling guilty. She supposed it was normal to want to know more about Markus, but he was just the last thing she wanted to think about. She finally led Ryder to the small coffee shop, and he wasted no time to open the door for her.

"Guess chivalry isn't dead after all," Charlotte said, handing him his sunglasses.

"Not as long as I'm alive," Ryder responded, putting them back on.

Charlotte walked in and Ryder followed suit. Inside, Charlotte was greeted by the friendly and familiar aromas of the coffee shop. The usual classical music made the place a den of tranquility.

Maxine was the one behind the counter at the moment. "Charlotte! Good to see you! Who's the boy you dragged in?" she asked loudly.

"This is Ryder!" Charlotte called out.

He raised his hand in an awkward wave. "Are we gonna order or..."

"You want the usual?" Maxine called out.

"Yeah! Make that two!" she called out, leading Ryder over to two chairs facing the window to the shop. They both took their seats while they waited for their drinks. Ryder looked around the shop curiously, and she noticed his eyes glowing steadily under his glasses.

"Guessing you're a regular?" he asked. "That lady knew what you wanted instantly."

"Yeah, I love this place," Charlotte said.

"What did you order, anyway?"

"Two caramel macchiatos with white chocolate shavings," she said, placing her hands on the table.

"Really? Don't know if I've ever heard of that before."

"It's kind of my unique drink. Nothing too crazy but I go bonkers over it."

"Bonkers, huh?" Ryder said, notable whimsy in his words.

Thinking about the drinks made her realize she had forgotten something; she patted down her jeans and was met with only the curved surfaces of her legs. "Shoot!"

"What?"

"I didn't bring any money!"

"Don't worry about it, I got it," Ryder reassured.

"You got cash?"

Ryder reached into his own jeans and brought out a satisfying-looking fold of money bills. "Courtesy of Spencer, of course."

"Dude, why did he give you that much?" she asked.

"I don't know, he just told me to go and have fun. Not sure

what his idea of fun would look like."

"Do I look that expensive to him?"

"Girls are just expensive in general."

She gave him a look of menace. "Oh, really now?"

He looked up at her, his face unflinching. "Don't look at me like that—his words not mine."

"Do you agree with him?"

"Can't. Don't know much about that kind of thing. But as for you? Nah, I don't think so."

"That's better," Charlotte said.

Ryder leaned on their table and tapped it like he'd done nervously the day before. "Okay, be straight with me here. Is this an actual date you tricked me into?"

Charlotte felt her heart begin to throb. "Maybe, or we're just two friends grabbing a coffee together. It's whatever you want it to be. You're the one blurting out that you're my boyfriend."

"I'm sorry about that all right?" Ryder groaned. "Besides, if this were a date, I wouldn't even know where to start. Most of the company I'm used to being around normally have claws, guns, and a real bad case of Time Rider derangement syndrome. Not exactly prime candidates for candlelit dinners and flowers."

"You've dated before, right? Surely you have, you're a good-looking guy." Even with the glasses, Charlotte saw the telltale glare of his eyes growing brighter.

"That's nice of you to say," he said timidly. "But no, not really. I was never that lucky. Girls at school always wanted something a little more macho."

"School?" Charlotte asked, confused.

"Yes, Charlotte, school," he said smugly. "Believe it or not I was a high-school student like you once."

"What was that like for you then?"

"Well, I went to school in the noughties. I don't really know about the ins and outs of what goes on these days, but I'd imagine it was different ten years ago when I was still normal. For me it just... was. I liked it well enough, I guess. I had a real affinity for mathematics. I wanted to pursue a career in it after I graduated."

"You like math?" Charlotte squeaked.

"Sure," Ryder said brightly. "Math makes things make sense. It always works if you do it right. Starting small, using the formulas, getting a solution after it all. It makes sense to me. It's even fun."

"I'm gonna agree to disagree with you on that one."

"Eh, I know a ton of people struggle with it. That made me stand out so much back then. I was the scrawny, nerdy kid that liked numbers."

"Scrawny? You?"

"Yeah, I was a real string bean back then," Ryder said. "Probably weighed about as much as you do now."

"That's a load of baloney," Charlotte said.

"Nope, dead serious. I was skinny as a rail and had a real bad haircut. I mainly kept to myself back then. That first decade of the millennia was wild. It seemed like everyone my age was trying to get laid, get high or some other kind of crap. And then there was me, this Bible- thumping kid that wouldn't have any of that."

"Did you have any friends at least?"

Ryder grinned lightly. "I had one good friend, a bigger kid named Joey. Shy guy, but the most loyal buddy I could ask for. I remember going to find him after I got taken by the revenants. That was when I learned that I... that he didn't..." He paused for a moment. "I really miss him."

Before Charlotte could comment, Maxine walked over with the two drinks and sat them in front of the two of them. Maxine gave a sneaky wink to Charlotte walking away to continue her duties. Charlotte began to drink her drink immediately, relishing its flavor and warmth. Ryder just nudged his with a finger.

"Are you going to drink that or just poke it?"

"It's hot."

"It's supposed to be."

"I know, but I don't want to scald myself. I hate it when that happens."

"It's not that bad, go on," Charlotte insisted.

Ryder hesitated for a second and looked at her. She gestured with her hand for him to drink. He brought the cup to his mouth and gently took a sip. His throat almost immediately lurched, and he brought the cup down quickly.

"Ow! Holy crap!"

"What? Too hot?" Charlotte asked.

"Well, yeah! I'm gonna be feeling that the rest of the day," Ryder said, poking his tongue out a couple of times. "Are you meaning to tell me you just endure that?"

Charlotte shrugged. "Yeah."

Ryder looked at her in disbelief. "You're scary."

"Oh yeah, totally. I just terrify the masses," Charlotte said sarcastically. Ryder kept poking his tongue out like an oversized snake.

"Nathan, I've been curious about something else," Charlotte said.

"What's on your mind?"

"Your time away. What happened?"

Ryder froze in place, and Charlotte could see his eyes getting even brighter. "It's like I said, I can't say much."

"I mean maybe without spoilers. What was it like?" she insisted.

Ryder's face tensed up. "Hell. That's what it was."

The way he said that made her feel nervous. "That bad?" she asked quietly.

"Yes," Ryder said. "I don't want to go back there, in thought or in any way else. We're not going to talk about that, so stop trying to bring it up."

"I'm sorry, but I didn't know where you were for so long. All we had were those cryptic notes. I just want to know what happened, where you were. You know you can trust me, Na—"

"Did Spencer put you up to this?"

Charlotte felt fear stabbing into her heart hearing him speak to her like that. "Wha—no. I just wanted to know."

"So that's what Spencer was playing at. Listen to me, and you can tell Spencer this too. Just because it's you, doesn't mean I'm gonna spill all my dirty little secrets. My story is my own business. Do you understand?"

Charlotte stared, unsure what was going to happen. But after many moments of anxiety- inducing silence, he broke out of his red haze and plopped down in his seat. He took off his glasses and covered his face with his hands, then began to breathe heavily leaning on the table. It almost sounded like he was in tears.

"Nathan, I'm sorry. I didn't mean to—" Charlotte paused abruptly and began to cough violently, sending her mind into violent dizziness.

"Charlotte?"

She managed to readjust herself. "I'm good." She said, sputtering out a few lighter coughs. "I've had this nasty cough lately, I probably need to see a doctor about that but I..." Charlotte was once again hit by a torrent of sharp coughing, she covered her mouth and felt something fly into her hand, she brought it forward and saw her hand covered in bright crimson blood. Before the shock could register properly she suddenly became incapacitated by overwhelming fatigue and fell from her chair and onto the floor. She didn't even feel it.

Ryder was immediately down on the floor holding her up. The last thing she saw before blacking out was his frightened eyes, their lights slowly fading out like dying lamps.

CHAPTER 33

Brightside

Markus:

Markus remained back at the undercroft with nothing else to do. At the moment, he was lying on the sofa with his feet kicked up, casually throwing a baseball into the air and back down in a repetitive cycle. He was worn out enough to achieve a sense of mellowness. As a result, he ended up thinking about anything his mind felt like. Old memories and new ones, pictures and faces, sounds, and smells.

While he did that, Spencer had been hard at work fixing Ryder's A.M.R. It was standing on its own in a sort of x-shape, all four limbs erected with the limb braces wide open. Spencer was alternating between screwing parts back on and taking an industrial-grade polisher to its dark metal. He was also fiddling with some sort of measurement device. He called it an E.M.F reader.

Markus had no interest in the scanner, though he was admittedly intrigued by the A.M.R, which looked imposing even on its own. Considering how fun the skysurfer was, he was interested in seeing this A.M.R in action, but not really enthusiastic about seeing Ryder again. A part of him wanted to shake the disdain, but his pride was large enough to have its own area code. There was just no getting past it, not right now.

The door at the top of the undercroft opened and frantic metallic steps sounded out coming down the steps. Markus and Spencer immediately turned their attention to them as Ryder came into view. Charlotte was in his arms, limp as a noodle, and her face dripping blood from her nose.

Markus immediately rose to his feet, instinctual rage coming to the forefront of his mind. He rushed over and knelt next to Charlotte. "What happened? What did you do to her?!" Markus yelled.

"I didn't do anything!" Ryder answered frantically. "Something happened at the shop we were at; I didn't know what to do! Oh no,no,no…" he stammered, kneeling on the floor and propping her head onto his left shoulder.

"Why didn't you bring her to a hospital?" Spencer exclaimed, walking over.

"Something felt off, I felt—"

Before Ryder finished, a loud blare came from Spencer's workstation. The E.M.F reader Spencer worked on sounded like it was throwing a fit. It was lit up brightly, and a loud noise was coming off it.

"That feeling," Ryder finished.

Spencer rushed over and collected the small beige device and examined it. He rushed back over and held in vertically near Charlotte. The device was so loud at this point that Markus took a small step back out of fear the thing would detonate. It kept going and going, reaching an almost musical crescendo, then suddenly stopped. Charlotte's eyes fluttered open slowly and she groaned sadly, still weakly leaning against Ryder.

"Charlotte? Oh, thank God. Are you okay?" Ryder asked.

"No…" Charlotte mumbled weakly. "Everything hurts."

"What even happened?" Markus asked.

"We were talking in a coffee shop, and she started coughing really badly and fell over onto the floor. I dragged her back here as soon as I could. I even went into the Time Stream just to get back here in time."

"Did you get seen?" Spencer asked.

"Who cares!" Ryder yelled.

Charlotte was conscious, but she looked like she was in a limbo, her eyes were opening and closing lethargically, a look of extreme fatigue or powerful sickness on her face. She winced as Ryder lifted her up and moved her over to the sofa.

"Wha—Nathan. Nathan?" she murmured.

"I'm here, I'm right here," Ryder said softly, putting a hand to her forehead and kneeling next to her. Markus was angry seeing him even near her. The moment he was alone with her she ended up like this. It wasn't the time for this, but his selfishness was once again trying to be the center of attention.

Spencer stood still, looking at his E.M.F scanner in awe.

"Have you seen this before?" Markus asked.

"No," Spencer answered flatly. "I've never seen a spike like that before."

"It's because of us, right? Me and Markus?" Ryder asked.

"What do we have to do with it?" Markus asked.

"Time Riders give off electromagnetic fields," Spencer explained. "It's a small field but it does exist. Revenants are where the real ones are. With you two down here there would be a good signal, but Charlotte just now. I've never seen a signal that large before, then it just stopped." Spencer said, lingering on those last few words. "Ry, does she have her phone?" he asked.

Ryder looked down at her and her jean pockets. "Yeah."

"Okay get her mom on the line, make up an excuse to keep Charlotte down here for a while. Nothing that would cause any alarm though."

"You got it."

"And Markus?" Spencer said, turning to face him. "Just keep to yourself for now."

Markus immediately became frustrated. "Is there anything I can do? Anything at all? I want to help her too. I can't just sit on my hands."

"You can help by staying out of the way," Spencer said, barely acknowledging him and walking over to the sofa to put the EMF detector on the coffee table in front of Charlotte.

Stay out of the way? Was that all he was? An obstacle? He knew he had caused strife lately, but he just wanted to help figure out what had happened. He might not have been around as long as the other two, but he still cared about what happened to her.

Charlotte's fatigue caught up to her and she fell into a peaceful sleep, breathing softly as she lay on the sofa. Ryder was still on his knees next to her, his reluctance to leave her side blatant.

"Ry, you need to talk to her mom," Spencer reminded.

"Right, I just can't leave her right now," Ryder said.

"She's right there. We don't need mommy dearest getting the police involved again since she's out past her bedtime," Spencer ordered.

"Right, right," Ryder said forcing himself away from her and into the bedroom in the back.

"Markus, I need to pick up some fresh batteries for the detector upstairs. Keep an eye on her," Spencer ordered without even looking in his direction.

Markus walked over and sat on the coffee table in front of her. For a multitude of reasons, he felt awful. Not exactly an alien feeling, more-so the norm. But this wasn't just anger, it was sadness, a deep and solid sadness. Markus didn't feel that so much anymore since he normally didn't let himself.

But he couldn't help it seeing Charlotte Rowes, this little flower, this ray of sunshine, in pain and covered in blood. Seeing her like this made him feel uneasy, so much so that he went into the kitchen, wetted a washcloth, and returned to sitting on the coffee table. He leaned over and began wiping her face with it gently, cleaning up the dried blood. Before he could finish Charlotte woke up with a sudden start, almost like she was having a bad dream, Markus almost jumped himself. "Sorry didn't mean to wake you," he said.

"Markus?" Charlotte said weakly.

"The one, the only," Markus said. "Don't worry. Nate and Spencer aren't far away. I'm just watching you for now."

Charlotte dropped her head down and winced.

"Feeling bad?"

"No, I was practicing making my face look like yours," Charlotte wheezed.

Markus snorted. "Least you still got your sense of humor."

He reached over and quickly cleaned up the rest of the blood from her face. Charlotte reacted somewhat defensively. "What are you doing?"

"Just cleaning all that red off your face," Markus responded.

"Red? I was bleeding?"

"Yeah, it's gone now, though."

Charlotte tried to sit up but immediately fell back like her limbs were made of twigs. She groaned in frustration.

"Can I get you anything?" Markus asked.

"I'm fine," she hissed, trying to get up again, she fell back down and let out a high-pitched pained whine. Markus didn't say anything. "I'm cold," she said.

"Do you want a blanket?"

"Please."

Markus didn't hesitate to grab one laid out nearby. He came back and threw it over her, tucking it under her small body until she was completely covered by it, only her head stuck out. She blinked a few times, seeming slightly more comfortable.

"Snug as a bug in a rug?" Markus asked.

"Yeah, thanks," she said gratefully. "I guess you can be decent."

"I guess so," Markus said. "Kinda new to me to be honest."

"You don't say," Charlotte said quietly.

"Would you rather me get lost and leave you alone for a bit?"

"No, you're okay. Rather not be alone."

Markus was surprised to hear that. "Okay, if you say so."

Charlotte lay there; Markus sat only a few feet away on the coffee table. He felt the world and his mind grow quiet for the first time in a long time. It was a good feeling. "Hey, can I ask you something?" he asked.

"Shoot," Charlotte responded.

Markus looked down at her, a sense of mellowness in his gaze. "Am I a bad person?"

Charlotte looked over at him and Markus met her eyes, their rich green color felt like they saw right through him.

"I don't think your bad per-se, you're just difficult. You suck at talking to people and you run around like you've got a death wish. But as for if you're a bad person, I don't think it matters all that much."

"Don't think it matters?" Markus asked confused.

Charlotte closed her eyes as she spoke. "What's more important is who you want to be, if you don't like what you are, you change…" she trailed off as she began to fall into a slumber again, she began to breathe like a calm wind.

Markus reached over and moved a few rebellious strands of hair from her eyes and nose with his index finger, a feeling of stillness following. "Sleep tight Freckles."

Ryder soon came back into the room and Markus immediately backed away and sat again on the coffee table. Ryder rushed over and saw Charlotte cleaned up with the blanket wrapped around her. "Is she doing alright? You did all that?"

"Yeah, she was awake for a sec, but she's passed out again," Markus explained.

"What did she say?" Ryder asked.

"Not much, she just asked for the blanket. She was cold."

Ryder was already looking antsy. Markus reluctantly relinquished his spot in front of her and Ryder immediately filled it. Markus just went over next to the workstation and looked in the mirror that was installed next to it.

He looked at his glowing gaze staring back at him. He was looking at a stranger, he didn't even recognize himself. His shaggy hair and face looked rough, his sweatshirt looked different without the sleeves, the long cut on his arm stood out, and his eyes glowed their new hue. Markus didn't like this person he saw and lamented the fact this is what people would always see and think about when they thought about Markus Daniels.

He began to lean against the wall and think diligently about what Charlotte had said. He honestly didn't know what he wanted to be, or what he could be. He wasn't really inclined to align himself with any grand vision of a greater good or being noble, but now he was simply not content being there only for himself anymore. Being around someone like Ryder was interesting. In so many ways he was Markus's antithesis, his opposite, but at the same time, there was something they shared, something important.

He had thought about it so much that he'd lost count. But what he wanted, what he needed, was something that generation upon generations of men before and after him would seek. Something to fight and live for, and in some cases, die for. For some, it was family and loved ones, for everyone else it was ideals or fervor. Markus was just starting to remember what that felt like.

It was frustrating. What could a young man like him do? To fight and endure the long and uncertain road with no thanks, no reconciliation? What then would his purpose be? To live for only himself? No, not for Markus, not anymore. He had tried that. It was all he had ever done. He was ready to stick his neck on the line for something that was actually worth a damn. Maybe it was for helping people not get carved up by revenants, maybe it was giving Oracle the middle finger, but for now, the only thing he could see was Charlotte. If there was anything worth fighting for now, it was her.

He was willing to do away with his misgivings towards Ryder and Spencer for the time being. He always led his own path, his own wellbeing being center focus. But that was changing. He was changing. He still didn't know if he had the capacity to be a hero or anything cut from that line of cloth, but he knew he had to try.

CHAPTER 34

Truth

Ryder:

Why? Why her? Why now? After everything that had happened in Ryder's life, he had never been more struck with fear. When Charlotte tumbled out of her chair at that shop, he had fallen into an immediate panic attack. That tingle on his spine, that feeling in his heart. He knew something was very wrong. He had rushed back with her in his arms. She had been bleeding and was slack like a corpse. Subconsciously, it felt like she had actually died.

That wasn't the case, but that didn't stop the shaking in his hands or the rapid beating of his heart. She was stable now, fast asleep on the sofa in the undercroft, cleaned up and wrapped in a blanket like a newborn. He had to tell Mrs. Rowes that Charlotte would be late getting home. Fortunately, it seemed like she bought Ryder's lame excuse. She trusted him with her, but he was starting to wonder if that faith was misplaced.

Spencer fiddled nervously with his EMF detector, making sure it got the most accurate reading possible. He kept moving it near Ryder and Markus, getting frustrated if the reading wasn't consistent. Markus kept to himself, quietly leaning near the mirror by Spencer's workstation. Ryder was seated on the coffee table right in front of her.

"So can you explain what happened again?" Spencer asked.

"I told you, we were drinking coffee and just talking," Ryder explained with annoyance. "She went into a coughing fit and started hacking up blood. Next thing I knew she was passed out on the floor."

"Anything that would indicate anything unusual? Anything at all?" Spencer asked.

"No! I mean nothing I could see. She was just as bright and cheery as always!" Ryder exclaimed.

"Well, there is that cough," Markus added.

Spencer turned to face him. "Cough?"

"Well yeah, you heard it too. Yesterday, when Ryder came back, she started coughing like a chain smoker," Markus explained.

"And she coughed up blood at the coffee shop," Ryder said. "Is she sick?"

"That goes without saying. The question is what the sickness is," Spencer said flatly. "That E.M.F reading, that's the key here. Normal human beings don't give off fields like that. Whatever is happening to her, it has to do with the Time Stream."

Ryder didn't like the sound of that. "Well, what do you mean by that?"

"I'm not sure. I'm hoping it's just a nasty side effect of being around Time Riders so much. Your mild E.M.F.s might have finally added up."

"That doesn't make any sense," Markus said. "Have you felt sick like that? You've spent more time with both of us than she has."

"No, I haven't. I mean it could have to deal with age and levels of resistance, but in that case, I would likely be the one who is more susceptible." Spencer said.

Ryder was surprised he overlooked that. It wasn't like him to lose a detail like that, but it seemed like he was sugarcoating it. "Spence, what are you thinking it actually is?"

Spencer looked over at Ryder, a look of discontent and nervousness lingering about him. "The Progenitress. That signal Ry, even normal revvies don't have spikes that high. Something is affecting Charlotte, and it's not anything small."

Even hearing that cursed name brought back memories and experiences that Ryder thought would give anyone else substantial trauma. He wanted more than anything to be done with her. He wanted her to be dead, but deep down he knew the truth.

"Hold on a sec. Who's that again?" Markus asked.

"The Progenitress," Ryder said. "The revenants all answer to a woman, a queen of sorts. She's their leader, but she's really more of a mother. And all the revenants are her family."

"A mother?" Markus asked.

"She wanted to recruit me. She wanted me to join her. She gave it her all, but I refused." Ryder continued.

"You said she was a chick?"

"Yes," Ryder answered. "When we fell through that gateway in the arch? We swirled around the Time Stream for a long time. It was like we were skydiving or something. She clung to me like some crazy animal. I managed to get her off and she faded away, like she evaporated into mist. I haven't heard or seen her since. I honestly thought she died. Then I ended up in the future," Ryder explained.

"It wouldn't be safe to assume that, especially now. You might not be the only one who managed a comeback," Spencer said. "But she does appear to be absent, or at least lately she has," Spencer said. "The revvies haven't been acting normal since you left anyway. Variants like brawlers and knights are the ones who are by far the most aggressive. They're killers, not good at much else. Spikers stay at a range, cloakers keep it quiet, so on and so forth depending on their niche. It's only when scouts are present that they change their tactics and go for collection. Lately there have been wanderers. Mostly the aggressive variants going at it alone, unable to figure out what to do. Even the scouts seem to be operating randomly. There is no structure anymore in the way they operate."

"No one to boss them around, eh?" Markus asked.

"Exactly. Revenants are by far the most dangerous when there is more than one and they are on the same page. They just haven't been lately. They haven't had a legitimate command structure."

"Then what about the Apex?" Markus asked. "That thing is an army of one in and of itself. And it knows what it wants. Me! Or at least it did, I guess it wants Nate, too."

"That's another reason that thing gets under my skin. It popped up out of nowhere, far too confident for my liking. Like you said it knows what it wants. It has a goal, a mission. To kill you two, the Time Riders."

"And is willing to kill its buddies if they get in the way," Markus said.

"Right," Spencer answered.

"So, I'm guessing that invitation to join her now is invalid?"

"She creates all revenants, so it's safe to say that yeah, she doesn't want us drawing breath anymore. Hell hath no fury like a woman scorned..." Ryder said.

"Tell me about it," Markus said.

"Why do you ask? Looking to join up?" Spencer asked flatly.

Markus looked over. A sharp scowl beaming at Spencer. He got up from the wall with a sudden start. "Okay, enough all right! I know I've been acting like... well me. But get off my ass!"

"Give me one reason!" Spencer bellowed.

"Guys, please, can this wait? Or even better, not happen at all?" Ryder asked.

"No, this ends now! I've been treated like an unwanted pest since Ryder walked in the door!"

"You've been a liability! You want that attention you crave so bad, do something to earn it!" Spencer yelled.

"Earn it? I've nearly been killed by the Apex twice! Don't give me that crap about earning anything!"

"Let something be clear, Markus," Spencer started. "If I'd known the kind of person you were, I would never have let you in to begin with, but we needed you. And now that we have Ryder back, I'm starting to have second thoughts about you. Do you catch my drift?"

Markus's face went blank, like his brain locked up.

"Spencer! What's wrong with you? Why would you even think of saying that?" Ryder yelled in disbelief.

"Yeah, I catch your crummy drift! And you know what? Screw you! Screw all of you! I don't need this; I don't even need you to kick me out. I'll see myself out the door, thank you very much!"

Markus stormed over to his gear at the workstation and began to angrily equip all of it. Ryder rushed over, desperately trying to diffuse the situation.

"Markus! Markus, please! Can we just talk about this for a minute?" he pleaded.

"Get out of my way! I'm out of here!"

"Markus enough! Stop being an idiot! Talk to me!"

"There's nothing left to talk about! You've made your point clear enough. I'm not welcome here," Markus said, clicking his final strap on. "But so help me if I hear that anything happens to that girl over there, you'll be getting a visit from me, and you won't like what happens next. Comprendes? "

"What?"

"Smell you never, Ryder." Markus sneered, bumping into Ryder's arm roughly and running up the staircase.

Ryder lifted his hand to stop him, but he was already gone. Ryder could hear the door at the top of the staircase opening and closing behind.

"Crap..." Ryder growled under his breath.

"Just let him go Nathan," Spencer said.

"We need him! Markus!" Ryder ran up the undercroft staircase into the alley repeatedly yelling his name. Once outside Ryder just barely managed to see him flying away on that board he had. Entering the Time Stream, Ryder used the momentum to get up onto the store rooftop.

It was difficult to keep up, but Ryder managed using the rooftops to move quickly. Markus just flew along seemingly distracted for at least five minutes. After finding a building of proper elevation Ryder used the Time Stream once again to jump forward quickly and grabbed hold of Markus midair, causing the two of them to start spinning.

"What are you doing Ryder? Get off!" Markus yelled.

"Put this thing down! You're not leaving!" Ryder ordered.

The two of them struggled, the board going mad with each tussle. It eventually ended up arcing too low, causing the two boys to fall off and tumble onto a gravel covered rooftop.

They both landed on their stomachs. Ryder had all the air in his lungs emptied and he lay on the ground breathing rapidly. Just as he began to get up Markus ran over and punched him straight in his face.

"Stay down!" Markus yelled.

Despite the oppressive throbbing in his face Ryder immediately got to his feet and was met with another punch, sending him back down to the ground. Despite the pain becoming unbearable and blood on his face, Ryder chose to rise again, not backing down. One more punch flew his way, and he fell back down onto the gravel.

"Wha—what are you doing? Fight back! Don't just sit there!" Markus bellowed.

Markus swung once again and Ryder suddenly dodged, then threw his own fist to knock it away. With Markus off-balance, Ryder lifted his foot and sailed it through the Time Stream right into his gut. He flew into the air, landed on the gravel, and skidded before coming to the edge of the rooftop. He took off his mask and lay there groaning weakly, completely out of air, and holding his stomach.

Ryder wiped the blood from his face and flicked his hand to rid himself of it. "Don't feel bad, sometimes you just can't beat the original." Markus tried to recover on the ground and Ryder hoped he hadn't overdone it.

"You ready to talk?"

Markus was still writhing around on the ground. "I guess I got a little time," he wheezed

Ryder went over and offered him a hand. Markus stubbornly just sat there with a grumpy look on his face, but he relented and took his hand and was pulled to his feet.

"Gah, you hit like a semi," Markus groaned.

"That's the Time Stream for you. If I didn't pull back, I would have broken my foot, and all your ribs," Ryder said. "Why didn't you mention anything about Charlotte?"

"What does she have to do with anything?"

"You know what I mean. This is mostly about her, isn't it?"

Markus looked away and cleaned off his arms. "Not all of it but yeah I mean... it doesn't matter."

"Of course it matters, that's your heart we're talking about."

"Or what's left of it," Markus said, walking over to a ventilation unit and sitting down there next to it, propping his arms on his legs.

"Seriously, why didn't you say anything?" Ryder asked.

"Well, what was I supposed to say? Hey Nate, I got the hots for your girl? And what could I tell Spencer? That old fart would have done everything in his power to keep her away from me. I mean, I asked her about it and all she did was kick me in the shin. There was no chance I was ever going to be with her, no way in hell. But that doesn't mean I just stopped feeling that way. If anything, it got worse when you came back into the picture. It's stupid, but I kind of wish I'd never met her. It would have saved me all the aches."

Ryder let his words sink in. His usual empathy worked its magic. "I'm sorry. I'm really sorry man."

"For what? You're the lucky one here."

Ryder decided to sit down next to him on the ground. Down there, Ryder placed a hand on his shoulder in an attentive way. Markus just sat there quietly.

"Charlotte is not my girlfriend. We are close, but not that close. It's extremely complicated between us Markus. Don't get me wrong, I do care about her, and I'd be lying if I said I didn't ever think of her like that. But I don't know how far I can take it. It tears me apart thinking about it too much."

"What are you talking about?" Markus asked.

"The ageless factor. Do you want to know how I met her? I saved her from some scouts at an old playground. She was only five."

"Five? You've known her that long?"

"Not exactly. We didn't have any contact for the next decade. I had a small blunder where my A.M.R ran out of juice on an Oracle assault job. As a result, I ended up showing up on a traffic camera near the undercroft. She ended up seeing that footage somehow and that led her to us. The rest is history—crazy history, but history nonetheless."

"She said you two knew each other for only three days."

Ryder didn't know what to say in response. "Uh... sort of. We met up for three days, but we always thought about one another and... she fell in love with the idea of me, I'm not sure how else to put it."

"Okay," Markus said plainly. "And what does the ageless thing do for you two?"

"Well, think about it. I don't age. She does. Let's say hypothetically we dated or even married. Let's say she's forty and I'm still seventeen physically. You see the problem with that?"

"Oh... yeah, fair point."

"Like what you're saying now, about wishing you never met her? Part of me feels the same way right now."

"Seriously?"

"It's not because I hate her or anything, quite the opposite. I would love to pursue something with her, but any relationship we have would already be doomed."

"I mean, all relationships end Nate; everything ends."

"Not Time Riders."

"Sure, but that doesn't mean you can't live a little, y'know? In a you kind of way of course."

"I can't. I can't do that to her, or myself."

"She likes you man; she can barely hide it."

"I know…" Ryder said quietly. "That's what makes this so difficult. I've stolen her heart…"

The two of them sat in silence, Ryder's pain becoming numb. The aura of aggression surrounding him and his fellow Time Rider seemed to do the same. Markus was calmer than Ryder had ever seen him.

They both sat still for a few minutes, taking in the night air before Markus broke the silence. "Nate, what is the end game here? How do you want this to end for her?"

Ryder looked over at him. "Far away from me and everything else that wants to harm me. It's the only way for her to be safe. The only chance." He closed his eyes and exhaled into the air. "Hey, I uh, hate to break a good bonding moment, but are you going back with me? We could use the help."

Markus exhaled deeply. "I'll give it a shot. I don't mind you believing in me, but I don't think Spencer will feel the same way."

"I'll deal with Spencer; I'll vouch for you. Just don't do it for me or him, do it for her. Or better yet, do it for yourself. Maybe you find something you've lost."

"Okay, sure. I don't care to much about what I have, she's the one worth the trouble."

"Okay, just focus on that."

Markus let out a tired groan. "Sorry about messing up your face," Markus apologized.

"I heal easy, don't worry about it."

Markus collected his board from the ground and turned it on. It shot up and hovered upright. "Before we head back, there's something I've got to ask."

Ryder turned to face him. "Go ahead."

"Are you ever going to tell me about how I am in the future? Or is that still breaking the time travel rules?"

"Yeah. Pretty much, I'm afraid. But I will say one thing," Ryder said.

"And what's that?"

"Back there? You were the bravest person I had ever met, a real leader. I wanted to be more like you."

Markus was now surprised. "Is that so? You sure we were the same person?"

"Yes," Ryder answered. "You're a better person than you think you are Markus Daniels."

Markus let out a small snort. "I'll take your word for it, Nathaniel Ryder."

Ryder gritted his teeth upon hearing his name. "Okay, that's a tad bit weird."

"You started it," Markus responded. "Meet you back there?"

"Yeah, nice night for a stroll anyway."

"If you say so," Markus said jumping, back on his board. "Ciao."

He flew back towards the undercroft. Ryder wiped the fresh stream of blood from his face, feeling it was a worthy transaction for getting the truth out of Markus. He was most certainly upset and even infuriated with Ryder in his short time of acquaintance with him, but he couldn't deny how cathartic it was to have him here.

For so long Ryder was the only Time Rider. In all that time he felt like an anomaly, a misinput. If he were to view his condition factually, that's what he was. Ryder didn't want to jump to any rash declarations, but he believed they could meld well together. They could work together, fight together. No more solo acts would be needed, no more standing alone.

That sudden disdain Markus had for him was extremely alarming, not to mention random. But now Ryder understood what happened. Of course, Spencer and Charlotte were gonna pick favorites, and on top of that he had feelings for Charlotte as well. He couldn't fault him for that since he shared similar sentiments.

Ryder casually started walking along the rooftops back to the undercroft with his hands in his pockets, taking in the cool fall air, happy for a small win. He continued on with hope this was the beginning of something good for the both of them.

CHAPTER 35

Hell Hath No Fury....

Markus:

Markus returned to the undercroft with a strange sense of ease. He waited patiently for Ryder to get back before trying to enter. Once Ryder returned, he managed to convince Spencer to let both of them back in. Seeing the old-timer again made all those thoughts of turning heel come back in full swing, but Markus fought them off, telling himself he owned Ryder a solid for what he did tonight.

For someone like Markus, sometimes a good beatdown was a good way to start thinking clearly again, and this time it did just that. Seeing Ryder get up over and over after taking solid hits to the face completely nullified any indication Ryder was weak. Markus's punches weren't anywhere near soft, he'd knocked out people on many occasions doing the exact same thing, but Ryder still continued to get up, like he was only knocked over by the air.

And somehow, after all that, Ryder went back to playing Mr. Nice Guy. It seemed so sappy to him, but airing out how he felt did help. It was a powerful thing to try to bottle up and he was happy to be rid of it, even if it didn't go away completely.

The fact that someone even bothered to hear him out was a miracle in and of itself. There were countless times in his life when he had needed to just talk to someone like that, and it had never happened. Everyone else were too busy scolding him or lost in their own problems to do anything helpful, yet so simple.

He didn't exactly like Ryder yet, but he was starting to respect him. He figured if anyone was going to be with Charlotte, complicated or otherwise, he was far from a bad pick.

Charlotte herself still slept soundly on the sofa, looking so comfortable it could be felt just by seeing it. Spencer still fiddled with his E.M.F detector, his patience wearing as thin as a razor blade. He was so stressed that Markus was half-expecting boss music to play out of nowhere like a video game. He made a mental note to keep an eye on him in case Spencer decided to throw the device, figuring if anyone was gonna get something thrown at them, it was most certainly him.

Markus sat near the kitchen counter drinking a soda, and Ryder was doing the same next to him, nursing a can in his hands nervously.

"So, you've never seen her do anything like that before?" Markus asked Ryder.

"Nope."

"This is weird. What did you tell her mom?"

"That she wasn't feeling well and passed out on my sofa."

"So... the truth."

"Kinda, more of a lie of omission. She said she was cool with it, but I'm not so sure."

"How much time do you think that will buy us?"

"She told me to have Charlotte call immediately when she was up, so at least the rest of the night and early morning, give or take."

Markus looked over at the sofa and Charlotte. "I dunno, man. I wouldn't be surprised if she were in a coma at this rate."

"Aw man, don't say that." Ryder groaned.

"I mean, looking on the bright side, if she was in a coma that would give us plenty of time to figure it out and we would still technically be following her mom's request, y'know?"

"I guess," Ryder said laughing lightly. "But that's still not exactly the best-case scenario."

"What's the deal with this Projenatrish, anyway?"

"Progenitress? Bad news, that's her deal."

"How so? Is it just because you didn't join her exclusive club?"

"Pretty much. She's freaky, man. She appeared in my dreams and started showing up when I was awake. She whispered crap in my ear and all kinds of things. She really wanted me to join forces. Did weird stuff trying to."

"Like what?"

"She went after Charlotte and tried to get her killed, then she tried to seduce me."

Markus's eyebrows perked up. "Seduce? Like in the adult way?"

"It depended on what she felt like doing, but yeah, in an adult sensual way. Nothing too crazy, but that was definitely a card she played. It's her MO, her usual method."

"This is a chick we're talking about, right?"

"An adult woman. At least she was the last time I saw her."

Markus became more attentive. "Was she hot?"

"Beautiful. Why?"

Markus leaned back on the counter with his arms crossed. "Lucky…"

"No, not lucky!" Ryder exclaimed. "That was freakin' awful, damn Jezebel…"

"Hey! Can't be talking like that, don't wanna upset the J-man."

Ryder scoffed. "Coming from you, that's rich."

A loud yawn could be heard coming from the sofa. Ryder, Markus, and Spencer all looked over at where it was coming from and saw Charlotte rise like a vampire from the sofa. She sat up, got to her feet, and began to stretch her back and arms like a slick cat. Her back was turned to everyone else.

"Charlotte! You okay?" Ryder asked.

"Yo, you good?" Markus followed up.

Charlotte let out a long, overly feminine sigh and craned her head without turning around. "Swell. I am so very swell."

Markus looked over at Ryder with confusion, Ryder returned the expression.

"Okay, that's good I guess," Markus said.

"You were in a sorry state." Spencer started walking over to her, E.M.F detector in hand. "You looked like you had a stroke. Are you feeling nauseous? Dizzy? Anything like that?"

Spencer put a hand on her shoulder, but she didn't acknowledge it.

"Charlotte?"

The moment he got close enough Spencer's E.M.F detector

went haywire, its alarm blaring at full volume and sounding like a blood curdling scream. A chilling chuckle began to sound out from Charlotte's mouth.

"Spencer Carter, for all the intellect you possess, you have never ever been able to see what was right in front of you, ignorant fool."

"What?"

Within a flash Charlotte spun around and ripped Spencer's handgun from his holster and pushed him hard. He flew over the sofa and landed hard on the undercroft floor.

"Whoa! What the hell!" Markus yelled.

"Spencer!" Ryder exclaimed.

Markus and Ryder focused their attention right back to Charlotte, alarmed at what she had just done. She stood there, Spencer's handgun hung limply from her right hand, her head crooked to the side. An impossibly large smile was stretched across her face. Her eyes were no longer their normal green but now glowing a bright blue. They looked alight, like ethereal flames. Markus knew without effort that was not Charlotte Rowes standing in front of them. Not anymore.

"Miss me Nathan?"

"You!" Ryder yelled. "What did you do to her? What is this?" Ryder rushed forward towards her. Whoever was in control of her decided to jam the handgun right into her own head, Ryder stopped dead in his tracks. She just continued to smile, like she was putting on a cute act.

"Such a pretty head this one has; it'd be a true shame to have it splattered all over the wall."

"No... no don't you dare! Don't you dare!" Ryder yelled.

"Oh, such temptation, such temptation indeed. Watching your heart shatter so would bring me joy beyond measure."

"I'll kill you!" Ryder screamed. Markus had to hold him back from running over to her.

"Stop for a sec! Nate, who even is that? The hell is goin' on?" Markus asked.

"The Progenitress!" Ryder answered. "What did you do with her?" he screamed at her.

"Oh, this sweet little vessel?" the Progenitress asked. "You destroyed my last body, don't you remember? Such a pity. It was by far my favorite. I needed a replacement. Most certainly not my preferred choice, far too young and small, but knowing how much you care for her Nathan… it made this all the sweeter."

"Let her go! You let her go right now! She's innocent! She has nothing to do with this!" Ryder demanded.

"You and I both know she has everything to do with this, Nathan," the Progenitress said. "You should never have refused me, never hurt me. Because now, I'm going to hurt you, and when I'm done, you'll be begging for death. I won't even think twice about granting your request."

The Progenitress craned her head around and looked at Markus, her smile turned even more dastardly.

"Markus Daniels," she said brightly. "Looks like my little ones have been collecting others in my absence. I wasn't expecting to see you again so soon."

"Sorry, but I don't think we've met, lady," Markus said.

"Oh, but I know all about you," the Progenitress said. "The defiant lion, the one who would light the world ablaze if it meant he could be seen. I know your anger, your desire. Oh, how powerful it is Markus. Why do you seek refuge with these vermin? They cast you aside like you were obsolete. They hate you, just like everyone else. I'm not like them. I know how much you hurt. I can take it all away, I will never hurt you, never act like you aren't there. You want Charlotte Rowes? I can give her to you. You can have her all to yourself. Why not? You owe them nothing. What have they ever done for you besides order you around?"

"Don't listen to her!" Ryder exclaimed. "This is what she does! Don't let her play you!"

"He would say something like that wouldn't he?" the Progenitress asked. "He's afraid of you. He knows you're dangerous, Markus. He knows you're stronger. Don't let him hold you back."

"Shut up!" Ryder yelled. "Enough games! You let her go right now!"

The Progenitress laughed and walked along the side of the undercroft.

"Grand things are ahead. Today marks the beginning of a new era for our brood, and the world altogether. Once you two are dead and gone, we will do what we set out to do that night three months ago. I want you to remember that we gave you a chance to join us, because soon it will be far too late."

The Progenitress was now near the staircase, the gun still pointed at Charlotte's skull. "It would be foolish to follow me, Nathan. Don't think I would have second thoughts about expiring this girl. The world is full of far more impressive vessels. I must be going, however. Much work to be done. But don't worry we will meet again, though I doubt you will find it a pleasant experience."

She cocked her head slowly over to Markus, akin to the way a serpent would move. "Think about what I've told you, Markus. Nathan had his chance but chose to forsake me. I hope you are wiser. I can show you a world you can't even imagine."

The Progenitress began to ascend the staircase, waving playfully behind her. "Have a good night, boys," she said sardonically with a wink, then she laughed until she was outside. Painful silence fell upon the entire undercroft as she left the building and journeyed deep into the night.

Ryder tried to bolt out toward the staircase, but Markus held him back. He struggled and struggled trying to get loose, but Markus's grip was like a pristine vice. He didn't dare let go. She still had the gun and he believed the threat she had said, it was not worth the risk.

"No! No! Charlotte! CHARLOTTE! No..." Ryder cried out heartbreakingly as he collapsed on the floor and onto his knees, heavy tears dropping from his eyes.

She had Charlotte, leaving only shambles between the three that remained, all uncertain what to do next.

CHAPTER 36

Yorkshire:

Doctor Bartholemew Yorkshire felt like death. It was late into the night, and his eyes felt heavy. He was at a breaking point. He stood in the research and development department of the underground base gripping the wrist of his injured hand. It had received proper attention in the infirmary, but it still hurt quite badly, and that didn't even begin to cover the psychological damage. Having a limb stabbed through by a sharp object and pinned to another proved to be terrifying. Yorkshire was not a violent man; the sight of his own blood and injuries was not a common occurrence.

More than anything, he wanted to go back to his personal quarters, pour a chardonnay, and play his favorite vinyl until he drifted to sleep. But that would have to wait. The new Apex revenant variant was currently there with him; his scientists were all working in tandem running tests and taking notes. Yorkshire was told how it apparently was defeated by the lieutenants earlier in the day. He was partly excited to see how it ticked, but his shaky spirit eroded his enthusiasm. Eight fully armed operators were walking around the station around it, battle rifles in tow, weapons up and pointing at the body.

"Doctor Yorkshire!"

A young lab coat-clad young woman wearing large horn-rimmed glasses ran quickly behind the operators right up to Yorkshire, giddy as a child.

This was Aubrey Milina, Yorkshire's overeager assistant. Yorkshire had enthusiasm in his work as well—any scientist or engineer would—but hers dwarfed his. She was a young college graduate with the intelligence of a prodigy and the self-control of a toddler. She did her assignments well beyond expectations, but Yorkshire often found himself assigning her busy work just to keep her away long enough for him to get something done.

"Miss Milina, I thought you had settled for the night."

"I did! But once I heard the variant was captured, I just had to get back to work!"

"Wonderful..." Yorkshire moaned.

"Yes, it is!" Aubrey said happily, as she ran over to the large body of the revenant. "Look at its sheer mass, its physiology!" she rubbed its muscles. "Oh! Solid as stone. This is hardened zenaphosphorus resin, isn't it?" she said, knocking on it with her knuckles.

"Back away from there!" Yorkshire barked, pulling her back from it and clearing his throat. "But yes, hardened zenaphosphorus resin. Like molders, but this is different. This particular resin is far more durable and distinct than the mucus-like structures on molders. We can't even penetrate it in any way to see what's on the inside."

"What about those scorch marks? Its mouth looks charred as well..." Aubrey said reaching out.

"Don't touch it!" Yorkshire snapped.

Aubrey took a step back. "What's the danger, Doctor? It's expired."

Yorkshire took her shoulder and guided her away. "Miss Milina, can you tell me what happens when a revenant variant expires?"

Aubrey's eyebrows showed her deep in thought. Once she realized where Yorkshire was leading her, her face went stiff. "Upon the death of a variant, the entirety of the creature's matter... unravels."

"Precisely, and has this variant unraveled?"

"No, Doctor."

"What does this mean?"

"The subject has not expired. It's still alive."

"Right again."

Aubrey's smile formed into an open mouth; timidness began to show on her breath. "Doctor, are we in danger?"

"Most certainly," Yorkshire said facing the revenant. "At the moment, it's showing no signs of awakening, but that could change in a heartbeat. That's why we have this security detail, but traditional firearms won't be able to penetrate the resin...wait a minute where are the ZL23s? I requested the prototypes to be here and ready to use! That's the one of the only weapons that can harm it!"

"Currently on route!" An operator captain sounded out.

"Well, double time it! If the variant awakens before we can properly contain it, this lab will turn into a slaughterhouse!"

"Yes, sir!" the captain yelled.

"The spark rifles, sir?" Aubrey asked.

"Yes. See those scorch marks? Spartan and his men used them to great effect earlier today. Spartan himself caused the gas inside to ignite with one, that's what incapacitated it in the first place."

"Is it comatose?"

"In a sense. 'On the mend' would be a better way to put it. Like spikers and molders, great fatigue will befall any variant whose stores of zenaphosporus have depleted too much. Much like a human losing too much blood. If the gas reaches optimal levels, then the variant will awaken.

"So, we need to keep it to a minimum."

"Yes, we already have vacuum pumps going down its throat, trying to keep it as minimal as possible. But we still need to exercise caution. We don't know much."

"Then let's get to learning!" Aubrey said with glee.

"Let's be careful Miss Milina. You know the nature of these creatures is not traditional science."

"Sorry. Yes sir," she apologized.

Research into dimension Alpha-2 and the revenant variants was mind-bendingly frustrating even on a good day. The nature of it all defied logic and scientific theory constantly. The laws of relativity and matter were challenged the most frequently. The expiration of revenants that resulted in the disassembly of matter shouldn't even be possible. Science would say matter is not created nor destroyed, but with the variants, matter seemed to dissipate into nothing. And that's not even considering how often matter could change in the blink of an eye.

Researching the revenants proved to be very difficult and dangerous, since a revenant would disappear upon death there was never an ample way to conduct a proper autopsy. There had been a handful of successful operations, but they always resulted in the creature's death.

Most of the research conducted was trying to learn how the revenants' cells never deteriorated, or 'the ageless factor' as Marigold coined it. What had been learned was that the cells of revenant variants were suspended in a kind of superficial stasis. Yorkshire himself has wasted countless hours staring at their bright blue cells under a microscope, even after all these years, they fascinated him to no end.

Science had taught him it was the nature of the world that all lives would eventually die. Even the planet itself will eventually perish altogether. Cells grow old and die. Some are replaced, sometimes they aren't. But not the revenants. Revenants were cold-blooded creatures that never gave off any signs of vitals or brain activity, even though they were clearly capable of exponential cognitive thought. They seemed like they were already dead, physical ghosts that walked among the living and could interact with and harm others. Their cells, however, never showed signs of deterioration or age. They remained and always would. Even after decades their state never changed unless an outside force was introduced.

There was also research outside the ageless factor, mostly pertaining to behavioral studies of the revenants. What Yorkshire deemed to be the most fascinating and vital behaviors to study were ones pertaining to combat and hunting tactics. Due to some kind of deal or loophole he would rather not know the details of, Marigold had been able to secure a wealthy supply of human test subjects stemming from incarceration facilities within the Missouri state or elsewhere.

Yorkshire would often set up arenas within the base that would play out almost like a game, where he would act as the game's master. The most common experiments would feature a revenant let loose into a simulated environment with a handful of inmates. Then he and his fellow scientists could watch from afar as the carnage commenced. Sometimes the inmates would try to fight back, sometimes they would hide for hours on end, but it never mattered. The revenants would always find them. Sometimes Yorkshire would mix things up by adding new kinds of variants or maybe adding defensive assets for the inmates to use. But the results would always be the same, albeit with increasingly more fruitful and fascinating methods each time.

When examining the behaviors of the revenants, the animal kingdom was always the first place to draw comparisons. At most, revenant intelligence and behaviors resembled those from mammals. For instance, their methods of hunting and cornering pray were similar to dolphins' and could use tools and strategy like primates. They even attacked like large canines or big predatory cats.

But at the end of the day, there was always one blatant elephant in the room. The one truth scientists didn't like to talk about. The truth that drew the obvious relationship between revenant intelligence and humans. It was no secret the revenant creatures were once human beings, but for one reason or the other, it was something of a taboo among the staff. They didn't like to think of revenants as creatures that could think and plan or hold grudges. But the research they had conducted was definitive. Some arenas had come installed with electric lights, but the revenants would sometimes find a way to destroy the lights or cut the power to gain an advantage on the inmates. When Oracle scientists initially discovered this, it kept everyone on edge for weeks. Everyone began to assume the worst. If even one of the variant specimens escaped the arenas, it would come for them next.

Not to mention that revenants had a way of communicating with one another, and in their own language, SpecterSpeak. Yorkshire's team had worked for almost decade now trying to decipher it. He was always proud to admit there was substantial progress in deciphering it, but the fact they could speak at all wasn't much of a comfort.

All this research paled in comparison to the one variant that had eluded them all these years. The Time Riders were the unique variant that Yorkshire and the entire corporation had the most interest in. They were mostly human but had the ageless factor. Neither one of them had shown any interest in aiding the research because of the nature of Oracle Incorporated. He didn't blame them.

"How did it even make its way underground, anyway?" Aubrey asked.

"It used the main service tunnel, and carved its way through the service door, and made its way down here."

"It knew how to get down here?"

"Yes."

"But... how? The variants are clever, but not *that* clever."

"This one has shown exponentially more intelligence compared to the others. It's a unique specimen to say the least, it's making me wonder."

"Wonder about what?"

Yorkshire looked over at his assistant. "The variants have a matriarch. The Progenitress, to be exact. She's the head of the spear. Revenants always act as part of a hive mind, with her as the lead."

"And?"

"Well, look at the way this revenant looks," Yorkshire said waving his hand over the creature's body. "The resin isn't a blotchy mess like molders, you can see muscles and veins. But this is completely solid. The creature looks like it could be displayed as a work by Michelangelo."

Aubrey looked confused. "Are you saying it was... sculpted?"

"Created. Diligently, methodically. No other variant looks like this on their own. Aside from the integrity of the mold, the musculature here is purely aesthetic."

"Are you saying the Progenitress created this?"

"Yes. I am. Like an artist."

"With respect, Doctor, that is simply not possible. Evolution, environmental conditions, and genetics determine what organisms even look like. What you're saying would be the result of something like creationism. Implying this here would say that this variant is the result of something not scientific, but supernatural."

Yorkshire looked over one last time. "This research is anything but natural. If there's anything I've learned, it's how little we know about what is really out there."

"Hmm?"

Yorkshire and Aubrey turned to their left and saw a young girl with messy red hair and beaming blue eyes slightly knelt over waving to the two of them.

"Could I bother you for your attention?" the girl asked.

Yorkshire took one good look at her before recognizing her. "Charlotte Rowes?"

"Guess again Barty," she said grinning.

"Wait...The Progenitress?"

The girl groaned with annoyance. "I wouldn't mind killing the ingrate that named me something so convoluted."

"It is you!" Yorkshire yelled. "What do you want?"

"I want my child back," he Progenitress said sternly.

"Child?"

The revenant behind them began to stir and thrash its limbs; it grabbed one of the scientists and threw him forcefully in the air and into a wall. Other scientists fled back, some screamed. The variant began to roar and sputter fire sporadically. It was still in too much pain to move. The operators on standby all raised their weapons, ready to fire.

"Enough!" the Progenitress shrieked unnaturally loud. The operators all stood in place not moving a muscle. "If one more of you worms dare hurt him any further, I will have you all gutted!"

She ran over beside the creature's head and stroked it with her small hand, shushing softly as she did so. The creature immediately went still and quiet, drawing slow, heavy breaths.

"It's okay, my sweet, I'm back, I'm here now." she said softly. The Apex started to make a noise akin to a purr. The Progenitress examined its body gasped in horror at the sight of the scorch marks on its body.

"How did you do this? How did you hurt him?!" she yelled.

Everyone in the room looked at one another, but nobody said anything.

"Tell me!" she yelled again, throwing out her hand. Aubrey got lifted from the ground and into the air, an ear-splitting scream escaping her mouth.

The words caught in Yorkshire's mouth. He was in shock from it all. The girl now being the matriarch, the sudden awakening, the new behavior shown by this Apex variant, and Aubrey being lifted into the air was too much to process.

"Tell me how you did this!" the Progenitress yelled, throwing her hand down, Aubrey slammed into the floor landing on her arm, her bones could be heard breaking. The painful scream she cried out left Yorkshire feeling horrified.

The Progenitress scanned her head around quickly, waving her other hand around trying to coax an answer. "How...." she threw her hand upwards, and Aubrey went with. "Did..." she moved her hand right, and Aubrey slammed into a wall. "You..." Aubrey went flying into another wall. "Hurt..." Then another. "Him?!" Then back down to the floor. Aubrey wailed a mournful combination of weeping and pained screams.

"A weapon!" Yorkshire yelled. The Progenitress craned her head over in his direction.

"What kind of a weapon?" She asked.

"ZL23 spark rifles! A prototype of my creation."

The Progenitress's face showed signs of confusion. "Is that so? I didn't think that was going to happen. I must be more careful," she said to herself

Yorkshire had no idea what she was talking about, so all he did was stay where he was still as a statue. Aubrey remained weeping on the floor.

"Where are these weapons now?" the Progenitress asked.

"They should have been here by now."

Yorkshire noticed two scientists in the back with familiar black rifle cases lingering in the back of the room. The Progenitress noticed them as well. With one swift movement, the boxes flew out of her hands and landed at her feet with a handful of loud thuds.

"Can you stand sweetie?" the Progenitress asked, whipping her head over to the Apex. The revenant sat up and rose from the table weakly, gradually recovering as it did so. Once it stood up, its massive height and width dwarfed the small size of the Progenitress. The Apex noticed the weapon cases on the ground and stomped on them with visible anger, smashing them into a pile of useless salvage.

The Progenitress looked down at the remains of them and giggled. "Good riddance, good to see you have your strength back, we have work to do. Barty?"

Yorkshire focused and straightened immediately. "Yes?"

"Where is Esther Marigold?'"

Yorkshire's throat felt constricted, and his limbs began to shake.

"Upstairs… emergency meeting," he said shakily.

The Progenitress put her hands behind her back and walked forward, the Apex close behind.

"Lead the way, Doctor."

CHAPTER 37

Partnership

Marigold:

Esther Marigold had called another emergency meeting
late into the night at Oracle Tower. All four lieutenants
were seated in front of her at the large table. The room was
lit up with yellowish artificial lights. The dark night outside and
bright city lights within gave a calm ambience to everything inside,
even though the subject matter and inner turmoil among them
would mask that completely.

Artemis had a large bandage on her arm and was recovering
from burns she suffered from the Apex variants attack. Spartan
was extremely bruised and medicated on painkillers, which left
him in a lethargic, half-focused state. Quake was recovering from
an injury that Marigold had no desire to even think about. Legion
was the only one not injured in any way, but regardless, a Legion
deprived of sleep like this was not a state they were found to be the
most cooperative.

Alongside Marigold still recovering from her own injuries, this
painted a frustrating picture for her. All this talent, all these
professionals, and nothing to show for it. Even Quake didn't seem
to make much of a difference. Her anger was so potent she
couldn't even bring herself to yell or emote at all. All she could do
was speak quietly, the inner rage burning like a slow flame.

"Can someone here please tell me what happened?" she asked.

The lieutenants looked at one another, waiting to see who was brave enough to speak up.

"The Apex," Artemis said finally. "It breached the base, hunting the Time Rider."

"It attacked," Spartan said afterwards. "We took it down, but the kid slipped out while we were busy fighting it."

"So, you are telling me we lost not one, but two Time Riders this week?" Marigold snapped.

"Yes," Quake spoke up. "The blame falls on me, I was unable to stop him."

"And none of us were at the Eads bridge incident," Spartan added.

"You are all worthless!" Klara yelled. Everyone in the room stared at her.

Legions mask changed over to Annike's color. "Klara, not now."

"You can't tell me what to do anymore! Shut up Annike!"

Now it changed to red. "Enough child, your rage is misguided!"

"You wanted this! You wanted me to be like this! You don't get to say anything!"

"Enough!" Marigold yelled, slamming her good fist on the table repeatedly. "I had Yorkshire collect the Apex variant's body. He'll be doing his work in the meantime. What we need to focus on right now is the Time Riders! If Markus Daniels has learned how to combat us alongside the Ryder boy, we are at a significant disadvantage! You couldn't even manage one, how the hell are we going to best them now? Huh! I'm all ears!"

Before anyone answered, the lights in the room changed and an alarm began to blare. Everyone got up in the room with a start. The lieutenants all began muttering amongst themselves, trying to make sense of the situation. Before they could, the door to the room flung open and Yorkshire flew into the room with a yell. He slid on the table and fell off the other end landing at Marigold's feet.

"What the...!" Marigold exclaimed.

She lifted her eyes to the doorway and saw the Apex leaning in, its large body taking up the doorway, Marigold felt frozen where she stood. It moved aside and someone walked into the room: a small girl wearing jeans, sneakers, and a plaid shirt. Alongside her reddish hair, she had the glowing eyes of a revenant and was grinning ear to ear.

"Hello, Esther," she said brightly

This girl felt familiar to Marigold, then she remembered why. This was Charlotte Rowes, the girl that was detained here at Oracle tower three months ago. That hair and freckled face was a dead giveaway. But the mannerisms on display here were completely different, showing the actions of someone else. She had an unnatural air about her. The eyes, that damned smile, Marigold knew who this was. Somehow, someway, this girl was now the Progenitress.

"What? How are you here?!" Marigold yelled.

"Very long story love, but I'm here now," the Progenitress said walking into the room. The large revenant followed in behind and stood up straight once it could.

"What is the meaning of this? Why are you in the body of that girl?" Marigold exclaimed.

"Irrelevant detail. Let's just say that Nathan Ryder made a very poor choice," the Progenitress answered, walking right up to Marigold with her arms open wide. "Rejoice! We are here to help you. We share a common goal."

"The last time I trusted you, I was almost killed by you!"

The girl in front of her just chuckled. "Sorry about that. I needed you to come here, but some time away and one little breach helped me reach that goal. And now *you* need me."

"Need you? What do you have to offer that would make me even remotely consider collaborating with you?"

The Apex grew angry and opened its mouth wide, preparing to engulf the whole room in fire. All the lieutenants got up with a sudden start and began to yell and swear.

"It's okay, my sweet, they understand now," the Progenitress said stroking the Apex's leg. The creature closed its mouth and breathed softly. "Well, for one thing. If you want to keep your lives and not turn to charcoal, it would be wise to heed my request. Plus, you said it yourself, you couldn't even stop one, so how could you ever hope to stop two?"

Everyone in the room looked around at one another. No one had anything to say.

"Perhaps if we joined together, we would have results! The way you cooperated with Nathan Ryder to stop me was certainly effective."

"Excuse me?" Marigold asked.

"Oh. They haven't told you? They worked with him, closed the gate, and ruined my pristine vessel!" The Progenitress whined.

Marigold eyed all her lieutenants with a venomous gaze. "When were any of you going to tell me about this?"

"Leave them be, they did what they had to in order to survive. There's something worth admiring in that. There's strength in such actions. Water under the bridge! As they say."

Legion shot to their feet. "No deal! No deal! You get nothing hexe!"

"Quiet, Klara!" Fritz snapped.

"Hush!" Annike hissed.

Even with lit-up eyes, the Progenitress clearly looked surprised. "It's Klara, isn't it?" she asked. "My, my, aren't you an interesting specimen? Your delusion is a powerful thing. Funny to see your more innocent side lashing out like this. All these names, these versions of yourself you conjured. The human brain is truly a remarkable thing, isn't it? What it will do to protect itself from its most painful memories, what it will bury, what it will try to forget. You would know this more than anyone wouldn't you, Ava?"

Legion drew a blade angrily and pointed it at the Progenitress. "Don't you say that name. Don't you say that name! Don't say that name!"

Legion rushed forward across the table with the blade aimed towards the Progenitress, immediately protecting her, the Apex grabbed them and slammed them into the wall. Legion's mask began to malfunction and cycle through colors and personalities very quickly, leaving all four of them dazed.

"Tsk-tsk. Such aggression. You are certainly an apple that didn't fall far from the tree," The Progenitress said." Legion just whimpered while being pinned to the wall. "This is why you treat your children with love. Otherwise, they could turn into this."

"What are you proposing?" Marigold asked, desperate for some clarity.

"Like I said, Esther, we share the same goal. I want the Time Riders."

"And do you have any plans as to how we can reach that goal?"

Spartan asked.

"It is truly an odd thing. No matter what either one of us has done, the Time Riders still live. Even my treasured Apex here, has not seen victory over them, not even Markus Daniels. Especially him."

"What's special about him?" Artemis asked,

"Much," the Progenitress said. "His presence here has the potential to change everything."

"That street rat?" Marigold asked in disbelief. "What could he possibly change?"

"There is a play here. The Markus Daniels of then knew what I speak of. Nathan Ryder arrived in your future, where he remained until they found a way to return him here. The Markus Daniels that he knew took steps to make sure his former self would be in the position he is in now. He wanted to change things."

"Change what? Are you saying this boy traveled through time? That is not possible!" Quake said.

"There is little that is not possible in my home. You may not believe me now, but you most certainly will. It is vital we succeed. If there is anything your history as a species has shown, it's that it only takes one person to change all of history." Marigold and all the lieutenants stole gazes at one another. "You fear me now, hate me for what I am. I will not hide that my goals and intentions lie with my family and myself, that is the truth. But listen carefully. I am not the only one out there seeking control. I am in danger. There is something within my home. Within the very essence of time lies something far more terrible and dangerous than even me, and I plan on stopping it. But first, the Time Riders must die on my terms."

Everyone stared at one another again, this new info passing around like a disease, infecting each one with uncertainty and foreign fear.

The Progenitress just smiled and let out an airy sigh. "But worry not, I urge you all to rest. We will have a lot of work to do tomorrow. As for me, I'm going to need lodgings of my own and new clothing. What I have now is far too male. And this hair, truly atrocious! Esther? I trust you will provide me what I need?"

Marigold straightened herself and swallowed deeply. "Yes, it will be done."

"Good," the Progenitress said. "This partnership? I have good faith this will work out just fine."

CHAPTER 38

Project Siren

Markus:

Ryder was not in a good way back at the undercroft. In an ironic turn of events Ryder had trashed everything around the basement that he could. Spencer sat in his office chair letting him vent, while Markus moved around doing everything he could to not get caught in the crossfire.

"Yo can you calm down just a tad!? Wrecking the joint ain't gonna get us anywhere!" Markus yelled. Ryder just flipped the sofa in response with a pent-up yell.

"Aw geez... you got anything Spencer?" Markus asked.

"Do I got anything?" Spencer repeated. "You think I anticipated something like this?"

"I don't know but we gotta do something! We can't just let Charlotte get away from us like this!" Ryder let out a yell and threw a chair across the room, it slammed into the wall and came back down to the floor.

"What can we do? She picked Charlotte for a reason, she's using her like a damn meat shield, she knows we wouldn't dare lay a finger on her while she's driving her around like that."

"Well, we gotta get rid of her!" Markus proclaimed.

"How? You know something we don't Markus?"

"No, but there's gotta be something they don't like, something that'll make them jump ship."

"This isn't some run of the mill revvie, this is the Progenitress! The big kahuna, the tip of the iceberg. I'm not sure she can be dispelled or killed at all!"

Ryder stopped throwing things around for a moment and just dropped down and sat at the refrigerator holding his head in his hands.

"Nate, you've fought them more than anyone else, c'mon man there's gotta be something we can do. Fire? Electricity? Bad music? C'mon there's gotta be something that shakes em' up!"

Ryder lifted his head, his eyes burning a deep glow. "I...." he started. "She might be....gone...gone for good."

"Hey no, none of that crap! We're gonna get her back!"

"Markus you don't understand. There's an angle here, something you don't know. Taking her was more than just getting back at me."

Markus threw up his hands in frustration and disbelief. "You know what's going on? You have an idea what's going on and you are just sitting on it!? Are you for real Nate!"

"Like I said, it is dangerous, I was told--"

"Screw that!" Markus exclaimed. "Things are clearly not the same anyway, I was the one risk, right? Me being here is probably what caused this in the first place!" Ryder just looked down quietly. "C'mon man, show me the money here Nate. What did she see in you? I thought you were a fighter, someone strong, cause the guy I'm looking at right now is a friggin' pussy!"

"Shut up!" Ryder got to his feet quickly in a moment of fury and started to push Markus, Markus himself pushed back. Ryder gritted his teeth looking incredibly vicious. Spencer got up to step in, but Markus held his hand out to stop him.

"There you go Nate! Get a little angry! They took Charlotte man, your inamorata! So, what are you going to do about it? Cry about it or go knock some heads until you get your gal back?"

Ryder began to pant until he processed what he said, afterwards he dropped his hands and stepped back. "You're right, I'm not stopping till she's safe."

"Atta boy," Markus said clapping Ryder on the shoulder. "So, do you have any ideas here? Surely we can use something to our advantage?"

Ryder rubbed the back of his head, diligently thinking.

"Deterrent. Deterrent. I mean back there in the war...I don't know....maybe..."

"What?" Markus asked.

"Hey Spencer, does the term siren grenade mean anything to you?" Ryder asked.

Spencer's eyes lit up. "Did you say siren grenade? How do you even know about that?"

"I heard about it back in the war, a bunch of guys were whining about it, wished they had one, made a full-blown competition out of trying to make one, but they never could. Didn't have the resources, I heard the schematics, and conceptual notes were destroyed though, is that still the case?"

"Did you say war?" Markus asked.

"It shouldn't be," Spencer said disregarding Markus's question. "Project Siren was one of my shelved projects, it never got off the ground. Research should have been kept and stored in case further opportunity presented itself. Did these guys know what they were talking about? The concept of the grenade was hypothetical, nothing was concrete. Any talk about dramatic changes in frequency, sound waves. Anything like that?" Spencer asked.

"You don't know the half of it, they rigged an entire alarm system to act as a deterrent if the revvies ever got too close. I didn't fare too good when that thing was on, but it worked. They really wanted that effect to be portable, that's why so much time was given trying to make the grenade."

"So high pitched frequency does have an effect on them," Spencer said.

"You bet it does." Ryder said. "Freakin' sucks"

"What even is this grenade? I like the sound of it," Markus asked.

"I started it with the idea of making something similar to a flashbang grenade, but it ended up being more of a portable generator as opposed to a traditional hand thrown explosive," Spencer explained. "The idea is that you plop this thing down and it gives off consistent pulsating sound waves, high pitched in frequency. Suppose to scare off or immobilize revenants in their entirety. We never had a chance to perform proper experimentation with the correlation between sound and the revenants, but if Ry is telling the truth, it's legit."

"It is," Ryder followed up.

"How will this thing work on the Projenitrack or whatever?" Markus asked.

"These sound waves really rock your grill," Ryder explained. "I couldn't even move once it started, I'm thinking it would do the same thing to her."

"And?"

"And… if she can't move to get away, she might be forced to jump ship, you see where I'm going with this?"

All three of them were struck with a sudden epiphany. "Okay, that's a lead!" Spencer said brightly. "It's something. Let's run with it."

"Sounds pretty spunky to me. How about you Nate?" Markus said

Ryder looked over, his eyes emanated hope. "Yes, sounds spunky."

Markus smiled a mischievous grin.

"Do we have a plan Spence?" Ryder asked.

"You know me, I'm going to go database surfing, and find my file. Shelved projects are a trainwreck of code, but I will find it. You two need to rest, as much as you can. No matter how we cut this, getting that file is gonna get dangerous. You all need to stay sharp."

"I dunno if I'm ever gonna sleep again," Markus said.

"I feel that," Ryder followed up.

Spencer looked at the two Time Riders, his face turned authoritative. "Charlotte's life is in your hands' boys, maybe even more lives than we know. You want to get her back? Dig deep and do what you need to make sure you can do so. Get some rest. Tomorrow we are going to strike back, and we are going to strike back hard. Does that sound like a plan?"

"Yes," Ryder and Markus said simultaneously.

"Good, cause we're going to make the Progenitress regret showing her face around us again, and I'll see to it that she doesn't even think about doing so again."

CHAPTER 39

Takeover

Marigold:

As far as Marigold was concerned, the Progenitress outwore her welcome the moment she arrived at the door. For the rest of the night, she was reduced to acting as the Progenitress's chaperone. After the meeting, she immediately forced Marigold to close the tower and send a majority of the workers and engineers home for an unspecified leave of absence. Considering the number of employees on the payroll ranked in the thousands, it was a troublesome matter, to put it lightly. Many demanded answers and acknowledgement that Marigold simply couldn't give. Only personnel with knowledge of the higher-level clearance had access to information on research into dimension Alpha-2 and the revenants that lived within.

The Progenitress's second order was to release all captured revenant specimens within the underground base, even the aggressive variants. On her word, Marigold gave the order on the Progenitress's word that her "children" would not harm any personnel. The moment they humored her two knights gored and killed one of the higher-ranking operators within Spartan's ranks. When confronted about this the Progenitress just waved it off casually, apologizing for what she said was a minor fit from her offspring.

Thirdly, the Progenitress demanded an assortment of dark

dresses and beauty products for her own personal use. In a moment of utmost absurdity, PMC operators were the ones sent to retrieve these items out in the city. When they returned the Progenitress scooped up what she wanted and spent close to an hour working on her face and hair in the ladies' restroom. Once she came out Marigold immediately saw how she had changed herself. Her hair was now straight and shiny, as opposed to the relaxed, messier hair from before. She had dyed her hair midnight black, its artificial color standing out to the experienced eye. Makeup had also been applied expertly on her face, the freckles completely covered up and lip gloss and eye shadow, adding a healthy glow to her lips and eyes.

When presented with the clothing, she ran through them like a picky toddler, trying on many expensive dresses and being obnoxiously displeased with most of them. After two and a half more agonizing hours she had finally settled on a unique black party dress.

It was tailored in an exquisitely elegant style. Strapless, and colored black with slick silk covering her body up to her chest. The rest of her torso and arms were adorned with black mesh. By the time she had finished her makeover, she no longer resembled Charlotte Rowes in the slightest. She looked more akin to her former self, only smaller.

Marigold and the Progenitress were, at the moment, in the CEO office on the highest floor of Oracle Tower. The Progenitress was now standing in front of a mirror, twirling in her new dress and enjoying her new look, giggling like a schoolgirl. Marigold stood still near the desk, quietly livid. This all felt like the most unfunny joke in the world to her. When Marigold first met the Progenitress she had been like a god, coming to her in this same office and offering her a way out—a way to cheat death. She had felt powerful, awe-inspiring. And now she acted like a privileged bimbo.

It was like taking the body of an adolescent, she was obligated to act like one as well. The Progenitress just kept spinning and spinning with enthusiasm that made Marigold want to puke.

"I feel so light!" the Progenitress said excitedly with a giggle. "I feel like the wind could sweep me off my feet and make me fly away like a kite!"

"Do we have a plan on what to do about the Time Riders?" Marigold asked flatly.

The Progenitress turned around, her childlike attitude turning stone cold. "Don't get impatient with me Esther. We are doing this on my time."

"Of course," Marigold said, course-correcting.

The Progenitress's right arm began to shake rapidly out of nowhere, which made her stop dancing. She looked at the limb, confused, and began holding it with her left hand to stop it from moving. She let go of it after a while, and the right arm stopped moving.

She blew through her teeth. "Defunct meat puppet..." she growled. With a huff she began moving and walked across Marigold's office and stared out the window overlooking the city, the bright lights of nearby buildings shining pleasantly in view.

"Interesting place you call home, Esther. The world here sleeps. Nothing rests in my home, everything moves, nothing stops."

"In Alpha-2?"

The girl in front of her placed her hands behind her back and looked at Marigold from the side, one glowing blue eye beaming her down. "Yes, Alpha-2, as you call it. Here it's so quiet... too quiet. Your world is... dead."

"I can assure you; it is very alive," Marigold said.

The Progenitress scoffed rudely. "You don't even know what alive means. None of you do. Most of you don't even know who you are anymore, can't even find a reason to live."

"I'm in no rush to meet *my* demise," Marigold said. "That's why I need your blasted ageless factor."

"That's still something you desire, don't you? Our immortality. You wish to null death entirely, I don't blame you. You have something many lack, self-preservation, a desire to adhere to life. What's your reason to live Esther?"

"My own desires are inconsequential. The applications of such a formula could change the landscape of the very—"

"You can lie to me all you want Esther," the Progenitress interrupted. "But don't lie to yourself. Those are the most dangerous kinds of lies. This was never about your corporation or the grandeur of greater good. It's always been about you trying to defeat the inevitable. And you gave up everything to do so. For me to stand here, right here, right now?"

"Perhaps."

"Your own reputation gone, your joy ripped from your heart, the man you love driven away. Such a steep price to just survive. It's a funny thing, isn't it? Some would say the strongest emotion is fear. If one were to ask me, the strongest emotion is love, and it is by far the most treacherous. Fear will keep you away from the things that want to hurt you, but love will have you running right towards them. You and I have learned this lesson well."

Being reminded of her former fiancé felt like a sucker punch. Marigold had to bite her tongue in order not to scream.

"How is your illness? Still growing nice and slow?" the Progenitress asked, poking the side of her face with one of her index fingers. "It's a shame what's it's done to your face, it used to be so pretty. But I suppose that'll be the least of your problems once it wiggles through your skull," she said, prodding her temple with a middle finger.

Marigold became uncomfortably self-conscious of the necrotic boil on her face. She chose not to humor the Progenitress's question about it. "Do we have a plan on what to do with the Time Riders? What are our priorities?" she asked, desperate to change the subject.

"It is vital that both of them are found. They are dangerous, especially Nathan Ryder," The Progenitress said.

"Why him specifically?"

"He is the most dangerous in many ways, and he will be the hardest to take down. He might seem good and soft on the outside, but he hides a violent beast within. You mustn't underestimate him as you've done before. He limits himself with his flimsy excuse of righteousness, but if pushed to the edge he will forsake them. We don't want him to remain long enough to do so. Otherwise, your life may be the one that is taken."

Marigold didn't understand this. "The original Time Rider has never taken the life of one of my operators before. Sometimes he will inflict devastating and crippling injuries, but there have been no fatalities, not from him. The only deaths came from *your* revenants."

"Believe me, Esther, death is never far from Nathan Ryder."

Marigold didn't understand this either, but she had no desire to linger on the topic. "And Markus Daniels?"

The Progenitress raised her closed hand to her chin in contemplation, a small smile etched on her lips. "He's a rogue, but a cunning warrior. When it comes to Daniels, I have a special interest in him. When the opportunity presents itself, I'll handle him, offering him something he can't refuse."

"And what would that be?"

The Progenitress smiled sinisterly. "Me."

"Pardon?"

"Markus Daniels has always had a unique desire for females. It's almost an obsession, like all self-indulgence can be. It's a favored tool of mine for countless years, I've used these desires to control even the mightiest men. It's magic, there is nothing like a soft caress or a tender kiss to bring a young man to his knees. When I work my act, they can't control themselves. Then they become mine to do with as I please."

"You're going to… seduce him?"

"Mere smoke and mirrors my dear Esther, He'll seek me, but only find death or submission, as many before him have fallen prey to. And this girl I'm wearing…" the Progenitress started, looking at her hand. "This Charlotte Rowes, she is important to Nathan Ryder, it's why I chose her, but she is also important to Markus Daniels as well. Neither of them will dare to hurt me again."

Marigold was strangely indifferent to the idea. It seemed as good a plan as any. She knew how men were, how hungry they could be. It helped that she seemed to know what she was doing. If she were anyone else Marigold would have offered her a job, but she would settle for living at the moment. Though there was an ambitious part of her that wanted to play this in her favor, she wasn't seeking to be brash. Hopefully if she played her cards right, she would finally gain access to the ageless factor, finally beat her disease and market it for substantial profit. Being this close to the one that could give it to her made her excited, yet afraid.

Marigold had let everything go trying to find the ageless factor. It all meant something, it had too. Too much had been lost to go without justification. Too much of her limited time had been wasted. Marigold wouldn't let this disease kill her. If the price was the blood of two young boys that were never going to age anyway, so be it. It may as well have been a handful of change being asked of her.

"One last thing Esther,"

"Yes?" Marigold responded.

"I need you to drag out that Poindexter of yours when he wakes up. Have him look into Project Siren. It should be among your unused projects."

"What do you need with it?"

"It's a weapon, something that can be used against me. I want it destroyed. The prototype, the files, all of it."

"How do you even... surely it's safe here in the tower."

"Not likely. The last time Charlotte Rowes was here a Time Rider broke down the door in less than five hours. They are not intimidated by this place, and if they learn about it like I know they are going to, they will seek it out. Spencer Carter is a master at siphoning info out of you. Not much of a surprise, considering he designed your database."

"How do you know about it? Project Siren?"

The Progenitress stared out the window again into the dark city, Marigold could see the reflection of her eyes on the glass. "I need you to understand something Esther. What I am, my very being, is so much more than you can believe. I know the beginning, and I know the end. I know the days you were all born, and the days you will die. But nothing is set in stone; time is a fluid, ever-changing thing. One thing moved in any particular way can change the very course of your world. It could be the death of someone, or something as small as a butterfly flapping its wings. I would know. It happens every time I create one of my children. I see all of time. But that doesn't mean I can predict the future, I can see possibilities and outcomes, but they change rapidly. In the future one minute we succeed, the other we don't. And every time I see failure; I see that device."

"And what's the future now?"

The Progenitress let out a laugh. "Worry not. We are well on our way, but that could change. We must be careful. But I'm hopeful. I've played this game plenty of times before. And let me tell you, I'm *very* good at it."

Hearing this sent an uncomfortable chill down Marigold's spine. Most of this girl's babble at this point felt like the ramblings of a child, but when she spoke like this the sinister thing she really was made itself known.

The Progenitress yawned loudly and patted her mouth, the night meeting her where she stood. "Goodness. Tiredness, I haven't felt this in years. It's like I'm floating," she said hazily. "I will need to retire. I will be taking your personal quarters for the night, any objections?"

"None," Marigold responded.

"Good, pleasant dreams." The Progenitress said through another yawn heading for the side door in Marigold's office and closing the door behind her.

Project Siren? Marigold had completely forgotten about that. It was something Spencer Carter worked on years ago but never could find the time for experimentation. He described the device as being designed for incapacitation, not elimination. As a result, there was no interest in the device under an Oracle being headed by her.

The Progenitress mentioned it was something that could harm her, a weapon. Marigold's mind began swirling with ideas. She was not happy playing subsidiary to this operation. She imagined using this weapon to make the revenant mother submit to her authority, passing the chain of command back to her, making her guest give up the ageless factor by force.

Marigold walked outside the office and pulled the handheld radio on her belt, bringing it to her ear, and taking note to keep her voice down.

"Yorkshire," she whispered.

No response.

"Yorkshire!" she snapped.

Sudden shuffling came through on the line. "What—yes? Yes! Yes, Ms. Marigold?" Yorkshire said, startled.

"Have you recovered?" Marigold responded.

"Barely, I'm still in the infirmary. Is that girl gone?"

"No, she's still here. I need you to collect a file and prototype for me."

"What?" Yorkshire said quickly clearing his throat. "With respect Ms. Marigold, I don't believe I can do so safely if she is still here. Perhaps Spartan, or maybe Quake?"

"She won't harm you. She requested the project personally."

"Really? What is going on?"

"Project Siren, I need it as soon as possible, no questions."

"Project Siren? We shelved that fifteen years ago. Why do you…"

"No questions!" Marigold hissed.

Yorkshire huffed into the radio. "I will collect Project Siren, Ms. Marigold."

"Good, and one last thing?"

"Yes, Ms. Marigold?"

"I need you to wake Spartan and Artemis, tell them to meet me early tomorrow morning in the armory. I have a job for them, and them only. And if you encounter the girl, it is imperative you remain quiet about it."

"What are you planning, miss?"

"Putting an ace up our sleeve Yorkshire, Putting an ace up our sleeve."

CHAPTER 40

The Timeless Knight and the
Mistress of the Damned

Ryder:

It was war for Ryder to try to fall asleep that night, his **stress** and worry made it difficult to even sit still. He was desperate, hoping and praying sleep would meet him where he was. Hours and minutes passed, each with countless tosses and turns. He kept seeing Charlotte every time he closed his eyes, her eyes burning blue, the firearm pressed against her head, one idle thought away from ending her life right there in the undercroft. His mind felt like it was unraveling, his soul coming undone. He struggled and struggled until what he desired overtook him when he least expected it.

He found himself within a dream, an eerie yet familiar haze. He gazed around examining where he was. He now stood on a soft grassy median with playground equipment around the area, including a large swing set. Ryder immediately recognized it as the playground in front of Charlotte's apartment, the place where they had first met. But within the dream it felt wrong, artificial, inauthentic, cobbled together by memories of old and new. The median was surrounded by a sheer wall of flowing blue, leading out to a limitless abyss. The only thing that existed here was the playground.

"Hello Nathan."

Ryder spun around and saw Charlotte sitting on one of the swings, her hands on the chains—no, not Charlotte. The Progenitress. The wretch wearing her skin. She sat there calmly, her eyes glowing steadily like always. She was now clothed in a sort of black party dress, her hair now as dark as a void. Seeing her like this leaked uncanniness, it was all wrong. Ryder shifted his gaze away from her. The anger within him made it feel like he was going to explode. All there was within his mind was the desire to yell at her till his lungs collapsed. To scream every obscenity he knew until his lungs went empty. But he didn't move, his lips didn't utter anything on his mind. He could only ask one question.

"What do you want?"

The Progenitress sat up from the swing and began slowly walking towards him. His gaze remained away from her.

"I know you're angry but can you a least look at me?" she said.

"No," Ryder growled.

"Don't make me force you."

Ryder defiantly stayed in place. The Progenitress sighed and lifted a finger, and Ryder's head moved against his will until his eyes were level with hers. Being this close to her was agonizing. He could still make out Charlotte's face beneath all the fluff she put on it, its bittersweet nature was sickening.

The Progenitress smiled with menace. "That's better. It is difficult to conversate with someone who isn't even looking at me. Wouldn't you agree?"

"I have nothing to conversate with you."

"Now, that's just not true. You have questions, I know you do."

"Nothing I couldn't live without."

"Don't be like that, ask away."

Ryder remained silent. Nothing left his lips.

"Ask," the Progenitress demanded hotly.

Ryder was in no mood for games, but he wasn't left with much choice. "Why her?"

Her eyes lit up as she walked back in forth in front of him. She let Ryder move his head freely again. "Very good question. You know most of the answer, but there were many reasons. Firstly, I know you wouldn't live with yourself if you ever hurt this little rascal you like so much, and frankly, it serves you right for what you did. But mostly..." She started patting her stomach. "For safe keeping."

"Safe keeping?"

"Don't forget Nathan, I know how this story ends, for both of us."

"Then you know it doesn't end well for you."

"Things can change," she said quickly. "And that's exactly what I'm going to do."

"What are you planning?"

The Progenitress readjusted herself where she stood. "I want the same thing you do, I want to stop it, that dreadful future we both saw. It has to be stopped. Things have to happen to reach that outcome." The Progenitress just stared back plainly. "You know what I speak of."

Ryder looked down, the revelation within him eating away at him like a venom. "Yeah, I do."

"Then why haven't you done anything about it?"

Ryder chose not to say anything.

The Progenitress blew through her teeth spitefully. "You're afraid to do it."

"I am, but if you left Charlotte out of this, I would have done so happily," Ryder said. "You let her go; I'll give you what you want. Easy."

"I can't do that, Nathan."

"Why not?! Leave your little grudge with us, leave her out of it!"

"You had every chance to leave her out of it! If you'd joined me this never would have come to pass!"

"You're not going to pin this on me! If I did that, the same future would have happened, maybe worse!"

"No! No, it wouldn't have! I wanted beauty, not destruction. That hellscape will be your own doing boy! You're the one who will bring it to life! All that pain and death, it will all be you!"

Ryder looked away fuming, it became difficult to maintain his composure. "No, it won't. I won't let it. I will change it. My fate is my choice."

The Progenitress didn't say a word. She started walking slowly towards him, her small footsteps leading behind him. She lifted her hand and placed it on his shoulder. The gesture felt strangely warm, comforting even. Each word that came next made Ryder's spine shiver.

"Time knows no master. Even something like me has no dominion over it. Some things can change. But this fate you wish to stop, it is almost a certainty, an inevitability. There is only one way to stop it for good. There is only one way to stop *him*. Deep down, you know this."

"That doesn't mean I'm not going to try. There's always another way."

"Not this time Nathan. Not this time."

Ryder felt uneasy, not from what she said, but what he knew. He should have been angry, furious, but he couldn't help but feel a strong camaraderie with her. They were both on the same lifeboat in treacherous waters.

He could feel her power—it was a vibrant, ancient thing— he could feel something different, too, something he couldn't understand. Regret? Fear? Hurt? It didn't matter. They were both trying to change this story, their story, by molding it into something else. Ryder had no plans of being second place.

"Can I ask you something?" Ryder asked.

"Yes," the Progenitress answered.

"What is your name? Your real name. Who are you? What are you?"

She held a lengthy pause; her unease could be felt in her grasp. "I've been named many names by many different people. Persephone, Lilith, Hel, The Progenitress… but my true name? If I ever had one, it's been long forgotten. As for what I am?" she stepped back away and faced him, her bright eyes stared right into him, precise and intimidating. "I am the kiss of death, every dark desire that leads humanity to the abyss with a smile."

Ryder's heart began to beat faster, fueled by a twisted cocktail of desire and fear. "You're a succubus, a demon."

The Progenitress lifted her hand and caressed the side of his face, its warmth bringing comfort and disgust simultaneously. She continued to stare, a curious yet loving gaze in her eyes. "I'm not a demon, I'm like you. I'm someone who chose to love." She walked away, taking her hand away from his face in the process. Ryder exhaled a breath he didn't even know he had been holding.

"Have you ever heard the saying; 'no parent should have to bury their child'?" she asked. "Well, I've buried plenty, far too many. And I'm not just talking about the ones you and Marigold's army have destroyed."

"What do you mean?" Ryder asked.

She craned her head over slowly, ignoring the question. "After all that has happened, you must think I hate normal human beings. But I really don't. Quite the contrary! Humans are so fascinating and loveable. If I'm being frank, they are simply delightful, mostly."

"Then why have you killed so many?" Ryder asked hotly.

"My goal is never to kill without reason," the Progenitress snapped. "Unlike you, I wish to preserve, not destroy."

Ryder looked back at her. She looked like she was close to crying. "Do you know if you can change it? Stop your death? Or is it just as inevitable as you say my story is?" he asked.

"I don't know…" the Progenitress whispered. She began to grip his shoulder tighter, and her arm trembled. Ryder hated this woman, this being, but something was changing. Within her words was a puzzle, a riddle to solve. A hidden testimony in her tone, a cry for help within her touch. All stemming from a lonely god with nothing left to her existence but monsters. If the circumstances were different, Ryder might have even felt pity.

She ended up letting go of his shoulder, then walked forward and lightly wrapped her arms around Ryder's abdomen. Then she placed her head on his shoulder gently, silently asking to be held. But Ryder went stiff, his own arms remaining at his sides.

"I… I don't want to be the villain," she said. "I never wanted this for you. If you had changed like the others, you would have known a bliss that you would have never been able to believe. But you didn't. You gained our gift, but you were still aware, just like me. You view your time with our gift as something akin to a millennia. But eventually, it will seem like that amount of time will pass as quickly as a breath. Then you'll truly see what it means to be something infinite in a finite world. You'll never be able to stop and smell the roses, because the roses will turn to ash in your hand before you can even take one whiff."

Ryder remained still like he was made of stone. "You chose this, you chose to be the villain. You don't smell the roses because you're too busy trampling them," he growled.

A hateful scowl formed on her face, and she pushed against

him, then backed away in a manic backstep, "I won't die. I won't let that happen! You're the one who needs to die! You!"

"Not happening."

"Why didn't you join me? We could have been together and safe! Choosing this worthless girl over me was the greatest mistake you've ever made!"

"No, you're the one who made the mistake! Charlotte Rowes is not worthless, someone like her is worth dying for. And you daring to harm her is the greatest mistake you've ever made; you will pay for threatening her."

"You're a fool! A stupid child! I won't let you win! I won't!"

"I'm a lot of things, but I'm not a fool. And I know you're not going to win this. Because we are not stopping until you lose."

The Progenitress gnashed her teeth, growling with anger. "Even after a decade you are still just a clueless young boy. Well, it's time to grow up."

She rushed forward and pushed Ryder hard into the endless blue void that surrounded the playground. He got swept up and taken up into it, swirling madly in a torrent of blue light. And then there was blackness, with slumber continuing as if the dream never happened.

CHAPTER 41

The Time Rider Returns

Ryder:

Ryder awoke the next morning to the sound of Spencer assaulting his door with a balled fist. "Ry! Ry! Get up!" he yelled.

Ryder struggled to wake up, frustrated by the racket. "What gives? Give me a sec!"

"I've got a hot lead on Project Siren!" Spencer said.

Ryder's door flung open, and he stepped out, his dark hair a forest of tangles. "Well, whatcha got?" he asked adamantly.

"Hold on," Spencer said. "Markus! Get up now!" Spencer yelled, running over to the sofa and grabbing Markus's sweatshirt.

"A yo! What did I do? Where's the fire?" Markus croaked out in confusion.

"Got a lead on Project Siren," Spencer told him. Markus sat up on the couch, just as eager to hear the news. "It's being moved—the files and prototype I cooked up years ago—by helicopter."

"A chopper? Where are they taking it?" Ryder asked.

"Likely offsite out of the city, most likely to their branch in Chicago; that's the closest."

"Chicago!" Markus yelled.

"Intercept?" Ryder asked. "Like while it's flying?"

"Preferably while it's on the ground, but that will be the only time we will see all of this outside the tower. If they get too far it will be gone for good. It's a small window but it's all we've got."

"Okay, noted. How's the A.M.R?"

Spencer smiled. "She's back, Ry. Haven't evaluated it yet, but everything is in the green on the diagnostic."

"Could it just sputter out again?" Ryder asked.

"That's always been a possibility, you know that. I'm not a miracle worker. But it's working now, and that's good news in and of itself considering the state it was in."

The last thing Ryder needed while doing this was for another critical malfunction to occur with the A.M.R, but he knew well enough there wasn't much legroom for complaints. "Guess that'll do."

Markus came over and joined the conversation. "So, what's the master plan here? We just roll up there, snag your little toy and dip?" he asked.

"Maybe not like that exactly, but yes. You intercept and steal the project before that whirlybird takes off," Spencer explained.

"Sounds too simple," Ryder said.

"Yes, there will likely be an escort—one of the lieutenants if it's considered a high enough priority. Well, let me rephrase that. It *is* a top priority."

"Great…" Ryder muttered. "Which one?"

"Only two would work, Legion and that new one would be no good in a helicopter."

"So, a ranged lieutenant."

"Yes."

"Artemis and Spartan?"

"Certainly, it's fifty-fifty. A coin flip. Could be either or."

Ryder let out an unamused exhale "Never cared much for gambling."

"Who cares? Whoever is there is gonna get a bona fide beatdown! They'll hand it over if they like all their bones unsnapped!" Markus exclaimed.

"We need to plan a little. Somehow this will go south, these things always do," Ryder said.

"While you're planning, Spooky Chick is wearin' Charlotte around like a catsuit! I'm done waiting around, let's do something about it!"

Hearing that delivered a fresh dose of anger into Ryder's mind.

"Screw it, we'll take the punches as they come, adapt on the fly. Like the old days."

"Now you're talkin' Nate."

Ryder quickly walked over to the washer and dryer in the undercroft and pulled out his black undersuit. It was partially stained by the copious amount of dirt that was on it but still had its dark color. The light armor on it was repaired, returning its look of sports or police gear.

"What time is this all going down?" Ryder asked.

"Eleven A.M," Spencer said. "That's when Project Siren leaves the tower."

"That's an hour away! Why are we even talking about this?" Markus asked.

"Why do you think I woke you two up?" Spencer retorted.

"Man, we got places to be! Get your hook-shooty thingy and let's get to work, Nate! C'mon!" Markus exclaimed madly, running over to the workstation and strapping into his skysurfer pack like a child about to go to an amusement park.

"He's not one to waste time," Ryder said taking this as a cue. He quickly ran back into his room and changed into his undersuit. After a minute he returned to the middle of the undercroft.

"You ready for this?" Spencer asked. "You haven't done proper field work in a while."

"I'm good. Might be a little rusty on the old A.M.R., but I'll get back to it in no time," Ryder said walking over to the rig.

The device stood upright with two leg and arm limbs open in an x shape and standing on its own. Ryder turned around and aligned his own limbs into the device's braces and they closed onto them and began to adjust automatically to his height.

"Try to keep your head about you, okay? Don't let that anger get to you, that's what she wants," Spencer said to him. The device went slack, and Ryder was able to move about freely, the limbs aligned with his own. A large storage box was suspended on his back housing metal cable.

"I know..." Ryder said quietly dipping his head. "I did this to her, didn't I? To Charlotte?"

"Ry, cut that out. Throwing a pity party for yourself every time something goes wrong isn't doing you any favors. You never intended this, you're not the one at fault."

"I don't know…"

"Knock it off," Spencer ordered harshly. "No more feeling sorry for yourself. Get your head in the game."

Even after everything Ryder had done, doubt sat in his brain like a parasite, siphoning what little pride and confidence remained. But Spencer was right, enough was enough. He'd been through too much and survived too long. There was no room left for pity. This wasn't about pride. It was about being strong enough to protect the ones he loved. That alone would be enough.

"Yeah, no more, I'm done. No more pity parties, just what needs to be done."

Spencer gave out a rare smile. "Atta boy."

"Nate!" Markus yelled at the top of the undercroft's staircase. "Let's go! Chicks to save and all y'know!"

"Coming!" Ryder replied, running to the staircase.

"Ryder!" Spencer yelled at him.

Ryder whipped his head around at the sound of his last name being used fully. Spencer opened the cabinet near the workstation and brought something down, then tossed it to him. He instinctually caught it and looked at the object. What he saw was the face of his old helmet staring right into him. The familiar equipment sent a triumphant pride back into his heart. Aside from a bullet indent, it looked just as pristine as ever.

Ryder threw up the helmet, placing it on his head and turned it on. The interface inside booted up quickly, connected to the A.M.R and the internal global positioning system came to life. A small laugh formed inside Ryder's throat. He never realized how much he missed this until now.

Spencer let out a bold laugh as well. "Welcome back Ry, are we back in action?"

Ryder threw his hand upwards in a sharp motion and a grappling-control grip flew into his hand, and a large hook on the end of it. Ryder pressed one of its buttons and the hook began to spin smoothly on the top of it. Old familiar instincts returned in the form of an itchy trigger finger.

"Yeah, the Time Rider is back in action."

"Nate! C'mon we need to get a move on! Ándale! C'mon, Pronto!" Markus yelled.

"Get going Nathan, we need that device," Spencer ordered.

"Yes, sir," Ryder responded.

He ran back up the stairs and met Markus outside. He was already on his board, itching to fly into the morning sky. His mask was on, and his sweatshirt hood rose up on his head. Upon seeing Ryder in his full set of gear, he looked him up and down, then returned to his original position.

"Holy hell Nate, you a space marine now?" Markus asked.

"Just a Time Rider," Ryder said. "You know how to get to Oracle Tower from here?"

"You bet; that do-hickey of yours any good? This board of mine can sail quite fast."

Ryder lifted his right wrist and flicked it in an upward motion, the hook apparatus flying into his hand and spinning up in the air. "I think I'll manage."

"Kay, kay, meet you there," Markus said launching himself into the air and flying away. "Try not to choke too bad on my dust."

Ryder flicked his wrist and aimed a hook at a nearby rooftop. He pulled the trigger and the hook shot out with a rush of air, connecting flawlessly into the brick. The line went rigid. So, he let go of the trigger and was pulled to the rooftop. As he moved, he planted his feet on the wall and hung there for a moment. Planning out his next few shots, he jumped from the roof and shot again and again, moving at incredible speed with each shot. Once he gained enough momentum, he threw himself through the Time Stream, moving even faster.

The exhilaration filled him with courage that he had forgotten about. It felt good, powerful, to once again be fully kitted zipping through the city. The Time Rider was back—Ryder was back—and he had every intention of letting Oracle and the Progenitress know it.

He kept going until he was right behind Markus, who was surprised to see him catch up and proceeded to fly faster on his board, seemingly offering Ryder a challenge. Ryder obliged and kept zipping around on the rooftops, flying through the air with grace. Markus flew close and maintained speed, keeping low to the roofs.

If the situation were any different, this would be a fun race, but not now, there was a job to do, a girl to save, and a package to collect. Ryder was so certain of his success he could already feel it in his hands. This wasn't pride, it was drive. Drive he would carry to fruition, no matter what stood in his way.

CHAPTER 42

Interception

Artemis:

Farai Omari and Edgar Talon awoke early in the morning and prepped their respective gear. They were currently heading for the top of Oracle Tower, making way to Marigold's private helipad. Late the previous night, they had been awoken by Doctor Yorkshire and asked to meet Marigold in the armory. Begrudgingly, both parties awoke and made their way down into the empty sprawling base to meet her. Once there, Marigold told them she had devised a small plan that was a work in progress. She said they had acquired a device that could be used as a form of defense against the Progenitress.

They were not given specifics, but this form of defense was stored in a military-grade box that was planned to be hidden in a specific location and collected at a specific time the next morning. Talon collected the package and Farai met up with him. The two lieutenants walked together, nearing the door leading out to the helipad. Farai had her bow slung over her shoulder, and Talon had his gauntlets on his wrists, a rifle on his back, and the weapon case in his right hand.

"So, we are heading to Chicago?" Farai asked.

"Yes," Talon responded. "Marigold wants this thing away from here as soon as possible. So, the tech junkies over at the Chicago branch can work on and assemble this thing."

"Do you think they can even do that? Apparently, Carter was the one who conceived this thing."

"Doubt it," Talon said. "It's a legit branch, no ties to the PMC, just the tech stuff. Even Yorkshire doesn't know what to do with half the stuff that nut cooked up, but it's better than nothing, especially if it gives us an edge."

"Stay quiet about that," Farai hissed.

The two of them arrived at the helipad where a helicopter was being prepped for takeoff, all at Marigold's request. Farai and Talon both entered the flying vehicle and took seats parallel to one another before putting on their radio/ear protection sets.

"When we're green, take off!" Talon yelled to the pilot on the headset. "We have a tight schedule!"

"Yes Commander!" The pilot responded. He flicked an assortment of controls and grabbed his flight stick between his legs. The helicopter quickly began to ascend high into the air. Once at a high enough altitude the pilot pressed forward hard and the helicopter dipped forward, flying at a high speed through the skyline of St. Louis. Talon and Farai both held on to something as they flew, the city beneath them glistening in the morning sun.

"Stop me if I've said it before, but I'm not getting paid enough for this," Talon said, his voice sounding in Farai's headset.

"Say it as much as you want. I don't remember anything about taking orders from an otherworldly teenager in the fine print of my contract," Farai responded.

"The hell is even going on? It's that woman from the arch, isn't it? The one in the black dress. Why is she that girl we interrogated?" Talon asked.

"I haven't the slightest clue, but it obviously has something to do with the Time Riders. It's always the damn Time Riders."

"Retaliation maybe?"

"Your guess is as good as mine."

Spartan let out a tired exhale. "Remember, once we touch down in Illinois, we let Marigold know we delivered the package. In and out quick, shouldn't take more than a quarter of the day."

"Rodger," Farai said looking out the window down at the building below, the early morning haze and the stress of the predicament not melding well together.

"How are you holding up Farai?" Talon asked.

"Not well," she responded. "I have a bad feeling about this. Do you think Carter knows what we are doing?"

"Don't see how he could, we dug all this up last night," Talon said. "Even if he did, we're out of the city in twenty minutes. What can those two kids even do up here?"

"We need to take this seriously. We should know more than anyone these are not normal children, they're dangerous."

"I know, that's why we are both here," Talon said. "I'll tell you what, we don't have to get back to Missouri right away. There's a bar I like in Chicago, visited there with some army buddies back in our hay day. Why don't I treat you to something to help take the edge off? I can use a stiff one too. It doesn't have to be anything more than that."

He was doing this now? If Edgar Talon was anything, it was persistent. If it were a standard business day, it would have been a hard no. But at the moment staying out of St. Louis and away from the Progenitress sounded amazing, even if it were Talon she would be with. At this time, it didn't seem terrible.

"We have a job to do, but once it's done ask me again. I might let it slide for once."

Talon smiled boldly where he sat. "You got it."

They were interrupted by the sound of something hitting the bottom of the helicopter, a loud noise emanating about the cabin.

"What the—what was that?" Spartan asked.

"Probably a bird," the pilot said. "Happens once in a while."

"What kind of bird would make a noise like that?" Farai asked.

"I don't know, what else would be up here?" the pilot asked.

Farai thought about it. There weren't that many large bird species in the area. Before she could figure it out, she saw something in her peripheral vision. She quickly turned her head toward her door and saw a masked figure staring at her from outside the window, his red sweatshirt and messy blonde hair blowing in the wind, blue eyes glowing brightly from his mask. The figure waved at her playfully as Farai sat staring. It was Markus Daniels.

Then another loud noise bounced around the cabin, and another figure showed up, this time at Talon's window. It was Nathan Ryder, adorned with his original bulletproof helmet and mobility device, he was currently latched on to the side of the helicopter, his feet planted in the side of the door.

Both Talon and Farai got defensive. She readied her bow horizontally toward Daniels, and Spartan chambered his rifle and pointed it at Ryder. Both Time Riders continued to stare in. Based on their head movements they seemed to be communicating with one another through the windows, but as for what they were saying, there was no way to know.

Then their movements became more aggressive. They began gesturing harshly and rudely at one another through the cabin, as if in an intense argument. Talon and Farai just looked at one another, confused about what do make of this. Then Ryder flicked his free hand upward, summoning his hook apparatus, then spun the hook on the end of the grip. Then he hit the glass rapidly, hitting it over and over again with flashes of blue light as he sent them into dimension Alpha-2. Each hit began to crack the glass.

Talon readied his weapon and aimed right at Ryder's head, the boy didn't even notice and just kept hitting the glass.

"Keep an eye on the other one!" Talon ordered, pointing with his right hand.

Farai obeyed and saw Markus Daniels seemingly cheering Ryder on with a pumped fist, encouraging him to continue. She suddenly became nervous. She wanted to look back to see what Ryder was doing but didn't. Markus just kept the encouraging gestures up, getting progressively more excited as the seconds went on. She couldn't resist anymore, and she looked behind her at Ryder. Once she did, he stopped, recalled his hook and made an L loser gesture on his helmet.

The door behind her opened wide and Farai accidentally let go of her drawstring. The arrow sailed past Markus harmlessly as he stood crouched on the edge, his board flying back into his hand and being stowed on his back.

"What's cookin' good lookin'?" he yelled over the helicopter blades.

He dove into the helicopter, aiming right for the suitcase in Talon's grasp. Once he got ahold of it, Talon immediately fought for it, dropping his rifle and pulling it with both hands. Ryder opened his door and jumped in himself, punching Talon right in the mouth with a solid hook. Both the lieutenants and the Time Riders fought inside the helicopter like a drunken mosh pit, each scrambling and throwing punches at one another, all taking turns wrestling for the case.

The fighting caused the helicopter to tetter back and forth like a rowboat in a storm. The pilot up front was now stricken with confusion and did everything he could to straighten out but could only manage to dive lower among the tall buildings in the city.

Farai and Markus were interlocked in a struggle. She let loose of his grasp and punched Markus right in the face causing his mask to fly off. He scrunched his nose and sneered in spite.

"Don't start throwing heat, babe! You do not want to be hit by..."

Farai swung her right hand and slapped Markus across the face loudly.

"Ow! Really?" he yelled as Farai grabbed her bow and used it to pin Markus to the other side of the cabin. She pushed with all her might against his neck, hoping to cut off air flow. Markus began to choke.

But then he began to push back hard and got the bow away from her. They both struggled but somehow the boy's strength proved to be too much compared to Farai's. When it got far enough, Markus let go and threw a punch through the Time Stream right into her head. Farai immediately went slack and fell onto the floor in pain and dizziness. Markus looked down with immediate regret as Ryder and Talon continued their own struggle.

"Aw, man! That's a bad look for me..." Markus muttered putting his mask back on.

"Heyo, Marko? Little help?" Ryder asked behind Talon, currently holding him in a lock from behind. Talon grunted in frustration as he continued to fight, even angrier after what just happened to Farai. Markus went for the case and Talon grabbed hold as well, struggling with one hand. Farai tried to recover but was still in far too much pain to do anything more than remain on the floor of the helicopter on her arms.

"Gah... c'mon!... Let go, G.I. Jerkoff!" Markus exclaimed.

It was slow, but Farai was recovering. She managed to get up onto a knee and began to climb to her feet. Talon backed up quickly, slamming the back of Ryder's head into the roof, causing him to lose his grip and slip down onto the floor. He nearly fell out of the open door. Farai was now on her feet, and she grabbed

Markus by the back of his sweatshirt and kicked him hard in the chest. He flew back towards the open door but managed to grab the frame with both hands before he fell out.

Following up, Talon readied the gauntlet on his free hand, charged it up and hit Markus's center mass. The Time Rider got launched into the air and flew out of the helicopter, falling through the air and screaming loudly.

"Markus!" Ryder yelled. He desperately fired a hook at him using his device. The hook sailed out the window and descended out of sight. Farai thought Markus would surely fall to his death out there, then she heard a sharp *tink* noise and Ryder's line showed signs of struggle. Somehow, he managed to snag his ally on the line. Farai didn't let herself think about it too much, this was an ample opportunity to deal with the other one.

Talon picked up Ryder and tried to throw him out of the helicopter. Before that happened Ryder planted his feet on the top of the roof's frame and pushed back through the Time Stream causing Talon to scrape his head along the roof and hit the back of it on the parallel frame. He fell to a knee and held the back of his skull.

Ryder reached for the prototype box, his unfree hand making it clear it was not going to be able to be used. In the moment, Ryder tried to pull up Markus to no avail and reached for the box which was just out of reach. He brought up his free hook and scrapped it forward, trying to use the wings of the hook to snag it.

Talon recovered before he could do so and picked up Ryder again. Farai gripped him afterward and secured his legs. Together they held on tightly to the young man as he struggled and they threw him out the other side of the helicopter.

As he fell, the hook cable began to grind quickly against the floor. What happened was so fast both lieutenants didn't even process it immediately. When Markus came back into the chopper he snagged the briefcase in the blink of an eye, and both Time Riders began plummeting into free fall.

CHAPTER 43

High Wire

Ryder:

It was difficult to focus, falling out of that helicopter. For **Ryder** everything felt like it was spinning. He just managed to make out the black silhouette of the helicopter above him when he aimed to the best of his ability with his only free hook and fired upward. The hook found its mark, and everything came to a pressured halt. Ryder went horizontal in the air with one hook fired into the helicopter and the other connected to Markus's skysurfer pack, all the weight caused the line to go straight.

Markus thrashed around wildly, shaking his legs in the air and gripping his pack. "Hey, man, I'm not liking this! I have the thing, get us down!" he yelled in Ryders headset, using a few choice words of profanity afterwards.

"You have the Siren grenade?" Ryder asked.

"Yeah! Yeah! Get us down, we're gonna hit a building!"

Markus was right. The chopper was so low it flew close to the buildings in the city. Navigating the free space between them, Markus and Ryder were hanging below at the mercy of the chopper's momentum.

"Can you use your board?" Ryder asked frantically, trying to conjure a means of escape that didn't involve hitting the ground at breakneck speed.

"No!" Markus responded. "It's just beeping if I try! Your line is in the way!"

"I got to get it loose. I'm going to try and pull you up! Oka—"

Ryder didn't finish because of the bullets that began to sail past them. He looked up and saw Spartan perched outside the helicopter, rifle in hand, pointing at the two of them. Artemis was up now, too, on the other side, her bow at the ready.

Ryder was forced to struggle about and start swinging in an attempt to avoid the sudden fall of bullets and arrows. He caused them to move about so sporadically that when the chopper pilot decided to make a turn, they flew high into the air with Markus almost getting mulched by the helicopter blades.

"Get me down! Get me down! Get me down!" Markus yelled frantically.

Ryder had to do something. This was getting way too dangerous. He recalled his hook, and Markus slowly began to ascend, as he did so Ryder nearly got impaled by one of Artemis's arrows. Markus did manage to get pulled up all the way up to him without being shot in any way.

"Drop your hook, let's get outta here!" Markus yelled close enough to be heard clearly.

"Can you get your board loose mid-air?

"I don't friggin' know! Not exactly something I went out of my way to learn!"

"You have to try—gotta do something!" Ryder exclaimed.

"Don't you dare drop me!"

"I'm trying not to! Work with me here, I gotta…" Ryder said, not completing his thought. Even as he moved, something over the horizon of the skyscrapers caught his eye, he barely picked it up, but it was something he had taught himself to see. Near the buildings he could make out movements in the air, moving about just enough to catch in his peripheral vision. Focusing on them revealed they were the flapping of wings; multiple sets were coming right towards them as they hung from the helicopter. When Ryder realized what he was looking at, panic immediately stunned him.

"Ra—raptors!" he yelled.

"Wha—the dinosaur? Whaddya goin' off about now?" Markus exclaimed.

"No! Flying revvies!"

"Flying?"

As they got closer, six raptors could be made out. Each one looking like grey humans with leathery wings, eyes glowing the familiar blue, they were like monsters of urban legend.

"Kill them! Destroy the weapon!" the raptor in the front hissed in SpecterSpeak.

One of them dove through the Time Stream and slammed into Markus and Ryder causing them to spin wildly on the A.M.R cable. The two boys yelled loudly in response to the impact. Three raptors began to circle Ryder and Markus down below. The other three were circling above near the helicopter where Spartan and Artemis sat.

The raptors on the Time Rider's level took turns making grabs towards Markus and the weapon case he was grasping for dear life. They kept pushing forward, swiping and grabbing. One of the raptors hit the two of them dead on and caused them to start swinging again. Markus went for a few mad swings with the case and successfully ended up hitting one in the head. The creature let out a high-pitched whine of pain in response.

One raptor went for another grab, then got ahold of the weapon case and pulled away hard. Markus didn't relent his own grip starting an aerial game of tug-of-war, pulling them around in a massive circle.

"Buzz off!" Markus yelled.

The raptor kept pulling hard over and over. Markus yelled in pain as his arms got yanked. After enough tries, his grip slacked on the case and the raptor flew away with its prize.

"No! Nate do something! It got the thing!"

Ryder thought quickly. He saw a rooftop the two of them were fast approaching, and he began to swing him and Markus over in its direction. When they passed by overhead, he released the hook with a metallic clink. Markus fell a short way down, flailing as he did so, before landing on the roof and tumbling a few times.

Once Ryder recalled his hook he detached from the helicopter and zipped up a taller building, launching himself high into the air using the Time Stream. Up in the air, Ryder's senses were razor sharp. He saw the whole flock of raptors flying away attempting an escape, he managed to see the one with the case, gripping the container with a pale hand.

He found an antenna and used the A.M.R to launch himself through it and into the air, the helicopter passed by him, still flying low. He seized the opportunity and fired some more lines into the flying vehicle before launching himself through the open doors out onto the other side, giving Artemis and Spartan a drive-by hit on the way through.

The momentum was enough to launch him toward the other raptors. When close enough, he fired another A.M.R hook and clipped one of the raptor's leathery wings. The creature wailed in pain as Ryder pulled himself up towards the descending revenant. Once they were at the same level, he climbed onto its back and jumped off hard, punching a diving raptor that came to its kindred's aid midair. The container revenant noticed him attacking the others and began to quickly fly away.

Ryder continued moving fast aiming another hook past the creature, focusing even more on angling his next move correctly. Once it felt right, he fired into the office building past the raptor and zipped forward, colliding with the raptor midair and grabbing hold of it firmly. Both he and the raptor began to plummet down, going right for one of the office windows on the building.

They crashed through it and landed hard on a carpeted floor, the raptor being the unfortunate one and taking the brunt of it. Ryder began to throw punches over and over through the Time Stream, mightily striking at the raptor's head. All the raptor could do was screech in pain. He hit again and again until the creature went limp and faded into a fine blue mist, causing Ryder to fall back down to the floor, the case sat right next to him. He remained on the ground, holding himself up on his knees and hands breathing heavily. After a moment, he looked up and was met with the shocked gaze of an entire group of office workers gazing at him, some with papers and other supplies in their hands.

Ryder got to his feet quickly and brushed off the dull remains of revenant dust on his body suit. Taking a look around the room, he suddenly became nervous because of his new audience.

Ryder cleared his throat. "Um… that's uh, one way to mix up the nine to five, right?" No one responded to him. "That thing…" he said, pointing down at the floor. "Don't look too hard into this all right? Believe me that is a rabbit hole you don't wanna go down. And, uh, sorry about the window, but the company pays for that kinda thing right? Yeah, for sure."

"NATE!" Ryder looked out the hole he had made to see Markus flying about on his board, being attacked by the two other raptors.

"Aw, crap..." Ryder muttered turning around and facing the workers. "Okay, everyone! Have a nice day and don't work too hard, aight? Make sure to tell your family you love 'em and have a blessed day!"

Ryder ran to another side of the building as office workers quickly got out of the way. He ran through the Time Stream turning the new space into a runway and launched himself out of the window. He zipped forward toward Markus, knocking one of the raptors down. Markus proceeded to sucker punch another in midair. Ryder shot a hook into another building and hung there, planting his feet in the side of it. Markus flew over to meet him.

"Are you all right? Do you have the case?" he asked.

"Yeah, fit as a fiddle. Happy early Christmas," Ryder said handing the case to Markus.

"Awesome! Let's get the hell outta here! Er—I mean get the heck outta here."

"You got it."

A loud boom could be heard over the horizon and the helicopter started spinning out of control. Raptors could be seen as the culprits of the malfunction as they pulled the craft apart piece by piece. The helicopter landed in a street and nearly fell over a guardrail that led into the Mississippi river. The civilians around began to panic as a small car pile-up formed trying to not hit the wreckage. Within seconds the area had become covered in black smoke, fire, and piled up cars.

Marcus whistled loudly. "Crash and burn, sucks to be them. C'mon let's get back."

"No!" Ryder exclaimed.

"Whaddya mean, 'no'?"

"You go ahead; I'm going to help them out. I'll catch up."

Ryder nearly shot forward again and would have if Markus didn't catch him. "You high? Are you forgetting they just tried to kill us?"

"Course I didn't! But I'm not gonna just sit back and watch them drown in that thing!"

"Heroics are nice and all Nate, but we don't have time!

Remember Charlotte? We have every reason to scoot on out of here."

"Not me."

Ryder jumped from the roof and detached his grappling hook, going into a dive down into the street. Markus yelled something he couldn't hear from above. Before he struck the ground Ryder used his A.M.R to go for a string of shots, propelling him just above the street right to where the helicopter landed. Once there, he diligently searched the wreckage, taking mind not to burn himself or choke on the fresh flames and smoke that surrounded the area.

"Edgar! Farai!" Ryder called out.

"In here!" responded Artemis's muffled voice could be heard.

Ryder's helmet kept his vision somewhat clear, but he still kept his hands up in order to block the oppressive heat. He ducked his head into the wreck. He saw both Spartan and Artemis inside, both in a sorry state. Artemis had a large gash on her head, and blood was pouring profusely down her face. Spartan held his arm, blood seeping from a wound he also sustained. The pilot up front lay limp in his seat, dead.

"Guys, you need to get out of there! Can you move!?" Ryder asked.

"Wha—you?" Spartan said weakly.

"Yes me! Your favorite person ever! Can you move out of there or not?

"I'm fine," Artemis answered.

"I'm not," Spartan grumbled.

He groaned in pain, still holding his arm. Artemis tried to get under his arm to hoist him up but found it difficult. All Spartan could do was yell in pain.

"Come on Talon! You need to get your thick hide up!" Farai yelled.

"Farai, just get… get out!" Spartan exclaimed.

"Quiet! Get up!" Farai yelled, pulling him even more.

A large metallic creaking sound started as wreckage started to give way, falling over the guard rail and sliding down into the river.

"No!" Ryder yelled, running to the front and firing both his A.M.R hooks into the hull, the remains of the helicopter falling quickly dragging Ryder against the street. Sparks began flying up from the metallic parts of the rig dragging along the pavement. He dragged until he managed to angle himself and planted his feet into an undamaged part of the moat. The A.M.R hooks immediately went stiff, and Ryder began to hold the entirety of the wreckage on his rig. His feet dug into the concrete barrier, The A.M.R hydraulic system in the legs were taking most of the weight, but Ryder's legs began to burn immensely from the effort and were stricken with pain. He groaned as he tried to hold it up.

He let go of his triggers and began to recall the hooks pulling up the wreckage. The A.M.R began blaring its cautionary alarms, the monitor on his left wrist began to flash red. The hydraulic system in his legs whined, suffering under the immense pressure. But Ryder didn't let up. The wreckage was slowly moving up. The A.M.R. was one bad moment away from completely falling apart. The wreckage kept moving. Ryder's limbs all felt like they were on fire. The A.M.R.'s alarms numbed his ears. But he kept holding it all up. The wreckage eventually climbed up over the hole again and Spartan and Artemis came into view.

"Get out! Get out!" Ryder yelled just as the hydraulic system in his legs gave out and pressure tanks and springs shot from his legs. Artemis and Talon jumped out just as Ryders legs gave way, and he was forced to release the hooks and drop the wreckage into the river below.

After he let it go Ryder fell back onto his back, the hooks and lines laying limply beside him as he sprawled open in the street. He could hardly focus as the pain came back for a second wave. Artemis helped Spartan to his feet and began walking him away from any prying eyes, calling it even with the Time Riders. Ryder barely heard Markus drop down next to him from above. He gaped down above him.

"Good friggin' lord…" Markus said slowly. "You good?"

"No…" Ryder grumbled from the ground. "Why are you even here?"

"Not much of a listener. Can you move?"

"I'll try," Ryder said trying to get to his feet, his legs immediately went wobbly, and he fell to a knee.

"Here, let me help you up," Markus offered.

"I'm fine," Ryder said waving him off. He tried a second time and fell back down to the road onto his wrist.

"Play stupid games, get stupid prizes. Hold this, Nate." Markus handed Ryder the weapon case. "Okay back to the undercroft we go."

"Wait a sec—what are you…Woah, hey!"

Markus lifted Ryder and threw him over his shoulder so he could carry him. "Markus! Put me down!"

"Dude, you can't even walk. Just chill out and enjoy the ride."

"Enjoy? I feel like an idiot!"

"You look like one too," Markus chastised. "Hang in there, we got a bit of a ways to go. Don't throw too much of a hissy fit, okay? Gotta headache already."

Markus walked with Ryder slung over him. His A.M.R hooks scraping loudly across the pavement.

CHAPTER 44

Breach

Markus:

"**Y**OU BROKE IT AGAIN!?"
The A.M.R sat sadly in front of Spencer on the workbench. He may as well have had steam shooting from his ears from how angry he was. Ryder was lying on the sofa, doing his best not to move his injured legs. Markus leaned against the monitor tables smugly, taking in all the smoke.

"Tell me again, I want to hear it. What did you do?" Spencer barked.

Ryder just closed his eyes and winced.

"Go on, say it!"

"I held up a helicopter…"

"A whole damn helicopter!" Spencer yelled. "What were you thinking?"

"I didn't, they needed help. They would have fallen into the river and drowned," Ryder responded weakly.

"Well use your head next time, yeah? Can't win a war by saving the enemy, now can we!"

"Don't start that, Spence, you know why I did that."

Spencer huffed. "You're still trying to be a boy scout out there? What are you trying to prove?"

"Nothing," Ryder muttered. "Just doing the right thing."

"The righ—oh brother…" Spencer grumbled.

"You should have seen him, though," Markus chided in. "He zipped around, took names, and even crashed into an office window! That was freaking bonkers man!" he said, a laugh intertwined with the words.

"Don't remind me..." Spencer said.

"Besides, we did get the thing right? Your alarm grenade?" Markus asked.

"Siren, and yes, you did get it. But not exactly with discretion."

"Where's the fun in that?"

Spencer lifted a finger, about to say something but stopped and turned his attention to the weapon case. He started to examine the scuffed-up box. Markus peaked over as well, and Ryder started making attempts to get up.

"No, you rest. Stay down on the sofa," Spencer said, lifting a hand.

"Aw, c'mon..." Ryder grumbled.

"Your legs are shot, you're lucky they didn't break like chicken bones with all that weight."

Ryder grumbled again, but Spencer just flicked the latches on the box and opened it up. Inside there were two items. To the right was a pile of papers and files all laminated in clear plastic, and to the left was a silver, circular device housed in black foam. Spencer first took out the papers and flipped through a few. Some were elaborate schematics, others handwritten notes.

"Huh, my personal notes," Spencer said reminiscing. "These take me back. I spent hours planning and theorizing on paper like this, always laminating them for good measure. Es would always joke that she had to compete for time with these to..." Spencer explained, stopping suddenly.

"Who?" Markus asked.

"Nobody. Let's see what we got here," Spencer said dismissively.

Spencer turned his attention to the silver device to the right. He carefully put his fingers under it and lifted it up. It was a pancake-shaped device with symmetrical metallic pieces arching upwards, looking like an elaborate land mine.

"That's it?" Markus asked.

"That's it," Spencer confirmed.

Spencer began to fiddle with the device and flicked a few

switches on its side. After flicking one of them, the room suddenly became engulfed by powerful sound waves that made Markus's ears burn intensely and painfully. Both he and Ryder yelled in extreme pain. Ryder tried to hide his head under a pillow and Markus fell to the ground, covering his ears. Spencer managed to power through it and turn off the device.

"Markus, Ry? Are you alright?" Spencer asked.

Markus squirmed on the floor and brought his hand away from his ears, his fingertips covered in blood.

"Oh no. Hey, Markus, can you hear me?" Spencer yelled kneeling down next to him.

"Wha—kinda, can you try not whispering?" Markus said.

"Nathan, how about you?"

"Man, I don't dig that *at all*!" Ryder yelled.

Spencer let out a sigh of relief. "I thought I blew both of your eardrums out. I didn't even know I... oh, yeah, now I remember."

"Remember what?" Markus asked grumpily, getting to his feet.

"I did complete the prototype. I just didn't test it. Couldn't have even known if it worked."

"Well now you know! Friggin' a..."

Markus began to pace around the room. He and Ryder still groaned in pain. Spencer was recovering far better.

He began to box up the device and snapped the box close before taking it over to one of the desks and kneeling under it. He began to twist and turn something on the floor and opened a small hatch conveniently just out of view.

"This is good news, we can skip a few steps. I'll need to do some tinkering later to make sure this tech is green, but now all we should need is a plan of action." He dropped the box into the hatch and closed it back up.

"Yep. Just say the word," Ryder said sitting up.

"You'll be sitting this out Ry," Spencer said.

Ryder looked over at them, a deadly look in his eyes. "Excuse me?"

"You heard what I said."

"Like hell!" Ryder yelled. "This is Charlotte we're talking about. I'm not gonna just sit back with my feet kicked up. Are you kidding me?"

"Use your head," Spencer said. "You're hurt, and you're

A.M.R. is fried. You don't have options here."

Ryder grimaced as the reality of the situation set in, putting his head back down on the sofa and closing his eyes tightly. "So, this is what you meant Markus? This is why you need to be here. Why didn't you just tell me?"

"Ry, what are you talking about?" Spencer asked.

"Markus is the one who needs to do this. He needs to save her."

Spencer and Markus looked at one another, a cold sweat dripping down the boy's brow. If this was really coming to a head, the stakes had just gotten much higher. Markus went over and sat near Ryder on the coffee table.

"Nate, be straight here, I don't care what kinda time travel consequential hoopla could happen. What happens man? What do I need to stop?"

Ryder sat quietly, a look of dread forming on his brow. "I can't, it's… it's too much."

"That's not good enough, tell me the truth, now!"

Ryder's eyes began to glow with an aura of melancholy. "She dies, Markus. Charlotte dies," he said quietly as he closed his eyes.

Markus's heart dropped, his breath becoming quick. Just the idea of her getting hurt was difficult to swallow, and this notion was too much. His gut felt impaled at only the thought of it. Considering how he was taking it, Markus figured it would be too daunting to even try to understand how Ryder took it.

"I wasn't there to stop the Progenitress in time, and she died. That's where this all would begin. That's why you wanted to be here, you wanted to stop it. You wanted to do what I couldn't."

"Who? My future self?" Markus asked.

"Yes."

"So, he just laid this all out for you to not tell me till now?"

"It was your idea. I just listened to you."

Markus started shaking his head. "Freakin' dick."

"This can't happen again Markus, it can't. We can stop it this time. You can stop it."

Spencer walked over and placed his hands on the edge of the sofa. "Okay, let me get this straight," he started. "You're meaning to tell me Charlotte *dies*? Is that why the Progenitress took her over? What is so important about one girl?"

"I can't say anything!" Ryder yelled. "Everything has already changed! There is no way of knowing now if..."

He stopped talking upon hearing the door to the undercroft suddenly open. All three of them stopped in their tracks and went deathly quiet. Spencer quickly drew his pistol and quietly pulled back the slide on it. He gestured for Markus to stay back as he inched closer and closer to the edge of the staircase, gun at the ready. Time seemed to slow as they all waited for something to happen. Other than the hum of the computers and other mechanical noises, it was quiet.

Then, out of nowhere, a canister was thrown down the staircase, the metallic noise of its landing causing Markus to jump. It detonated into a storm of loud noises that quickly erupted over and over, completely shutting down Markus's senses. His vision became a series of snapshots of an entire group of armed men clothed in beige uniforms stormed down into the undercroft, knocking Spencer down to the ground with the butt of a rifle and restraining him. Then they pulled Ryder away from the sofa and did the same to him before finally doing the same to Markus. On the floor all Markus could see was wafting smoke, flashlight beams, and a multitude of dark figures. One of them stood over him as Markus lay on his stomach. Another looked down at him, rifle in his right hand, handheld radio in the other held high.

"Ms. Marigold, Spencer Carter and the Time Rider's have been detained. Requesting new orders."

Marigold spoke through the radio. "Find the Project Siren Case. Carter should have hidden it in that basement. Do not return until you have it. Coax the information out of him if you need to. All methods are authorized."

The operator looked back at Spencer, who was on his stomach the same way Markus was. He currently looked like he was stuck in a coma. "Carter has been rendered unconscious Ms. Marigold."

"Unconscious? Bollocks!" she yelled through the radio. "Get the Time Riders and Carter back here *alive*. You turn over that basement Corporal! Do not return until you have found that weapon. Without it, we have no chance of succeeding against her! Do you copy?"

"Affirmative, copy," the operator said. "Bag 'em up, get them back to the tower. We have a short window, make wake!"

"Affirmative!" everyone else sounded off. They began to lift

Spencer and Ryder up onto their backs and carried them out of the undercroft. Then another one came over and with difficulty lifted up Markus roughly.

"Be a little more gentle would you buddy? I ain't in the mood for horseplay," Markus managed. The operator next to him responded by throwing a sack over his head and forcing him to his feet, then struck him across the head.

CHAPTER 44

Breach

Markus:

"**YOU BROKE IT AGAIN!?**"
The A.M.R sat sadly in front of Spencer on the workbench. He may as well have had steam shooting from his ears from how angry he was. Ryder was lying on the sofa, doing his best not to move his injured legs. Markus leaned against the monitor tables smugly, taking in all the smoke.

"Tell me again, I want to hear it. What did you do?" Spencer barked.

Ryder just closed his eyes and winced.

"Go on, say it!"

"I held up a helicopter…"

"A whole damn helicopter!" Spencer yelled. "What were you thinking?"

"I didn't, they needed help. They would have fallen into the river and drowned," Ryder responded weakly.

"Well use your head next time, yeah? Can't win a war by saving the enemy, now can we!"

"Don't start that, Spence, you know why I did that."

Spencer huffed. "You're still trying to be a boy scout out there? What are you trying to prove?"

"Nothing," Ryder muttered. "Just doing the right thing."

"The righ—oh brother…" Spencer grumbled.

"You should have seen him, though," Markus chided in. "He zipped around, took names, and even crashed into an office window! That was freaking bonkers man!" he said, a laugh intertwined with the words.

"Don't remind me..." Spencer said.

"Besides, we did get the thing right? Your alarm grenade?" Markus asked.

"Siren, and yes, you did get it. But not exactly with discretion."

"Where's the fun in that?"

Spencer lifted a finger, about to say something but stopped and turned his attention to the weapon case. He started to examine the scuffed-up box. Markus peaked over as well, and Ryder started making attempts to get up.

"No, you rest. Stay down on the sofa," Spencer said, lifting a hand.

"Aw, c'mon..." Ryder grumbled.

"Your legs are shot, you're lucky they didn't break like chicken bones with all that weight."

Ryder grumbled again, but Spencer just flicked the latches on the box and opened it up. Inside there were two items. To the right was a pile of papers and files all laminated in clear plastic, and to the left was a silver, circular device housed in black foam. Spencer first took out the papers and flipped through a few. Some were elaborate schematics, others handwritten notes.

"Huh, my personal notes," Spencer said reminiscing. "These take me back. I spent hours planning and theorizing on paper like this, always laminating them for good measure. Es would always joke that she had to compete for time with these to..." Spencer explained, stopping suddenly.

"Who?" Markus asked.

"Nobody. Let's see what we got here," Spencer said dismissively.

Spencer turned his attention to the silver device to the right. He carefully put his fingers under it and lifted it up. It was a pancake-shaped device with symmetrical metallic pieces arching upwards, looking like an elaborate land mine.

"That's it?" Markus asked.

"That's it," Spencer confirmed.

Spencer began to fiddle with the device and flicked a few

switches on its side. After flicking one of them, the room suddenly became engulfed by powerful sound waves that made Markus's ears burn intensely and painfully. Both he and Ryder yelled in extreme pain. Ryder tried to hide his head under a pillow and Markus fell to the ground, covering his ears. Spencer managed to power through it and turn off the device.

"Markus, Ry? Are you alright?" Spencer asked.

Markus squirmed on the floor and brought his hand away from his ears, his fingertips covered in blood.

"Oh no. Hey, Markus, can you hear me?" Spencer yelled kneeling down next to him.

"Wha—kinda, can you try not whispering?" Markus said.

"Nathan, how about you?"

"Man, I don't dig that *at all*!" Ryder yelled.

Spencer let out a sigh of relief. "I thought I blew both of your eardrums out. I didn't even know I... oh, yeah, now I remember."

"Remember what?" Markus asked grumpily, getting to his feet.

"I did complete the prototype. I just didn't test it. Couldn't have even known if it worked."

"Well now you know! Friggin' a..."

Markus began to pace around the room. He and Ryder still groaned in pain. Spencer was recovering far better.

He began to box up the device and snapped the box close before taking it over to one of the desks and kneeling under it. He began to twist and turn something on the floor and opened a small hatch conveniently just out of view.

"This is good news, we can skip a few steps. I'll need to do some tinkering later to make sure this tech is green, but now all we should need is a plan of action." He dropped the box into the hatch and closed it back up.

"Yep. Just say the word," Ryder said sitting up.

"You'll be sitting this out Ry," Spencer said.

Ryder looked over at them, a deadly look in his eyes. "Excuse me?"

"You heard what I said."

"Like hell!" Ryder yelled. "This is Charlotte we're talking about. I'm not gonna just sit back with my feet kicked up. Are you kidding me?"

"Use your head," Spencer said. "You're hurt, and you're

A.M.R. is fried. You don't have options here."

Ryder grimaced as the reality of the situation set in, putting his head back down on the sofa and closing his eyes tightly. "So, this is what you meant Markus? This is why you need to be here. Why didn't you just tell me?"

"Ry, what are you talking about?" Spencer asked.

"Markus is the one who needs to do this. He needs to save her."

Spencer and Markus looked at one another, a cold sweat dripping down the boy's brow. If this was really coming to a head, the stakes had just gotten much higher. Markus went over and sat near Ryder on the coffee table.

"Nate, be straight here, I don't care what kinda time travel consequential hoopla could happen. What happens man? What do I need to stop?"

Ryder sat quietly, a look of dread forming on his brow. "I can't, it's… it's too much."

"That's not good enough, tell me the truth, now!"

Ryder's eyes began to glow with an aura of melancholy. "She dies, Markus. Charlotte dies," he said quietly as he closed his eyes.

Markus's heart dropped, his breath becoming quick. Just the idea of her getting hurt was difficult to swallow, and this notion was too much. His gut felt impaled at only the thought of it. Considering how he was taking it, Markus figured it would be too daunting to even try to understand how Ryder took it.

"I wasn't there to stop the Progenitress in time, and she died. That's where this all would begin. That's why you wanted to be here, you wanted to stop it. You wanted to do what I couldn't."

"Who? My future self?" Markus asked.

"Yes."

"So, he just laid this all out for you to not tell me till now?"

"It was your idea. I just listened to you."

Markus started shaking his head. "Freakin' dick."

"This can't happen again Markus, it can't. We can stop it this time. You can stop it."

Spencer walked over and placed his hands on the edge of the sofa. "Okay, let me get this straight," he started. "You're meaning to tell me Charlotte *dies*? Is that why the Progenitress took her over? What is so important about one girl?"

"I can't say anything!" Ryder yelled. "Everything has already changed! There is no way of knowing now if…"

He stopped talking upon hearing the door to the undercroft suddenly open. All three of them stopped in their tracks and went deathly quiet. Spencer quickly drew his pistol and quietly pulled back the slide on it. He gestured for Markus to stay back as he inched closer and closer to the edge of the staircase, gun at the ready. Time seemed to slow as they all waited for something to happen. Other than the hum of the computers and other mechanical noises, it was quiet.

Then, out of nowhere, a canister was thrown down the staircase, the metallic noise of its landing causing Markus to jump. It detonated into a storm of loud noises that quickly erupted over and over, completely shutting down Markus's senses. His vision became a series of snapshots of an entire group of armed men clothed in beige uniforms stormed down into the undercroft, knocking Spencer down to the ground with the butt of a rifle and restraining him. Then they pulled Ryder away from the sofa and did the same to him before finally doing the same to Markus. On the floor all Markus could see was wafting smoke, flashlight beams, and a multitude of dark figures. One of them stood over him as Markus lay on his stomach. Another looked down at him, rifle in his right hand, handheld radio in the other held high.

"Ms. Marigold, Spencer Carter and the Time Rider's have been detained. Requesting new orders."

Marigold spoke through the radio. "Find the Project Siren Case. Carter should have hidden it in that basement. Do not return until you have it. Coax the information out of him if you need to. All methods are authorized."

The operator looked back at Spencer, who was on his stomach the same way Markus was. He currently looked like he was stuck in a coma. "Carter has been rendered unconscious Ms. Marigold."

"Unconscious? Bollocks!" she yelled through the radio. "Get the Time Riders and Carter back here *alive*. You turn over that basement Corporal! Do not return until you have found that weapon. Without it, we have no chance of succeeding against her! Do you copy?"

"Affirmative, copy," the operator said. "Bag 'em up, get them back to the tower. We have a short window, make wake!"

"Affirmative!" everyone else sounded off. They began to lift

Spencer and Ryder up onto their backs and carried them out of the undercroft. Then another one came over and with difficulty lifted up Markus roughly.

"Be a little more gentle would you buddy? I ain't in the mood for horseplay," Markus managed. The operator next to him responded by throwing a sack over his head and forcing him to his feet, then struck him across the head.

CHAPTER 46

The Tribulation

Markus:

When Markus awoke next, he didn't even initially realize it. His vision was a slideshow of black and blur. It was like he was a drunkard in need of glasses. His vision waned and adjusted painfully as everything came into focus. He tried to move his limbs and suddenly became stricken and alert, his eyes shot open. He saw his wrists and legs bound to some sort of high-end office chair with metal chains, but he continued to try to move them. They didn't budge in the slightest.

"If I get knocked out one more time..." he muttered.

He looked up and saw where he actually was. He was seated at the end of a very long wooden table. Glass windows surrounded him on the left and right. He appeared to be in some sort of conference room, based on a trademark office scent and the atmosphere of lavish luxury that made Markus feel violently ill. He assumed he was up high somewhere in Oracle's big tower overlooking the river. He continued to perceive his surroundings, shocked when he realized he wasn't alone. On the left side of the table was Ryder, bound and chained. He grunted and kept fighting against his restraints on all fronts, his eyes burning bright in distress. Curiously, Markus wasn't bound at the mouth himself. Next to Ryder was Spencer, bound but still unconscious. His head drooped lethargically in front of him.

Parallel to Ryder on Markus's right, was the Apex, standing on its own with its claws pulled up to its chest and knelt down slightly, slowly peering at Markus now that he was awake. It was calm, but something about it seemed to say it wasn't doing so of its own volition. Like it was a trained animal waiting for someone to sick it on someone. Right in front of the Apex sat Esther Marigold, the CEO. Bound up like everything else, she was conscious but looked extremely confused or distracted. Then, looking slightly downwards, Markus saw there was something wrong with her left arm. It was bent at an unnatural angle, black and blue. Markus realized her face conveyed pain, not confusion. He started to feel sick to his stomach just looking at her.

"Markus, you're finally awake!"

He looked forward to the source of the voice and saw someone at the end of the table, parallel to himself. It was the Progenitress, seated nonchalantly on an office chair like his. She was currently eating something in such a manner that her cheeks were enlarged like a chipmunk. Markus then noticed an Imo's pizza box placed next to her at the table, a plastic plate stacked to the brim right next to it. If this were still Charlotte, the sight of her blown-up face would have been hysterical. But since this wasn't her. It was anything but.

Plates had been placed in front of everyone at the table, all with pizza sloppily thrown on. Markus found it odd—they were all tied up at every limb, two of them were incapacitated for one reason or another and one had his mouth gagged. Markus didn't know if this was some sort of joke or blatant disrespect, he figured it was an unholy combination of both.

The Progenitress swallowed deeply, rubbed her stomach and let out a small belch. "Excuse me," she said. "This vessel is quite fond of St. Louis-style pizza. As it turns out, they use something called provel cheese for the top when making it." She began circling a slice with her finger as she talked. "I have absolutely no idea what that even is, but it's like sin. It's so good!"

She grabbed another slice and began to gorge on it. Markus just looked on, transfixed. She swallowed it all down and laughed quickly. "You are quite right Markus. There really is nothing like good old pepperoni."

Something ended up bumping the back of her chair and caused

her to jump forward, a look of tepid annoyance forming on her face. She turned around and looked down at the floor. "Quit it!" she whined. "That body isn't going anywhere! Eat slowly!"

Her chair rocked forward again, and her face went rigid. She pointed at the source. "Door Dash driver, my ilk doesn't need to eat. But when given the chance to do so they can be quite gluttonous."

A snarling noise sounded off behind her and something flew into the air and landed on the table. After a moment everyone could see it was a chewed-up severed hand. Ryder recoiled in disgust; Markus just looked on in shock. The Progenitress stared at it blankly, only blinking a few times in response. "That's one way to ruin an appetite." She picked it up by the index finger, using two of her own fingers and flung it behind her.

Markus was unnerved. Even without limbs flying about, this kind of enthusiasm coming from her made him uncomfortable. Even Charlotte herself was never this cheery.

"I'm a pizza connoisseur as much as the next guy, but, uh, why are... why am I..." he started

"Still drawing breath?" she interrupted. "I'll be the first to admit, had my plan been followed through correctly you and that little heartache next to you would have been dead many moons ago. I even crafted a perfect hunter for the two of you, the one who would be the downfall of the two of you. He was my magnum opus, my *Apex*."

The creature to Markus's right hissed in disapproval. "But alas, like roaches after the fall of an atom bomb, you both live. It's like I'm fighting fate itself. It feels like the two of you have gained favoritism of the universe at large."

"And your plan changed?" Markus asked.

"Yes. Let's just say Esther Marigold here is a little snake." She sneered over at the woman to her left. "She tried going behind my back, hoping to save her own skin. She had the audacity to not trust me. Tried to overthrow me, can you believe that? Well, I caught her and taught her a valuable lesson. Hopefully, lesson learned." She placed her elbows on the table and crossed her fingers. "But we'll get to that in due time. For now, let's start with a question, I want your opinion on something."

"My opinion?" Markus asked raising his eyebrow.

The Progenitress stood up and made a few small spins where she stood, her black hair and dress flowed gracefully about. A big smile etched on her face glistened in the light. "How do you like the new look?"

Markus wasn't even sure why, perhaps it was something instinctual, but he actually humored her question. The whole pseudo-goth thing that the Progenitress did with Charlotte's look was jarring for him. She looked very beautiful, but at the same time it was like an elegant mask. There was no escaping the fact this was clearly an outer layer hiding something underneath.

"I mean, it's definitely got some spice to it, real hot. But that isn't your look now, is it?"

"Of course it is silly, I've taken the claim," the Progenitress said, sitting back down. "I'm wondering how I look to a male your age. I take pride in the way I fix up my vessels. You would have loved my last one. She was a little servant I found back in the early nineteen hundreds. Nicked her from a rich family from Italy. She was older than this one, about twenty-six. But she was so beautiful. Perfect skin, perfect face, perfect bosom, perfect all the way around. It's a shame *someone* had to go and ruin it." She scowled over at Ryder, who looked at her with a look of equal disdain. "This new one is wildly imperfect. The face is pretty but far too bratty looking, the body is premature, and the hair. Don't even get me started! It was a nightmare trying to get it under control. And *red* hair?" She made a face of disgust. "Deplorable. At least it's as cute as a button with enough work."

"*It* has a name. Her name is Charlotte. That's a human being you're talking about."

The Progenitress let out an airy exhale. "Markus, dear, this whole situation is more than one painfully average girl. Believe me if she weren't so important, I would have just killed her."

"Ouch," Markus said. "If that were the case, why bother? Why not leave her be? Why is she so important?"

"For one thing, getting back at Nathan has been sweeter than the finest wine. But mainly for safekeeping."

"Safekeeping?"

The Progenitress stared blankly. "What do you know about where Nathan and I ended up? Hm? What did he tell you?"

Markus looked over at Ryder, who had gone still with a wide-eyed look. With a perceptive eye, it was possible to even see sweat dripping from his brow.

"Not too much," Markus said. "Just that it wasn't a prime spot for a picnic."

"That's putting it mildly," The Progenitress said. "It was horrendous. Anything else?"

"That's really about it."

Ryder darted his eyes between him and her. Nervousness was coming off him like a space heater. He wasn't the one in control of the narrative anymore, and it was getting to him.

"Let me guess, Nathan here said he couldn't say much about it. No surprise there, it's not like the truth paints him in a good light." Markus kept his mouth closed, despite his curiosity urging him to engage with her. "You want to know what really happened? Or rather *what* will happen?" she asked.

Ryder continued to struggle, but nothing was changing. Even trying to knock himself onto the ground wasn't working. The Apex kept looking at him but gave off nothing that would indicate it was alarmed in any capacity. It felt akin to betrayal trying to coax this information out of her, but at this rate there were simply too many unanswered questions to keep playing by Ryder's rules. He needed the full picture.

"Well, we have to go back to that night back at that arch. Esther here was kind enough to take the time to open a door for me and my children into this world. But of course, Mr. Ryder here couldn't let me have a nice thing, so he forced me back into it, where we both got caught in the current of time. It was rough enough that my vessel dissipated completely. Nathan was the lucky one there. If he had gotten caught in it the same way I had he wouldn't be sitting next to you right now. We probably would have been stuck in that swirl forever, spinning round and round until the end of time and all over again. But against all odds, the door opened again. Briefly, but just enough for us to slip through."

"It opened again?" Markus asked. "Like, someone made a breach?"

"Yes," she said. "A whole setup was rigged and a whole menagerie of power generators were used to recreate a small opening. I flew away from area once I got loose, Nathan fell like a brick all the way down." She snickered. "Serves him right."

"You can fly?"

"Without a vessel, I can do all sorts of things!" the Progenitress said enthusiastically. "But not having one does, unfortunately, have its limits, obviously mostly of the physical variety. That's why I need a body here in your world. A girl can only do so much when the most she can do is play peeping Tom in people's lives as what could only be described as an invisible puff of smoke."

"So, you were a ghost?"

"In a manner of speaking. More of a whisper in the wind, a state of being, but not being."

"So, a ghost."

The Progenitress groaned. "It's whatever you want it to be." She straightened herself. "Anyhow, as it turns out we ended up back where we started, up high near the middle of the arch. We didn't travel through space, but through time. We didn't travel an inch, but we certainly went far." Her demeanor seemed to go somewhat quiet, almost as if this was a touchy subject. "We were back in this city, but it was *very* different."

"Different how?" Markus asked slowly.

She looked up. "Your world... had died."

Markus felt his heart sink "What do you mean, 'died'?"

"Everything was wrong. Your buildings were ruins, there were no people, no trees, nothing. Even the sky had taken a sickening shade of orange. It was mortifying to see it all, even for me."

Markus's thoughts all felt like they were sinking in sand. She didn't appear to be lying, though part of him wished she were. What she described sounded like some sort of doomsday. St. Louis was already ugly to him on a bad day, but this seemed beyond pale. And with Ryder being so coy about it since he returned, it all fit like a glove.

"And why was it like that? I mean, what happened?" he asked.

"That's the first question I asked myself. It was like a bomb had gone off, or at least some kind of war. My brood is certainly destructive, but I would never let it go as far as what happened. I knew it wasn't my doing. My children were still there in the city, abundant in number, but they didn't answer to me anymore. They answered to something else, leaving nothing living in their wake."

"Something else? Like a new head honcho?"

"You could say that. A patriarch to be precise. *The* Patriarch."

Ryder let out a sound akin to a squeal beneath his gag.

"Patriarch? Like a dude?" Markus asked.

The Progenitress nodded. She was resting her head on a hand, looking sad. Ryder looked like he was an inkling away from a full-blown panic attack. Markus found himself thinking about something Ryder had told him earlier. He had said that he had met him there, in this future. A picture was gradually being painted, and Markus became stricken with a need to get the full canvas, color, and all.

"And who is this guy? The Patriarch?"

"A devil," The Progenitress said. "When I searched around the city, I didn't find much initially. Just a seemingly never-ending necropolis. It took me ages, but I found him. As it turns out he was like you. Somewhere between my home and yours. Another little accident."

Markus's eyebrows rose in surprise. "A Time Rider?"

"Yes," The Progenitress said. "A real nasty piece of work. Had himself a little fiefdom set up in the city, with all his little monster spawn making a mess of everything."

"Monster spawns? Nice to see the irony isn't lost on you Honey Bun."

"Silence," The Progenitress hissed hotly. "I know how to raise my spawn. You think they're mindless monsters, but they are living, thinking beings and I know what they can handle and what they cannot. I know where to place limits and provide direction. The Patriarch did not. He didn't care to."

"So, he was incompetent?"

"No, he reveled in their disorder. Their lives meant nothing to him. All were excess and disposable. There was no love in his heart for them, they were all fodder to him!"

Little by little, Markus was connecting the dots.

"Look," he said. "I'm willing to work something out here, let bygones be bygones and all that jazz. This Patriarch Time Rider doesn't sound like someone I'm gonna dig. Why don't we work together to stop him? Yeah? All I ask right now is you let Charlotte go."

"I've told you, Markus, I can't do that. As much as it pains me, she needs to be protected."

"Protected from what? You?"

"No, not me." She reached for something on the floor next to her. "But the one who owns *this*."

She tossed it onto the table, and it slid down in front of him and Ryder. It looked to be some sort of mask, crudely constructed from darkened steel, welding veins snaking all around it. It was created to resemble a human skull, with large eyeholes and a horrid bone-chilling smile installed into the metal, complete with silver teeth. It was an evil, viscous smile. The smile of a killer. Just looking at it made Markus's blood run cold.

Ryder erupted into a spasm and fought his chair with even more ferocity. The Apex snarled at him, trying to simmer him down. The Progenitress stood upright and just stared. Markus looked at the mask as well, somehow even more confused than before.

"That mask, that's the Patriarch's I'm guessing?"

"Yes," The Progenitress said. "A little souvenir. A whole world of people feared this mask. It's a real shame a girly like me had to go and steal it." She giggled. "I literally stole his face. And that's not even the best part. Can you guess what that is?"

Markus took a moment to think, then produced nothing. "No, but I have a feeling you're going to tell me."

She began to walk around the table on Markus's left down toward Ryder. He was still going ballistic out in his chair, powerless against his restraints. The Progenitress walked up behind his chair and spun it so that Ryder faced him. She stood behind him, placed her hands on his shoulders, and knelt so that her head was just above Ryder's.

"The best part is," she started, "That the Patriarch has been sitting right here the whole time."

CHAPTER 47

Revelation

Markus:

"**H**old on, what!?"

"You heard me," the Progenitress said.

"So he... he's the one who took control? He's the one with the mask?"

"Yes."

"I don't... what? Are you saying he caused everything to go topsy-turvy? Nate? I call BS, that guy is a blow hard peace-monger. Pretty boy would save Hitler if given the chance."

"You would think," the Progenitress groaned. She gripped Ryder's chair and began yelling in his ear. "I came here because I wanted to enrich this world with my children, but one little girl dies, and Nathan here has a full-blown meltdown! Forsakes his friends, his God, his entire code—and for what? To become a tyrant? A self-elected Caesar of your own sad excuse for an empire!"

"I haven't heard a shred of proof come out of your mouth," Markus said.

She grabbed Ryder's face and forced it toward Markus's direction. "Look at him! He is falling apart. He knows the truth! He hates what he will become! He would have kept it for himself for as long as he could." She pulled his face close to hers. "Nathan thought he could change things when he returned here. He wanted to save the girl, and himself. But what he doesn't understand is that no matter how behaved a mutt may be, once it bites, it will do so again. The Patriarch is not an if, but a when."

She forcibly threw Ryder's head away and walked closer to Markus. "What would have happened without all this intervention is that me and Nathan would return like we have, but I *understandably*, would take it upon myself to kill Charlotte Rowes in retaliation. What happened from that moment was a domino effect of Nathan losing himself. Taking control and killing hundreds, if not thousands of people who stood in his way, including me!"

Markus wasn't able to amass enough energy to even conjure a thought that didn't feel hazy. All he could think to himself was how this could all go bad so fast. How was all this even happening? He would have paid any price for it to be some sort of narcotic-induced fever dream. All he wanted was to wake up in his foster parents' home, grab his phone and call Cassandra to apologize up and down until his lungs went empty. But there was the pain behind his eyes, the aching of his heart, and the fear in his mind that made it all potently explicit. This was all real, and it was not going to go away. The world was going to change for the worse, and Ryder would be the tip of the spear. There was no lie leaving this girl's lips.

"What about me? What do I have to do with all this?" he asked.

"You change, just like you already have. But you wouldn't participate in this tale until later. By then it would be far too late. After the worst of the downfall, you live. You live long enough to be a threat. In the great scourge brought upon the world, you stood defiantly as the resistance, the rebel. You alone stood against Nathan and his rule, you fought against him with whatever you had, and whoever you had. There was an ongoing war between you and him. You were the only resistance."

"Me? A resistance leader? That's funny."

"I'm not deceiving you, Markus. You have a role to play here too, and a prominent one at that. You're the hero of this story, not him."

Markus began to recall what Ryder had said about his future self. "He wanted me to be found."

"Your future self and Nathan have an agenda. They wanted you to gain proficiency early or at least didn't want you to be killed. As luck would have it you seemed to be faring nicely. Even my Apex here couldn't snuff you out."

"Why do you want me dead? What'd I do to piss you off?"

"Nothing," she chimed. "But you are a threat regardless, all 'Time Riders' are. You could be an asset in my demise as well. I don't need to be the one to tell you that the existence of even one of you is a great threat to all that lives." She walked up closer to Markus. Her nearing presence made Markus feel nervous. "You need to see the big picture. That was always Nathan's mistake. Our immortality is a gift, but a savage curse if allowed to be so. Nathan here is like me, a lover. He cares about his flock and cherishes them to no end. They are his purpose, his life. He would die for them without a second thought. His love for others outweighs his fear of death. That was why I chose him to be one of my own in the beginning. He would have been my most beautiful child, my greatest warrior. But he chose to love the futile ones, the ones who will wither away and die. Time after time, he would try to be the hero but ultimately fail. The truth of the matter is that all humans die. From the moment they draw their first breath they are doomed to draw their last. An immortal being cherishing and loving them is the actions of a fool. Loss is the only reward for playing that kind of game." She walked behind Ryder again. "And what happens when someone has already lost so much? Well, to be frank, if Nathan loses even one more life that is precious to him, we all pay the price. We all lose the game."

The air felt heavy. Markus's limbs were sweaty under the chains. This was far out of his league, way too far. He wanted to know why he had to be the one here in this room. What had he done to warrant this kind of weight, this kind of responsibility? He wasn't some kind of soldier, certainly no resistance leader. He couldn't lead anything. Not anyone else, and certainly not himself. Oracle, these revenant monsters, they all hated him, wanted him dead and gone. Just like everyone before.

The Baymores, every teacher he had in school, Cassandra, even his own parents. They wanted him gone, wanted him to never exist. And now they had finally got their wish, but it still wasn't enough. More had to be taken.

He remained silent, stoically sitting in place. The Progenitress tilted her head curiously, like a puppy that had heard a funny noise.

"You're upset," she said sadly.

It was like she could see right through him, read him like a book. To say this unsettled Markus would be putting it mildly. He didn't realize how much of a luxury it was having his thoughts kept to himself until he wasn't able to keep them a secret.

The Progenitress's next course of action involved her walking over to Markus's right side, skimming her hand along the top of his chair. She pulled Markus away from the table, then turned around and softly hopped onto his leg, scooted until she sat completely in his lap. Then she took both of her hands and wrapped them around his neck.

Ryder looked at the two of them with a heated gaze. The Apex stared on with equal disdain, growling like a truck engine. This sudden warmth from her cursed Markus with a sense of vertigo. He felt energized, like electricity raced through his veins. A feminine touch never failed to excite him, but this felt different. It was like a drug-filled stupor far stronger than anything Markus knew. He felt warmth in her legs, arms, and her breath, which despite still smelling of pizza, surprisingly didn't repulse him in the slightest. He couldn't help but feel relaxed and invigorated.

He didn't know what she was doing. He didn't know if she was playing him for a sap or trying to get on Ryder's nerves by curling up to him in Charlotte's body. Either way, it all felt like too much of a good thing. She began to rest her head on his shoulder and breathe softly onto it, letting out relaxed exhales.

"So cozy, I feel like I could cling to you forever," she said pulling her arms around him even tighter.

"Does the word consent mean anything to you?" Markus choked out.

"Oh, there's no need. I know you want this."

"Get off me," Markus demanded.

"No, I want to stay."

"Get the hell off of m—!"

She put her index finger to his lips and shushed him softly, each one sending shivers up his spine. "Don't talk, just relax."

Ryder started fighting against his chair again, making loud shrieks from under his gag and tittering back and forth in his chair.

"Oh, hush, Nathan. You had your chance." She turned her gaze back to Markus. "Now it's his turn."

"You get your arms off me. Get off my lap or so help me..." Markus growled.

"Or you'll do what?"

Markus didn't respond.

"You're always fighting, fighting on and on and on. Ever since you were a little baby." She began to trace her index finger playfully across his chest. "I've seen it. All those families, all those fights. All those nights you were so angry you wanted to put your fist through a wall, burn it all down. But most of all, I remember every time you wondered who those parents of yours always were, and why they left you on that doorstep."

Markus swallowed deeply, trying to regain control. "I can live without it; it doesn't mean anything to me who they were."

"Don't lie to yourself, Markus," the Progenitress snapped. "There's no gain in doing that."

"I'll agree to disagree on that one. Lying is great. Makes it all go down a little easier."

"Lying is hiding, and only cowards hide. Are you a coward Markus?"

Markus tried to steady his breath, remain calm, but she was making it nearly impossible. Making matters worse, she'd decided to lay her head against his shoulder again, letting out a few airy exhales for what seemed to be dramatic effect.

"Your mother's name was Janine. Janine Daniels. Sweet girl. Skinny, pretty face, always kept that blonde hair of hers up in a ponytail. She was someone with an impressive amount of prospects. She had a high grade point average and a healthy amount of friends. She was even going to school to become a psychologist. That all changed the night she met your father."

Markus began to assemble a picture of her in his head, exactly as the Progenitress described. He imagined her smiling, the sun beaming past her. Just the idea of her felt tranquil.

"And who was my dad?" he asked.

The Progenitress grunted in disapproval.

"Timothy Grisham," she growled. "He was a felon, a miscreant, but mostly an absolute bastard. He came up to your mother one night at a bar. He'd taken a liking to her, asked her a few questions. Offered a few drinks and all the usual transactions.

Janine was always a perceptive person, but not perceptive enough to see what he slipped into her drink when she excused herself for a few minutes to use the restroom."

"What did you say?" Markus asked.

"Eventually that drug took over and she lost consciousness. He took her back to his apartment and... well. Let's just say the word consent didn't mean anything to him, either."

Markus's stomach dropped like an anvil.

"She didn't know what to do after that," the Progenitress continued. "She went to the police afterward and had your father arrested, but the damage had already been done. She had to drop out of her studies and find out what to do with you. Her parents wanted her to do away with you and have a procedure done, but dear Janine couldn't go through with it. So, she carried you for a grueling nine months. Then she had you, tried her hand at motherhood and found out she didn't have what it took. Being reminded of what had happened every time she saw you proved to be too much. That's why she left you on that doorstep, Markus, only leaving that grimy sweatshirt and a little postcard with your name in the pocket. It killed her to do it. Even though you were the result of something heinous, she loved you. She never forgave herself for what she did. Not even for one day."

After all this time he would have killed for this information that had just been spoken to him. But now he wondered if it would have been better not knowing after all. The way she described his father, it scared him. There was something about him that hit too close to home. Even Ryder looked stricken with shock sitting across from him, almost like he could feel the same things Markus was feeling.

"Your mother left a hole in your heart that you've been trying to fill with whatever you could find. Girls, illicit substances, troublemaking. But nothing has fixed it, has it? It still hurts. Do you really see a family in these people you've stumbled across? Nathan here is a mopey child playing hero, Spencer Carter is damaged goods and a drunk. And Charlotte Rowes? Well, she's mine now. She can be yours, too, if you wish. We can fill that hole in your heart. I can take that hurt away and make sure it never comes back. What do you say? Do I have *your* consent?"

Every syllable spoken was as soft as velvet going down

Markus's ears. He closed his eyes and slowed his own breathing; her breath became the only thing on which he could focus. He felt her constrict herself even more around him, making him feel even warmer. He had never felt so broken, so vulnerable. There was no fighting back, not against her. He just wanted to stay here with her clinging to him. It felt good, like pressure he'd been holding on to for as long as he could remember, exited him like gaseous vapor. He felt himself drifting off as the moments passed, The Progenitress softly hummed what sounded like a lullaby, urging him to close his eyes, softly asking him to drift away into nothing.

Suddenly, the Progenitress's eyes went wide out of nowhere, causing Markus's to do the same in surprise as he looked at her. She shook her head, softly at first, then faster until she held her head still with a hand. He had no clue what she was doing.

"Even now, you are still thrashing?" she asked rhetorically. "I'll give you one thing girl I've never had a vessel end up being this troublesome bef... get off of him!"

She threw herself off Markus and began having a spasm on the ground. Both Ryder and Markus gawked at her like their eyes were glued to her. Markus himself began to feel disturbed seeing her in such a state. After a painstaking minute, her spasm stopped and she lay still on the floor, curled up in a fetal position. Then she began to whimper softly and climb onto her knees. As her dark hair parted her face, Markus could see it was contorted in an expression of immense discomfort, but something changed. Her eyes were no longer glowing blue, they now glistened an earthly green, mixed in with a few tears that had begun to streak her makeup.

"Charlotte?" Markus asked.

She cried out and held her stomach like she'd just been stabbed, crying mournful tears of pain afterwards. The Apex let out a sharp growl and began hissing so loud it hurt Markus's ears. Ryder began to panic again, much more desperately this time.

"What have you done?" the Apex demanded to know in SpecterSpeak. "Where is she?"

"I put her in time out. It's my turn!" Charlotte growled through her teeth.

"Bring her back! You bring her back or I'll rip your friends apart!"

Biting down her teeth, Charlotte shot to her feet, grabbed

Ryder's chair, and swung it towards Markus's until they mashed together in front of the door leading out of the room, she jumped in front of both of them and spread her arms.

"You want to kill them? You'll have to kill me! Then mommy goes bye-bye and disappears all over again!"

The Apex snarled, then stopped abruptly, as though it was being more careful about its next move. Charlotte began patting her chest until she reached down into her dress and withdrew two keys. Then, while still gritting her teeth, she managed to unlock Markus's chair. Then she shrieked in pain again and her eyes began to flicker glowing blue, then back to green. She breathed deeply and put the keys in Markus's sweatshirt pocket.

"Please... I can't keep her... get Nathan out... get him out!"

Whatever control she had was quickly being relinquished. "We're going to get out of this. We are going to get you back!" Markus exclaimed.

"Please, it hurts..." Charlotte whimpered. "Leave!"

She ran over to the doors, opened them, and swung them open, then she collapsed off into a corner holding her stomach. Markus looked outside the room and down the hall, dragging Ryder's chair with him. With instinctual perception, he noticed there was an elevator down at the end of the long hallway, still open from its last trip upstairs.

Without even thinking about it, in a quick motion that felt like it wasn't more than a second, Markus grabbed one end of Ryder's chair, wheeled it back, then threw it through the Time Stream, causing the chair to fly down the hallway at a high speed. Ryder yelled out as he sailed down the hallway and spun around in circles until he came to a sudden stop when it slammed into the open elevator car down the hall.

"Kill them both! Rip them asunder!"

Markus turned around to see the Progenitress fully back in control, standing and unfathomably furious. Her eyes glowed brighter than Markus had ever seen before. He wasted no time going into the Time Stream and ran down the hallway toward the elevator as fast as he could. The Apex was now out of the room running forward in a mad sprint, claws outstretched and mouth open.

Ryder began hitting the floor buttons with his foot as it sprinted down after Markus in the hallway. The elevator doors began to close painfully slowly as the chase continued. When Markus was close enough, he slid like a baseball player into the elevator just as the doors finally closed completely and were forcibly bent toward him as the Apex slammed into it with a loud, screeching thud. A few more hits on the door followed as the elevator car began to descend.

Markus and Ryder just sat there as an inappropriately pleasant elevator tune played inside. For a moment, everything was stuck in an ironic stillness, and even the Apex's roars felt distant. Markus put his hand in his pocket quickly and took out the key Charlotte had shoved in his pocket. He unlocked Ryder's chains, and they all clattered to the floor. Then Ryder took off his gag and began breathing manically.

"She's still there, she's still there," he muttered over and over again.

"You got that right, and she gave us the second chance we need to win this," Markus said.

Ryder stood up from the chair, it only took a few seconds before his legs went wobbly and he plummeted to the floor with a yelp of pain. "Ow! that smarts…"

"Wait, your legs are still messed up, aren't they?" Markus asked.

"Unfortunately," Ryder whimpered.

"Would it kill you to not be a cripple for a few minutes?"

A horrid howl filled the entire building outside of the elevator, echoing like a cry of the damned in every direction. The nature of the call sounded like it had a purpose, like a call with the intention to alert. Soon after, many hoots and howls followed in response. The elevator finally reached the ground floor and Markus scrambled to his feet, lifting Ryder onto his shoulder and running out with an awkward haste between the two of them until they were in the middle of the main lobby. That same cry sounded out again and revenants of all types began sloppily running into the area through the doors, sliding on the slick tile, and knocking over plant fixtures and the few desks that littered the area, sending papers and utensils flying. One look up revealed even more of them jumping from the higher floors and landing on the floor below.

They wasted no time in rushing toward the front doors through the Time Stream. Markus muttered panicked obscenities as he moved with Ryder toward the glass revolving doors at the entrance, the oncoming horde not far behind. He slammed the two of them against one and they both fell on the other side onto the pavement. The revenants began to pile up on the glass like a swarm of insects, unable to use the doors. They climbed on each other piling high, forming a storm of gnashing claws fighting against the glass.

Markus helped Ryder up to his feet as he looked on in shock and scrambled away as the glass bent back and forth, scratching in some places, cracking in others. He helped Ryder down the small concrete staircase out front, then down over a second. He stopped in his tracks when he saw the car parked right in front of him. It was convertible sports car, elegant in design and in a bright baby blue. A Ferrari 44 Pista Spider. Markus had seen this kind of car on the internet before, he just never imagined he would actually see one.

Markus threw Ryder over the passenger door and jumped over him into the car's driver's seat. He immediately ducked below the steering wheel and popped a piece of plastic loose, fiddling with the wires.

"What are you doing?" Ryder yelled.

"What's it look like? I'm hot wiring!"

"We don't have time for that! Do you even know what you are doing?"

"Do you have the key Nate?"

Behind him, he heard the glass of the entrance shatter, the expected growling and gnashing behind it following suit. After splitting the correct wire, Markus began to strike them together.

"Whatever you're doing, hurry up!" Ryder yelled.

"I am! Shut up! I just don't know if...." The engine of the car suddenly roared to life in the most satisfying way possible, humming like a majestic beast. Markus couldn't help but smile in triumph.

"Thank you, Tina Shrew!" he yelled.

The Apex finally made its appearance and howled high into the sky in all its earsplitting glory. It ran forward and jumped, landing right next to the vehicle as Markus sat up, then put the car in gear.

The Apex howled and slashed at one side of the car, knocking the back of it into the air and back down onto the ground again. Markus shot his foot down onto the accelerator, spun the car's tires on the ground, and swerved right into the Apex's leg, knocking it off balance. The other revenants began to swarm over the staircases, and an armored clawed revenant managed to jump on the back of the car but was thrown off just as quickly when Markus sped off down the street. Neither he nor Ryder dared to look in the rearview mirror once he went onto the main road.

CHAPTER 48

Focal Point

Markus:

Of all the things that Markus could do, driving wasn't what could be considered his strong suit. And being burdened by a clouded mind didn't make it any easier. It was past rush hour, so the streets were as open as they were ever going to be this time of day, but that didn't mean he didn't almost repeatedly get into a collision or pop up onto the curb like he was going for a record. Ryder sat quietly next to him the whole time, seemingly suffering from similar mental afflictions, oblivious to the poor driving. Markus himself was so stressed that even if he was an experienced driver, he would likely be struggling in the driver's seat. Memories of the Apex, the Progenitress, and everything else kept popping into his head every few seconds, triggering a subdued form of panic in his gut.

He knew he and Ryder had to get back to the undercroft. Within the fragmented memories of being captured, he remembered Marigold barking up a storm about the Siren grenade. In a single-minded pursuit, Markus knew he needed that device. He just hoped that the Oracle drones hadn't found where Spencer had hidden it.

He took his time driving there, trying to slow everything down. He slowed the car, his breathing, and his mind. After a while, he finally found the store and pulled up to it. The sign above it had been turned off signaling it was closed. Continuing, Markus pulled into the alley and turned off the vehicle. He jumped out of the car, then helped Ryder do the same. After he put himself under Ryder to support him, they both moved quietly towards the back of the store.

When they arrived at the bunker door, Markus saw that the panel outside had been tampered with, an assortment of wiring and a micro-chip hanging loosely from it. It appeared the operators had damaged it in such a way that the bunker door was unable to close. Noticing the open door, he helped Ryder down the stairs into the undercroft. When they reached the bottom, they were faced with a room that had been completely ransacked. Everything from the computers to the refrigerator was toppled and thrown about the room. The floor was matted with paper, old machine parts, and other clutter. Even the flat-screen television hadn't survived. It was currently on the floor, shattered. The emptiness of the place left Markus feeling somewhat melancholy.

He helped Ryder take a seat on the downed refrigerator. After wincing slightly, Ryder's eyes furrowed into a sad expression as he looked around at what had happened to his home. Markus felt like he was one inconvenience away from completely losing it, but he couldn't even begin to contemplate what was going through Ryder's mind with the combination of Charlotte, the Patriarch that the Progenitress mentioned, and the undercroft in a bad state. He figured Ryder and the undercroft were one in the same at this moment, scattered and broken.

He scrambled over to where he had seen Spencer hide the Siren grenade earlier. Getting down on his knees, he moved some papers away and found the secret hatch, opening it in a moment of quick anticipation. He found the device sitting in there, as pristine as ever. He took it out and mulled it over with his hands. As far as he could see, it was perfectly fine. He let out a sigh of relief and jammed the device into his sweatshirt pocket.

"It was still there?" Ryder asked.

Markus quickly took it out of his pocket, flourished it in his hand, then put it back in his sweatshirt. This time Ryder was the one to sigh with relief.

"Finally, some good luck," he said.

"Say that for those in the back," Markus said in agreement. As he stood up his shoe ended up nudging a light container on the ground. Looking down at it he saw it was a carton of cigarettes, colored red and white, still wrapped in plastic. He picked it up and examined it, flipping it over and back again. He considered it a safe bet to assume this had belonged to Spencer. It more than likely had fallen out of one of the desks when the operators threw its contents all over the place.

He then scanned his eyes along the ground until he found a lighter that had also been thrown onto the floor. He took it and plopped down on an especially large chunk of clutter to Ryder's left, tearing the plastic off the box. He pulled out a cigarette, then stuck it in his mouth. He lit the cigarette and breathed in deeply. The nicotine rush started in the shoulders and then traveled throughout his body; its sensation was welcoming as it stood juxtaposed to all the stress that plagued him.

He sat quietly smoking, trying not to think. All he bothered to do was look at the floor stuck in a sort of daydream or just focused on the smell of the cigarette. All the chaos of the last few days was finally taking its toll. His body ached and his head throbbed. He was burned out and ready to wake up from this nightmare. As far as he could tell, the Progenitress had won this battle. She had Charlotte and Spencer. Oracle was in cahoots with her as well. Even though Markus was a Time Rider, he only had himself and an injured ally to lean on. Aside from that he had no backup and no plan. It was a miracle he had survived this long. But his luck was draining like the sand in an hourglass, inevitably fading into nothing. All he could do was sit and wait.

Ryder stared at him stupidly as he smoked, lethargic but somehow judgmental. Markus rolled his eyes. "I don't want to hear it."

"I'm not saying anything," Ryder said quietly.

"Your mouth isn't, but your face is."

"My face has a ton to say right now, ignore it. When did you start to care what I think, anyway?" Ryder growled.

Markus thought about it, then shook his head dismissively. "I don't, just don't feel like getting preached at."

"I'm not preaching, even if cigarette smoke is the last thing I want to smell right now."

"Good, keep it that way," Markus said, taking another drag and puffing it out of his lungs.

He looked at his fellow Time Rider with contemplation, he was breathing softly and holding his arm. The hue of his eyes glowed sharply. "I'm guessing you want to talk about what you heard back there?" Ryder asked.

"Hell no," Markus said. "That's the last thing I want to do right now."

"You sure? I mean, that was a lot, Are you okay after all that?"

"Am I *okay*?" Markus exclaimed. "Do I look okay? You're not my shrink, Nate, stop trying to take me through the motions."

"But about that future, where I was…"

"You go evil, I know, I was there. And I'm the bastard child of some douchebag, so yeah. Happy fun times for both of us. Real friggin' peachy. Wish I could say I was surprised." He took another deep drag of his cigarette. "Charlotte was right about me all along."

"The Progenitress could have been lying." Ryder said.

"I know she wasn't," Markus huffed. "She's a piece of work, to say the least, but she doesn't strike me as a liar. The truth was far more powerful, and she used it against us. It explains a lot about the way I turned out."

"You're not your dad, that doesn't explain anything."

"It explains everything! Apple doesn't fall far from the tree, right? A scumbag spawns a scumbag son. It ain't rocket science."

"You're responsible for yourself," Ryder snapped. "You don't have to like what you've done but you need to be accountable."

"Accountable? Are you for real? That's real cute coming from you, Mr. Patriarch of the Apocalypse."

Ryder's eyes lit bright like high beams. "Do not *ever* call me that! I know my future, but I won't let myself become that monster! I don't like where I'm going, so I'm going to change it. Maybe you should do the same!"

Markus stormed to his feet and rushed over to Ryder through the Time Stream until he grabbed his bodysuit by the front and pulled him towards his face.

"You don't know me, asshole! Shut up about your stupid morals or I'll snuff out the Patriarch right here, right now! How's that sound pretty boy?"

Ryder's eyes still glowed with a high intensity, but his face remained still as stone and as cold as a corpse. His gaze met

Markus's eyes, staring with quiet anger. He began to speak, each word deathly monotone.

"If you really want me dead, do it. Kill me, spare the world all the trouble. Because if you don't, one day I'm going to be the one who snuffs *you* out."

Markus felt locked up, maybe even paralyzed. Something about Ryder's voice chilled his very blood. "Well? What are you waiting for?" Ryder yelled. "Come on, badass! Kill me!"

Markus dropped him onto the debris and backed away quickly. He began breathing rapidly, completely caught off-guard by his demeanor. Ryder blinked and softened his gaze, the hue of his eyes dimming slightly, then evened out.

"You didn't mean that, right?" Markus asked. "You don't actually want to die."

Ryder stared at the floor sadly, seemingly afraid to look up. "It's the only way to prevent the Patriarch from happening for sure. The world would be better off if I'm dead."

"Dude, what the hell..."

Ryder wiped his eyes and let out a shaky breath. "I'm sorry."

Markus shook his head and breathed in deep, trying to steer out of the matter. "Forget it, I'm the one who should be sorry. You're right, it's all my fault. The only reason I became a Time Rider in the first place was because I screwed around, doing something I wasn't supposed to do. I'm the one to blame. I've always been the one to blame."

Ryder looked down again. Markus went over and knelt in front of him "Nate, you aren't a bad guy. What causes everything to go so bad for you like that? I know losing someone can be tough, but is that it? What causes you to become the Patriarch?"

Ryder's face tensed up as he took in a deep breath, a single tear sliding down the left side of his cheek.

"I'm scared, Markus. I've been scared for so long, even when I learned to fight back. Eventually, I became angry at it all. I wanted answers, a sign. Some vindication that what I was doing was right. But nothing ever changed. And now, every so often I begin to wonder what it's like to let it all go, go my own way. Be my own God."

Markus remained still but was completely attentive as he continued. "I can choose to be good, but the world never will be.

The harsh truth is that it's difficult to be good, and too easy to be bad. And if I lose Charlotte, that desire... that anger in me will claw its way out of me and take over. The good part of me will die, leaving nothing but the devil inside."

"Nothing but the Patriarch," Markus whispered. "I get it."

"You do?"

"I know what it's like to be angry," Markus answered. "I've let my own devil out more times than I can count. I wish I could say it helped, made things easier. All it did was lead me here." He sat on the floor, letting his arms rest on his legs. "The world needs people like you. It's people like me that the world would be better off without. I'd be the one better off dead."

He looked up at face level, remained still in a moment of contemplation, then looked around until he found the skysurfer pack lying on its side in the corner of the room. He went over to the pack, brushed it off, and began to strap into it.

"You won't be able to help her now, but I can," he said snapping in his final buckle.

"Whoa, whoa. Wait a minute. You're planning on getting her back alone?" Ryder asked.

"What choice do we have? We've been kneecapped. Spencer is gone and you're still hurt, I'm the only one in commission. There's not a debate here."

Something shiny managed to catch Markus's eye. Looking over at it, he could just barely make out the handle of the aluminum bat he had used earlier. It was currently lodged under the refrigerator Ryder sat on. Walking over to it, Markus knelt next to it. He began tugging on it, but it didn't budge. He pulled more forcibly with both hands. After a few unsuccessful attempts, he managed to pull it free and was immediately greeted by the misshapen end. It was bent at an awkward angle, making it resemble a hockey stick more than a baseball bat.

"Oh, well ain't that a biatch," he muttered. "That won't do."

He wasn't going to be able to hurt anything with something like this, and he didn't have the luxury or time to look for a replacement. In addition, he didn't think a run-of-the-mill aluminum bat was going to be enough for what he was about to face. He was suddenly blessed with an idea. He looked first at the bat, then at the workbench in the corner which had an abundance of clutter on it.

Markus immediately began to move shelves and other detritus away until it was sufficiently cleared. "This is as good a start as any," he said to himself.

"What are you doing?" Ryder asked.

"Does Spencer have acetylene?" Markus asked.

"What?"

"Acetylene! Like a blowtorch, does he have one?"

"Yeah, I think… check below the bench."

Markus dropped the broken bat onto the workbench and immediately began rifling through the bottom of it rather clumsily. He found a welding mask and the acetylene torch. Then he turned his attention to some of the old dirty milk crates he had moved beside him. He knelt down and began to rummage through them, tossing old rusty parts aside.

Some were what he was looking for, but too small. Others were too big, or too old, but he quickly found the exact thing he was looking for. A large hexagonal metal piece that was around the same length as the base of the bat. He smiled and grabbed a handful of random parts alongside it and threw them onto the workbench.

"Maybe taking shop class wasn't a complete waste of time after all," he said.

He put on the welding mask and turned on the welding torch. He wasted no time getting to work. He pressed the torch to the base of the aluminum bat and loosened the steel with the heat, then carefully realigned the piece back into its original shape. Whilst gripping the handle, he slid the bat into the hexagonal piece onto the base. Once it was aligned, he jammed as much metallic scrap into the base of the handle before welding it all together.

Taking off the mask and turning off the torch, Markus took a step back from the bench and got a broader look at his work. As far as he could see, it was exactly what he wanted. A heavier, more reinforced bat. It sat on one of its flat sides, still smoking slightly. It was the ugliest, yet the most beautiful thing he had ever seen. It remained hot for a few solid minutes, but once it had cooled enough, Markus took it by the handle and lifted it up.

It was far heavier than a normal bat and ended up dipping and falling to the ground with a metallic clang. Then he took both his hands and lifted it, adapting to its new mass. He looked at his new weapon with astonishment.

"I call it... the heater-beater."

"Good Lord..." Ryder said.

Markus let out an exhale and faced Ryder "You believe in redemption, right? I'm going to do this. And hopefully with an excess in over-the-top style."

"Over-the-top style? Do you have a plan? Anything at all?" Ryder asked.

"Nope," Markus said casually. "Plans cramp my style."

He lifted the bat over his head and placed it near the back of his pack. It stuck instantly to the magnets near the base and remained stowed next to the board.

"You're going to get yourself killed if you're not careful," Ryder said loudly.

"I don't plan on dying. They haven't killed me yet. If that's what's going to happen to me, so be it. If push comes to shove, I won't make it easy. But that's not what's going to happen. I'm going to draw her out, get her back. That's as good a plan as any."

"This is our last play, our last chance," Ryder said. "If we don't win here, the Progenitress will. And the Patriarch will be the least of our problems."

"I wanted this remember? Back in the future, I wanted me to be the ace up our sleeve we all needed!"

"We can't will this win into existence, you're only one person."

"And you're not?" Markus asked. "We're not just kids, we're Time Riders. If that were any different, we'd be dead."

Ryder furrowed his brow and scratched his head. "What am I going to do?"

"You're going to chillax until I get back. I hate to bench you, buddy, but there's not much you can do."

"So, I'm just going to stay here? No phone, no TV, not a thing to let me know what's going on out there. Not knowing if you'll be back or not."

"Yeppers. It's not ideal, but it's all we got."

Ryder exhaled deeply. "I guess we don't have a choice," he said. "Promise me, Markus. Promise me you'll be alive when this is all over."

"I'll do you one better. I'll keep living, and I'll have Charlotte back safe and sound. I might even put a little bow on her head for you."

Ryder smiled lightly. Markus walked forward a few steps, and something round bumped against his foot. He looked down to see the baseball he had played with earlier at his feet. He leaned over, picked it up and examined it brightly in his free hand. Then he took a look at his new bat. After taking a moment to think, he began to smile, starting small, then growing larger.

"What are you smiling about?" Ryder asked.

"I'm smiling," Markus started, "because I'm about to become the best thing for the Cardinals since Albert Pujols."

CHAPTER 49

Surviving Embers.

Spencer:

When Spencer Carter finally regained consciousness, **he** awoke in a room he had not been in a very long time. He was in the conference room at Oracle Tower. Eleventh floor, down the hall from the elevator, he remembered it well. He was sitting in an office chair facing the beautiful wood table. Esther Marigold sat parallel to him on the other side. As his eyes opened, it initially felt like he had fallen into a cruel dream, almost as if his mind were unearthing a memory he had no desire to relive. The conference room, Esther, the smells of vacuumed carpet, polished wood, and filtered air all felt bittersweet as it was processed through his mind, like honey and ash stuck in a blender on puree.

But to his shock, his focus returned and he woke up. He realized he wasn't living out a memory—he was actually in the tower. But something was wrong. He was bound to his chair in chains, and just one look at Esther sitting across from him was enough to strike his mind with fright. Her hair was a messy blob of spider legs. Her face and eyes contorted in extreme pain, nearly ready to sprout ugly tears.

The necrosis on her face stood out vividly like a parasitical black mold in the late evening sun. Her right arm was bound up in chains, pinning it to her chest like the wrapping of a mummy. Her left arm was bent at an alarming angle, the skin around it bruised and black. It looked like a mannequin arm that had been jammed haphazardly into a junk box.

Spencer didn't know what had happened. The last thing he remembered was the flashbang coming down the stairwell into the undercroft, the flashbang going off, and being knocked unconscious. Next thing he knew he had awoken to this horrific scene, his head throbbing and his old spark horribly mangled in front of him. Emotional sensory overload enveloped him.

He began to struggle in his chair, desperately hoping to regain control of the situation. Esther lifted her head slowly upon realizing that Spencer was now awake.

"Spencer," she said quietly, barely audible. Despite not hearing exactly what she said, Spencer immediately recognized her soft whisper.

"Esther. What did they do to you?" There was an anger in his words he didn't expect to hear.

"I tried to secure the weapon," Marigold started, her words tense. "You took it away, and once she found out what I tried to do she broke my bloody arm!" she cried out. She began to hyperventilate, tears mixing with her heavy breaths.

It felt like some unseen hand was gripping Spencer's heart and squeezing with all its might. It was almost as if he shared her injuries. Or at least seeing her hurt was hurting him as well. "Es— the boys, what happened to them, are they dead?"

"No," Marigold said. "They escaped from here. The Progenitress... she lost control."

"Lost control?"

"Yes, the girl... she somehow took her body back."

"Charlotte? She took back control of herself?"

"Briefly," she said quietly. "Just enough to send the Time Riders on their way. She regained herself, fought back."

Spencer leaned back in his chair, letting himself relax slightly. "That girl continues to surprise."

"Spencer, Project Siren, where is it?" Marigold hissed.

"Your men didn't find it?"

"No, they didn't! Where is it?" she yelled.

Spencer didn't consider his secret hatch a foolproof plan of protection for the Siren grenade. But from what Marigold said, it fared quite nicely. He didn't know whether it was that efficient of a hiding spot or if the operators she sent to the undercroft just weren't up to snuff.

"It's safe, hidden away."

"We need it. Where is it? We need to drive her out."

A flicker of hope found its way into his chest. "We finally on the same page?" he asked.

"I have no use for dead Time Riders! I don't give a damn about the girl, but the boys need to live if I am to find their cellular stasis."

This was not a call to partnership. Marigold was merely an enemy of Spencer's enemy. The doors to the room opened and Spencer looked over to see Spartan entering the room, a hand holding onto his stomach.

"Marigold," he muttered, running over to his CEO. He looked at her chains and pulled on them slightly to test their integrity, she yelped in pain and Spartan backed up with his hands raised.

"What is it?"

"It's my arm you dolt!"

He moved over quickly to her side, saw her injured arm, and recoiled. "Oh damn…"

"Get me out of this chair Edgar!" Marigold yelled.

Spartan groaned and pulled out his handgun. He aimed and shot at the lock on her chair, filling the room with the sharp noise of a high caliber gunshot. Marigold's chains fell to the ground, and she leaned forward in her chair, holding her arm as much as she could, still whimpering.

"Where is she?" she asked.

"No clue. She's been all over the tower since the kids slipped out, gathering all her revenants. She even sent that big one out looking for them again. God knows where they slipped off too. But she won't be pleased with anything less than their heads on pikes at this rate. C'mon up, we need to get you down to Doc Watson."

"They're going back to the undercroft," Spencer said. Both Marigold and Spartan looked over at him. "They are going for the Siren grenade, they have to. They know where it is."

Marigold and Spartan exchanged glances, stayed silent for a few seconds. Then Marigold nodded her head. "Get him loose."

Spartan looked alarmed. "You want to let *Carter* loose?"

"Yes," Marigold snarled. "Do it. *Now*."

He didn't look entirely sure of himself, but despite whatever he was feeling he walked over to Spencer and shot his lock off his chains as well. Spencer felt them drop and clatter to the ground. He took his wrists and began to rub them tenderly. "Thank you, Edgar."

"Sure," Spartan said plainly.

Spencer looked across at Marigold. There was a fiery, hateful look in her eye. She was angry, but not entirely at him. She could tell the real cause of her spite was the Progenitress.

"I need to get back out to the undercroft before the Apex gets there," he said.

"That might not be a race you can win, Spencer," Marigold said softly.

"I have to try. There's too much riding on this."

She looked over at Spartan. "Get Tyke on the line, Spartan. Get Spencer a vehicle, anything you can spare quickly."

"Are you sure you're just going to let him slip through the ropes?" Spartan asked.

"As far as I can see it, our little war is over. We have a new enemy. You have your orders."

Spartan stole one last glance at Spencer, then brought his radio from his hip to his ear. "Donovan, you copy?"

"Go ahead, Spartan," a voice said faintly from his radio.

"How are our transports looking?"

"The transports? Whatever we have on the lineup is good to go. What do you need?"

"Something on the lighter side, we need to get to the other side of the city yesterday."

"On the lighter side? Sure, will the taxi cover vehicle work? That's as light as you're going to get."

"That'll work. You know the drill, get it moving out of the base and park it in the front. I'll meet you there, usual ETA?"

"I'll do you better, five minutes. You'll be there?"

"Affirmative." Spartan began to put his radio away before Tyke managed to say something else.

"There's one more thing sir," he said

Spartan put the device back to his ear. "What is it?"

"She found out about the Charon." Spartan put the radio back closer to his ear, like he didn't believe what he had just heard.

"What do you mean she found out about it?" he barked.

"The kid in the black dress," Tyke said. "She found it and told me to deploy it. One of your squads is driving around the city right now looking for Marigold's car and the Time Riders."

"You deployed the Charon?"

"She started hurting my mechanics, I wasn't left with any choice."

Spartan bit his tongue and dipped his head. "Copy that." He took his radio away from his face and put it back on his belt, then he gestured sharply with his head toward the front door. Spencer got up from his chair but stopped on a dime in the entrance to the room. Though it was not in his best interest, he couldn't help but look back at Marigold. She remained slouched in her chair, one of her arms in a cast, the other horrendously broken.

He didn't want to leave her on her own like this, but he knew time was short. Marigold looked up and saw his hesitation.

"Don't waste time on me Carter, worry about the Progenitress. I can live with another broken limb if it means she's gone."

Spencer felt like he was playing an invisible game of tug-of-war. He knew he needed to leave, but part of him didn't want to. What happened next occurred without thinking. After letting himself relax slightly, he allowed himself to walk over to her, bend over, and kiss her on the forehead—a gesture he had done many times before, but not for a long time.

Once he leaned back from her head Marigold blinked a few times. Her face was still but her one good eye seemed brighter, livelier. She stared back at him with a quiet, but attentive gaze. For a moment, the one grey eye that stared back at him glowed, beautiful once more.

"Hey, you don't have time for lovey-lovey. You need to get to that basement," Spartan barked. "If my squad in the Charon finds them, they are not going to survive."

"Can you get her to Patricia?" Spencer asked.

"Doc Watson?" Spartan asked. "Yeah, I'll get her there. Just do your part Carter." Spencer remained still staring at Marigold. She continued to look at him with a loving gaze, a small smile etched on her lips. "Get a move on handsome."

Spencer began to smile so wide it was painful. "You got it, Es."

He turned around and left the room in almost a sprint. Once he got there, he descended the massive staircase at the end of the hall and began to run through the main lobby until he stopped in surprise at the entrance. Where the revolving doors and front windows usually were, was a mass of glass and bent steel. What was left of the windows were shattered into fine particles that littered the ground like grains of sand. He took only a moment to ponder on it before going through the glass and shimming through the median where the revolving doors used to be.

Once they got outside, a stocky black man with a buzzcut and sunglasses stood in front of a taxi parked at the sidewalk near the staircase. Spencer walked down to meet him.

"Fancy seeing you again Spencer," he said.

"I'd agree Donovan."

"This ride for you?"

"Yes."

Tyke threw the keys and Spencer caught them flawlessly in the air. He opened the door of the taxi and climbed into the driver's seat, then placed the keys in the ignition. Tyke put his hands on the open windowsill of the car.

"You got a plan Spencer? I don't know why you're back but I'm hoping you're here to get rid of that girl."

"That's the plan."

"Well, do it. All I could do was sit there as she hurt my boys. You better make her pay for that," Tyke hissed.

"Excuse me!"

They both stopped what they were doing and turned their attention near the stairwell. Spencer suddenly began to feel feverish. The Progenitress was near the staircase, walking down, hands behind her back. "Looking to go somewhere?"

"It's no business of yours kid," Tyke's voice declared with authority. He stepped in front of Spencer's door like he was a personal bodyguard. The Progenitress scoffed, opened her mouth with shock, and clasped an open hand against her chest. "Excuse me? Kid? I'll have you know I am over a millennia old, you cretin! Who taught you to speak to a woman like that?"

"Woman? You don't look a day over fourteen!"

The Progenitress craned her head sharply, then clenched her hand in a crushing motion. Something audibly cracked in Tyke's chest, and he fell to a knee. Then she thrust her hand outwards, and he flew onto the hood of the taxi and onto the ground.

The Progenitress balled both her fists and began shaking with anger. "The vessel is sixteen," she growled through her teeth. "I know it's too damn young."

She noticed Spencer sitting in the seat of the taxi and rushed forward until she was right at the window of the driver's side door. She gripped both her hands on it. Her fingers drifted inside the cabin. "And where do you think *you're* going?"

Spencer faced forward. She was so close now that even looking in her general direction was like staring down a flashlight because of her eyes.

"Nah—no, wait. Let me guess." She lifted a finger. "Evening drive? Maybe getting some takeout? Ice cream?" Spencer didn't acknowledge her. She brought her finger to her chin and began to tap it. "Or maybe... just maybe... you're going after the Siren grenade again." Spencer remained silent. "Not you, surely you wouldn't do that." She brought up an arm horizontally on the door and rested on her hand. "You're a smarty pants. I mean you don't have the foresight I do, of course, but surely you can tell this isn't going to go in your favor. You can't save her." Her eyebrows arched upward and she giggled. "Oh, I'm a poet and I didn't even know it."

Spencer gripped the steering wheel of the taxi like a vice, biting down on his tongue in order not to say anything. It was like sitting cross legged in a minefield with her so close. One wrong gesture and everything felt like it would blow sky-high. He wasn't afraid as much as he was extremely unhappy with being in such a position.

"Do you want to know how this is going to go?" she asked. "Well, for starters. Let's take into account all the little things that can change an outcome. The number of ways is so vast it may as well be infinite. But mostly it ends in... well, violent death!" she said brightly. "The only desirable outcomes that are even feasible for you I could count on one hand. And even so, that's not accounting for the probability of it going wrong later. The house always wins, sweety, and I've got a golden throne at the tippy top. I mean... y'know, now that I think about it, there is one outcome, but surely not."

She was immediately interrupted by the sound of a car horn blaring past the taxi. Her face went still. The honking continued until she stood back up from the window and walked around the car to see where the commotion was coming from. Spencer let his curiosity get the better of him and he did the same, stepping out of the taxi and looking over the roof and out onto the other side.

Spencer looked and saw another car parked around twenty feet away. It was Marigold's convertible sports car. Its engine hummed like a growling dog. What he didn't expect was who was sitting in the driver's seat.

"Markus?"

"Heyo, Progenatramp! I'm looking for a hot date!" Markus yelled. The Progenitress just stayed still. Markus stood up in his seat and brought up a baseball that was in his right hand and began tossing it up and catching it in his hand. "I got a ticket or two to the ball game at Busch stadium. You interested?"

"Ball game?" the Progenitress said. "What are you blabbering abo…"

"Think fast!" Markus threw the baseball, and it collided bluntly with the Progenitress's nose. She recoiled and held her face with her hands, grunting in obscene anger.

Markus let out a tricksters laugh. "Bada-bing! Bada friggin' boom! The Rebel with Wings finds his mark!" he hollered. Then he put on his mask, jumped down into the seat, and began flipping her off with a sharp middle finger.

He pushed down on the gas and sped off in the car, hitting a median with a loud crash and speeding off into the streets ahead. The Progenitress yelled vilely, like a scorned demon.

"I will tear you apart!" she yelled. "I've had it up to *here* with unruly children," she hissed.

As her anger grew, she began to hover off the ground, her eyes glowing brighter and her feet and hands showed the Time Stream floating past her like flames in the wind. She floated forward, then sped off into the sky like an aircraft until she was out of sight.

After the whimsy of seeing her fly had worn off enough, Spencer managed to collect his thoughts enough to finally get a grasp of what was happening. He pieced everything together, one thing at a time. Markus was there in the car, but Ryder wasn't. He had the skysurfer pack on so he had to have gone back to the undercroft. Did he have the Siren grenade? He thought he had seen him hide it, but he wasn't sure. Par for the course, he had no idea what Markus was thinking. He seemed like he wanted to draw the Progenitress toward him, but for what? Does that mean he had the grenade? Either way, he had mentioned Busch stadium.

He quickly got out of the car and ran over to Tyke on the ground. To his surprise, he wasn't dead, but he was clearly substantially injured.

"Donnie!" Spencer called out. "You need to get to the infirmary."

"Don't waste time on me you old fool!" Tyke exclaimed. "Make wake! Get after them!"

Begrudgingly, Spencer got to his feet, climbed into the driver's seat, and closed the door. He turned on the engine, then shifted the taxi into gear and slammed his foot on the accelerator. He took off in the general direction of the undercroft, hoping that he would be able to catch up with Markus before it was too late.

CHAPTER 50

Lovely Dose of Chaos

Markus:

All things considered Markus was having the time of his life. If anyone were to tell him he was going to start a full-blown car chase in the personal vehicle of Oracle's CEO, he never would have believed it. Yet here he was, driving as crazy as possible, living out a punk anarchist's dream. The addictive rush was back, and he rode the high with every fiber of his being, laughing and hollering like a villain.

He accelerated until the speedometer in the car kept spiking to one hundred miles per hour. He tried to avoid any cars on the road and did everything he could to avoid popping onto the sidewalk and hitting an innocent pedestrian. After a while, Markus began to hear sirens and looked in the rearview mirror. He saw the pulsating blue and red of police lights, speeding after him.

"Uh oh. Five-O," Markus said to himself with a twinge of excitement.

Markus sped down the street like a freak on drugs, dodging cars and nearly being hit by others. The police were hot on his tail, but they struggled to keep up with the high-end vehicle, and if they got too close, Markus just went through the Time Stream. If it weren't for the spoiler in the back, the vehicle would have taken flight.

As he continued his little race, a helicopter came into the area with a camera, filming the whole debacle, and Markus was on board for all of it. It was all going according to plan until one of his tires popped loudly, almost causing him to hit somebody.

"What? Really, she went for the cheap tires? Are you for real right now?" Markus complained. Then the front window shattered, startling him even further, and he looked back at the rearview mirror as he was driving. He saw a new vehicle behind him: a large mammoth of a contraption, black in color and speeding right towards him and keeping pace.

It looked like a large black tank with massive wheels. Something about it seemed like an oversized homemade remote-controlled car. Markus could hear its engine from where he was, sounding like an absurdly loud diesel engine. An operator fired a machine gun from a gunner's seat to the vehicle's right. As they drove, the operator pointed the weapon at him and pulled the trigger. The sound of gunfire cracked through the air as bullets whizzed past Markus's head.

"Whoa! What the—!" he yelled, trying to swerve slightly trying and avoid getting pelted in the head. One last look behind him revealed another gunner's seat open on the left side of the vehicle, parallel to the other.

"Oh, piss off with that!" Markus ducked his head as low as he could to avoid the torrent of ballistics that began to slam into the back of the car and through the shattered windshield. Between the popped tire and lack of visibility, controlling the car proved to be a nearly impossible task. For a few minutes that felt like hours, Markus had to fight the urge to raise his head into danger in order to see where he was going. This was not going to last. If it persisted this was going to end in a massive crash or with a bullet caving open the back of his skull.

Before he could conjure a plan, something down the street caught his eyes. Large police vans were closing off the road with a few cruisers alongside them. Officers took cover behind with weapons at the ready.

A blockade. Markus had enough knowledge about police to know what to expect next. If they had set this up, they expected Markus to stop, and they were going to do it by force. He acted quickly. He kicked through the Time Stream until the pedal became lodged and stuck on the floorboard, then climbed up onto the hood of the car as it kept moving forward at extreme speed.

Markus lay down on the hood as he felt the engine scream through the hood. He felt close to slipping off but managed to stay clinging. Closing his eyes and focusing, Markus took himself and the sports car into the Time Stream, making it go exponentially faster. He stole a glance forward and just barely saw the spike strip he was anticipating.

The car ran over the strip at an unsafe speed and the vehicle flipped, shooting Markus through the air. As he careened up high, he slammed the gauge on his glove, and the skysurfer flew under his feet. He took flight, almost losing his balance in the process. The car cartwheeled into a large crash, sending the officers at the barricade scattering to avoid the debris. The large black tank vehicle behind crashed right through over the strips and into the law enforcement vehicles, completely unaffected.

Markus flew as fast as he could while trying to maintain control as the gunners continued to fire at him in the air. Bullets flew past him and hit the windows of the massive office buildings next to him. Glass began to rain down on him, grazing his arms and landing in his hair. In response he did an evasive maneuver away to avoid the sharp particles. Once he was out of the open, he crouched down and leaned forward, causing him to descend at a high speed.

Getting closer to the ground, Markus was harshly pulled back by an unseen force. His legs flew into the air, and the skysurfer flew forward without him, but he didn't fall. Instead, he was turned around and faced forward with the Progenitress. She flew with him like a dark angel. One hand raised in a clenched gesture. She pulled him closer, a manic bloodlust in her gaze.

"There will be no future for you, Markus Daniels!" she screeched.

The skysurfer kept pushing forward, then did a one eighty midair and flew back toward Markus and the Progenitress until it slid right under his feet once more. Feeling its weight, he pushed it upward with his feet until the flames from the board were right in front of her face. She let out a scream and let go of him and backed away quickly in the air, but not quickly enough to prevent her hair from catching fire.

She flew away in a panic, like a burning tree branch caught in the wind. Markus screamed loudly as he plummeted down to the street below. He eventually landed on something—not the concrete he expected, but something metallic and nearly as hard. All the air in his lungs exited the moment he landed. Trying to regain his composure, he realized that whatever he had landed on was moving. Sitting up, he saw the street going by in front of him and two massive wheels to his left and right. There were two more up front. When he realized what he was on, his lungs felt even more empty.

He'd landed on the vehicle that had been pursuing him this whole time. A hatch on the top opened to reveal a helmeted operator rising out of the vehicle and looking right at Markus. He jumped, pulled a pistol from his side, and pulled back its slide. Markus, still sitting, kicked the operator's arm instinctively. The sound of one gunshot rang out as the weapon flipped through the air and down onto the city street behind them. The operator jumped out of the hatch and forced his hands on Markus's throat. Still recovering from the fall, his lungs began to burn like they were filled with fire.

Mustering the last of his energy, he pushed forward in another desperate kick through the Time Stream. The operator flew behind Markus when he kicked away. He began rolling until he was over the front of the vehicle, next to the two windows serving as a windshield. Markus rolled over to the left side at the same time.

Grabbing onto the only thing he could, he got a grip on one of the machine guns that was attached to the gunner's seat. It moved fluidly on its pedestal as Markus's shoes dragged on the street. The vehicle began to swerve as the operator on the front obstructed the driver's view, causing Markus to move around rapidly like the end of a wet mop. His grip began to feel weaker moment by moment.

He heard a scream from the front as the operator fell and landed in front of the vehicle. A loud boom sounded as he was hit and driven over. The tires went over him and popped up in the air, causing Markus to go up with it before gravity brought him back down onto the street. He was hit with sharp pain in his arms and cried out as his grip slipped down the end of the machine guns barrel.

Looking ahead of him, he saw the skysurfer still following behind him as he moved. It wasn't catching up, but it managed to keep pace as everything remained in motion. The operator in the gunner's seat reached forward and tried to reach for the trigger of the machine gun, hoping to fire the weapon while the barrel was aimed right at the middle of Markus's body.

In a panic, Markus exerted himself to his limit and pulled himself up from the barrel and grabbed hold of the gunner's tactical vest. The operator let out a small scream as he was pulled from the seat and began rolling on the road below. He managed to get his foot on top of the gun and used it to push himself onto the seat and inside the vehicle.

On the inside, an entire squad sat to his left, and the driver and the passenger seats were to his right. He knelt down and quickly moved towards the driver's seat before anyone realized that he'd managed to get inside with them.

"You got a visual?" the driver asked. "Anything?"

"I don't know, something happened up top," the operator in the passenger seat said. "Maybe he went under a wheel?"

"Or maybe he's right behind you! Wouldn't that be crazy?" Markus asked.

"*What the*?!" The driver yelled.

"Mind if I borrow this?" Markus grabbed the steering wheel up front and turned it sharply to the right. Everyone inside was thrown from their seats and to the left into a pile on the floor. The driver began to fight fiercely against Markus for control of the wheel. All the while, he had to duck and dodge punches coming from the operator in the passenger's seat.

As they wrestled, the vehicle went everywhere except the middle of the street. They drove on the sidewalk, colliding with four light poles before going back into the road. Then another yank on the wheel from Markus sent them all crashing through the windows of the first floor of an office building, driving through a cubicle area until they crashed through another set of windows out and into the street once more.

Then Markus forced his head into the Time Stream and headbutted the driver without even thinking about it. He immediately became dizzy and began to see stars. He looked around as he began to see double, trying to articulate where the wheel was, or which one was the real one. He waved his hand, reaching out at all the wheels he could see, until his hand struck something tangible. He gripped hard and brought it down in the right direction.

The vehicle crashed into another building and began to grind into it, making an earsplitting noise and sending showers of sparks flying into the air. Gritting his teeth and ignoring the new throbbing in his head, Markus climbed to his feet, kicked an operator out of the way, and climbed up out the hatch and onto the top and back outside. Once he brought himself all the way out, he adjusted to the change in light and avoided the sparks as the transport drilled into the side of the building and began to tilt on its axis.

He looked behind and saw the skysurfer was still in hot pursuit behind, still trying to get back to its pack. Realizing what he had to do, Markus steadied himself as best he could and focused on the still-moving board as everything began to move horizontally. One, two, three seconds passed. His eyes remained glued to it for every single one. The transport groaned and tilted even more.

"Tally friggin' ho," he said to himself. Letting out three breaths in rapid succession, Markus jumped and let out a yell, moved down through the air, and landed on the board whilst barely keeping his balance. He immediately put his feet up in the air to stop as he looked to see the vehicle reach the side of the building and topple over onto its side, then clumsily onto its top. The wheels jutted upward into the sky like it was an upturned turtle with a square shell. Everyday civilians began to appear cautiously around, trying to figure out what happened. Markus remained suspended in the air on the skysurfer, one end of it higher than the other.

Fair amounts of people started to crowd both the Oracle transport and Markus. Some brought out cell phones, others just looked on in shock. Many sets of eyes gawked at him, like he was some sort of messianic figure. They whispered in each other's ears and murmured amongst themselves. Markus was always willing to be the center of attention, but as the crowd around him was proving to be almost too much. *Almost.* Not sure what else to do, Markus waved around like a celebrity posing for a photoshoot. All things considered, he quite enjoyed it, maybe even too much.

"Make a path! Make way!"

Markus stopped his façade and looked over to see a grey-haired police officer and two younger ones formally making a path through the assembling crowd. They were in full uniform, pistols in hand and teeth gnashing. All three of them raised their weapons at him as he remained suspended in the air.

"Come down off that device and get down on the street! Hands where I could see them Daniels!"

Markus was hit with a sense of déjà vu, when he realized he recognized the officer up front. "Heya, Officer Holt," he greeted. "Didn't think I'd see you again. In truth I was hoping not to."

"Get off that board and onto the ground!" Holt demanded.

"You think I'm the threat? What about the needle dicks that flipped their oversized cereal box over there?" he said gesturing towards the flipped transport. "Y'know, the guys with possibly illegally owned machine guns and all that fun stuff?"

"Get down now! I'm not going to ask again!"

"You really want to shoot me Holt? Get in line."

"On the count of three, you are going too…"

A horrid screech filled the air, and everyone including the officers held their ears in order to block out the high-pitched drone. Markus saw Progenitress overhead, her hair finally extinguished. She looked down and began diving toward them like a flying witch. As she descended many of the civilians ducked down and let out startled screams. Markus took to the air and kept a distance between him and the Progenitress who was flying just above, a desperate desire to finally reach his destination swarming his mind.

CHAPTER 51

The Battle of Busch Stadium

Markus:

The Progenitress sailed through the air like a runaway kite, flying after Markus in hot pursuit like a needle through water. Both he and the Progenitress went into the Time Stream to gain speed. While still within it, she began to dive low into the city skyline through the many buildings. At the rapid speed they were both going, the buildings they passed were nothing more than a blur. One wrong move would have either one of them obliterated on impact against the structures. He followed close behind, consciously tracing his path to avoid any potential danger. Once they both navigated through the buildings safely and came to a clearing, Markus cranked his gauge and put his acceleration on full blast.

He moved faster and faster, getting closer and closer until he was close to where he needed to be. When close enough the Progenitress leaped forward and grabbed hold of the Markus midair. He screamed in surprise and both of them went into a barrel roll, slowly but surely descending. They kept spinning, unsuccessfully trying to get loose.

The next thing Markus knew he fell back down to earth and rolled a few times onto soft green grass. He was blinded by large bright lights. An announcer's voice sounded, masses of people sitting in bright red seats looking in at where he sat. The more he adjusted, the better he could see the handful of people in the area wearing baseball uniforms, most of them clad in red and white, their caps depicting a red cardinal perched on a baseball bat. Markus then knew exactly where he was.

"Finally! Busch Stadium!" he said brightly as the skysurfer returned to its pack.

Markus shot to his feet as the team gawked at him. The Progenitress did the same, manically screaming like a mad feline at anyone that was close.

"He's mine!" she yelled pushing a few players out of the way.

Stadium security was now on the field right behind her. Upon noticing them she spun around and threw her hands outward. The guards went flying into the air. The audience gasped collectively. Even the players backed away from her. She turned her steaming gaze toward a mascot who was on the field, dressed in a bipedal cardinal costume. The mascot ran away and the Progenitress threw her hands towards him. The mascot went flying high into the crowd and crashed into a few patrons.

"Oh, for the love of—leave Fred bird alone, you Philistine!" Markus yelled.

She rushed towards Markus through the Time Stream and tried to find his throat. Wrestling for a moment, he managed to kick her off him and she went flying down onto the grass. He rushed forward, hoping to restrain her.

Now on the ground she turned to face Markus again, holding her hands up, her palms facing forward. "Not any closer!" she screamed.

"Or what? You'll jedi push me? Sit still!" Markus said, trying to get the Siren grenade out of his pocket. The Progenitress screamed again, and a horrible roar filled the stadium.

Markus turned his head to the source in the backfield. The Apex was there on the roof of the stadium. Its eyes glowed at a distance and its imposing size easily seen. It proceeded to jump down into the chairs, running through them like they were bowling pins and jumped onto the field, rushing through the Time Stream toward Markus. Markus jumped out of the way as it went for a wild hook in his general direction. The Apex then placed itself between him and the Progenitress. The audience screamed and all the remaining players on the field fled.

The Progenitress lay on the ground winded and breathed

heavily. She looked up, a burning hatred in her eyes.

"Kill him! Rip him asunder!" she yelled to the Apex.

The Apex let out another brain-rattling roar and walked towards Markus. He began to back up slowly towards home plate until his foot bumped into a bat on the ground. The Apex inched closer, mouth agape.

Being this close to both success and failure filled Markus with drive, but now the Apex stood between him and his goal. He told himself that it didn't matter if he was torn to shreds or killed. He wasn't going to run, not this time. He looked up at its head, despite the nature of its eyes, Markus felt it meet his own.

"Let's roll, Chompers. We gotta audience to entertain."

The Apex roared again, and Markus flicked the bat at his feet up into the air with his foot, catching it in midair. The Apex then went for a powerful swipe again and Markus bashed at its hand with a Time Stream guided swing of the bat. The creature's hand got knocked back with a solid crack that could be heard all over the field, then he began pummeling its legs. The Apex seemed to grow aggravated with each swing smashing against its solid flesh, and it took a few swings of its own with its claws. Markus got away from each of them and kept hitting its legs until the bat snapped in half, sending splinters flying in every direction.

The Apex opened its maw, revealing the forming inferno in its throat. Markus found a baseball at his feet and chucked it right into the Apex's throat. It began to choke and only a few stray flames escaped from its mouth. The ball dropped from its throat and onto the ground smoldering and on fire.

Markus took the heater-beater from his back and readied it to swing. The Apex rushed forward again, and he struck the darker part of its leg with the bat. It howled in pain and stood back holding its leg. Its flesh noticeably became cracked like an eggshell, exposing bare, glistening blue flesh beneath it.

He was surprised by this welcome revelation. Most attacks just angered it, but now he had hurt it. He noticed the Apex was covered in these black spots, like there were parts of its anatomy that consisted of brittle charcoal. They were randomly located at various spots from its legs all the way to the creature's neck.

He rushed forward with his new bat and struck a black spot on its second leg. Its flesh shattered like molded clay, and the monster once again howled in pain. The audience that remained began to applaud and cheer. Markus and the Apex were being projected on the large screen in the back of the field. He took a quick look around, holding the bat on his shoulder.

"Hey! Hey! Always wanted to be in the big leagues!" Markus said cheerfully.

The Apex roared again, its frustration peaking. It began to swing wildly around with its clawed hands, trying to hit Markus in a swan song. He backed away and hopped on his feet around the Apex, making mental notes whenever he saw a black spot. The Apex shot some more blue flames out of its mouth at him, scorching the dirt and grass.

Rushing forward again, he jumped. Smashing a spot on its shoulder and arm, knocking the Apex down to one knee, then onto the ground. Then he moved over to the creature's front and began hitting its head over and over with passion, repaying a debt of retribution. Having to endure the waves of hits, the Apex struggled to get up, and the audience remained in an excited uproar cheering Markus on.

As the Apex's head moved back and forth with each swing, Markus noticed one more black spot, waving along the creature's neck. Noticing this, he started hitting in an upward motion, forcing the creature's head up. He continued doing this, taking a swing at exposed flesh. After three successful hits the Apex began screeching in fear, but Markus didn't relent. After one especially powerful blow while the creature's head was high in the air, he conjured all the strength he could and sailed the bat through the Time Stream, yelling and throwing all the strength he could into his swing as the bat was about to connect with The Apex's head one last time.

Just before it did, out of nowhere he became enveloped in a thick blue cloud and everything around him surrounded him in an infinite black. All of Markus's mind suffered a debilitating spiral. What once was sensical became abstract. It was like he was plucked from reality and thrown into a nightmare. He heard the Progenitress's voice dance among the shadows. It was single, quiet voice that called out from the void, quiet and feminine. She only spoke two words.

"No more."

Out of the fog came a spectral figure, seemingly made out of fog or smoke. As it drew closer, a figure revealed itself. But she no longer looked like Charlotte, she was something different now. Something belonging to unreality. She resembled a woman, donning a curvaceous figure and a sea of wispy white hair which seemed to flow above her. Then as she drew closer, Markus immediately became afraid. Her face resembled the front of a monstrous skull. Rows of long sharp teeth were housed in its jaw, and a skeletal hole was in the place of a nose. The eyes glowed a blinding blue in their sockets.

"No more, Markus Daniels."

With one movement of a hand the cloud flew towards Markus and enveloped him where he sat. His lungs became filled with a potent noxious gas that caused him to cough violently and fall to his knees. Something inside him began to change. His veins felt like they were pumping acid, and his muscles began to move and contort painfully. His head was ravaged by the worst headache he'd ever experienced. All he could do on the ground was scream in pain.

"As you can see, this gas is much stronger than what you are used to. You may have avoided changing, but who's to say if all you needed was one more little push?"

Markus threw off his mask as his eyes burned hot in his skull. His back bloated as if something was trying to break its way out of his spine. His vision flashed between his dimension and the Time Stream.

"I restrained myself out of love. I wanted you to come to me—I want all my children to come to me. But I'm done asking now. I'm done being nice."

Markus fell over and lifted his hands as his fingernails began to split and black blunt claws replaced them. Warm blood began pouring from the newly formed appendages.

"You will be mine. You will help me prevent the Patriarch from taking control. We will snuff him out in his crib, end him before he even begins. Nathan Ryder, your new friend, your new brother, will die by your hand."

Markus felt hard growth breaking his skin all over his body. His arms, legs, torso, and back became enveloped in tiny, symmetrical boney armor.

"You are an ugly little bit of nothing, Markus Daniels. You are the child no one wanted. But *I* want you, and I will make you something beautiful."

Among the pain, her words were understood clearly. And even so, something else festered, something that took control of everything he had. Anger was now in control. There was a time he had accepted this position as truth, he had believed he was the one nobody wanted, but something was different now. He didn't believe it, and he didn't *want* to believe it. He wasn't a hinderance, he was Markus Daniels, flaws and all. This was his choice. He wasn't going to be anything else.

"Shut up," Markus growled, almost inaudibly.

"What was that?" she asked.

"I said shut up!" Markus screamed, getting to his feet. He wobbled but remained standing. He grunted and hissed through his teeth, powering through the pain.

"Still fighting, the audacity! Why do you keep defying me?"

"I don't call myself the Rebel with Wings for nothin' sugar tits. I rebel, it's what I do."

"Well, no longer, I am beyond finished with you and your nonsense."

She moved forward, hand outstretched. Markus raised his head to the sky and let out another scream. It came out differently than the others. As if it was the cry of a massive bird or a reptile. Then two more spots of immense pain erupted as two growths shot out of his back and tore through the back of his sweatshirt. Once he opened his eyes, the fog had cleared, and he was still in the middle of Busch stadium. The Apex remained in front of him, startled. The Progenitress lay on her side in the grass behind him, back in Charlotte's body.

The audience gasped in prolonged surprise across the stadium. Markus's mind went into vertigo, and he felt like he was processing more than he initially had to. After trying to focus, he began to see the light around him change and the sound of a cloth-like object filled the air, akin to that sound of a flag dancing in the wind. He looked up and nearly fainted when he saw the leathery wings flapping passively to his left and right.

As he moved them, they responded to his every thought, just like his arms and legs. He swayed with them, bent them in and out.

He even began to clap with them as best as he could. As odd as it was, it was like he had been born with them.

"Okay, wow! That... that is gnarly. Holy crap!"

The Apex snarled and took a swipe at him. Markus flapped his wings instinctually and propelled himself backward into the air. He began to flail about in the air as he went back and forth. The Apex jumped up and tried to bite him in the air, but not before Markus managed to fly off to the side, throwing his weight. He began flapping his wings in accordance with his opponent's movements, carrying himself through a crash course of learning how to use his new ability for aviation.

The Apex kept trying to get a hold on Markus, and it felt like a dog trying to bite down on a fly buzzing overhead. With every passing moment, he was growing more proficient. So much so that the audience began cheering Markus on, hoping to urge him to victory.

In the air Markus began to look at his blood-soaked hands and noticed the claws that now were in place of his fingertips. Lifting his right hand up high, Markus swooped in and swiped at the Apex's face through the Time Stream, knocking it back off its feet. Once he readjusted himself, he swiped back and forth over and over. The Apex retaliated each time to no avail each time.

He continued encircling his opponent, to home in on a new opportunity to cause some damage. The Apex shot more flames into the sky and hit one of Markus's wings. He felt the fire hit his new limb and he yelled out in pain and plummeted to the ground. He held his wing like he'd burned his hand on a stove. The Apex sensed its advantage and charged forward as the audience gasped in horror.

Despite his pain, Markus gritted his teeth, flew up and forward toward it, made an evasive maneuver, and slammed into its back. He clung to it as he began swiping at it with his claws at animalistic speeds, chipping away at the burnt armor on its neck. While Markus was on its back, the Apex couldn't use its own claws or jaws. All it managed to do was shake and jump in circles, trying to get him off. Eventually Markus chipped away enough to get to a patch of dark flesh that sat exposed beneath it all. He lifted one of his hands and plunged it into the wound with a yell.

The Apex's mouth went wide as it wailed in pain. Markus

attacked again and again until it fell onto its knees. Then, he flew up off its back, went back up, and came back down hard on its back with his feet, knocking it face first in the dirt. He landed in front of it, and began attacking the neck once again. Bits of hardened stone like armor flew around like it was being attacked with a jackhammer. The creature's head swayed back as the attacks persisted. When the neck was completely exposed, Markus focused and began to attack that. Within seconds the flesh was cut and torn almost completely by Markus's claws.

The flesh inside glowed like a wall of sapphires and zenaphosporus began to leak out of its body. The Apex coughed and gagged. Then Markus flew up again and wrapped his arms around its head from behind, beginning to pull. Using the strength in his wings and the Time Stream, he pulled with all his might. After a few seconds Markus could feel the flesh tear as he continued. The Apex groaned in pain and desperation. With one last mighty heave, the head came loose, and Markus flew into the air with its decapitated head in his arms.

The audience of the stadium gasped in shock. In disgust, Markus immediately dropped it, and it hit its own body on the way down, rolling onto the ground like an uncooked pot roast. The rest of the body fell over and began to unravel completely, dissipating into dust.

He flew back down to the ground and tried to remember how to use his feet as he began to process what had just happened. The crowd began a loud and outstanding cheer. Everyone left was hooting and hollering on their feet. Markus turned around to see masses of people all applauding him, then he realized that a camera was filming him, and he was up on the big prompter in the middle of the field. He also realized that since that was the case, he was likely being aired on television as well. He raised his arms and wings, leading them all, an immediate ego trip going right to his head.

"No... *noooo!*"

Markus turned around and saw the Progenitress flying towards him, hands out. She slammed into him and knocked him to the ground, choking him with both of her hands. The audience gasped. He tried to throw her off, but somehow her strength surpassed him. Markus could only look up at her as his airflow became constricted. Looking up at her, she showed the raw rage on her face. Her teeth were grinding, and she growled like a wild animal.

"Why do you keep doing this?! Why do you keep hurting me and all that I love?"

Markus's thoughts couldn't complete. He couldn't breathe, couldn't focus. He wouldn't last much longer like this. She raised his head and slammed it into the Earth, which is when Markus could feel something fall out of his pocket. Then his thoughts were realigned just enough to remember what it was. The Siren grenade.

"I never wanted this! I wanted us to be together, to be a family! That's all I wanted; that's what *you* wanted! Why couldn't any of you just say yes? Why couldn't you just love me the way I loved you?"

Markus let his right hand loose, constricting his throat even further. He frantically tried to grab the device and found its mark. He closed his eyes and used the last of his energy to focus on finding the switch that Spencer showed him. For five more agonizing seconds he searched for it. Then her grip loosened ever-so-slightly. He was still being choked, but her grip was losing vigor. Her eyes began to flicker like a damaged light fixture, going between glowing blue and emerald. He could picture her internal struggle, as her hands' restrictions varied. Using the last of his breath, Markus began to speak.

"Char… the button. Hit the button!"

Her eyes shut tightly, and her teeth began to grind. Opening them, her eyes showed green once more. With a loud, pained scream, she balled her fist and slammed it into the Siren grenade. Markus's eyesight and hearing went wild. The noise became unbearably painful, and his vision went wavy. The Progenitress got to her feet and began screaming, her voice a muffled, haunting drone along the waves. She struggled in place unable to move. It was difficult to see but Markus thought he saw something smoke-like manifest in front of him, looking like the haunting spirit of a woman he'd seen moments earlier. This spirit let out one last scream and flew away into the sky, her body plummeted to the ground. Markus lost his ability to think, then lay on the ground and closed his eyes.

CHAPTER 52

Free Once More

Markus

Markus didn't recover right away. His vision was blurry and his ears were ringing. Slowly, everything came back into focus, and Charlotte's face came into view. At first, he thought he was dreaming, but time showed him it was her. Her face was still made-up, and her hair was black and singed, but her eyes were back to green. She was shaking him desperately, trying to wake him up.

"Markus! Markus! Wake up! Please!" she cried, some tears streaking her makeup.

He let his mouth form a smug smile. "Heya, Freckles, missed ya," he said weakly.

"Oh, thank God! Are you okay?" she cried.

Markus sat up; her voice sounded muffled. His ears were stinging and reaching over to touch them revealed they were bleeding.

"That's not good," he muttered, then gave her a thumbs up and a let out a choked laugh. "Other than my ears leaking I'm thinking I feel pretty swanky."

"You idiot," Charlotte said throwing her arms around his neck tightly. Even in his state Markus suddenly felt giddy. He didn't move a limb while she latched to him.

"Hey, uh, I think you're a bit confused."

"Don't be stupid Markus," Charlotte said lightly.

He let himself wrap his arms around her, hugging her back. "Yeah, I guess I am being stupid."

The audience cheered and hollered in celebration. Even though Markus's hearing was not completely back yet, he could hear it clear as day.

Charlotte backed away from him and sat on her knees, looking like a bundle of nerves. Even in the Progenitress's getup it was easy to see this was Charlotte—she was back. She looked up and started to gape at something above Markus's head. She began pointing and struggled to speak. "Markus, you… have… wings? You have wings!" she exclaimed.

He looked above them and lowered his wings, almost embarrassed.

"Don't ask," he said.

Charlotte blinked a few times, as if trying to scrub her memory of his new appendages. "You saved me," she said. "Thank you."

"You kidding? You saved both of us! You hit the Siren grenade."

"I guess, I mean… where are we?" she asked looking around. As she took it all in her eyes widened. "Are we at the baseball stadium?" she asked.

A police helicopter flew overhead, beaming down a searchlight on the two of them.

"Yep, and we have people looking for us," Markus said. "We need to book it on out of here. Are you feeling all right?" Markus asked, climbing to his feet and helping Charlotte do the same.

"I think, just shaky," she said.

"Good enough," Markus said.

"How are we going to get out of here? We don't have a way out!"

"Yeah, we do," Markus said. He went over to Charlotte, grabbing her legs from behind and threw her onto the skysurfer pack on his back.

She yelped sharply. "Hey, what are you doing?"

"Flyin' us outta here. Hold on tight, okay?" Markus ordered, and she wrapped her arms around his neck from behind. "Hang on, I'm kind of new to this. But after I get it down, then we're home free, you got that?" Markus asked.

"Yes! Lead the way!"

"You got it!" Markus flapped his wings and flew out of the field and into the sky. He lifted the two of them with ease, and he went as fast as he could in order to dodge the authorities. Once they did, Markus quickly wasted no time in returning to the undercroft. He kept them high in the sky, the cold night air clinging to them. Charlotte remained latched on, seemingly having a good time despite everything else. She would occasionally start cheering or let out excited screams as Markus swooped and swayed in flight.

He was enjoying it too, but a problem presented itself. Everything was becoming disjointed, and he began to feel drowsy, overly fatigued. In a matter of minutes, it felt like Markus had not slept in a week. He began dipping lower and lower. He fought against it, but it was slowly overtaking him. He blinked rapidly, hoping the night air would aid him, but it did little.

He knew he was close to the undercroft— he had to be. He powered through it as much as he could, hanging on, but once he couldn't, he plummeted. Charlotte let out a scream of fear instead of surprise as the wings glided him toward the ground until they landed in a pile on a sidewalk, Markus taking most of the fall. Charlotte exclaimed something, but Markus didn't process it. All he wanted to do was sleep. He couldn't help but close his eyes and drift off on the sidewalk.

Markus, for the first time in what felt like an eternity, began to dream. He dreamt of an open sea, lush forests, a vast tundra. Beautiful places, places of tranquility. That changed the moment his eyes opened. He found himself staring at a roof. He sat there with no desire to move, finding himself strangely comfortable where he was.

After an unknown amount of time passed, sudden pain in his left hand caused him to shoot up in alarm. Sitting up, he was greeted by the sight of Spencer holding up his arms, urging him to slow down.

"Spencer?" he asked groggily.

"Yes, it's me."

"Where did you come from? How am I...?"

"Oracle let me borrow a taxi. Picked you two up after you nosedived. Brought you home."

"Home?" Markus said. He tried to sit up and every bit of his body that hurt made itself known. "Easy, I was just bandaging your hands," Spencer said.

"My hands?" Markus asked groggily. He brought them up and saw that nine of his fingers had a bandage on their tips. Only the pinky on his left hand did not. Tenderly moving it revealed the pinkish flesh that was where his fingernail used to be, but there was no claw anymore. Spencer took his hand and began to apply a bandage to it.

"Spontaneous physiological growth of additional limbs and appendages," Spencer said. "That's a new one. They completely wrecked your body in the process."

"But they're gone...?" Markus asked.

"Receded," Spencer said. "Somehow, you were hit with an exceptional amount of zenaphosporus back at that stadium, triggering the dormant revenant procreation process. When the element left your bloodstream, you fell into a coma and your growths dissipated."

"I was becoming a revenant?"

"Yes, a raptor from the looks of it."

"But it didn't go all the way through, again. Why?"

"I couldn't tell you. All we know is that there is still a risk of Time Riders turning now."

"Time Riders..." Markus murmured. "Where's Nate? And Charlotte?"

Spencer smiled and gestured with his head in another direction. Markus looked over and saw he was in the undercroft on the coffee table, the sofa mere inches away from him.

In the middle of the undercroft both Charlotte and Ryder were both quietly holding one. It appeared that not even Ryder's injury could keep him from pulling Charlotte into his arms and holding her close for a very long time. They both were a weeping mess, crying into each other like she'd come back from war. If this were yesterday, Markus would have hated this. But not this time.

"They've been like that since we got her back to him. I'm going to have to get the pry bar if they don't break it off soon."

Charlotte opened her eyes after she had come around and saw Markus had awakened. "Markus!" she called out. "Hey, wait a minute, don't..." Ryder started.

She let go of him, and he nearly toppled to the floor because of his legs. She put her hand to her mouth in shock and immediately got under Ryder's shoulder and began helping him back over to the sofa.

"Sorry," she said through her teeth.

After they settled, they all sat around the sofa and coffee table, discussing what had happened. Spencer's next project was examining Markus's ears. His hearing was mostly back but a consistent and obnoxious ring remained. Charlotte tucked herself under Ryder's arm on the sofa. She had taken the time to clean up her face and wore one of Ryder's sweatshirts over her dress.

"Nice to see the grenade worked," Spencer said.

"You bet it did, nearly blew my eardrums out," Markus complained. "Why wasn't Charlotte hurt so bad by it?"

"It mostly effects revenants. For normal people it's annoying, but it's no worse than attending a concert," Spencer said rifling through a first aid box that sat next to Markus.

"Got to admit, I put on quite the show didn't I—*yawoo!*" Markus yelled as Spencer poked his ear with a cotton swab.

"Sorry," Spencer muttered. "And speaking of that, all of St Louis and most likely the whole world probably knows about us by now. It's blowing up on television, social media, and news outlets. Everything. They are just as interested as they are confused about the whole thing."

"Well, they don't know *everything,*" Markus said.

"They know enough. Enough to draw prying eyes. We're going to have to be extra careful now."

"And what about Oracle?" Ryder asked.

"Well, let's say things are going to change for them too. They won't be able to run ops normally after this, they'll have to be more creative. And I think it might be time to kiss the undercroft goodbye."

"Wait, what?" Markus asked.

"Why?" Ryder asked.

"We've been made, and we got raided. We have the leverage, but that's not going to stop them if they get desperate. And when they come back, they will come back hard. Rudy will be caught in the middle of it. I can't do that to him. Besides, I got bigger ambitions than this smelly old basement."

Ryder and Charlotte both took interest in this. "Like what?"

Charlotte asked.

"Yeah, what do you mean?" Ryder followed up.

"I've been property searching, gathering capital. I want to get out of here anyway. And now that we have two full-fledged Time Riders, well... I'd say it's time for an upgrade. It'll take some time to do it right, but we will be moving our operations elsewhere. Getting this mess cleaned up is going to be project in and of itself."

"We're leaving?" Ryder asked sadly.

"Yeah. What? Do you like it down here?" Spencer asked.

"Well, you know it's, uh... sentimental."

Spencer exhaled loudly. "This place wore out sentimentality ten years ago. I'm done working in a basement."

Ryder dipped his head down in slight disappointment. Charlotte nudged him a few times trying to steer him out of the mood.

"It's almost morning, isn't it?" he asked.

"It should be, why?" Spencer asked.

"I just want to see the sunrise outside."

"Sunrise? Like from the roof?" Charlotte asked.

"Yeah. I liked that view, went up there a lot when I first started. Like I said it's kinda sentimental."

"I'd say," Markus said.

"I'll be up there for a bit if you need me," Ryder said moving away from Charlotte and getting to his feet.

"Hey, don't hurt yourself Ry. There's no way your legs are good enough yet," Spencer said.

"I'll be good, I need this right now."

"Hey if you're hurt, you should take it easy Nathan," Charlotte said, concerned.

"It'll be fine. You're welcome to join me, if you're ready."

Charlotte didn't seem to understand the invitation, but Ryder left without saying anything else as he hobbled up the staircase, leaving Spencer, Markus, and Charlotte alone down there.

"Hey Spencer, is there anything you need to be doing right now?" Charlotte asked.

Spencer started to look confused. "Why?"

"I just want a moment with Markus." Spencer looked over at Markus, then back to Charlotte, staring blankly at her. "I'm not going behind Nathan's back, I just want to talk," she said.

"I didn't say anything like that."

"You have that look."

"What look?"

Charlotte groaned. "C'mon, it's me Spencer."

Spencer tapped his foot a few times. "Alright, I'll go check up with Autumn upstairs. I'm dumbfounded she didn't pop her cage with all that happened."

He stood up from the coffee table and quickly left up the staircase out of the undercroft, leaving both Charlotte and Markus alone. She remained on the sofa, Markus remained on the coffee table, one leg propped up on it.

"So, what did you wanna talk about?" he asked.

Charlotte looked either nervous or sad, Markus couldn't tell. "Well, I just wanted to say thanks again."

"Don't worry about it."

"No, you don't understand." Charlotte rushed to respond. "She dressed me up like a doll, hurt people, and I just... I almost killed you, Markus!" she exclaimed, that shakiness from the baseball field returning. "She started choking you to death."

"Hey, none of that. I know that wasn't you."

"I could feel you, Markus. It was like I was asleep and dreaming, I don't even remember all of it. It's all broken up. But somehow, I knew when she interacted with people. I felt them. She used me to hurt people, used me to hurt you."

"Charlotte, it wasn't you, it was the tramp. Don't waste your breath on crap that ain't your fault. You and Nate are horrible about that."

She sunk back down onto the sofa. "There's something else I need to ask you."

"What's that?"

"Spencer told me she's a seductress of some kind. I remember feeling you being... closer." Markus felt a stinging in his heart. He didn't want to talk about this. "Yeah, you could say that."

"What did she do? Did she do anything... bad?"

Markus suddenly remembered what the Progenitress had done back at the tower, the way she clung to him, the way she felt, even her smell. In retrospect the memory made him feel ill and uncomfortable.

"You probably don't want to know," he said.

Charlotte looked sickly in the face and crossed her arms over her chest. "You didn't see me naked, did you?"

"Wha—no! Hell, no! She didn't lose your layers or anything like that."

"Honest?"

"Yeah, honest," Markus said sternly. "The worst she did was sit on my lap and wrap your arms around me. She didn't go that risqué on me. It was adjacent at worst, but it wasn't a bunch of hanky-panky."

Charlotte exhaled in relief. "It's bad enough she put me in this stupid dress. I'm not used to not wearing pants..." She cleared her throat and placed her hands on her lap. "Also, while we're on that topic, there's something else I wanted to talk to you about." Her words turned quaky as she spoke them.

"What now?"

Charlotte sat up and stared right into Markus's eyes. "Markus, do you really have feelings for me?"

He tensed up, afraid to answer. "Yeah."

"So, what you were saying after your flight around the city, that was legit? I thought you were just trying to get an easy kiss out of me or something."

"Yeah, it was legit."

Charlotte looked away and crossed her arms, sadness enveloping her eyes. "I'm sorry Markus."

"For what? You didn't do nothin.' All you did was be you. That's all it was Charlotte. You were just you, and you're just a real loveable gal."

A small smile formed on her face and disappeared just as fast. "Look... I don't wanna... I can't..."

"It's okay," Markus interrupted. "I care for you, but not as much as Nate does, not by a long shot. You two have history, I ain't gonna screw with that. You mean the world to him, y'know?"

"Markus, we really don't even know what we are. We're just..."

"He's your hero, and that makes you feel safe." Markus interrupted.

"Yeah," she said, slight delight intertwined with her words. It was like she was waiting for someone to finally say that.

"I wouldn't sweat it. It's not a competition where you're the prize. Besides, I think I've worn out the steamy stuff, I'm looking forward to embracing stuff that's more... wholesome, I guess."

"What do you mean?"

"Well, as weird as it seems, between you, Nate, and Spencer. It's almost like I have a family now. I honestly thought I wouldn't have anything like that ever again. I may not have you as my ladylove, but I'd be more than happy to be your friend, maybe even a brother if you need one."

"Brother? Does that make me your little sister?" Charlotte asked with a head tilt.

Markus scrunched up his face. "Maybe not exactly, but something along those lines. More like someone you could trust like kin. Does that sound like something nice?"

Her gaze softened. "Yeah, that does sound nice."

A small laugh of satisfaction went through Markus's throat. "Good to hear."

"And with Nathan, I, uh..."

"You'll figure that out. Speaking of which. Nate wanted to see you up top for something right?"

Charlotte shook her head slightly and looked behind her at the staircase. "Yeah, he did." Markus got up and offered his hands to her. She placed her own in his and he lifted her to her feet.

"Thanks, Markus," she said

"Get a move on, Freckles. You can't get much better than a sunrise, now scoot on out of here and see what he wants, yeah?"

Charlotte nodded to him and quickly ran up the stairs out of the undercroft. Markus plopped down onto the sofa, threw his hands behind his head and began lounging. He turned on the tv and just casually started watching the news, knowing that what was going to be said upstairs needed to happen.

CHAPTER 53

The Dawn

Charlotte:

Charlotte left the undercroft and immediately found the ladder behind Rudy's store and scaled it, nervousness and excitement racing in her heart. Once she got to the top, she plopped down onto the gravel and saw Ryder leaning on the guard rail staring out over the city skyline, an orange glow emanating from his direction.

She slowly walked over to him and joined him, leaning against the rail and looking where he was looking. It was a beautiful sight. The early morning sky radiated warmly, like an artful painting come to life. Her heart swelled even more, all Charlotte's life she'd lived in the city, but she'd never seen it like this.

"Heckuva thing, huh?" Ryder said, not looking over at her.

"Yeah, it sure is something. I think the arch is a bit of an eyesore though."

"What's wrong with the arch?"

"Well, considering what happened…"

Ryder laughed. "It'll take more than that to get me to hate the arch. It's St. Louis's symbol, an American symbol. It's home."

Charlotte looked over at Ryder, who was still staring out at the horizon with a small, satisfied grin on his lips, his short hair blowing in the wind. He looked breathtaking. He noticed her staring and returned his gaze.

"What?" he asked.

"You're smiling."

Ryder grinned even more. "Yeah, I guess I am."

"You should do it more often; it's a good look for you."

"I'll give it a try," Ryder said, looking away and back at her. "Are you doing okay?"

"A lot better," Charlotte said. "Being controlled by some interdimensional pick-me was a miserable experience."

Ryder let out a surprised snort. "Geez, that's just foul."

"She deserves a lot worse than that!" Charlotte exclaimed. "If I see her again, she's gonna get a bona-fide bitch-slap!"

"Language," Ryder scolded "But yeah, have at it. I won't stop you if it comes to that."

"You got that right," Charlotte said asserted.

"But you *are* okay right?"

Charlotte looked forward. "I may be small, but I'm tougher than I look."

"You don't need to tell me," Ryder said. "But you didn't answer my question."

Charlotte groaned. "I'm fine now, but as for tomorrow or any other time, I don't know. I've never felt so humiliated and scared before in my life. I'm not going to forget that anytime soon."

"Do you remember anything?"

"Not really," Charlotte said. "Have you ever had a real bad fever dream? Like one that screws with reality for you? It was like that, what I do remember is stuff I don't even know was real. I knew she had taken me, and I regained control for a bit, but after she took control again it was like falling back into the dream. It was like a void, like I was nothing."

"Yeah…" Ryder said quietly. "I had no idea she could do something like that. Scared me half to death."

"I know," Charlotte said. "And what about you? You hanging in there?"

Ryder went still. "Me? Not really, I'm just grateful you're okay, really grateful. But this is far from over. There is so much that needs to be done, so much I'm going to have to fix."

"I'd be surprised if there wasn't," Charlotte said. She leaned forward farther on the railing, stealing one more glance at him. He began staring off, like he was deep in thought. "What's on your mind?" she asked.

He blinked and looked over at her again. "Me? I, uh... deep stuff I guess."

"Deep stuff? Like what?"

Ryder lifted his hand into the air and blue energy waves whooshed from his fingertips and trailed like smoke in the wind. Charlotte gazed at them curiously, the bright color catching her eye.

"Time, it just keeps going, doesn't it? It's never resting, never sleeping. It just keeps going despite everyone. Always moving, always changing. Changing the world and changing people. People like me."

"Nathan?"

Ryder closed his fist and the bright blue waves ceased. Then a furrow formed on his brow. "Sorry, I trail off like that sometimes. Pay it no mind."

"What are you really thinking about?"

Ryder frowned. "I know this is a weird question, but do I seem... *real* to you?"

Charlotte became very confused. "Yeah? what kind of question is that supposed to be?"

"Well, think about it. When the revenants got me, I ceased to exist. Nathan Ryder ceased to exist. I can't help but feel I'm just a mirage, an echo of him. Something living that should be dead. I'm... a revenant. I don't even know if I'm alive. Not really. Maybe I'm also stuck in a fever dream."

They held each other's gaze until she took her right index finger and pressed it against her thumb. Then she brought it up to Ryder's face and flicked him right in the nose.

He recoiled in surprise and covered his nose. "Ow! Wha—what was that for?"

"You seem real enough to me, so shut up. You need to stop being poetically mopey all the time. It's depressing."

Ryder let his hand down and scrunched his nose. His annoyance caused his eyes to glow. "Fine. What's your deal with hitting people? There's never a good reason to do that."

"Oh really? Way for the pot to call the kettle black there, Mr. Time Rider," Charlotte said sarcastically.

"You know what I mean!" Ryder retorted. "Geez, you're a real handful, you know that?"

"And you wouldn't have it any other way." Charlotte smiled at him.

Ryder returned to the railing. "Yeah, I guess not." He leaned over and dropped his head, letting out an exhale.

"I don't get you. The moment we have time to breathe your having an existential crisis. What's up with that?"

"It's not just that," Ryder said without looking up.

"What else is there?"

He raised his head with a small groan, his eyes flaring in color. "I'm just torn, Charlotte. You've been a blessing to me you know? I mean, if I'm gonna be completely honest when it comes to this Time Rider work, I'd lost my faith. When I started all of this, I did it because I had nothing left. I did it to make light of a really, really messed up situation. I really wanted to help. I did. I'm not a fighter. I hate hurting people. But I did it to do the right thing. For ten years I was going back and forth, saving some, losing others. It was tough."

"You told me about that. Right after Legion attacked you in that warehouse."

"Right, but I kept going. For as long as I could. But eventually I couldn't help but feel what we were fighting for was a lost cause, there just would never really be a way of knowing how many revenants there were. I had no clue if what I was doing was even making a difference or even a dent worth mentioning. No matter how many revenants I destroyed, no matter how many Oracle operators I dealt with, there would always be more. It would never stop. What I realized was what me and Spencer did, it was pointless. Pointless... until you came back."

Charlotte took a few steps forward, focusing on what he was saying. "Me? What do you mean? Why am I special?"

"You are something tangible. You weren't some abstract goal I didn't even know could be achieved. You were right in front of me, flesh and blood. But then again maybe I just took a real shine to you. My guess is that it's a bit of both. I'm not sure if that makes any sense."

"It does, actually. For me, you went from abstract to real life real fast. Meeting you again was like falling into a film, last action hero-style. I still can't believe I found you the way I did."

"Yeah, I don't know why the good Lord decided to let you come back into my life like that. Maybe he decided to finally answer my prayers, maybe he wanted me to find that faith again that I'd lost. Whatever it is, I can't help but feel like I failed."

"How have you failed?"

Ryder looked over at her, his radiant gaze staring right through her. "In the short amount of time we've been together, you've been in danger. Your life has been at risk. I was able to stop it the first time when Oracle kidnapped you, but not the second time. Markus had to do the heavy lifting this time."

"I don't blame you for that."

"It's not about blame," Ryder said. "It's about being honest with ourselves. Being with us has put a target on your back. And not just from Oracle, but Progenitress as well. Part of me wants you to leave and never come back here, have it to where you would never see me again. I don't want it to be that way but…"

"It wouldn't make a difference," Charlotte interrupted. "There is still a high chance they would use me again to get to you."

"Right, exactly," Ryder said.

Charlotte leaned back over the railing, a mild annoyance simmering in her gut. "So, I'm the perpetual damsel in distress, groovy."

"I don't know if I'd put it that way," Ryder said, joining her on the railing. "You're just… high demand now. Popular, because of me."

"Popular?" Charlotte shook her head. "That's hysterical."

"Just trying to be optimistic. Take a glass half-full approach. Give or take."

"We could use more of that. What are we going to do now? Do we have a plan?"

"The same plan as always. I'm going to get back to work, get back to doing what I do best. But more than anything else, we stick together," Ryder said. "We might need to be subtle at times, but me and Markus are going to be around. Keeping an eye on you, making sure you don't get snatched up again or get into real trouble."

"Trouble? Little old me?"

"Yeah, *you*," Ryder said tensely. "It's not even worth joking about how much trouble has come your way."

"I guess, you have to admit it's kind of fun."

"Fun? You're starting to sound like Markus."

"Glass half-full right?"

Ryder made a face. "Touché," he said. "Are you going to keep that look?"

"What do you mean?"

"Your hair, are you going to keep it black?"

"What, this?" Charlotte said, taking a few strands of her hair in her hands. "Ew, no."

"You sure?" Ryder asked. "I dunno, you kind of pull off the emo look quite nicely."

"Emo? Oh, don't even go there!"

"Come on, think about it. You could start a band and everything. You could call it like uh... Charlotte's Woes or something," Ryder suggested.

"That's the dumbest thing I've ever heard!" Charlotte exclaimed. Ryder began giggling under his breath.

"I'd pay to see that," a voice behind them said.

Both Ryder and Charlotte turned around to see Markus standing behind them on the roof, smiling with his hands in his sweatshirt pockets. "What do you think, Nate? Would you go to her first concert?"

"V.I.P front row ticket," Ryder said smugly.

"Man, you both suck," Charlotte huffed.

"Don't feel bad. Just look at Nate. If he grew his hair out and wore that dress, he would look identical to you. To be honest I'm surprised the tramp didn't use him for a vessel and really home in on that feminine vibe."

"Man, screw you!" Ryder exclaimed.

"Just a joke, Pretty Boy, don't get bent outta shape," Markus said, walking over to them and taking his place next to Charlotte on the railing, leaning his back against it. "But seriously, are you going to keep that color? Right now, you look like Nate's sister."

Charlotte bit her lip and thought about it. "Definitely not keeping the black, but maybe I could go for brown or something. What do you think, Nathan?"

"What's wrong with your normal hair color?" Ryder asked.

"That red color? No one likes red heads."

"I like red heads."

"Well of course *you* do," Charlotte responded whimsically. "What about you, Markus? What do you think?"

"I dunno, wouldn't ya say blondes have more fun?" Markus said, flourishing his hand toward his own hair.

Charlotte raised an eyebrow smugly. "Too much fun."

"You don't know the half of it," Markus said, grinning. He leaned his head back, letting his hair slope over the building. "So, what now? What are we going to do from here on out?"

"Well, we got to get you up to snuff for, starters. We are going to have our work cut out for us real soon," Ryder said.

"From what? Anything in particular?"

"Bad luck," Ryder said lightly. "Always prepare for the worst possible outcome, because revvies always meet it."

"No days off for Time Riders, huh?"

"Not one. But hey, at least you won't be doing it alone."

"Yup, that'll be fun. I'll have all the time in the world to annoy the ever-living crap out of you."

Ryder sneered slightly. "Looking forward to it."

Charlotte rolled her eyes. "You boys are ridiculous."

Markus laughed out loud. "Ridiculous? Be careful tempting me like that. The Rebel with Wings is officially off the chain," he said proudly.

"And the Timeless Knight is going to work overtime trying to prevent him from getting himself killed," Ryder groaned.

"Timeless Knight?" Charlotte asked with a twinge of amazement. "Did you just come up with that?"

"I need a nickname too," Ryder said. "Too corny?"

"I don't think so," Charlotte said. "The Timeless Knight and the Rebel with Wings. I dig it."

"The Great Freckled One has spoken," Markus said sarcastically.

"That she has," Charlotte said leaning forward on the railing.

Markus and Ryder looked back out at the sunset. Charlotte took in the calm breeze and the soft morning glow. The presence of the two Time Riders next to her was comfortably prominent in her senses. She wrapped an arm around the two of them, pulling them close to her. In response, they both wrapped an arm around her, connecting the three of them in an interlocked embrace.

"Keep going, keep believing. Right, Nathan?" Charlotte asked.

"That's right," Ryder responded.

"Believe in what?" Markus asked.

Neither Ryder nor Charlotte responded. But she knew the answer. Even after the night had fallen and the terror made itself known, the morning sky came to greet her all the same. It reminded her of her mother, her warmth and brightness following in the morning. It reminded her of her new allies, the loyal friends that held her on that rooftop. What started as a subliminal saying ended as a truth. A truth that is best never forgotten.

Believe there is always a new morning.

ABOUT THE AUTHOR

Gage Copeland is a young man aspiring to become a proficient storyteller. He is a High School graduate working through college off and on. He currently works a humble job and lives with his family in the small town of Nixa, Missouri.

Gage is someone who has struggled long and hard with mental illness, and still battles it to this day. He is no stranger to the darkness that lives within his own head. But he believes in doing the best with what one is given.

He is a Christian and a student of the teachings of the Holy Bible. Though his actions are not foolproof, and far from perfection. He knows there is no other hope, no other way besides the teachings of Jesus Christ.

But for a good long while, Gage was away from the Bible's teachings. He was initially inspired by the imaginative minds and works of filmmakers like Steven Spielberg and James Cameron, as well as writers like Michael Crichton and Sam Lake.

Over the years Gage had become an avid connoisseur of all forms of media. Film, books, music, and even video games. He believes that all mediums carry the potential of incredible storytelling. All which fueled a dream to create stories of his own. Fiction had a way of comforting him and helping him understand the person he wanted to be when no other wisdom could be found. And he hopes to create works that can help others through their struggle the same way fiction has helped him.